THE RISING ORDER

THE
RISING
✶✶✶✶
ORDER

A NOVEL

CLAIRE ISENTHAL

GREENLEAF
BOOK GROUP PRESS

Published by Greenleaf Book Group Press
Austin, Texas
www.gbgpress.com

Distributed by Greenleaf Book Group

For ordering information or special discounts for bulk purchases, please contact Greenleaf Book Group at PO Box 91869, Austin, TX 78709, 512.891.6100.

Design and composition by Greenleaf Book Group
Cover design by Greenleaf Book Group
Cover images used under license from ©Shutterstock/m-agention, ©Shutterstock/atk work, ©Shutterstock/Nadia Chi, and ©Shutterstock/Pogorelova Olga

Publisher's Cataloging-in-Publication data is available.

Print ISBN: 979-8-88645-088-0

eBook ISBN: 979-8-88645-089-7

To offset the number of trees consumed in the printing of our books, Greenleaf donates a portion of the proceeds from each printing to the Arbor Day Foundation. Greenleaf Book Group has replaced over 50,000 trees since 2007.

Printed in the United States of America on acid-free paper

23 24 25 26 27 28 29 30   10 9 8 7 6 5 4 3 2 1

First Edition

To the matriarchs of my life—my mother, my grandmothers, my sister, and my aunts—who taught me to never take no for an answer. I stand on your shoulders.

★ ★ ★ ★

To Mrs. Vesely, my fifth-grade language arts teacher, who taught me Aristotle and grammar. As promised, this is for you.

AUTHOR'S NOTE AND CONTENT ADVISORY

I started this book over seven years ago. It began as a way to process the Orlando nightclub shooting, in 2016, and has since evolved to encompass the growing violence that will now be interwoven into my children's daily lives. I started writing this before the Manchester Arena Ariana Grande concert. Before the First Baptist Church of Sutherland Springs Sunday service. Before Uvalde. There have been so many others in between.

Please take into consideration that this book contains acts of violence and mass shootings, and it explores themes around trauma. My intention is never to glorify this violence, but to instead depict how it is present and inescapable in places and parts of our lives we once considered the most sacred and safe.

PART ONE

★ ★ ★ ★

THE CATALYST

1

WOLF

Killing had always been easy for Wolf.

Pulling a trigger . . . easy.

Slight pressure. Release. Slight pressure.

Release.

Easy. Satisfying. Predictable—the sounds of chaos the exact same every time. The thrill of pain inflicting more pain. It would never get old. How the air would sizzle in each round's wake, a tingle of exhilaration rippling outward. Like a wizard with a wand, Wolf could control a crowd, summoning a stampede with a single wave.

Tonight, it begins. My life's work. My masterpiece.

Bass notes low enough to vibrate the entire stadium pulsed through him. Lights dimmed in unison, fading until darkness swallowed Soldier Field whole. Pinpricks of light materialized as cell phone flashlights bobbed and swayed, creating the illusion of stars dancing in the night sky. Thousands of cheers echoed throughout the open arena, drowning out the rain. A sold-out concert, exactly as planned.

Wolf stood guard on the outskirts, next to a sound booth tucked in the football field's back corner, careful to avoid the spotlights now swirling over the crowd. Illuminated faces stacked in the stands above him blurred together. "Green Line. Green Line. Green Line," they chanted.

He couldn't believe this many people would actually pay to see a band with such a dipshit name. Heavy raindrops slid over the edge of his hood, spilling a wet trail down the collar of his orange work crew jacket. Nerves raw from adrenaline, sweat clinging to a concealed suicide vest strapped to his body. Just in case. He inhaled, relishing the moment, tasting the cool air in the back of his throat. The tiny hairs on the back of his hands stood on end.

I'm ready. For years, I've been ready.

Two dead audio techs lay at his feet. Blood oozing from their slit throats glistened black in the dark. His concentration wasn't on the shrieking crowd or their pumping arms. It wasn't on *who* would die, but how many. Saliva filled his mouth as if he'd just bitten into a sweet summer plum.

I can't wait to kill the rest of them, he thought. *To seal the fate they made for themselves.*

Blue numbers glowed from the face of Wolf's watch. "Sixty seconds, Falcon." He glanced over his shoulder, shifting to shield Falcon. Protecting the mission's commander came above all else. Duty first. Self last. A mantra that had been ingrained in him years ago.

Falcon stooped over a large crate, cracking open its latches. "This is the one."

He tossed the lid aside and pulled out blocks of dense foam and several AK-47s. He passed a rifle to Wolf's eager hands. Wolf slung the strap over his chest and reached for another. Warm and familiar, the weapon's weight wrapped around his shoulders. Elation coursed through his veins, igniting every cell. His skin was on fire.

Now this . . . this is what pure joy feels like.

Falcon hooked a grenade launcher beneath the barrel of his AK-47. A beam of light glided over his face, illuminating a soft smile. "Alright, masks on. It's time."

Wolf's heart thrashed in his eardrums, muffling Falcon's voice. The silky fabric conformed to his face. Behind it, a concealed part of him roared to life. By tomorrow, the world would fear the masks' crimson color. He jammed the magazine into the rifle and pulled back on the charging handle. The round clicked into the chamber. His finger hovered over the trigger.

Slight pressure. Release.

Now, the world will finally have to see me, he thought. *And this time, they won't forget.*

2

FLYNN

Blood rose to the surface of Flynn's skin. Beaded droplets paved a sluggish ruby trail down her arms. Shattered glass covered her like powdered sugar, but she was oblivious to any pain. Another explosion reverberated down the main hallway connecting the row of box seats, shocking her ragged breathing into silence. A seismic quake trembled the concrete beneath her.

I'm going to die, she thought. *Strange. I never saw it happening this way.*

Terrified to move, she lifted her gaze to the monster before her. No sweet memories scrolled through her mind. No familiar faces flashed before her. Disembodied shrieks floated in and out of her consciousness.

The man staring down at her held some sort of rifle to her forehead. She'd expected a terrorist's eyes to be shadowed and dark, windows into an empty shell. Instead, they were a bright, unsettling green. Familiar, almost. Her scalp prickled as he studied her with strange intensity.

What are you waiting for? she wanted to scream. *Kill me now. Get it over with.*

Tears streamed down her cheeks, not from sadness, but from the acrid smoke engulfing them. Digging deep into herself, she tried to channel terror into strength. How ironic, that her most life-defining moment would occur only seconds before she died. She'd spent years waiting for her life to change. All she'd wanted was to transform it into something new.

As she focused on the gun's narrow mouth, her shock subsided. Begging for her life was pointless. No one could reason with a monster.

"Goodbye," she whispered, not to the man, but to the world.

Pain ripped through her skull.

Everything went black.

3

WOLF

Although Wolf was now twenty-seven, well past his teenage years, he sometimes cringed when he thought back on them. Not for the reasons many probably had while reflecting on awkward adolescences, but because of how weak he'd been—how passive he'd been, despite his anger. Throughout his childhood he'd lived with the resounding echo of all the reasons he would never be good enough. But when REDS saved him right before his eighteenth birthday, everything changed. Ironically enough, Wolf had been living in a reform center at the time. Funny how life could be shit for so long and then change course in a day.

It was an afternoon like any other until one of the center's volunteers found him heading to his housing ward after school. Wringing her hands, the middle-aged woman had difficulty meeting his gaze. Her watery eyes skirted around his face when she told him he had a visitor in the guest lounge.

Yeah, fucking right. "You've got the wrong person," Wolf sneered.

He'd never received a visitor in his seven years at Abbott Juvenile Reform Center. But she wouldn't know that. The volunteers were usually stay-at-home moms with nothing better to do with their boring days. Volunteering at Abbott was just another way to "give back" to the community that didn't involve being on the Parent-Teacher Council. They usually steered clear of the teenagers and stuck to the younger boys.

She glanced down at the plastic identification bracelet encircling his wrist. "Um . . . your member number is 1730 from Men's Ward C, correct?"

His eyes narrowed. "So what?"

She shrank back as if he'd threatened her. People had a tendency to cower around him. It only reinforced his glowering disposition. "Well, then come with me, young man," she blustered. "Your guest said you should be getting home from school right around now."

Pivoting on her heel, she hurried back down the hallway, eager to stretch the distance between them. Wolf trailed after her, mumbling profanities under his breath. This had to be a mistake . . . and a waste of time.

The volunteer stopped at the guest lounge door. She nodded toward a tall man seated at a cafeteria table in the far-left corner of the room.

"See? There's your guest, right over there. Enjoy!" Her voice pitched to an unnatural soprano.

"Wait," he said as she sidestepped around him. "I don't know who that is."

Ignoring him, she scurried away, ponytail flicking behind her like an agitated metronome. Squinting through the rectangular slab of glass, Wolf tried to pinpoint the man. He had his back to the door so it was impossible to identify him. No one knew Wolf lived here except the school. He didn't have any friends. Was he in trouble? Yeah, he'd stolen that prick's cell phone today in class, but he tossed it down the toilet. No way they could prove it was him.

Squaring his shoulders, he stalked into the center's most hideous room. Paintings of rainbows and butterfly cutouts attempted to hide dreary walls. Kids' arts and crafts were a pathetic effort to create an inviting façade. Even the *Mona Lisa* wouldn't be enough to distract from the shabbiness of peeling wallpaper, flickering fluorescent lights, and cracked laminate flooring.

Maybe he hated the guest lounge because he never received visitors, or maybe it was the bullshit fictitious cheerfulness plastered everywhere.

The man sat erectly, shoulders drawn back in impeccable posture. Wolf's footsteps slowed, echoing on the sticky plastic tiles, as he waited for the man to turn. Instead, he remained unnaturally still. Wolf came to a stop behind him, staring at the back of his head. He wasn't a cop. Definitely wasn't from the school's administration. Hell, he sure knew all those assholes.

Dropping his chin, Wolf lowered his voice to sound more threatening. "Do I know you?"

"Have a seat."

Accustomed to scaring the shit out of people, Wolf scratched the back of his neck. "Look—"

"I said," interrupted the man, "have a seat." His tone insinuated refusal was not an option.

Who the hell does this guy think he is? Rolling his eyes, Wolf stormed around the table, and threw himself into a chair. Looking the man up and down, he took in his broad shoulders, emphasized and shaped by a perfectly tailored navy blazer. A pressed, stark white shirt underneath gave his bronze complexion the illusion of sandy gold. Dark stubble dotted his strong, square jawline. His immaculate appearance was a blatant contrast to Wolf's baggy sweatshirt and grungy jeans.

This douche has to be loaded.

"What do you want?" Wolf refused to blink, determined not to break the stranger's unsettling gaze. His eyes were so dark it was hard to tell if he had pupils.

Asshole wasted no time getting straight to the point. "I'm here to extend an offer on behalf of my employer. It's our understanding that your eighteenth birthday is a few days away. You are on the verge of legal adulthood."

"What? You with the Army or something? I don't even know who you are." Crossing his arms, Wolf paused in brief consideration, intrigue itching the back of his throat. "What kind of offer?"

This guy's boss was probably sponsoring some charity just to receive a government subsidy. The possibility made Wolf hate him even more. His pulse thumped against his windpipe, sending his blood surging through the artery extending down his neck. He didn't need anybody's sympathy.

"It's an offer to join our organization. We have observed you and selected you as a potential candidate."

Eyebrows rising, Wolf's head tilted to the side. "I don't need you or your bullshit organization. Stay away from me and stop watching me, creeper." Slamming his hands on the table, he pushed himself back to his feet.

Asshole's mouth ironed into a stern line, face hard and ominous. "Member 1730, tell me about the future you have here. Are you going to continue living in Ward C until they throw you on the streets? Is that where you belong?"

Speechless, Wolf stared, his eyes widening. He'd never been spoken to like that.

"Sit. Back. Down." The man's words sliced through Wolf like a cleaver, reverberating through his bones.

He was right. Wolf had come to terms with his fucked future a long time ago. Not much to it other than rotting away in a center for delinquent boys until they booted him out. Shaking his head, Wolf sat, running his hands through greasy hair.

"What do you want from me?" Wolf tried to keep his voice calm, but it wavered. "Who are you, and why the hell are you watching me?"

"If you would let me finish," the man began, "you might find out the answers to those questions." A sharp edge lingered in his voice.

Wolf forced himself to look into the dark tunnels of his eyes again. "I just want to be left alone."

"You really think you can survive in this world alone?"

His gaze burned a scorching hole through Wolf's forehead, as if judging his most vulnerable thoughts and fears. Wolf lifted his chin. "I've done alright so far."

Asshole studied him. Wolf was suddenly acutely aware of his slouched form. He straightened. "In three days, when you become a legal adult, you will meet me at five o'clock sharp at the Central and Oak Street intersection. There's a bus stop. Wait on the bench. A green pickup truck will come for you. When you join us"—he paused—"*that* is when your life will finally begin."

"Join who? You?"

For the first time, the man's body moved. He gave a small shrug. "You'll have to see."

"You expect me to leave here and wait for you at a bus stop with no idea about what you plan to do to me or where I'm going? What's in it for me?"

"I assure you, it will be worth it."

"I'm supposed to trust that?" Wolf asked.

"What other choice do you have? It's that or *this*." He nodded toward the four walls of the visitation room, a prophecy equivalent to death itself. "You're smart and articulate, despite your efforts to hide it. We chose you. Soon, you will see that our invitation is an honor. It's not offered to many."

It was as if the stranger had backed Wolf into a corner he'd run into a thousand times, but maybe this time, there was an escape. He held up a crystal ball showing Wolf the unavoidable image of his future, forcing him to confront his life's empty depths if he stayed here. How had they known he had nothing to live for? That he hated his existence? A lifeline seemed too good to be true. He'd been fucked over and over again, bounced from one foster home to another until he'd landed here. What's to say it wouldn't happen again? Wolf's throat stuck together, preventing words from forming.

Asshole stood, buttoning the front of his blazer.

"Remember, five o' clock sharp. Otherwise, you forfeit this opportunity. Bring nothing with you but yourself."

Cracking his neck, Wolf stared at the table. "You know, you're not very convincing in rallying me for your cause . . . whatever the hell that is."

"Ah, thank you for reminding me. There's one condition I'm required to share before you join us."

Wolf glanced up. "Who says I've agreed to anything?"

A small smile played on the man's lips. "*When* you join us, your identity as Member 1730 of Abbott Juvenile Reform Center will be obsolete. It will cease to exist." The stranger turned to leave, offering no name or phone number. As he walked away, he called over his shoulder, "Leaving that person behind should be incentive enough."

4

FLYNN

"What?" Flynn shoved a giant piece of sushi into her mouth. She chewed slowly, giving herself a second or two to come up with a response. "Don't you think it's a tad over the top?"

Cori's eyes almost disappeared into the back of her head. "Uh, maybe, but who cares? Welcome to corporate America. I mean, it's Green Line. You've been obsessed with them forever. You have no legit reason not to go."

Raindrops streamed down their apartment windows like racing tears. Perched on stools they'd fished out of a dumpster when they first moved to Chicago, the two women were eating takeout at their kitchen bar. It had been raining all week. Typical Midwest spring weather.

Flynn had lived with her best friend since they'd both graduated college five years ago. Since then, they'd battled through the stages of early adulting together, surviving a seemingly endless roller coaster of boyfriends and job-related triumphs and disasters. They often joked about who was a worse influence on the other, and the verdict would swing in either direction depending on the day.

"It's been a long week." Dunking a pod of edamame into soy sauce, she jabbed her chopstick at Cori. "I'm tired."

"I'm tired," Cori mimicked in a whiney voice. "So lame. Your whole team is going." A thin headband pulled her blonde bangs off her forehead.

Her full lips pursed together, curving downward. Usually warm and inviting, her striking face turned haughty and rigid. Cori had a scary ability to transform from charming to fierce within seconds.

"Don't give me that look. You know I don't care; I hate team outings."

"As our wise friend Justin Bieber always says, 'YOLO.' They're box seats. The show is sold out. Why wouldn't you go?"

Flynn dragged a spicy tuna roll across her plate, smearing a brown ring around its perimeter. Eyeing Cori, she tried unsuccessfully to repress a groan. Her stomach seized, dread squeezing it into a tight ball. "One of the managers is going too. He's a total sleaze . . . He's asked for my number, like, seven times. Se-ven!" Flynn enunciated each syllable for effect. "He won't take the hint that I'm not interested. Now it's just getting awkward and weird."

"What's his name again?" Cori asked.

"Ted. Creepy Ted."

Cori scrunched her nose in distaste. "Ew. So, you're going to let this douchebag Ted get in the way of seeing your favorite band? Just ignore him."

Flynn considered this for a second, tugging at a strand of her dark wavy hair. A familiar sludge of worry poured over her and hardened like concrete. "It's kind of hard to ignore a manager when he won't leave you alone. He's the one with the upper hand here."

"You know, it's crazy to me that sexual harassment still happens at a place like Magnetic," Cori said. "You would think *the* number one tech company in the world would be able to weed these creeps out."

"Why do you think they need to be 'weeded' out? They're everywhere. And they never really go away."

"Can you bring another guy as a date?"

"Yeah," Flynn snorted into her cup of water. "Let me just whip one up out of nowhere."

Cori lifted a bony shoulder. "That's why you gotta keep a stacked bench, my friend, so you can call in the reserves."

"We both know dating isn't really my strong suit."

"That's because you don't apply yourself." Cori snagged the last shred of ginger from their Styrofoam takeout box, dropping it into her mouth like a bird gulping a worm. "You've got to stand up for yourself, Flynn. Go. Have fun, and if he pulls any moves, say something."

Say something. In theory it sounded easy. The problem was no one ever listened to what you have to say when you are twenty-seven. It's an awkward age. The age when life smacks you in the face. An age that, when Flynn was eighteen, sent a tremor of dread through her at how old the number sounded. Everyone assumes that when you're twenty-seven, you're finally hopping over the cusp of immaturity and getting your shit together. Except for Flynn, getting your shit together meant conforming to who the world told her she should be. A world run by men. A world where women, especially Jewish women, are reminded every day they don't belong.

"Fine. Fine, I'll go." Her hands leapt toward the ceiling, inadvertently flinging soy sauce in Cori's face. "Are you happy now? Can I eat my sushi in peace?"

Cori's mouth twisted into a smug smile. "Yes. Yes, you can. One day, you will thank me." Swiveling on the stool, she gave Flynn's knee a quick pat before getting up. "I'm going to shower."

It felt like there was rice stuck to Flynn's throat, glued to its walls with clumps of wasabi wafting fiery steam into her sinuses. Cori could never understand. She thrived on being seen, standing out. Her entire life, Flynn had wanted nothing more than to blend in.

"Dibs on your suede skirt," she yelled after Cori as she waltzed into the bathroom.

"Fine. But it probably won't do much for that pancake booty."

Snatching her phone from the counter, Flynn scrolled through her text messages. She tried to ignore the twinge of fear needling its way into her thoughts.

"This'll be fun," she said out loud to no one. The word hung in the air, full of empty promises. *Fun, fun, fun . . .*

* * * *

At work the next morning, Flynn hunched over her gaping file cabinet, waiting for her computer to come to life. She was trying to shut the drawer, but a candidate's file had gotten stuck.

"Goood morning!"

She recoiled from the shadow looming over her keyboard. The cheesy voice was too enthusiastic for 8 a.m. Glancing up, she forced a smile.

"Hey, Ted."

"On a scale of one to ten"—he paused, leaning against her cube divider—"how pumped are you for tonight?"

Ted was a lot to swallow. His polished side part, flashy TAG Heuer watch, and calculated grin screamed: ego. Anxiety built in the bottom well of her stomach.

"Oh, you know," she said, yanking the file loose and then slamming the drawer shut, "probably an eight. Green Line is my favorite."

He winked, reaching to grasp her shoulder. His hand lingered, and he rubbed his thumb in a small circle over her black sweater. "I was hoping for a ten."

She stared at him, her lips frozen into a grimace, etched into her face like dry mud. *Play it cool, Flynn,* she reminded herself. *Don't panic.* Resisting a shudder, she shrugged and sat back in her chair.

He gave her outfit a once-over. "You're changing first, right?"

Flynn scanned her brown suede skirt and black tights. She squeezed her knees together. "Umm . . . I wasn't planning on it."

"Ah, okay. No worries. I mean, you look great but this whole outfit vibe doesn't really scream concert, you know?"

Seriously? What does that even mean? She bit her tongue so hard a metallic tang overpowered the burnt coffee taste. Why did it always seem like she was biting her tongue? Why did *she* have to worry about losing her job, while this loser got away with being a total prick? *Say something,* Cori's voice urged, protruding from her memory. Flynn opened her mouth, heart thundering, but no sound emerged. Frustrated by her conditioned silence, she turned to her computer, signaling the conversation was over.

"Oh." He faltered, taken aback by her abrupt aloofness. "Okay, guess I'll swing by your desk later to talk timing."

"I'm planning on heading out whenever everyone else does." Eyes creasing into a squint, she scanned her computer screen, fixated on her stacked calendar. Five phone screens. One interview training for an internal team. Only a small block of time for outreach emails. Oy. Just thinking about the day made her voice hurt. Sometimes she wondered why she'd gravitated toward a career in recruiting. She wasn't a natural extrovert and she hated chitchat. But, in her opinion, it was the most important job at a company—an undercover opportunity to shape the culture and try to create a more diverse and inclusive workplace.

After Ted finally sauntered away, her fingers danced across the keyboard in a flurry of taps, logging into her email's chat.

> **FLYNN:** I'm so annoyed.
>
> **CORI:** Already? It's not even 9 a.m.
>
> **FLYNN:** Creepy Ted just asked me if this is *actually* what I'm wearing to the concert tonight!!
>
> **CORI:** Wait, I'm offended. I helped you pick out that outfit. That's my fav skirt. What's wrong with it???
>
> **FLYNN:** IDK. That's what I thought . . .
>
> **CORI:** W/e. Who cares what he thinks. Bright side, it'll be so loud you don't have to hear him speak.

This will be fun, Flynn silently recited over and over. Groaning, she plopped her chin into her clammy palm. *Fun.*

"Now, if that doesn't sound like pure enthusiasm, I don't know what does." Nate Turner grinned over the low partition separating their desks, dark hazel eyes twinkling. Propping a forearm on the cubicle divider, he pulled a hand over perfectly groomed stubble.

"Nate, it's already been a painful morning. I'm not mentally prepared for your unbearable sarcasm."

Smirking, he folded his arms over his chest. "Fraternizing with managers now? I guess that's one way to get what you want around here. Should

I ask Tracy to go as my date? I mean, yeah, she's our director, but it might give me that edge I finally need for promo."

Flynn straightened, her body taut with instant rage. She and Nate had always vied for the top spot of placing the most candidates each month, so they often found it impossible not to constantly dig into each other. "Do you really need to be an asshole so early in the morning? I don't actually *want* to go to this concert tonight."

"Exactly my point," he taunted, disappearing from view.

Typical, she thought. *Of course, he's turning this around on me.* Fuming, she struggled to summon an adequate comeback. One that would knock him on his ass. Yet again, conditioned silence won. *What's the point?* she asked herself. *Anything I say will just egg him on.*

* * * *

As the end of the workday loomed, Flynn took a break from reviewing candidates to refill her water bottle in the sixth-floor kitchenette. She usually loved her job, but sometimes she couldn't stand its repetitive, cyclical tasks. Lost in thought, she jumped when Ted snuck up on her from behind, startling her yet again.

"Oops, sorry." He grinned, sheepish, watching droplets of water spill onto her cashmere. "Almost ready to go?"

Something in her snapped. She wiped her sweater with a paper towel. "Not yet. I have a couple interviews I need to wrap up first."

"Oh, come on. It's a Thursday; leave it for tomorrow."

Taking a sip of water, she shrugged. "I need to get these positions filled."

As Ted walked Flynn back to her desk, his hand grazed her lower back.

A shiver pulsed through her, as if a pointy talon had slid down her spine. Her pace accelerated, increasing the space between them.

Oh god. Please let no one have seen that.

His potent cologne followed her, a cloud of masculinity. Of course she'd lied—there were no more interviews; she just wasn't ready to start the evening with Ted yet.

"Try to hurry it along," Ted urged.

Sinking into her chair, she shot furtive glances over her shoulder, swallowing hard. There had to be a way to sneak out of here without him noticing.

She wiggled her mouse, reawakening her computer screen, and clicked back into her email. A new bolded memo from Magnetic's CEO sat at the top of her inbox. The subject line prompted an inward cringe: PROTECTING OUR MISSION AND OUR USERS.

Over fifteen years after our genesis, we have a lot to be proud of. Although we began as a search engine, last year we accomplished a groundbreaking achievement when we pioneered the first connected IT infrastructure of our time. We revolutionized the entire home ecosystem and built a new family -modeled network, unifying all of our devices onto the same backend system. Our future is bright as we continue bringing our customers closer to harmony and security . . .

Flynn rolled her eyes and pressed Delete before she finished reading. *Whatever.*

Ignoring the rest of her inbox, she opened a new browser and navigated to BuzzFeed. Anything to occupy herself for the next hour. Headlines flashed over last night's debate between the Republican candidates. While she skimmed an editorial on a celebrity's sudden engagement, a video in the far-right corner caught her eye. A short blurb called attention to recent criminal activity by some organization referring to itself as REDS.

Strange . . . never heard of them before. What a weird name.

She clicked into the link. According to the article, the group originated as a radical gang in the Midwest, gradually becoming more aggressive and lethal as their following grew. Their attacks seemed random—bank and shopping mall robberies—with no apparent connection to each other, but they were happening more frequently. The article reported:

Illinois Governor Evelyn Meloche claims these incidents of violence are isolated, and likely an attempt to expand their drug and weapon trafficking territory. "These thugs are determined to wreak havoc and must be held responsible. Local police are well-positioned to deal with disturbed individuals," said Meloche.

Flynn chewed her thumbnail, wondering if she should have removed last week's chipping manicure, and pressed Play on the video. It showed REDS followers raiding a bank in suburban Illinois. Clothed in black, two hulking figures smashed through security glass and reached into tills, while another held onlookers at gunpoint. Under the black hoods shrouding their heads, ruby-red masks covered their faces, creating an illusion of phantom blood. The footage appeared to have been taken on someone's phone. The images wobbled and then, without warning, tumbled to the ground with a loud clatter.

Strange . . . and creepy.

Didn't drug lords try to fly under the radar? Based on Flynn's limited knowledge of the drug ecosystem, which admittedly consisted of binging Netflix documentaries and dramas, it seemed pretty critical to a cartel business not to bring attention to themselves with robberies.

"Fucked up, isn't it?" Nate materialized behind Flynn without warning. "Read about that this morning. I'm surprised it didn't make more headlines. Looks way more calculated than a group of 'disturbed individuals.'"

Closing her eyes, she exhaled slowly. "Any chance you can stay in your own cube for one day? Just one day is all I ask."

"But that would be no fun, now would it?" She hated that mock sympathetic smile of his. "Here comes your date."

"He's *not* my date," she hissed through gritted teeth.

There was Ted hurrying in their direction. The office open floor plan was an invitation for invasion. Designed to inspire collaboration, in reality, it ensured no one got any privacy. It also meant the whole floor reeked if someone burned popcorn in the microwave. "Wonderful! Looks like you're done."

Flynn held in a sigh, wondering if this was how a caged animal felt—resigned to a life of walls and unfamiliar rules. "Yup." She pushed back from her desk. "Let me grab my jacket."

"You won't need that. We're sitting in a box, remember?"

It took every ounce of self-control not to snarl, *Why do you care what I'm wearing?* "It might get chilly," she said instead. "These places always blast the air-conditioning."

Ted and Nate made small talk while Flynn retrieved her black bomber from the coat closet, her legs dragging like concrete blocks the whole way. The two tall men stood eye to eye, both dressed in similar dark jeans and button-down shirts. Nate's muscular form filled his clothes impressively, in contrast to Ted's lanky frame.

"Is the rest of the team meeting us?" Nate asked. "I still gotta pick up my date."

"Yeah. A bunch of people already left," Ted said. He flicked his wrist, flashing his expensive watch. "Why don't we just meet you there? We're already running late."

"Nahhh," Nate said. "We should split a cab. Besides, it'll take forever to get there in this weather." He nodded toward the window, raising his eyebrows at the threatening rain clouds looming on the horizon.

Flynn returned, zipping up her jacket. "Good idea. Let's all go together." She glanced at Nate, hopeful. She couldn't tell if he had sensed her intense discomfort and swooped in to save her or if he simply didn't want to expense the cab, but regardless she wanted to throw her arms around him. Anything was better than being left alone with Ted.

"Uh . . . alright, I guess." Ted didn't attempt to hide his reluctance.

Nate beamed, nudging Ted. "Nothing like kicking it together in box seats, boss."

Ted huffed, the wind sucked from his flapping sails. The disappointment on his face prompted the first real grin from Flynn all day.

5

FLYNN

After being squished between two tall men in the back of a cramped cab, Flynn wasn't sure which turn of events would be worse—being alone with Ted and forcing conversation or having to endure Nate's sarcastic commentary all night.

Seconds felt like hours as they inched through the Chicago Loop, making an unbearably long detour to pick up Nate's date. Flynn's stomach churned from the car's jerky motions.

"Glad you found us so fast, babe," Nate said dryly, as a leggy blonde finally climbed into the front seat of the cab. Despite giving her explicit instructions to meet them at the intersection of Randolph and State streets, they'd spent ten minutes searching for her, watching their cab fare climb steadily higher. Impatient car horns blared behind them, agitated by rush hour traffic.

"Oh, good! I thought I took forever. I couldn't figure out what you meant when you said *south* of the river. I'm so directionally challenged." She flashed a dazzling bleached smile back at them.

"Wow, Nate," Flynn whispered under her breath, "what a winner."

"Yeah, you're one to talk."

She shook her head. How many times did she have to tell him that she and Ted were *not* an item?

Five minutes of uncomfortable silence passed as the cab crawled toward the highway.

"Well, since Nate forgot to introduce us, I'm Victoria," the blonde chirped, craning her long neck to face them.

"Hello," Ted and Flynn echoed in hollow unison.

"You two must be Nate's coworkers?" The grin plastered on her face seemed permanent. "Sooo cool you guys work for Magnetic."

Flynn nodded, her cheeks aching with the effort of stretching her lips into a similar expression.

"Eh, I wouldn't quite call us 'coworkers.' I'm peers with Nate's *boss*." Ted's tone was notably condescending as he reached forward, extending a manicured hand. "Ted Flanker. Nice to meet you."

"Ohhh, *you're* Ted?" Her eyebrows ticked upward, attempting to lift to the center of her forehead, but Botox ensured her expression remained placid. "You're not at all what I expected."

Flynn did her best to cover her abrupt laugh with a cough, enjoying a brief moment of smugness.

Victoria's attention slid to Flynn's face. "And you are?"

"Oh, sorry. I'm Flynn Zarytsky. I work with Nate."

"Zay-ritz-wah?" She squinted her eyes, as if her vision became blurry, lasering in on the small Jewish star hanging from Flynn's neck.

Nate's body tensed. His fingers, drumming on the windowsill, froze.

Flynn cleared her throat. "It's Ukrainian." Although she received this question often, the words barely wriggled through her clenched teeth.

Ignoring the awkward silence, Victoria swiveled back around to face forward. "Let's listen to some jams to get pumped!" Flicking her sheet of blonde hair over her shoulder, she twisted the volume dial sharply. The small, already claustrophobic vehicle became even more confining.

Chin dropping to her chest, Flynn glared at Nate. He refused to look in her direction. Ted reached over and placed his hand on her leg, squeezing her knee. Every instinctual urge in her body begged to knock it off. Her skin itched, panic-induced hives threatening to bubble up on her arms. Nate seemed to be taking advantage of the opportunity to deflect attention from his date.

"So, how long have you guys been together now?" he asked.

Yup, it's official. This cab ride cannot get any worse. Cocking the edge of her heeled boot, she jammed it onto his foot.

"Ow! Flynn!"

"Oops, *so* sorry; it's tight in here."

"Well, we're not really together." Ted glanced at Nate, gifting him a coy wink before giving Flynn's knee another firm squeeze.

A second wave of nausea swept over her. Heat blistered up her neck, amplified by the hot air blasting from the cab's vents. She could hear Cori screaming at her. Staring at his hand, Flynn counted backward in her head. Fifteen more seconds before she threw an elbow to his balls.

"That's probably best. Must be some kind of HR violation, right? It would look pretty shady if things were to go south, especially for a manager," Nate said.

Ted stopped rubbing her leg and placed his hand back in his lap. He didn't speak to Nate the rest of the cab ride. Flynn considered coughing up forty dollars and asking the driver to take her home.

When they pulled up to the drop-off at Soldier Field stadium, Flynn practically shoved Ted out of the back seat. Stumbling from the car, she tilted her face to the sky, gulping the fresh air. Sprinkling rain had started to fall, dashing them with tiny droplets. Concertgoers swarmed around the entrance, the narrow funnel filling with recent arrivals.

Ted ushered Flynn toward the doors, trying to steer her away from Nate and Victoria. But they stayed right on their heels, following them through the packed security checkpoint and into the elevator up to the stadium's box seats. Victoria squealed at least twice about the rain, bitching about how it would ruin her keratin blowout. Flynn could relate, although not exactly. Her hair never cooperated in any weather. Wavy curls formed at the slightest indication of moisture or humidity.

They flashed their work badges to a security guard policing the door and stripped off their jackets while the opening band finished a set. The box was glamorous, offering a panoramic view of the stadium through floor-to-ceiling glass windows. A huge stage at the far end of the field completely obscured any evidence that people might come here to watch a football game. A narrow aisle stuck out from its center like a tongue, providing a runway for the band to waltz into the crowd. Fans hooded in plastic ponchos jostled to get as close as possible to the front, unfazed by the rain falling through the gaping oval opening above them. Metal barricades separated the standing-room-only section from rows of grandstand seating placed on the field to accommodate even more people. Flynn repressed a shudder at the sight of so many people massed together. A huge crowd coupled with cold rain was not her idea of a good time, even to see Green Line.

To one side of their box, steam wafted from hot chafing dishes of food, carrying the smell of fried chicken and barbeque. Flynn's stomach wobbled. A bartender served cocktails to the mingling crowd, his mouth drooping with boredom. Everyone was white, of course. The group's blended complexion came very close to matching the cream-colored carpet. And even though Flynn looked as if she belonged, a familiar nagging sensation drifted over her, reminding her that she was an outsider. At events like this she couldn't help but feel as if she was an imposter, observing the scene before her from behind an invisible barrier.

"I'll grab some drinks. What do you want?" Ted asked as they settled into plush seats next to the team, his back to Nate and his date.

"Any white wine would be great."

Victoria and Nate claimed seats in the row in front of them. Victoria eyed her date, batting long, faux lashes as she shifted her body closer to his. Nate pulled out his phone, checking the score on the Cubs' game. Visibly annoyed, Victoria stood, puffing out her chest before strutting off to join Ted at the bar.

Flynn leaned forward and tapped Nate on the shoulder. "Seriously? You're not going to at least get your date a drink?"

He shrugged, eyes still glued to the phone screen. "I brought her here, didn't I? Drinks are free. She's a very capable woman."

"I'm sure she is." Flynn glanced over her shoulder, examining Victoria's attempt to flirt with Ted. Her overly tan complexion took on an orange hue in the box's dim glow. "Not too hard to predict the outcome of your night."

"You're okay with one of our managers touching you like Ted did in the cab?" Nate propped an elbow on the back of his chair, angling to face her.

Typical Nate deflection. "What was I supposed to do?" Flynn said. "Verbally assault him or keep my job?"

Ted returned at that moment and handed Flynn a glass of red wine in a tall, stemmed glass. Victoria trailed behind him, rejected once again. She folded her lean body into a seat, attempting to cuddle up to Nate while sipping a clear beverage. Hesitating, Flynn stared into the wine glass, then set it aside.

"I asked for white wine, actually."

Ted didn't respond. He checked his cell phone and wrapped his arm around the back of Flynn's seat. She pulled herself in tighter.

"You seem to have a hard time relaxing," Ted observed.

Flynn dragged her hair over her shoulder, raking her fingers through its thick, curling ends. "You seem to have a hard time listening."

"Well, *you* take everything so seriously."

Her chest tightened, defensive. She glanced at him for the first time all night and tried to settle down. "I would think you'd want that in a direct report."

"It's not a bad thing." He took a swig of beer. "If anything, it's actually sexy. But it must mean you enjoy life a little less."

A round of polite applause rippled through the stadium as the opening band exited the stage. Bristling, she frowned. It was hard not to interpret Ted's comment as an attack on her character. "It's how I've always been. I'm not a relationship person. I have a few close people in my life and that's all I need."

"You don't care if people don't like you?" Ted asked.

"Not really." She tasted the lie on her tongue. At least, she pretended like she didn't care. Deep inside, she knew it was a defense mechanism fortified over time.

Nate extracted himself from Victoria and headed to the bar. As he walked away, Flynn couldn't help but stare. Although he could be infuriating, even she had to admire the way his shirt clung to him in all the right places.

"And how do you decide which people are worthy of a relationship?" Ted pressed, attempting to draw her attention back.

"If they're genuine. Real. I'm good at reading people. It's why I'm a recruiter."

Without warning, the lights dimmed, and fireworks shot into the sky like miniature rockets. Explosions ignited around the arena's perimeter, pouring a fountain of sparks onto the stage in a cascading waterfall. The rain's steady stream riled fans into a crazed frenzy, their yells mingling into one deafening roar. Blinding lights swirled over the crowd, illuminating a curtain of glittering raindrops. Music blasted around the stadium, accompanying the band members' appearance onstage. They emerged from beneath the platform on risers, tiny figures shimmering among a haze of confetti.

The lead singer threw his head back, strumming chords on his electric Fender. "Helloooo, Chicago!" he yelled into his microphone. "Feels good to be back in our hometown. Thanks for showing up for us tonight. We won't let a little rain ruin our parade!" The crowd went wild. Flynn leapt to her feet, a contagious energy buzzing through her. All of her anxiety from the evening melted away.

Amid the fans' cheers, three loud booms shook the stadium and a slew of what looked like more fireworks erupted, but this time they were aimed at the field—straight into the mass of spectators near the stage. Flynn couldn't decide whether this was strange or cool. Was it part of the show? It seemed a little extreme. Maybe something had gone wrong with the pyrotechnics.

Standing on tiptoe, Flynn froze, hands stretched mid-clap. Pulsing strobe lights flashed over people falling to the ground. In between each burst, she caught a brief glimpse of people scrambling over each other. She grabbed Ted's arm, but he hadn't noticed the sudden atmosphere shift. He plugged two fingers into his mouth, emitting a shrill whistle.

"Ted!" Flynn shouted above the reverberating speakers. "Ted, I think something's wrong!"

He pumped his fists in the air, mistaking her yells as excitement.

Flynn looked around. Was she the only one seeing this? Victoria had an elbow crooked around Nate's neck with her other arm outstretched to take a selfie on her phone. Both seemed oblivious. Flynn bounced on the balls of her feet, jumping to see past them. Then she heard it. Roaring cheers turned into screams. Not the earlier screams of excitement. These were higher, more urgent. Strained. Desperate.

Screams of panic.

What's happening? The thought drifted through her mind, sluggish and confused, as if she had drunk several glasses of wine instead of barely sipping one.

Waves of people surged away from the stadium's center, shoving to fit through narrow rows of seating. Blinking lights cut in and out, skipping over moments in time so everyone appeared to be moving in slow motion.

A shocked quiet settled over the box, and everyone froze. Victoria's grip around her glass slackened. It slid through her fingertips, dropping to the carpet with a dull thud. Nate leapt out of his seat, and Flynn followed, her feet involuntarily carrying her down riser steps to the paneling separating them from the stage below. A massive explosion bathed the arena in blinding orange light. Walls shook from its deafening boom. Victoria released a shrill scream. Throwing their arms over their heads, they crouched away from the shivering glass. Crowds stampeded in multiple directions, the stadium awakening, crawling like an anthill.

Victoria bolted across the room to the box entrance. "Victoria!" Nate yelled after her. "Wait! Nobody's told us where to go!"

It was too late; she was already gone.

This can't be happening, Flynn thought. With her heartbeat thundering in her chest, panic seized hold of her limbs.

Smoke bulged into the sky, mingling with rain and clouding the arena. Their view from the box was almost completely obscured. Above the muffled screaming, a much sharper sound rang through the stadium.

Ratta-tat-tat-tat-tat-tat-tat-tat-tat-tat.

Tiny bumps swelled up her arms. She turned to Nate. "Is that . . . is"— she choked on the words—"is that a gun?"

Nate grabbed her waist. His voice echoed, seemingly far away, as if thick wool clogged her ears. Her legs wouldn't move. "Come on! Flynn! Let's go. We gotta get out of here! Now!"

She stared at the ashy fog that was wafting up from the field and enclosing them.

Ratta-tat-tat-tat-tat-tat.

A spray of bullets shattered the glass front of their box. Nate threw himself on top of Flynn, pinning her to the ground. Scrambling to his feet, he dragged her up beside him, guiding her to the door. He flung it open, leaping backward as people spilled past him. Smoke billowed into the wide hallway, transforming it into a dark, narrow tunnel. People were piling out of neighboring boxes, pushing and ping-ponging toward various exits. Ted dashed by and disappeared.

Is this a dream? Some movie? A video game? It can't be real life. It can't be.

Nate wrapped his fingers around hers, yanking her along behind him. "Come on, Flynn. We need to get out of here. MOVE!"

The floor beneath them trembled from the impact of more giant explosions. Shrieks heightened into more screams. The persistent hammering of nearby machine guns intensified. Wading through a sea of people, they blindly followed the clamor of bodies. Suddenly, the crowd turned, pushing back like an opposing wave.

"Turn around!"

"They're coming!"

RAT-TAT-TAT-TAT-TAT-TAT-TAT.

People dove, covering their heads. A spray of bullets ricocheted off a wall. Tripping, pitching forward, they staggered over each other, desperate to escape the sound of impending death. One by one, people fell to their knees, blood blooming over their clothes like vibrant dye.

Nate shoved Flynn in the opposite direction, away from the stairs. "Run! The next exit!"

The shots weren't stopping. They were gaining speed. A blur of bodies enclosed them, trapping them. Nate's hand was all that grounded her to earth.

Two young boys stood in the center of the stampede's path, separated from their parents. Wearing matching Green Line T-shirts, they clutched each other, sobbing, faces swollen. Nate let go of her, swooping down to pick up the children. Stumbling, she reached for him.

"Nate, don't . . . don't let go." The frantic crowd, a wild and raging river, ripped them apart.

"FLYNN. Stay right behind me!" But the distance between them grew. Tightly packed bursts of machine-gun fire unloaded behind them.

Nate looked back, searching for her. Neck straining, Flynn opened her mouth to scream. Her throat squeezed, an iron fist unable to produce sound. Arms clasped around the boys, Nate struggled toward the only possible escape.

"Flynn!" he shouted.

She fought to stay close but was unable to extract herself from the flow of tangled limbs.

"Nate!" she called. A blast masked her voice. Agony-filled moans collided with ringing ammunition fire. Endless rounds drummed against her ears, pounding them with mounting pressure.

Diving sideways, she scrambled behind an abandoned concession stand. Dark blood covered the ground, streaking like slippery lava. A man crawled after her. Flynn reached for him, a floating life raft. Their eyes met, forged together by similar wild desperation.

Rat-tat-tat-tat-tat-tat-tat.

A spray of bullets drove straight into his back. His body jolted from the impact. Face slack, he collapsed. The world spun, as if it had been thrown out of orbit. Tears streamed down her face, catching on her lips. Bitter saltiness mingled with the acidic taste of bile rising in her throat.

Suddenly a popcorn machine shattered on the counter over her head. Glass shards cascaded over her shoulders, slicing her arms through her thin sweater. A crisscross pattern of blood rose to the surface. She flattened her back against her concession stand bunker, jaw clenched. Something nearby was on fire, and a thick, putrid cloud of smoke burned her nostrils and seared her eyes. She couldn't breathe. She pressed her head between her knees, her fingers fastening behind her neck.

It's over. I'll never live through this. Just let it end quickly.

Several seconds passed before Flynn realized the gunfire had stopped. She glanced up from her lap, her heart thudding into her stomach. A pair of heavy black boots stood before her.

Her gaze crept upward, over the black cargo pants and bulletproof vest to the dark red mask covering the towering person's face. Slowly, he raised his gun to her head.

I'm going to die.

The man studied her, unreadable beneath his costumed façade.

Staring into the endless barrel, one last whisper fell from her lips.

"Goodbye."

Pain ripped through her skull.

Everything went black.

6

WOLF

Wolf's finger hovered over the trigger of his AK-47. Sweat poured down his neck and adrenaline tripled his heartbeat, making it impossible to catch his breath. Two eyes stared up at him, freezing him in place. His body had responded first, without him understanding why, until it clicked.

He'd seen those eyes before. And he never thought he would see them again.

A work badge looped around her neck displayed a picture of her smiling face. Underneath it, printed in bold text: Flynn Zarytsky, Magnetic.

Flynn.

Wolf had met Flynn for the first time about a year after he'd joined REDS, although he hadn't known her name then. The encounter was brief, and it happened so long ago there was no chance she remembered, but he never forgot.

Despite the fact that almost a decade had passed, the day haunted him. He'd been sitting in a discreet café on the outskirts of the suburb where the reform center was located. The town had been swarming with his old high school classmates, now college douchebags home for summer, bloated from inflated egos and too much beer. He'd hated everything about them.

He had chosen a table by the café's storefront window, offering a view of fat-ass waddling strip-mall shoppers sweating from the walk across the parking lot in the summer heat. Suburbanites with so much time on their hands all they did was eat. Hunched over the beginnings of his new project, Wolf diligently studied an electrical engineering textbook. Numbers jammed in the lined paper's sidebar produced complicated equations, overlapping with cramped notes scribbled into his binder—all prep for his first official pitch to REDS's executive committee. This was his shot to prove himself, to bring their manifesto to life, to assist in building a new empire with REDS at the helm.

"Good morning," said an overtly cheery voice, catching him off guard.

A girl in a light blue apron stood over him, a pen and pad poised in her hands. Ignoring her, he fixated on his book. She didn't move. "Hardly morning anymore," he sneered into the pages.

"Oh." The girl shifted her weight onto one hip. "I like to think of any time before noon as morning."

Well, I don't give a fuck what you think, he thought.

He continued to ignore her.

"Can I get you anything?" she persisted. "Or are you just loitering in my section?"

Releasing a forceful exhale from his nose, he dropped his pen. *Could this bitch not take a fucking hint?* Glancing up, he prepared to flash her his usual steely glare. Instead, his stomach dropped to the cracked linoleum floor.

Flynn was beautiful, but not in a typical, predictable way. Her striking features made it difficult not to stare. Thick, dark eyebrows and long, mascaraed eyelashes framed light gray eyes. The rays of sunlight slanting through the windows reflected off her irises, making them shine like a sheet of ice on a bright winter day.

Wolf froze, glued to his chair. Faint beads of sweat formed on his upper lip. An alarm screamed in his head, blaring as an unfamiliar emotion hypnotized him. A sudden urge to sprint from the café hijacked his legs. Both his knees bobbed, injected with shots of adrenaline, heels tapping frantic Morse code under the table.

"Coffee," he managed. His tongue and vocal cords refused to work together, turning his voice thick and raspy.

Undeterred by his aloofness, a practiced smile spread effortlessly across Flynn's face. "Easy enough."

She had two rows of straight, white teeth, likely made perfect by years of intense pre-teen orthodontics. Eyes dropping back to his notes, Wolf pretended to read what he'd just written. His heart pinballed around his chest. Mouth moving around silent words, he summoned months of training to smother the response he had to this meaningless stranger.

Forget about her, he told himself. *She's no one. With no feeling comes absolute power. Focus.*

Returning too soon, Flynn placed a steaming mug of coffee on his table, alongside a miniature pitcher of cream. The sharp, burnt smell relaxed the muscles wound tightly across his back.

She peered over his textbook. "Taking a summer class?"

"No." He covered his book with an elbow so she couldn't read the chapter title. *Mind your own fucking business*, he thought.

"Oh, well where do you go to school?"

She ignored his iciness with impressive indifference. Scowling up at her, he immediately regretted it. Her top lip had the most perfect Cupid's bow. A springy chunk of her dark hair fell over an eye, obscuring one side of her face.

"I'm not in college."

"Got it." Clutching her metal carafe awkwardly, she seemed determined not to let him end this on a bad note. "Are you having a good summer then?"

"I hate summertime." Forcing himself to break her gaze, he turned back to his calculator.

A bell tinkled behind her, signaling new customers' arrival. Three guys sauntered toward them. Although close in age to Wolf, they looked as if they were still peaking puberty. Their torsos were too narrow, and their shoulders had no breadth but carried artificial bulk from skinny muscle. Wisps of facial hair sprouted from soft-skinned chins, matching baby faces lacking distinct jawlines.

"Hey, babe. We wanted to come check you out on the job," the pack leader said to Flynn. He talked out of one side of his mouth, which, instead of making him appear cool, made him sound like he had a slurry speech impediment.

Flynn turned to face them. "Check me out?"

"Yeah. Well, we also gotta go meet Brian's brother." He inclined his head toward the puniest guy. "He picked us up some booze for tonight."

"Cool. I just started my shift and I close tonight, so I won't be off 'til six."

"Alright." He eyed the pastry display behind her. "Any chance you can sneak us some of those cinnamon rolls? They look dope."

Wolf snorted into his book. This prick was too pathetic not to laugh. Uncomfortable silence lingered in its wake. The guy approached his table, feet shuffling in unlaced shoes one size too big. Wolf glanced up. The kid looked vaguely familiar.

Typical jock asshole thinks he runs shit, he thought to himself.

"I know you," the guy said, lifting his chin to give himself more height. Instead, it offered Wolf an unpleasant view up his large nostrils. "You're the *dick* who stole my phone in high school." He hocked a loogie and launched it forcefully. It arched in the air, landing right on Wolf's notebook pages.

Before Wolf could react, Flynn shoved the asshole. Hard. "Reid!" she screeched. "What the hell is wrong with you?"

"This fucking loser stole my phone! He's trash."

Wolf's training had taught him restraint, but it took every ounce of strength not to smash this dickwad's face in. He hadn't even had the balls to spit on him.

"*You're* trash for thinking it's okay to treat someone that way," she snarled. "Grow up. Oh, and get outta here unless you want to *pay* for a cinnamon roll."

"Your girlfriend's got a major stick up her ass," one of Reid's friends mumbled as they turned to leave.

"Girlfriend?" One eyebrow disappeared behind her thick, side-swept bangs. "Who said I was your girlfriend? I sure as heck never did."

"Oh, come on, babe. You don't even know that guy. He's a huge asshole."

"Better to be an asshole than a bully, *babe*," she sneered.

Flynn stood in front of Wolf, bunched knuckles pressed into her hips. A force field of rage sizzled from her small frame. Finally taking the goddamn hint, the rat pack left, rolling their eyes and muttering "whatevers." Without looking at Wolf, Flynn passed him a napkin and stormed off behind the counter to busy herself with rolling silverware.

As he wiped the spit from his notebook, Wolf's mind buzzed like fuzzy static on a television screen. No one had stood up for him before. Ever. He couldn't understand his mind's reaction to this person—this girl. Since initiation, Wolf had considered himself immune to emotion. Hadn't that been the fucking point? Other recruits struggled to destroy the connections they had to the outside world, but for him it had been the easiest part of training. He'd spent his entire life practicing detachment, perfecting it. Now, it was basically second nature.

Twenty minutes later his head ached, and his eyes were exhausted from unsuccessfully trying to process the meaningless sentences in his textbook. His focus was shot, but every time he mustered the strength to leave, he would catch a glimpse of Flynn and freeze in his chair. When she approached him with the check, he resisted, cringing. His coffee sat untouched on the table. Suddenly, her fingertips grazed his shoulder, skimming his thin T-shirt. He jumped. Face and neck burning, he clutched his pen so tightly his nail beds turned white.

She hesitated, extending the bill and then withdrew it. "I've been there too," she said, her voice soft. "Coffee's on the house."

As she walked away, he stared out the café window, shoulder tingling. Gathering his materials, he left as fast as he could, wishing he'd never stepped foot in there in the first place.

* * * *

Wolf never went back to that café. Although his memory of the girl in the light blue apron dulled, he couldn't forget how, for a second, she'd made him feel seen for the first time in his life. A few nights he'd dreamed about her, waking with a faint recognition of her Cupid's bow, only to forget her face again seconds later. Yet in a few rare moments of calm, he wondered about her. What was she doing right at that moment? He punished himself when he let this happen, swearing that would be the last time he thought about her.

Now, eight years later, standing amid the chaos in the Chicago stadium, the weight of the heavy rifle in his hands, he was the most powerful, godly asshole in existence. Until he turned a corner at the popcorn concession stand and saw a pair of gray eyes staring up at him. The same sleet-colored eyes that had greeted him in the coffee shop so many years ago.

7

FLYNN

Flynn woke slowly. So slowly it seemed impossible to escape the eerie, dreamlike state consuming her mind and body. Disjointed pieces of a conversation floated by, close yet far away, like an ocean fog rolling over the shoreline. She tried to open her eyes, but pain exploded through her head. Her limbs were glued together, so stiff she wondered if the circulation in them might be permanently damaged. A strip of coarse burlap fabric tied tightly around her mouth parched her tongue and chafed her lips.

Despite the sharp throb drilling through her temple, she eased her eyes open. Her eyelashes grazed a piece of cloth blindfolding her. It took a second or two to process whether she was alive. Darkness threatened to collapse on top of her in a suffocating rockslide. Panic squeezed her chest, burying her alive.

Two men, nearby, shouted at each other. Their argument grew louder and more heated, distracting Flynn from her paralyzed body. "You disobeyed my orders. Why the fuck didn't you kill her? Now we're stuck with a hostage. Do you realize how vulnerable you've made us?"

"We've dealt with this before. We won't be discovered. If anything, this will draw out more press coverage. We *need* this money."

Something was thrown against a surface right by her head. A loud clang of metal hitting metal shook the room. A scream wrenched from her raw throat, but its sound couldn't be heard over more clanging and shouting. Vibrating cymbals tapered through her eardrums.

"Not after a large-scale attack like we just pulled. This was never part of the plan! All of our work—all of it—could be compromised because of your fucking stupidity."

Are they talking about me? Her thoughts floated around her head, butterflies twirling from flower to flower, dancing out of reach right before she could swipe them into a net. She closed her eyes, channeling her dwindling energy toward absorbing what the men were saying.

"Spider, she works for Magnetic. This is the last piece to my puzzle. I've been waiting for an opportunity like this. I need her to get in."

"And how are you planning on delivering her? She already knows too much to be your mole. The Feds will be watching her like a hawk. She's not right. We'll find someone else. Pick anyone from that company and we can make them work for us."

"If we kidnap someone else and they tie it back to us, they'll know Magnetic is our target. Our mission will be blown. We had to take another hostage sooner or later. This kills two birds with one stone. And the timing gives us leverage. We can squeeze more money out of them. The government needs to smooth things over. Panic's already spreading."

Silence. Flynn's brain sent a signal to move her hands, but they were unresponsive, numb.

"How do you know she works for Magnetic?"

"I did a full background check already. She's a recruiter; it couldn't be more perfect."

"And you knew this *before* taking her?"

"I saw her identification badge. It was around her neck."

Silence again, except her heart pummeling her sternum.

"We'll discuss it with the group. If there's dissent—any at all—we kill her."

"Everyone knows we need this money."

"Discretion is more important than money, Wolf, especially now. Think about all the progress we've made."

The gag constricted her airflow, forcing her breathing to become shallower.

Spider? Wolf? How did I get here? My parents. My sister. Cori. Does my family know I'm alive? I never got a chance to say goodbye . . . to tell them I love them more than the world itself.

Clammy sweat dampened her forehead and hairline. Footsteps approached, echoing ominously. The cold cement floor reverberated under her cheek. Keys scraped against a lock. As the door screeched open, her muscles contracted, tensing in anticipation. Two leathery fingers pressed into the skin right beneath her jaw, checking for a pulse. Involuntarily, she shuddered, terrified her racing heart would betray her. The urge to scream built in the back of her throat, but it was too late.

No one can hear me. If he's going to kill me, let it be quick.

A sharp point pricked her neck and then, blissful, painless darkness.

* * * *

When Flynn regained consciousness again, she was seated in an upright position. Hard ground rested beneath her feet. Her head hung heavy like a bowling ball from her aching neck. She struggled to lift it; every movement was excruciating. Someone untied the gag.

"Can you confirm your name is Flynn Zarytsky?"

It was the same deep, threatening voice she'd heard earlier. The one that wanted her dead. Her tongue was swollen and useless. Forming sentences was near impossible, but she croaked a hoarse "Yes."

"And you work for Magnetic?"

Words lodged in her throat. Flynn didn't respond. A blow across her face knocked the entire chair over. Her body smashed to the ground, a cry ripping from her lungs. Her head struck the tile, and bright flashes burst behind her eyes. The world blurred even though she still couldn't see.

"I asked you a question. If I were you, I would think very carefully before you decide not to respond again," the voice said calmly. She was left on the floor unable to move. "Let's try this one more time. That's all you get." Footsteps circled her. "Do you, or do you not, work for Magnetic?"

A sticky pool of liquid expanded beneath her cheek. *Please don't let Da and Mom find me like this*, she thought. *Brutalized. Dead.*

"I do," she whispered. Her lips barely moved. Stomach pitching, she tasted metallic blood as it seeped into the corner of her mouth.

"That's more like it!" The cold voice separated and merged around her swimming thoughts. "Alright now, let's make this as quick and simple as possible. We've decided to make you an offer, an offer too good to refuse. We would love to have you join our organization. But there's one small catch: our terms are unconditional."

The gears in her brain worked to process what he was asking.

"So, what do you say? You in?"

Before she could respond, she felt a swish of air and something in her rib cage cracked. Scorching fire flooded her abdomen. She was a ghost, departed from her body, watching from above as she screamed until she felt nothing.

8

WOLF

It felt like a pack of rabid dogs threw themselves against Wolf's back when Spider's steel-toed boot came into contact with Flynn's stomach. Their jaws ripped into his spine, paralyzing him. It took everything in his power not to double over and clutch his head between his knees to avoid hearing her scream. Panic rose inside him.

I should've killed her, he thought. *Weak. I'm so fucking weak.*

Wolf had learned in the early stages of initiation that emotions were the gateway to self-destruction. They deteriorated years of carefully crafted defenses. Now, he finally understood why. It was as if someone were carving into his sternum with a blunt knife.

After he'd taken Flynn back to headquarters, he slipped her Magnetic work badge from her neck. Her name still rested on the tip of his tongue. He'd wanted to say it out loud, wondered what it tasted like.

I never thought I'd see her again, he thought.

Staring at Flynn, broken in a pool of her own blood, was torture more brutal than the worst days of initiation. REDS had taught them to embrace physical pain—to condition their minds to eradicate any fear associated with it. But this was different, and holy shit did it hurt. It took over, shredding his insides into tattered, indecipherable pieces. Something deep and innate longed to protect her.

Spider crossed the cell to Wolf until the two of them stood centimeters apart. Freezing his muscles in place, Wolf fought to maintain his composure. The outline of Spider's face blurred, blending into their surroundings.

"You want her? Fine. Up to you to make sure she doesn't die." Spider's heavy footsteps clicked over the cement. He shoved the Containment Room door open and paused. "Your plan better fucking work, Wolf."

His posture rigid, Wolf averted his eyes from Flynn's motionless form. The door slammed closed. As he exhaled, his shoulders sagged. Pinching the bridge of his nose, he shook his head.

Damnit. Damn my idiotic, fucking stupidity. What've I started? Walking toward her slowly, his usual confident stride deflated with every step. *I should kill her now. End this misery. It could all be over in a split second . . .*

As he knelt to untie her hands and legs from the chair, his fingers trembled. Wolf turned her over, careful to avoid looking at her face. As he scooped her up, a faint scent, mingled with her sweat and blood, startled him. Fumbling, he almost dropped her sagging body. A long-forgotten fragrance plumed from her hair. It smelled familiar. Floral.

He placed Flynn on a bench in the corner of her tiny cell. Blood oozed from a gash above her temple. Hands shaking, Wolf locked them behind his neck. Her chest barely lifted and fell. Pacing up and down, he cast furtive glances in her direction as if she might jump to her feet and attack.

If Spider knew, if *any* of them knew the effect she had on him, they'd kill her and, to be honest, it would be for the better. Bending over, he checked for a pulse. Flynn's skin was clammy, but her slow rhythmic heartbeat thumped beneath his fingertips. He yanked his hand away.

I can't believe it's her. His eyes finally skimmed over her blindfolded face and lingered there. *After all these years.*

Peering over his shoulder toward the door, he removed his jacket and ripped off one of the sleeves to staunch the blood flow. He balled up the remaining fabric and tucked it under her head. Hesitating, he probed around her rib cage. Definitely broken bones. Probably internal bleeding as well.

Shit. Shit. Shit . . . Not good. Not good at all, he thought. She needed help fast or she could die. Maybe that'd been Spider's plan all along. *Does he know how I feel? Can he read me like the open book I am?*

A weak moan disrupted his paranoia. Flynn coughed, then yelped in pain. Wolf flipped her on her side in one swift motion. Water. She needed water. Slipping out of the cell, he hurried to a trough sink in the corner of the room. When he returned with a full canteen, her breathing was raspy and labored. He removed the burlap gag, freeing her airway. One of the broken ribs might've punctured a lung.

She couldn't drink by herself with the blindfold. Holding his breath, he reached down to touch her. Flynn twitched, thrashing her legs to push herself away from him. Shushing her urgently, Wolf grabbed her right before she fell off the bench. She yelped again.

"Relax," he whispered. "I'm going to give you some water."

Flynn stayed very still, her jaw clenched. He brought the canteen to her lips, cushioning her head with his hand and lifting. A trail of water sloshed down her chin. She gulped thirstily, choking. Blood stained one side of her face. The other had shadows of swollen purple bruises, transforming her symmetrical features into unrecognizable shapes.

"Who are you?" Her meek voice rang through his memory like a familiar song.

Leaning over her, he tightened the sleeve wrapped around her head, hiding his face from the cameras hovering over them.

"Listen to me," Wolf said, voice icy. "You think this'll be a quick death? A bullet right through your head? No. You will be ripped apart. We have no rules. No. Rules."

"What do you want from me? I have nothing. I know nothing." Her words quivered.

"Tell them you work for Magnetic and you'll do whatever they want." His eyes remained fixated on the door in the corner of the Containment Room.

"I work in recruiting," she breathed. "I can't help you."

"You're exactly what I've been looking for. You need medical help, and this is your only shot at getting out of here."

"What if I can't get you what you want?"

"Do what I say and there won't be any problems, got it?"

Her teeth gritted against what must have been a fresh wave of pain, her legs tensing and releasing. "I'm not going to be part of your fucked-up plans," she spat.

"Listen." His lips dipped closer to her ear, voice lowering. "You want to die? Fine. Not my fucking problem. But if I were you, I'd want it to be on my own terms and not in here. Trust me. You will suffer."

"You're evil," she said weakly. "Go to hell."

Well, she's got balls, I'll give her that, he thought.

"Hell suits me just fine. And let's not be so quick to throw judgment around. You're the one about to get tortured to death. You think we'll end with you? Your family, your friends . . . they're all part of this equation now, and if you want them to stay alive, you'll do what we say."

She took a minute to respond. Her skin grew paler, her fight waning.

"You can't make me kill anyone. I won't do it. I'll bleed to death first."

She recoiled from the harsh sound of his laugh.

"We don't need *you* to do any killing. What kind of pussies do you think we are? You're going to get us into Magnetic." He paused. "It's your only chance at staying alive."

She was silent. Wolf resisted shaking her. *What the fuck is wrong with her?* he wondered. *How can she not grasp who she's up against?*

"If you want to stay alive, agree to our terms, keep your mouth shut, and do what you're fucking told. Got it?" He said each word slowly and deliberately so he could be sure his point stuck.

Her whisper was so soft he almost missed it. "What do you want me to do?"

It was the answer he'd been waiting for.

* * * *

Wolf found Spider in the arena, eating with other executive members. He approached him from the side, careful to stay in his line of vision. Spider once beat someone to death after they'd surprised him from behind. Poor bastard never stood a chance. Dangerous reflexes and quiet stealth earned Spider his alias. It was in Wolf's best interest not to test those skills.

Standing at attention, Wolf waited for Spider to acknowledge him. He gave a small nod, permission to speak. "I have an update on the hostage," Wolf said.

Spider's eyes flicked toward him, but he continued staring at his plate, lifting a forkful of food to his mouth. "Better be good."

"I'm making progress. She's cooperating."

Spider took a long sip from his mug. "She understands our conditions?"

"I'll keep working on her."

Shifting, he straddled the bench. "Don't make me regret this, Wolf."

Wolf nodded, the tips of his fingers tingling. "This is it—the last piece of our puzzle. She'll get me into the right division."

Spider shrugged a shoulder. "We'll see about that, won't we?"

"Have you given the Feds a heads-up about our hostage?"

"They know."

"Where's drop-off?"

"Depends on which one you're referring to. The one we told the Feds, or the real one?"

9

FLYNN

Flynn hovered precariously over the fine line separating unconsciousness and what might be reality. The excruciating pain gripping her abdomen hinted at which it could be.

What did I do to deserve ending up in this hell?

The jarring movement and rhythmic vibrations of a vehicle's tires hummed beneath her. Her eardrums ached, as if they were stuffed with sharp gravel. Muffled voices drifted by, hard to decipher and interpret. Speaking with fluid urgency, no idle conversation or laughter lingered between their tones. Every word knew its purpose. A slew of warnings bubbled to the surface of her memory.

"Speak of us and we kill you. Mention our name and we kill you."

"If you tell anyone what happened, we'll slaughter everyone you ever cared about. Once that's done, we'll kill you."

"You can't hide from us."

"We'll find you when we need you."

"If you want to live, if you want your family to live, this is what you have to do."

Flynn knew she should be afraid of what awaited her, but she was too exhausted. Cautious hope flitted deep within her, a tiny spark waiting to grow. She might escape them, even if it was just for a short time.

"Alright. All clear, no five-O within two miles, according to the radar."

Grooves of hard plastic dug into her spine, unforgiving. The vehicle decelerated, gradually rolling to a stop. Doors slammed. Her heart pounded in her chest, creeping upward to rest in the base of her throat. Moments later, a light breeze caressed her face. She inhaled the fresh air, tears springing to the corners of her blindfolded eyes.

"We're two miles away. Knock her out here?"

"Not yet. Wait 'til we get a little closer."

The voice's silky roughness was familiar, like chocolate milk coating a sore throat. *It's the one that gave me water*, she realized. *How long ago was that now?*

"Any word from the crew on the east side?"

He didn't answer right away. "No. Pickup isn't gonna be easy. Especially with her here in case things go south."

"Alright, let's keep moving. Here's the phone. We've got five minutes to ditch her and bail."

"I'll stay with her in the back. Once you stop, I'll knock her out and then we can get outta there. Make sure to go to the exact spot we planned to avoid cameras. If anyone is there, do a quick perimeter until they leave."

"Got it."

The floor of what seemed like a cargo van tilted toward the heavy weight of another body climbing in beside her. Terror dripped down her aching neck, spreading into her bound limbs. Doors on unoiled hinges squeaked closed. The van's engine coughed back to life.

"Don't forget, you're alive for a fucking reason." His voice close to her ear caused Flynn to jump. "We'll find you when things quiet down, once there's less attention on you." The same hands that tended to her wounds fastened something around her arm. His words were barely audible over the rattling wheels racing down an unpaved road. "Don't try to run from us. Don't speak of anything you heard or have been asked to do. We'll know everything. We see everything. We hear *everything*. You can't escape us." An underlying warning threaded through his threats.

The burlap around her mouth loosened. Sticky bile coated the walls of her throat, gluing it shut. "How am I supposed to believe you?" she whispered.

"You don't have a choice."

The vehicle bounced over an uneven surface, dipping and tilting around frequent bumps. Flynn clenched her teeth to suppress a groan. "Where are we going?"

"What the fuck did I tell you about asking questions?"

The brakes whined in protest as the van slowed to a stop. Heavy steps rocked the floor, scattering pain like buckshot inside her rib cage. She yelled out.

"Shut up!"

The man lifted Flynn as if she were a feather pillow, his touch surprisingly gentle. His body was so hot it burned her raw skin. He pressed against the object secured to her arm as if he were dialing on a keypad. Another sharp needle pricked the side of her neck.

"See you soon."

The warmth vanished. Hard ground beneath her. Sprinting footsteps. Squealing wheels. Distant sirens. Then nothing.

✳ ✳ ✳ ✳

When Flynn woke again, fear gripped her chest in a familiar suffocating bind. She gasped, choking on the lump of panic wedged within her throat.

I'm not dead yet? Please no, her mind raced. *No more. No more torture.*

Brightness rested against her heavy lids. It took her a moment to process that she was lying on a soft bed. Cautiously, she cracked open her eyes, afraid of what might greet her. Sunrays peeked through blinds, saturating the small hospital room in dazzling morning light. Pain pounded at her temple, reverberating through her skull like a mallet to a gong.

Where am I?

Struggling to sit up, she released a small cry as her abs contracted. She sank back into her pillow, gingerly rubbing her torso. Thick bandages wrapped her arms. Tubes hooked to whirring machines protruded from hidden veins. Mounting dread spilled into her stomach, filling it with churning nausea. The memory of glass showering over her shoulders flashed before her.

Trapped. I'm trapped.

A monitor started beeping frantically as it picked up her accelerating heart rate, summoning a middle-aged nurse into her room. "Well, look who's awake." The thin lines spoking her shriveled lips deepened into a welcoming smile. "Mornin', doll."

Flynn blinked at her. Anxiety thundered into her bloodstream, spreading throughout her body.

"My name's Melissa. I'm one of your nurses. We've been taking extra good care of you." She bustled over to the contraptions next to Flynn and examined them closely. As she turned to grab a clipboard, Melissa's hip knocked against Flynn's bed, setting off a fresh chain reaction of pain. "Don't you worry, though, nothing too serious."

"Where am I?" Flynn asked, her voice raspy. Her tongue and the roof of her mouth still felt raw from the gag.

"You're at Northwestern Hospital, honey. I'll call the doctor in, tell her you're awake. She'll want to go over your injuries with you, and I'm sure you've got loads more questions." The shrill beeping took off again, picking up speed. Nurse Melissa studied the monitor, deep in thought, then turned her attention to Flynn. "Come to think of it, your family's here. They've been waiting to see you. Why don't I go bring them in first?"

She left the room, returning with Flynn's parents, Sean and Rachel; her sister, Fiella; and best friend, Cori, in tow. After a few dazed seconds, relief flooded their gray faces. Their eyes sagged with exhaustion, but their joyful grins quelled the terror building inside her.

"Flynn!" They rushed toward her, shoulders jostling each other to get to her first.

Nurse Melissa intercepted them. "Now, hold on a second. Don't dogpile her. She's been through a lot. Four broken ribs, a punctured lung, and a serious concussion. Dr. Martin mandated limited contact over the next few days to avoid further injury."

"Do we need to worry about her breathing?" her mother asked, pressing both palms over her own heart.

"The doctor will be in shortly to explain," Nurse Melissa answered. "But please be careful with any physical contact."

Everyone nodded fervently and surrounded her bed, reaching out to touch her in gentle reassurance. It was as if she'd died and come back to life. She couldn't believe it. She never thought she'd see them again. Their presence enveloped her, like she was sinking into a warm bath.

"I'm okay," Flynn said hoarsely, even though she wasn't.

"Oh, Flynn!" Her mother squeezed Flynn's hand, holding it against her cheek, tears streaming from light gray eyes. The same eyes as her own. "After the attack, we didn't think those psychotic people would ever give you back. Terrorists, that's what they are. And they call themselves REDS? After the color? I mean, come on, talk about bizarre." The words poured from her mother's mouth as if they had been building inside of her for days.

REDS? Where had she heard that name before? It circled around inside her head, a buzzing fly she couldn't catch, until out of nowhere she snatched it midair. *That group from the BuzzFeed article. Those men were from REDS?*

Suddenly, a voice whispered from the back of her memory. *Mention our name and we kill you.*

"Flynn," Cori said as she sat on the end of her mattress, resting a few fingers on her shin. Flynn jumped, startled from her reverie. "I'm so sorry. I never should've made you go to that concert." Her hair was tangled into a messy knot on top of her head. Disheveled bangs splayed across her forehead.

Flynn tried to smile despite her throbbing head. "You didn't make me go, Cor."

Purple circles formed a ring around her dark brown eyes. "I pressured you into it and now look where you are."

Her sister, Fiella, wrapped an arm around Cori and reached for Flynn's free hand. "We have to be strong, Cor. If you start, we'll all start. She's alive! It's all going to be okay now."

"What happened?" Flynn asked. "How long has it been since the concert?"

"Six days." Her father cupped her cheek with his palm. His thick Irish accent muddled his voice with emotion. "The young man you were with—Nate—he reported you missing. Then the government told us REDS took you as a hostage."

"Nate . . ." An anvil slammed onto her chest. "Is he okay?"

"Yes, sweetheart. He's fine. He's asked to see you."

"They wanted ten million dollars for you, Flynn." Her mother's Long Island twang sounded brash compared to her father's drawl, every syllable urgent and hurried. Along with a tendency to wear her wide spectrum of emotions on her sleeve, her mother could get overwhelming and exhausting. Flynn often wondered if her mother's overtly dramatic personality was why she was so reserved when it came to expressing herself. "There was complete panic. We were terrified. When they showed up without you, we were sure you were—" She gasped, several tears catching in her long eyelashes. "We were sure you were d-d-dead." Her mother sobbed into Flynn's father's shoulder. "Oh, Sean, I can't bear the thought."

Vague bleariness jumbled Flynn's thoughts. Trying to concentrate hurt her head even more. "*They* showed up without me? These REDS terrorists did?"

"Rachel, can you please pull yourself together?" Her father shushed her mother. His fair, freckled complexion usually showed amazing resistance toward age, but fresh wrinkles webbed his skin. "Flynn's been through enough these past few days without having you pile this on her all at once." He sighed, downturned eyes serious behind round glasses. "Well, sweetheart, REDS identified themselves quickly after the terrorist attack. They used *you* as proof of their claimed responsibility. When the time came to exchange you for the ransom money, all they found was some sort of fake dummy."

"You paid ten million dollars?" Flynn's mind went blank. Pain piled upon more pain. "Where did you . . . ?" She shook her head. "I don't understand." Her family didn't have that kind of money.

"The FBI got involved, of course. They wire-transferred the money, and then all REDS left behind was a note with a list of clues. Almost like a sick game to throw everyone off their scent. The FBI tracked you down, but it was difficult."

"A note?" Flynn asked, bewildered. Frustration squeezed her lungs, making it difficult to breathe. She felt like a toddler who couldn't understand anything her parents were saying. They were saying words and gesturing, but none of the pieces clicked.

Pressing her lips together to smother a fresh sob, her mother hiccupped. Her father helped her to a chair, rubbing her back in robotic circles. Despite her parents' differences, Flynn had never once doubted their devotion to each other. When his Irish Catholic parents disowned him for marrying a Jew, he chose her mother without regret, even taking on her family name. Flynn searched his worried face now.

"Yes, a note," he said. "It had ten riddles leading to different places around the city. Each had a number. After putting them together, the FBI was able to connect to the cell phone REDS had attached to you."

More memories of threats flooded over her in a rush of cold chills. She could hear the same distant voice muttering in her ear, *Don't forget, you're alive for a fucking reason.*

"Not one of them was caught?" she asked.

Fear crept up from the bottom of her stomach. Even though her family was there beside her, she swirled through an orbit a hundred miles away.

"The FBI is all over it," Fiella jumped in to say. She eased onto the edge of the bed by Flynn's hip. "There's a lot of pressure to catch these fuc . . . err, jerks." She glanced at their parents. "Don't worry. They'll get to the bottom of this."

Nurse Melissa returned, pointing at her wristwatch. "Alright, crew, it's time to give our patient some rest." She scurried around the small group, attempting to usher everyone to the door. "Dr. Martin needs to come in and have a look at her. The authorities have been hounding her about questioning Flynn."

"Questioning? Already?" Her mother became frantic again. "Can't that wait?"

"Once the doctor evaluates her condition, that's up to her, Mrs. Zarytsky. I'm sure you've noticed the FBI presence around here. They're desperate to talk to her."

"Can I have a few more minutes with my daughter alone?" Sean asked. Nurse Melissa pursed her pruney lips. "It will be quick, I promise."

She sighed. "Fine. But five is all you get."

Fiella leaned down to plant a kiss on Flynn's forehead before retrieving their mother. They wore jubilant grins, faces glowing with jittery relief. Even though Flynn was battered, bruised, and broken, she was alive. They had no idea of the damage she now bore beneath her skin's surface. Flynn winced as Cori gave her foot a quick squeeze. Mouthing a silent sorry, Cori allowed Nurse Melissa to herd her back to the waiting room.

"Sweetheart, I know how overwhelming this must be for you," Sean said once everyone else had gone.

Flynn nodded, biting her tongue. She wished she could cry. She wished at least a single tear would fall. That would be a normal response to this madness. Not anger. Not dread. Maybe tears would release the building pressure, a pinprick to an inflating balloon.

Why me? she wanted to ask, but couldn't.

Her father enveloped her hand between his own, warming away the sticky chill clinging to her fingers. "Do you have any questions you want to ask me? While no one else is around?"

She studied the veins tunneling from his wrist to his cracked knuckles. His dull, chipped nails revealed the years of hard labor he'd poured into his contracting business. When he was only eleven, her father and his Catholic family had fled Ireland during the worst of the 1980s bombings. He instantly fell in love with America, its freedom of religion, its civility. "There's so much I don't understand. Who are these REDS people?"

"Well, that's what the authorities are trying to figure out. No one's heard of them until recently. There are a lot of terms being thrown around. Extremists. Radicals. *Disturbed* individuals."

"What do you think?"

His eyes drifted around the room in search of words. "I think that's a bunch of blarney. They're bloody terrorists. And they're smart."

The pain hacking into her head bordered on a migraine. "What do they want?"

"The FBI claim they're a small gang committing random acts of violence. They don't think REDS has an agenda other than to stir things up. *I* think they're just saying that to keep everyone calm."

"You think they're more . . . strategic?"

"Strategic, yes, although I can't say for certain. But REDS seem much larger and more sophisticated than government officials are making them out to be. They're dangerous, ruthless even. Why else would they attack an entire concert full of people? To show their power. To scare the living daylights outta everyone. And it worked. I was just a kid when we left Ireland, but I remember my own da telling us about the Guards downplaying the IRA and what they were capable of." He paused. "Speaking of which, there's something I want to ask you. Is, uh—is there anything you want to tell me, sweetie?"

A caramel voice breathed into her mind. *You're going to get us into Magnetic. It's your only chance at staying alive.*

"What do you mean?"

Her father collapsed his hands over hers, squeezing. "It's strange . . . after killing so many innocent people, they chose to keep *you* alive as their hostage. If there's anything they told you or you overheard, you can tell me. I would do anything to protect you."

You're exactly what I've been looking for, the voice whispered again.

"I know, Da," she stumbled. She hadn't prepared for this. She hadn't prepared for the questions. "Everything's such a blur. Maybe it'll come back to me at some point."

✷ ✷ ✷ ✷

Dr. Martin conducted a thorough evaluation before informing Flynn that her concussion was improving. Briefing her on the side effects of the injuries that would accompany her for a while, she prescribed more medication to reduce the brain swelling. Only time could mend the broken ribs, she said, and her breathing would likely be impaired until her lung recovered from surgery. Until then, she'd continue wearing a chest tube to help re-inflate the organ while it healed. In the interim, plenty of drugs numbed the endless throbbing.

"How's your memory?" Dr. Martin asked, shining a bright light into Flynn's pupils.

"Uh, pretty hazy," she lied. Bloodied bodies, exploding and falling in fleshy heaps, played before her like a horror movie every time she closed her eyes.

"Well, long-term memory doesn't appear to be impacted. Events will start to come back to you as your brain heals. You took quite a blow to the head."

She didn't respond.

Scribbling notes on her chart, Dr. Martin's scratching pen pricked the silence. "Are you comfortable talking to the authorities yet? They've been asking to speak with you."

"Not really . . . I don't have much to tell them. I can't remember anything. Maybe it'll come back to me in a few days."

Dr. Martin gave her a warm smile. "Alright, let's prescribe you another day of rest before you speak with anyone."

* * * *

Flynn's parents, sister, and Cori returned and didn't leave her side, but she wasn't allowed any other visitors. Deciding how to buffer her from the onslaught of media outreach became their most pressing task. All the major TV networks were desperate to cover her story, but the hospital deflected their efforts. They wouldn't be able to protect her forever.

"Oy vey. I'm telling you, they're animals," her mother fumed over a steaming cup of tea later that evening at Flynn's bedside. Her thick accent exaggerated her abrasive tone. "I mean, have they no respect? She only woke up this morning and now we can't even get to our car to drive to the hotel. How are we supposed to get a change of clothes?"

"Ma, they're looking for answers." Fiella rolled her blue eyes. She was the spitting image of their father, while Flynn had inherited her mother's angular, dark features. "There's never been a terrorist attack like this in Chicago. The entire country is petrified."

"What happened to Nate?" Flynn interrupted, suddenly remembering how he'd tried to lead her to safety.

"He's fine, hon," her mother soothed. "Both Ted and Nathaniel came by to see you. Ted seems rather persistent. I had no idea you were seeing someone. You two work together?"

"I'm not seeing him."

"You can tell us these things, hon," she pressed.

"There's nothing to tell."

"Rachel, stop berating your daughter about her dating life. Now is hardly the time," her father scolded.

As if lifted by an invisible marionette string, Flynn's shoulders rose to her ears while her family bickered warmly about her nonexistent dating life. Fear stirred in her chest, awakening regularly like a starving baby. Pulling her lips back into a forced smile, she nodded when her parents looked to her for approval. Her insides ached, reaching toward distant normalcy. She'd do anything to forget this past week and move on. Sinking her teeth into the soft inside of her cheek, she squashed the temptation to unburden herself of these secrets.

She couldn't tell anyone. REDS had vowed to kill her family, and she had no doubt they would.

She had to protect them, even if it meant losing part of herself.

10

WOLF

Wolf was thirteen when he'd stood in front of the reform center for the first time. His stomach swirled as he took in the squat, ugly building. Good thing he'd been living off morsels of food, or else he might have hurled all over the sidewalk. He'd been bounced out of the foster care system, and this was his last option. *It's such bullshit*, he thought. *All of it is bullshit.*

A faded yellow sign announced the location, and below it a brief description read: Behavioral Health System. Throughout his five years there, he could never figure out what that meant. Behavioral health? As if behavior was something that could be diagnosed and then cured or controlled. Wolf had been alone his entire life. He didn't know how to behave or what constituted good behavior. He'd been more concerned with how to survive. But these instincts had taught him something. They'd taught him to trust his gut. He'd never had anyone to guide or mentor him until the moment Spider intercepted him from his hopeless future that one afternoon in the reform center guest lounge. The only person he'd been able to rely on up to that point was himself. Eventually, the more he learned to trust his instincts, the more he could predict an outcome *before* it happened. That was when things started changing for him. That was when he started to win.

His first day of initiation now seemed like a lifetime ago. He'd been a different person. Young, naïve, and eager, he'd been terrified when two escorts met him at the bus stop by the reform center in an old pickup truck. All he'd had was a small backpack filled with his only belongings, except for a special item, which he'd hidden in his baggy pants. The backpack and all its contents were taken from him, never to be seen again. They blindfolded him during transit to the recruit training center and made him wear headphones that muted any sound other than blaring death metal music. He had no idea where they were going or who these freaks were. When they arrived, a pair of rough hands herded him down a steep ramp. Directional shoves indicated approaching turns, but occasionally he scraped against a cold wall. His ears popped as they descended farther, and the dank smell of mold grew more pronounced.

Finally, his guide yanked him to an abrupt halt, removing his blindfold and headphones. Heavy silence hung in the unventilated air, an eerie contrast to the screaming music. He blinked, disoriented, while his eyes adjusted to the dimness. He found himself in a large chamber, with one overhead bulb casting a weak, circular glow over the room's center. Its deficient rays left the periphery cloaked in darkness. An occasional drip of water leaking from pipes echoed on metal grates embedded in the concrete floor. Wolf glanced around, his heart grappling out of his throat.

He counted sixteen teenagers on either side of him. They all looked to be around his same age—eighteen at the time. Some were short and dweebish, some tall and hefty. Each seemed to carry a familiar weight that slapped on about ten years to their countenance. In the shadows, six forms flanked an enormous beast of a man. He towered before them, dominating the small spotlight. The group withered under his gaze. Mangled red ridges crawled up both the man's arms, twisting around taut muscles, crisscrossing like reptilian scales. A tattooed snake coiled around his neck, curling up and over his left ear. He was completely bald, with thick eyebrows that canopied his glowering eyes.

"Congratulations, recruits!" he shouted. "By accepting our invitation, you've just made the best decision of your damn lives. I'm Cobra. I'll oversee your initiation training." He paced up and down their staggered line. Beneath a coarse, bushy beard, his thin upper lip curled into a sneer. "There are three rules. Only three damn rules for your puny little brains to remember. First, your old identity no longer exists. Under no circumstance will you mention your name. Don't care. Doesn't matter. Don't give any shits. Second, no fighting other recruits unless directed by members." Spittle flew from his mouth like a sprinkle of venom. "Third, never leave the training center's premises. If you do"—he paused, allowing the enormity of his words to settle—"you'll be executed." Wolf held his breath, concentrating hard on keeping his spine as rigid as possible. "Yeah, you heard me—killed. Finished. Kaput."

Cobra's piercing glare landed on a short, pimply boy whose face was gleaming in a sheen of sweat. He flinched as Cobra approached. "This isn't some bullshit fraternity. Our secrets are too critical to compromise—way more important than each of your measly lives."

A gangly boy next to Wolf began to tremble, emitting soft whimpers. *What the fuck have I gotten myself into? Some insane fight club?*

"REDS doesn't need a group of pussies. We need warriors. By the end of initiation, *if* you make it, that's what you'll be. A bona fide, ruthless warrior far superior to the rest of the pathetic human species." He grated his knobby knuckles against his palm. They were so round they looked like individual stones covered with leathery skin. He cracked them one by one, filling the silence with sharp pops. "Now, we've developed a program to weed out the winners from the losers. A *cultural* conditioning program to expose your most primitive emotions."

"What if I don't got no emotions?" asked a stocky teenager standing farther down the line. He crossed his arms over his chest, a smug expression plastered on his face.

Cobra looked him up and down with evident disgust. "Recruit, don't ever speak without permission." Turning back to the group, he ran a hand over his smooth head. He moved as if he had complete control over each muscle. "You *all* have emotions because they're necessary for survival. They prime us to take action against outside threats. Nature hardwires them into you from birth."

"Yeah, well, I'm not afraid of nothin'," the same boy blurted, squaring his body toward Cobra.

Within three steps, Cobra loomed over Dumbass. His eyes narrowed into vicious slits. Everyone drew in a collective breath, bracing for his response. He whipped a knife from his belt, flicked it into the air where it spun, blade winking, and caught the leather handle squarely in his palm. In a flash, he slashed the kid's throat. The group staggered backward, scattering like mice, as the boy fell to his knees, blood flowing from the gash gaping across his neck. Indecipherable words gurgled from his mouth, drowning in the thick liquid.

Wolf's heart leapt into his skull. It pounded so loudly against his eardrums he was sure everyone could hear it. He'd never seen anyone die before. Not right in front of him. His arms and legs went numb as the pressure of a scream built in his lungs. The pimply boy turned and threw up, vomit splashing over the cement.

"You all should be afraid," Cobra whispered. "You all should be very afraid. Disposable. That's what this group is right now—fucking disposable. Anyone else got somethin' to say?"

The entourage surrounding Cobra stepped forward, faces impassive as if they'd just watched someone stroll by in the park. The teens clustered into a tight circle, minnows shuddering in the shadow of a predator. Silence stretched throughout the chamber. Half the group stared at Cobra in awe, captivated by his forceful presence. The remaining recruits shrank back in terror. It was clear who'd succeed over the coming weeks.

Cobra casually wiped his knife's blade clean on the dead boy's pant leg before sliding it back into its sheath. "Be brave, recruits, but don't be fucking idiots. Everyone's afraid of something. If you're not, you ain't human." He shook his head in mock sympathy, then continued, voice upbeat. "But that's our goal! Squeeze the humanity outta you. Our conditioning program is highly personalized. Whoever is left at the end will be able to convert emotions from reactive to decisive action." He counted the heads in their group. "Well, lookey here. Now we've got an even number. You'll each have an assigned roommate throughout initiation. Figure out their emotional triggers." A slow smile spread across his face. "You wanna survive? You're gonna need to know them."

* * * *

The initiates' temporary housing was in an outpost close to REDS headquarters. No one had any idea where it was other than being below an abandoned warehouse on the outskirts of Chicago. Dim corridors connected the training facilities to their small holding cells, but there were no additional common spaces. Leadership discouraged socializing.

Living in close proximity to another boy for an extended period of time was reason enough for Wolf to reconsider joining REDS entirely. Not that leaving was an option. Cobra had made that pretty damn clear. But the promise of competing to become a warrior reaffirmed his determination to become a REDS Enforcer. He had no idea how to develop a relationship with someone for the purpose of using it to his advantage. Manipulation is a learned skill, one that requires emotional understanding—something he never got the chance to practice during his isolated childhood.

This was an opportunity.

Shifting his weight from foot to foot, Wolf glared at his new roommate. The other boy sat hunched on his cot, seemingly sizing up Wolf's tall, intimidating build. Their unit contained nothing but a sink and two cots pushed against opposite walls. Wolf had never worked well with others. Throughout his entire life, his sole responsibility had been to look out for himself. This guy was just another dick who'd get in the way.

"So, uh, where were you before this?" the guy asked.

Wolf tensed, shoulders tightening. No way was he going to spill his fucking guts to a complete stranger. "Nowhere important." He hadn't wanted to reciprocate the question, but in order to be successful in the coming tests, he had to get some sort of read on this prick. Where he came from seemed like a start. "What about you?"

Dude shrugged. "Foster parents."

Wolf's guard eased a fraction. He recognized shadows of familiar recluse characteristics in his new roommate. Maybe a little younger than Wolf, lanky and awkward, he still had some growing to do to fill into an adult physique. Shaggy brown hair flopped over shifty eyes.

They couldn't introduce themselves using their old names. Instead, they had to decide who would take their assigned temporary aliases: Alpha and Beta.

"I'll take Alpha." Jutting out his chin, Wolf dared the other boy to argue.

"Fine by me."

The corners of his lips crept upward. *That was easy.* If complacency was Beta's strategy, it wouldn't work in this process. "Guess you know how to pick your battles."

Beta returned the smile apprehensively. "I'm used to flying under the radar." He cleared his throat, then rubbed his chin. "So, uh, that kid . . . crazy, huh? I've never seen anyone do that . . . in real life, I mean. Movies don't count."

"What're you talking about?"

"Cobra just slit that guy's throat"—he snapped his fingers—"like that. No hesitation."

The image of black blood fanning over concrete still hovered before Wolf. But, as the shock waves had worn off, admiration sprouted from a newly planted seed. Cobra had wielded his power without hesitation. In a blink, he righted a wrong against him. No one fucked with him. He was indestructible. Wolf wanted that kind of power, craved it.

"So what?"

"I dunno. Seemed harsh is all," Beta said.

"Yeah, well, the world's harsh. You of all people should know that. Now we've finally got our chance to fight back."

11

WOLF

Throughout initiation, REDS severed all attachment the recruits might have held to their previous lives. The memory of Wolf's old, worthless existence faded. In its place, something else grew. Something hungry. REDS hadn't disclosed the organization's terminal objective. They'd only reveal that secret to those who survived 'til the end, those who proved themselves worthy of upholding such a profound duty. But no one had cared. They had what they needed for the time being—a newfound sense of belonging.

Initiation began with lectures, application of content, and physical conditioning in the training center's workout room. Vicious animals were REDS's main inspiration and served as the backbone of all their education. Initiates observed animal behavior, watching video after video, studying how predators rely on their natural instincts for brutality to survive.

Wolf's first opportunity to prove himself came a few weeks in. Leopard, one of the more senior REDS Enforcers, led daily trainings on carnivorous hunting techniques. He stalked around their group, green, catlike eyes glinting as he searched for his next victim. Tension collected in the cramped room, thick as a Midwest summer day. His white teeth flashed into a calculated smile.

"Recruits, if you take away anything from my lesson today, remember you are always the hunter, never the prey." Leopard stopped in front of

Wolf, rubbing his chin. His long fingernails, filed into pointed claws, grazed his pocked skin. They stood nose to nose. "I earned my alias because of resilience. You see, a leopard is an animal so powerful it becomes even more dangerous when wounded."

In an instant, he threw Wolf to the ground, knocking the wind out of him. Pressing his knee onto Wolf's chest, he pinned him in place, forearm jammed against his throat.

"Channel the pain," Leopard snarled. "Use it to fight back." He leaned forward, the tips of his incisors augmented by his dominant angle.

Gasping, Wolf thrashed his legs and twisted his core in an effort to unbalance Leopard. But Leopard was too strong. There was a moment between panic and pain when physical sensations took command of his body.

"Always attack your enemy as if they're threatening your life. What are your instincts telling you to do?" Leopard's breath stank like dead meat.

Curling his fingers, Wolf plunged them into Leopard's eye socket, scraping down his face, ripping his flesh. Leopard staggered backward. Air filled Wolf's lungs. He leapt into a crouched position, breathing heavily, bracing for the next attack. Instead, Leopard grinned, blood blossoming from deep nail tracks.

"Good, Alpha." Leopard addressed the tight circle, a red trickle dripping down his nose onto his lips. He showed no signs of pain, instead withdrawing calmly as though Wolf had offered him a handshake. "Instincts can't be taught. We'll see soon enough if you sorry assholes got 'em. If not, well," he laughed, a screeching sound, "you know how the saying goes—survival of the fittest."

The initiates continued to immerse themselves within the animal kingdom. They experimented with a viper's powerful hemotoxic venom, a poison that disables blood clotting so victims bleed out from every pore. They replicated a Komodo dragon's killing technique, ripping out small mammals' throats and retreating as they bled to death. Each physical test grew in intensity.

Beta surprised Wolf early on. He'd misjudged him as muted, submissive. But Beta was cunning. His subtlety was dangerous, disarming competitors who perceived him as weak. The two roommates maintained an aloof relationship, avoiding contact as much as possible except for evenings together in their holding cell. Until one day something between them changed.

Two months into training, Cobra called the remaining group together. "Recruits, time for your first partner challenge. Your roommate's life will be at stake throughout the entire test. If you fail to save him, you enter an elimination pool. We all know what that means—fight to the death." His words hit Wolf like a heavy blow to the chest. Not a chance in hell did he trust Beta to save his life. He'd probably let him die on purpose and risk the elimination pool. "The person with the fastest rescue time will be exempt from the next test. You'll be evaluated on both speed and demonstrated skills."

Beta's and Wolf's eyes meet. Beta inclined his head, their determination mirroring each other. Unexpected confidence surged through Wolf. *Shit, I've been wrong about him before; maybe this'll be the last time.*

"Save your partner at all costs," Cobra continued, deep voice cracking with malicious glee. "Look at the bright side—if you die trying, it'll be better than what's on the other side."

✳ ✳ ✳ ✳

Cobra didn't tell them anything about the challenge except that it consisted of three different themes—earth, water, and fire. He led them through a tunnel up into an old warehouse. Steel rafters supported a high ceiling. The recruits wove over and under rusted truck beds, stepping through the hollowed-out frames like a skeleton's rib cage. Rows of shattered windows were covered haphazardly with plywood slabs, forming a gap-toothed grimace. No one knew what time it was exactly, but it appeared to be late evening. An orange sky peered through the murky glass.

Wolf volunteered to go first, anxious to get it over with.

Everyone watched Cobra guide Beta away from the group. "Keep warming up, Alpha," Cobra called over his shoulder. "We'll get you when the time comes."

They disappeared behind a padlocked door.

The other pledges eyed Wolf, searching for cracks of fear. He smoothed his face into a conditioned mask. *Keep looking, assholes.* Insecurity meant a death sentence within these walls. He wasn't going to let that shit get the best of him. They'd trained fiercely over the past few weeks. Strengthening their bodies and their minds, they'd hardened both in preparation. Watching their peers fail, and die as a result, had changed them.

Wolf's attention locked onto the makeshift wall that had swallowed Beta. Shoulder blades stitched together, his abdomen contracted, he swung his arms back and forth, loosening his tense muscles. All moisture vanished from his mouth. He jumped in the air, tucking his legs to his chest. Finally, Cobra emerged alone.

"Alpha, you're up."

12

WOLF

When Cobra stepped aside to let Wolf pass, the others tightened into a semicircle. The door swung closed behind him, groaning in doomful foreshadowing. Wolf inched forward, squinting into endless black. Silence descended, sucking away all noise except his rapid breathing. It was impossible to make out the room's depth or width. He crouched, lowering his center of gravity. Sharp cold seared through thin Lycra fabric as his knees grazed the floor.

From far across the room, a small flame flickered to life. The expanding glow illuminated what appeared to be a low platform. He sprinted toward it, vigilant of seconds ticking by.

Beta has to be there.

After a few strides, he lurched forward, pitching into a shallow hole. A pool of knee-deep, gritty muck cushioned his fall. Leaping up, Wolf tried scaling the sloping bank, but the damp sand collapsed on top of him, sharp pieces of dirt and gravel spraying his face. Desperate, he lunged again, clawing every edge of his trap's small circumference trying to climb his way out. More avalanches piled over him, churning up a dusty mist.

His nostrils flaring, eyes watering, panic shot through his bloodstream. *I'm being buried alive.* The soft mud sucked him deeper, provoked by his desperate thrashing. He was soon up to his chest in muck. Sand fell in whispering waves, turning instantly into a cement-like substance upon contact with water. Its dense viscosity constricted his limbs, tightening around his torso in a suffocating bind. He lashed out, reaching for the hole's edge, coughing in choking heaves. Tiny, crystallized shards scratched his throat. Fear smothered all reason. He couldn't think.

What are you so afraid of? a quiet voice whispered. *Death? No. Fuck that. Failure. You're terrified of failure.*

The realization shocked him back to reality.

I can't fail. I won't fail.

Panic had exposed his trigger. His limbs froze. The sinking sensation slowed. Quieting his breathing, he focused on controlling his instinctual resistance to the muck. Cautiously, Wolf lifted his thighs up toward his waist, working to extract his legs. Fighting against gravity, he climbed through the thick layers, using the cascading sand as stairs.

Spreading his body over the mud to increase his buoyancy, he dragged himself onto solid ground, gasping. The heavy mixture still clung to his clothes, hardening into a suit of weighted armor. He sat back on his haunches, his splayed fingers gripping the frostbitten concrete. His stomach dropped. The individual flame had multiplied into a long line. Beta's outline stood on the platform, like a hazy mirage surrounded by a ring of heat. Scrambling to his feet, Wolf staggered forward, searching for an opening in the wall of fire.

Without warning, he plunged through black ice, straight into frigid water. He sucked in a breath just as the cold pushed all air from his lungs. His mud-caked clothes dragged him downward like a set of weights attached to his ankles.

Fumbling in the dark depths, he struggled to strip off his pants and shirt, but his arms could hardly move. His lips sealed shut, arctic liquid shoving against his nostrils, trying to gain entry. Once he'd freed himself from the fabric bonds, he thrust his legs powerfully to kick back to the surface. Instead of breaking through the shifting water, his outstretched hands struck a thick wall of ice.

Trapped.

Again, fear flashed before his eyes in a bolt of white light. Ignoring the burning sensation in his lungs, he pressed against the frozen barrier. Exiting where he fell in was his only chance of escape.

Fingers tingling on the verge of numbness, he propelled himself backward. The ice grew thinner until his head broke free. Spluttering, he slithered out of the water, careful to distribute his weight evenly across the crackling frozen sheet beneath him. Pieces of ice stuck to his skin and adhered to what remained of his soaked clothing. Wolf began to shake uncontrollably, his teeth stabbing at his tongue.

As he inhaled oxygen in deep gulps, putrid smoke singed the back of his throat. His heart flatlined. *Beta.* The flames had reached soaring heights and were quickly devouring the small platform where Beta was tied to a stake, a burlap sack covering his head. *Shit. Shit. SHIT.* He slid to his hands and knees across the ice, slipping as he crawled as fast as he could. When his fingers brushed solid ground, he staggered to the other end of the room.

Don't think about it; just do it. He plunged through the wall of fire, the sleeting mixture coating his body protecting him in sizzling triumph. He hurdled onto the platform in one leap. Eyes stinging, he tore at the knots securing Beta to the post. The rope fell to the floor, releasing a platform door beneath their feet. They dropped into a cellar, landing on a lumpy mat. The fire raging above them retreated, summoned back to the depths of hell. Wolf's chest heaved, piping fresh air into his lungs. Doubled over on his knees, Beta coughed uncontrollably.

Wolf pulled the burlap sack from his head and clapped him on the back. "Sorry 'bout that one. Took a bit longer than expected. I'm sure you understand."

* * * *

Later that evening, Beta and Wolf walked back to their cell in fatigued silence. A newfound easiness had formed between them. Beta shaved a minute off Wolf's time during his turn at the challenge. Too exhausted to care, Wolf focused his remaining energy on being grateful he was still breathing.

"You know, that was the first time I can remember depending on someone," Wolf confessed.

Beta glanced at him, unable to mask his surprise. Wolf never spoke voluntarily. Their footsteps echoed through the narrow hallway. Lit bulbs every five yards guided their way. Following closely behind, their shadows disappeared in the intermittent gaps of darkness.

Solemnness passed over Beta's face. "I understand what REDS is doing now," he said. "Exposing our fears so we can overcome them. We've gotta extract our emotions if we wanna destroy them."

"It's humbling," Wolf said. "I've never felt anything like that before. I always thought all that bullshit didn't apply to me."

Beta shrugged, eyes glued to his shuffling feet. "How could you know? You've been let down your whole life. No one ever gave you the chance to feel anything other than disappointment."

A gut-wrenching swirl of anger and resentment tornadoed through Wolf. He nodded. "What was your trigger?"

Beta took his time responding. "Darkness. Guess I'm scared of not knowing what's out there waiting for me."

"The unknown," Wolf repeated.

"Yeah. Paralyzed me the second that door closed."

"How'd you finish?" Wolf asked.

"I kept my eyes on the flames and ran like hell." He watched Wolf, as if he were waiting for him to pass judgment. "Sure helped my time though."

The corner of Wolf's mouth ticked upward. "Everyone has their thing. Mine was failure. I dunno what happened. The thought of failing just took over. I couldn't fucking think."

Wolf hadn't realized emotions were so personal. Like pus festering at an open wound, vulnerability needed to be squeezed out in order to overcome an infection. Exposing who he was required bravery. Way more than he'd expected.

They made it back to their cell and collapsed onto their cots.

"What made you want to do this? I mean . . . Why are you here?" Beta asked.

"I wanted to escape." Wolf's eyelids dragged closed.

"Escape what?"

"My life. Shit, if that's what you'd even call it. More like my existence." Wolf glanced in his direction. "What about you?"

Beta stared at the ceiling, his profile impassive. "Revenge. I wanna show people what their complacency created. I wanna make them feel the pain I've carried my whole life."

Eight years later, Wolf would have the opportunity to do just that.

13

FLYNN

Her second day in the hospital, Flynn feigned intense head pain to avoid talking to the authorities. Her family continued shielding her from the outside world. Newspapers and magazines were banned from the room. The television was never tuned to the news, talk shows, or any programming that might cover the attack. They tried so hard to protect her, and Flynn appeased them, even though she knew she would have to face her new reality at some point. Grateful, she embraced the isolation while she could.

By the fourth day, the FBI demanded to speak with her. Three agents in matching white shirts and black jackets crowded into her room. Shiny gold badges on lanyards hung from their necks. Despite her mother's very vocal protests, they barred her family from the room. The strangers scrutinized Flynn. Lying in bed, dressed in only a hospital gown, she wrapped her fingers around the edge of the bedsheet, desperate to yank the thin fabric over her head.

One of the agents, who introduced himself as Rich, kicked things off diplomatically. Eyes glued to a pad of paper in his hands, he said, "Ms. Zarytsky, we're sorry about the recent events. We hope we can get to the bottom of this and bring you some peace."

Peace? she scoffed in her head. *I'll never know peace again.*

"We need to ask you some questions about the evening of the Green Line concert and your kidnapping," Rich continued.

"I really don't remember much," she replied shortly. Throbbing pain lassoed around the crown of her head, pulverizing her brain into mush. Exhaustion dragged at her eyelids and limbs. Crafting words into sentences still seemed like an impossible task.

"Yes, we heard about the effects of your concussion from your doctor." Rich glanced at his colleagues. His flat cheekbones made his face look square and stern. "Can you tell us the last thing you remember?"

"Running away from one of the gunmen. To a stadium exit."

"Mind giving us a full debrief of the evening? From the time you got to Soldier Field until the last thing you remember," agent number two asked. She was pretty sure he'd introduced himself as Agent Craig.

I do mind, she thought, but doubted that would be an acceptable response.

Reliving that terror seemed worse than all her injuries combined. She swallowed hard. "I left the Magnetic office after work with my coworkers, Ted and Nate. We headed to the concert together in a cab, picking up Nate's date along the way. We all sat together in the same box at Soldier Field. When the concert began, I saw explosions in the crowd by the stage and realized they weren't part of the show. Bullets shattered the glass around our box, so we ran. People were stampeding in every direction . . ." Her heart accelerated as if she was back in the crowded corridor, sprinting away from the imminent machine guns—men stalking them like beasts, killing everyone in sight.

"When did you become separated from Mr. Turner and the other gentleman you were with?" Rich flipped through his notes, as if Flynn had recited a boring lecture.

"We lost Ted right away. There were, uh, too many people. Then we came across two young boys without their parents . . ." she faltered, her tongue unable to function. "Nate, uh, he picked them both up, and after that it was impossible to stick together." She shook her head, blinking back tears, using her hands clasped together on the bedsheet as a focal point. "Then I lost him." Her voice emerged as a hoarse whisper.

Rich rubbed the back of his neck. "And that's when you encountered the REDS member who took you hostage?"

"Yes. I hid behind a concession stand. The last thing I remember is one of the gunmen standing above me. Then everything went black."

Whenever Flynn used to imagine her death, she expected her life to flash before her like film scenes on an old movie projector. Instead, the green eyes from behind the terrorist's mask had mesmerized her. Shrieks of terror had echoed through the hallway as people sprinted past and fell, a slow-motion blur at the edges of her peripheral vision. But she hadn't been able to look away—all she could do was stare into those unsettling green eyes.

The third FBI agent had thinning salt-and-pepper hair and wooly brows that softened his demeanor. He reached forward and touched her arm. She flinched, withdrawing as if he had struck her. "A full rape evaluation was done when you were admitted to the hospital. Do you remember whether you were sexually assaulted?" His voice was gentle.

Her stomach twisted. "I was not. I mean, I don't think I was."

He thumbed through a file. "Based on your condition, it appears you were beaten brutally. Broken ribs, contusions over your entire body, cuts on both arms, a severe concussion." His sloping forehead creased, eyes shining with concern. She wanted to open up to him—to tell him everything—but her throat stuck together, jaw clenched against the words.

"Everything after I dove behind the concession stand is hazy. I don't really remember anything else."

"Do you remember voices or conversations?" Agent Rich interrupted. She shook her aching head. "Did you see any faces?"

Biting down hard on her lip, she met his gaze. "No. Whenever I woke up, I was blindfolded and gagged. They kept knocking me out. It disoriented me . . . I could never get a feel for where I was or what was happening."

Agent Craig paced from one end of the cramped room to the other. Flynn couldn't tell if he was stocky or chubby. She doubted her fingertips would touch if she wrapped both her hands around his thick, stubby neck. Chubby, she decided when he turned and she caught sight of the banana roll hanging over his belt. "Were you drugged? What does her blood work say?"

The kind agent with the soothing voice sighed. His mouth stretched into a thin line. "Only thing noticeable is high levels of Rohypnol. Likely to knock her out or keep her sedated."

"Roofies?" Agent Craig asked. "Why her? Why did they take her of all people? This group is far too calculating to take a random woman hostage. Did they mention your place of work? Do they know you work for Magnetic?"

Flynn's instinctual response was to tell the truth. She almost let "yes" slip, but caught herself. She slumped back into the pillows, drained. The torture, questioning, and pain collided in continuous blows. Unable to withstand the brewing storm, her resistance crumbled. "I don't think so. I don't know. Maybe they just really wanted the money?"

Agent Rich sat in a chair and leaned back, squeezing the bridge of his angular nose with his thumb and forefinger. "Based on your description of the night's events, it doesn't sound like you suffered the concussion until you came into contact with the REDS member, correct?"

She shrugged. "Yeah. That's when my memory gets hazy."

"What about your ribs?"

Her hand instinctively moved across her body to cover her midsection. "All I remember is pain. Excruciating pain. Then I blacked out again."

"It's not out of the ordinary for terrorists to torture victims senselessly," the gentle agent observed, turning to his peers. "Especially terrorists responsible for killing hundreds of innocent concertgoers."

It felt like the ceiling collapsed on top of her. Beeping from a nearby monitor spiked to match her own heart rate. "What did you say? Hundreds?"

Startled by her reaction, the men looked back and forth between each other, unsure how to respond. A glowering nurse pushed into the room, hurrying past them.

"Time to leave, gentlemen. You can come back for further questioning another time."

Mumbling their thanks, the agents shuffled out the door. Fussing over Flynn, the nurse injected more medication into her IV. Soothed by a calming sedative, the relentless anxiety gripping her stomach loosened. The nurse tucked her thin sheet around her, smiling warmly. Despite the bright sunlight streaming through the window, Flynn's skin prickled.

"Don't worry, dear," she said, "you can rest now."

14

FLYNN

Another lie. Another lie to ward off the incessant guilt snarling at her heels.

It's for self-preservation, Flynn told herself. *And the preservation of others* . . .

But the tally kept rising.

Mom would be so disappointed if she knew. Her mother, Rachel, had raised Flynn and Fiella to know better than to allow themselves to be manipulated. She forbade excuses, no exceptions.

Rachel had inherited her mother's intolerance for dishonesty and cheating. After her family immigrated to Poland from Ukraine to escape the pogroms, and then to the US to escape the Nazis, Flynn's grandparents had worked three jobs to support Rachel and her siblings. Other families may have had liars, cheaters, or drunks, but that kind of behavior was unthinkable in Rachel's childhood home.

As she later raised her own daughters, she'd generously passed on her mother's ethical standards. Every question had a right or wrong answer. Every choice was good or bad. Honesty and deceit were black and white, as if the decision between the two was easy.

When Rachel discovered Flynn's first lie back in middle school, she'd shown no mercy. Flynn had claimed she was too sick to go to school, but later that morning Rachel caught her rocking out to *Hannah Montana* on the

Disney Channel. Then it all came out—the truth. About the bus, about the boy who'd teased her. Rachel had pried the fear out of her.

"Flyynnn," Fuck Boy had taunted, "ewwww. Isn't that a boy's name? You're gonna go to hell, you know that, don't you? That's where all Jews go when they're dead."

The entire time he'd antagonized her, she'd stared straight through the grimy windshield, face on fire, guts melting into mush, wishing she could sink into the lumpy, russet-colored seat.

"Ma . . . please don't make me go." Flynn's fingers curled around her backpack straps, crushing the spongy mesh.

"Sweetie . . ." Wrapping her robe around her chest, Ma had sunk into a crouch, balancing on her toes. Her gray eyes were starch hard, and the single, razor-thin line slicing through her forehead deepened. "You're going to find that not everyone in this world shares the same morals as our family—to treat everyone with respect and decency, no matter who you are or where you come from."

Flynn choked back tears with each painful swallow. "Why not?" She hated riding that stupid bus and its perpetual moldy milk smell. She dreaded it so much she couldn't stomach eating breakfast before school.

"We can't lower ourselves to his standard, Flynn. It's easy to be cruel, but to be brave takes strength." Her mother traced a heart-shaped outline on Flynn's chest. "Real strength." Her mother's fingers traveled through her daughter's coarse hair, until she rested a cool palm on Flynn's cheek. "What does Da tell you?"

"Rise above them," Flynn mumbled, squirming, squeezing her backpack straps tighter. "Can't you drive me to school? Puhleasse, Ma, just this once." She used her little girl voice, the one she knew cut the air like scissors through paper.

"Some things in life you can't run away from, sweets." Ma raised her thick eyebrows, lips puckering. "You gotta stand up and show up. Be yourself. It will always be good enough." Up close, her steely irises were clear enough to fit the entire solar system inside. "If you don't confront your problems, they'll catch up to you."

So, that was what Flynn did. She showed up. Every single day. From that point on, she realized how hard it was to forget the horrible things people say, but how easy it was to forget the nice things. It must be some cruel brain trick, trapping in the negative but leaking out the positive. More storylines she convinced herself to believe. More lies injected into her brain.

Over time, Flynn grew out of her awkward middle-school stage. Later, Fuck Boy even tried to ask her out. How the tables turn. But she'd always remember him and his cruel leers. She'd always remember how he made her feel. Inferior. Some people thrive off that power. Sometimes it's all they have.

* * * *

A week passed and Flynn's family still refused to leave her side. Cori visited every other day, keeping her stocked with books and her favorite treats. They brought only temporary relief.

The three FBI agents returned twice more for questioning. According to them, her "story" aligned with Ted's and Nate's. Every time the men crowded into her room, she refused to cooperate, feigning amnesia. Still they tried to pry into the black hole of her memory in hopes of extracting evidence to piece together her hostage capture.

"Nothing is coming back to me," Flynn insisted. "I promise, I'll reach out if I remember anything."

Their skeptical faces suggested they could read straight through her empty assurance.

Normalcy attempted to creep into her hospital life. But every time she drifted toward its seductive, false sense of security, she shoved it away. Restless, residual fear haunted her from the second she opened her eyes in the morning to the minute she closed them at night—a relentless hot poker stoking the flames. Terror shaped her dreams, shading them a menacing crimson. Coiling around her chest, it suffocated her, dragging her from nightmares to bolt awake, gasping for air.

"PTSD," Dr. Martin said to her family one morning. They huddled around her bed, faces stricken. Each of the past five nights, she'd woken screaming until her throat burned. Her mother clutched her father's arm.

"Post-traumatic stress disorder," Da repeated quietly.

"It's to be expected after experiencing a horror like this." Removing her glasses, Dr. Martin squeezed her eyes shut, deep in thought.

"You mean like soldiers after a war? What do we do? I mean, how can we help her recover?" Her mother's pleading carried a hint of desperation, as if they were discussing an incurable sickness.

"Counseling is a good start. There are group therapy sessions being held here at the hospital. You should attend, Flynn. It can be helpful to find companionship and solace in the aftermath of trauma."

Flynn's head dropped back against the pillows stacked behind her. Folding her arms over her chest, she dug her fingernails into her skin. All everyone wanted her to do was talk. Talk and listen. No one understood how reliving anything about that evening reopened the wound, exposing an angry gash like a freshly ripped hangnail. She would do anything to avoid going back to the darkness, the ice-cold floor in the holding cell.

Of course, her mother forced her to go. Another item on her rigorous checklist, she followed up with the nurses daily to ensure Flynn attended. She barely remembered the first few sessions. Dazed and perplexed, her brain struggled to untangle the trauma that broke her in ways she didn't know was possible. Watching the therapist's mouth open and close, she thought it was impossible to grasp the atrocity that brought them together. Listening to others speak about their pain tightened the back of her throat until it hurt to swallow.

Inhale, exhale, she reminded herself. *Just keep breathing.* In the end, she was alone. A victim who always seemed to stumble off the path to recovery. She could never speak of her capture to anyone.

* * * *

Two weeks after the attack, Flynn was still stuck. Staring at the speckled gray linoleum floor, she waited for another hospital group session to begin, disembodied voices floating around her. Perched above the door, a clock's needle-thin second hand ticked by, quivering with each forward decimal. *TICK. TICK. TICK.* Round and round it moved, never stopping, never moving backward. Always the exact same monotone interval weighing over her head, reminding her of what was coming.

She groaned inwardly. *Here we go again.*

Other patients filed in, taking their seats slowly, joining the battered circle. It was sad, but by now she was immune to their expressions. Most were shocked, incapable of grasping their new reality.

A hand touched her shoulder lightly. She jumped, startled. Heat flooded her cheeks, creeping down to her collarbone. As she glanced behind her, her heart leapt out of her chest. Nate Turner stood over her, a sad smile on his face. His hazel eyes—the same light brown pools that had anchored her to this earth while everything around her was shattering—carried shadows of familiar exhaustion.

"Nate?"

"Hey, Flynn. They told me I might find you here." His shoulders sagged, and his usual charm and egotistical sarcasm had been leached from his being. Rising to her feet on wobbly legs, she reached out her arms, which were lighter than they'd felt in days. He wrapped her in a gentle embrace. Pitching forward, she fell into him, disarmed by the calm his scent and warmth offered. Her remaining fragile strength disappeared, and she finally surrendered to the waves of emotion she'd held inside so tightly. Quiet tears streamed down her face.

Silently, they held each other until everyone around them was seated. After helping Flynn to her seat, he pulled up a chair beside her. Sniffling, she wiped her wet cheeks with the back of her hand. Peace settled over her, and she sank into it like a soft bed.

Their therapist, Dr. Macy, smiled softly, clearing her throat and beginning her usual opening prose in an upbeat, singsong voice. "I'm glad to see many of you back. It also looks as though some new faces have joined us. Now, during these sessions, it's important to remember that this is a journey. There is no end point." Her wide eyes scanned the circle, chin bobbing up and down in small individual nods. "I hope you can find comfort in each other. We're all here together, so none of us have to face our pain alone. Let's be mindful of remaining open and honest. It's likely your respective thoughts and emotions are shared experiences that many here are also struggling to understand. We'll begin the usual way, with a quick round of introductions. I want everyone to feel comfortable speaking in this space."

They recited their names in a theme of robotic tones. Once everyone had a chance to introduce themselves, a regular attendee jumped straight into a recitation of her list of panicked concerns. Her fingers fidgeted, twitching every few seconds. "I want to know that I'm going to be okay. That these feelings will go away." Her eyes were wild, and her voice had a shaky edge. "What I'm saying is that I need to know this won't happen again."

"Well, Amber," urged Dr. Macy, "let's talk about what 'okay' means to you. Everyone might have a different interpretation. Does 'okay' mean not having the same fears or anxiety?"

"I need to know I'm safe," Amber responded flatly.

None of the other patients knew Flynn was the hostage victim. She could never feel safe again with REDS's threats looming over her like an invisible noxious gas.

"You *are* safe, Amber. They can't hurt you anymore," Dr. Macy soothed.

"Don't you understand?" A man slouching in his seat glared at Dr. Macy. His face contorted into a sneer. "The damage is done. Here. Out there. To all of us." Spittle flew from his lips. "We can't escape it. They'll never stop hurting us."

Familiar fear began to clog Flynn's throat. Resisting the impulse to reach for Nate's hand, she curled her fingers into a fist.

"Kyle, that's what trauma does to us. It makes past events seem like they are inescapable. That they define us," Dr. Macy responded gently.

"Then how do you escape it?" Nate's tone, usually wry and cynical, was hollow. Surprised by his question, Flynn glanced at him out of the corner of her eye. The thin lines of her palms filled with perspiration. She clenched the extra fabric bunched around the seams of her hospital pants.

"Well, one way is to confront it. You confront what haunts you because it already happened." Dr. Macy peered at Nate. "It's Nate, right? Welcome. Can you tell us one thing that haunts you from that night?"

Flynn was tempted to scream at Dr. Macy, to shake her until her head hurt as badly as hers still did from the concussion. How could they pinpoint just one moment that had derailed their collective sanity? What she wanted was to erase the entire evening from history.

Nate looked down at his hands clasped on his lap. His shoulders hunched, as if under an invisible weight. "Guilt," he said, voice tight. "Guilt that I survived."

"That night was beyond your control, Nate." Dr. Macy studied him over her round spectacles, the wrinkles around her beady eyes crumpling. "There was nothing you could have done differently to change the outcome."

"That's not true. I tried to save Flynn"—he gestured toward her—"and I tried to save two little boys. I had to choose, but instead I saved no one. Except myself." He paused, hesitating. It was so hard not to wrap him in her arms again. "One of the boys I was carrying got shot. He died in my arms, right in front of his big brother."

Flynn's ears rang. It took everything in her power not to bolt from the room. She gripped the sides of her chair and closed her eyes. A flash of explosions and black pools of blood streaking across a concrete floor unfolded before her.

"That bullet should've hit *me*," Nate continued. "I should be the one who is dead."

Flynn slowly turned her head to face him, scared of what emotion she might see. His complexion was ashen, hate etched so deeply into his features it devoured his eyes, replacing them with darkness.

"But, Nate, if it wasn't for you, that other little boy might be dead as well. You risked yourself to save them," Dr. Macy said.

He looked back at Flynn, lips pressed together, his jaw rigid. "I couldn't save Flynn." He dragged a trembling hand down the length of his face. "Maybe we should have stayed in our concert box and hid."

"Flynn is sitting right there, Nate, she's safe," Dr. Macy said pointedly.

"No, not before REDS took her. Not before they took her hostage and tortured her for five days."

The silence in the room was so deafening the ringing in Flynn's ears intensified.

Dr. Macy turned her attention to Flynn, unable to mask her surprise. "Flynn, you never mentioned this in our other sessions."

"I, uhh, I . . ." Her voice caught, lodged in her throat. "I don't remember anything." The lie rolled unnaturally off her tongue.

Everyone's attention locked onto her, riveted. This was exactly what she'd hoped to avoid. Nate reached toward her. "Flynn, I'm sorry. I thought people knew."

Shooting out of her chair, she involuntarily winced from the pain boomeranging between her head and body. Slicing heat scorched down her rib cage. She resisted the urge to double over, desperate to sprint from the room closing in on her.

"Flynn, wait," Dr. Macy called as she limped away. "We don't need to talk about it now; it can be on your own time."

Flynn pushed through the community room's swinging doors, slamming down on the handle of an emergency exit. Every step resurrected misery she thought had healed. She swerved into a wide stairwell and was down two flights before she had any idea where her feet were taking her. Ignoring the searing cramp in her side and the shortness of breath squeezing her chest, she threw herself against a door leading to the small hospital courtyard.

"Flynn." Nate appeared right behind her, clearly having had no issues keeping up thanks to her injuries.

He reached for her again, but she staggered backward, trying to even her shallow breathing. Everything was suddenly too bright. She covered her eyes, shielding them from the beating sunlight. A car horn blasted down the street, the outside world moving on without them.

"Nate, please, I can't do this right now."

"I'm sorry, Flynn. I'm sorry for everything. I'm still trying to wrap my head around what happened to us. How our lives changed in a matter of minutes. How our very beings changed." He stood before her, arms hanging by his sides. Just like her, he seemed lost and helpless.

She wanted him to be wrong. She wanted to be the same Flynn she was before the concert, no matter how boring she might've been. But he was right. That Flynn was gone forever. Even though she stood there alive, a part of her had died along with the hundreds of other victims at the stadium.

Sighing, she sank onto a bench overlooking a bubbling fountain at the center of the courtyard. With the bench toasted from the sun, its warmth seeped through her thin pants. A nearby wind chime sang merrily, jangling a song orchestrated by the breeze. "Do you think we'll ever find them again?" she asked after several minutes of silence, shoving her fingers underneath her legs. "Our old selves, I mean. I know we can't be those people again, but maybe we'll still see them from time to time."

Nate sat next to her, rubbing his palms along his jeans. "I would like to think we still have visitation rights." A shadow of his familiar crooked smile played across his lips. "My old self was a damn good time."

She allowed herself to relax against him, their shoulders and legs pressing together. For a brief moment the world stood still, pausing to watch them. Peace trickled through her, loosening the blockage of terror clogging her arteries.

We see everything. We hear everything.

The voice resurfaced, startling her.

"You okay?" Nate asked.

No. I'm not okay, she wanted to scream. *I'm trapped in a life that's no longer mine.*

"Yeah," she said. Another lie. Now that they'd started, they wouldn't stop. They couldn't stop. "We should probably head back inside." She stood, hugging herself, turning back to the protection of the building's four walls—away from invisible eyes scrutinizing her every move.

For Nate, each day was a step toward recovery. For her, each day was a waiting game, bringing her one step closer to a fate resting in someone else's hands.

15

WOLF

After Flynn's drop-off, days crawled by before Wolf could shake the tension stalking him like a starved animal. He'd spent almost a decade mastering complete control. In seconds, it had deteriorated. *Why now?* he asked himself. *Why her? So she stood up for you once when you were nineteen. Big fucking deal.*

Years ago, his favorite initiation lectures had been about poison. Watching how an unassuming substance became lethal had thrilled him. During one workshop, their group had gathered around a large glass case perched on a table. Inside, a scorpion had cornered a small rabbit, its tail poised to strike a lethal sting.

"Thirty to forty scorpion species possess venom strong enough to kill a person," REDS Master of Education, Eel, said. Pointy teeth and dark, protruding eyes personified his alias. His mouth hung slightly open, the result of an injury to his jaw. "There are many different types o' venom, tailored specially for the species' prey o' choice 'n' lifestyle." His scaly lips barely moved as he talked; his thick, raspy words were jumbled together.

In an instant, the scorpion released its tail, descending upon the rabbit faster than a snapped whip. Fascinated, Wolf froze. The scorpion's venom had paralyzed it mid-crouch.

"This venom," Eel drawled, "causes liquid to fill the creature's lungs." He blinked at them. "This rabbit's drowning, boys. As surely as if you'd forced its head underwater. Nothin' is mo' lethal than nature's secret weapons."

Now, Wolf drowned in his own thoughts. They poured over him, relentless. What had he done involving Flynn in their plan? He should've killed her under that shitty concession stand and moved on.

There was nothing special about her, other than when he first saw her, he couldn't look away. An energy radiated from her, just like it had when she dumped her boyfriend's sorry ass right in front of him at the café. He'd felt it as she lay on the floor of her holding cell—beaten and powerless. Even then she wasn't defeated. Her resilience was admirable. Uncompromising.

I gotta hand it to her, she's tough, Wolf admitted to himself.

Mind racing, he shoved a heavy stack of books into his backpack. He had to get the hell out of there. Escape for a bit. The malware he'd been working on needed testing and the community college library was nearby. A thick notebook slid from his cot to the floor, spilling papers under his bed.

"Damnit."

Dropping to his knees, he groped blindly for the stray sheets of paper. His hand brushed a metal grate's rough edges. Faltering, his breath slowed.

Is it still there? he wondered.

Inhaling deeply, he lowered to his stomach, using his forearms to drag the top half of his body underneath the bed. Cold leaked from the concrete through his clothes and into his skin like water seeping into a wetsuit. He pulled his knife from his pocket and slid the thin blade under the metal webbing. Flipping the lid open, he dug into the shallow drain until his fingers wrapped around a wad of damp, fleecy material.

Bear.

His oldest belonging. The little toy bear's peeling fur had grayed with age, its remaining stuffing lumpy from moisture. He had smuggled it into initiation under the waistband of his pants after he'd left the reform center. With no connections to his past, it was the one item he'd been able to call his own during his childhood. It was also the link to his only memory of his mother. When he touched the pilled fabric, he could still hear her, still feel her arms cradling him, still see her face before she turned around and left him forever.

The stuffed animal's remaining eye taunted him. *Fucking loser.*

He'd tried to burn it. Tried to *force* himself to do it, but he never could. He should destroy it now. Attachments were dangerous—a sign of weakness. If he couldn't abandon a fucking teddy bear, how was he supposed to kill Flynn?

Gritting his teeth, he gripped the bear's head, preparing to decapitate it. Several seconds passed. A tick kicked against his temple. Then he shoved it back into the drain and slammed the grate shut. *Piece of shit.* Turning onto his back, the rusty metal grid supporting his mattress gaped down at him.

What's happening? he asked himself. *Am I losing it? Come on, get it together. Don't let this bullshit rattle you.*

Unnerved, he blew a long stream of air out of puffed cheeks. Unsurprisingly, throwing the toy back into captivity did little to ease his churning stomach. Every time he thought he'd outrun his few displaced memories, they caught up, pouncing on him with no warning. No, he couldn't let his thoughts get the best of him. Not now. This was all just a mind fuck, and he wouldn't lose.

I can't lose.

* * * *

Spider was waiting for Wolf at the concealed underground entrance. He had an eerie ability to anticipate where Wolf was going, like he was watching from a web cast over the entire organization. Recognizing Spider's distinct form in the shadows of the stairwell, Wolf's body locked into immediate attention.

"Wolf, ever since Soldier Field you've been distracted. What's on your mind?"

Only seconds passed before Wolf responded. "I'm focused. Now's the time to push forward with my mission." His lips barely moved, controlling any vocal inflection that might reveal his lie. "We finally have an infiltrator—a way to plant the malware. An end is in sight; I can taste it."

The light was so dim only the white glint of Spider's eyes and the shape of his strong chin were visible. His hot breath brushed against Wolf's face.

"Patience. The Feds are watching the girl closely. They'll notice any advance. You must maintain your distance."

Wolf's chin dipped obediently. "I can wait. I've waited a long time for this."

"Your hunger is what I admire about you most, Wolf," Spider said. The ghost of a smile pulled his gaunt cheeks upward. "In a short time, you've earned the merits of your name." His words wrapped around Wolf, embracing him. Compliments from Spider were rare. "Did you know wolves begin feeding before their prey is even dead?"

"I did, Spider."

"While your hunger is worthy, it can be dangerous if you act too quickly." His heavy gaze scrutinized Wolf. "Do you remember the pledge you made during your naming ceremony?"

"I'll never forget it."

"Allow your alias to serve as a constant reminder of . . ." he recited, pausing to allow Wolf to finish the statement.

"The new order we strive to build as one."

"As *one*, Wolf. We are one." Spider stepped toward him, his body lean and long compared to Wolf's bulk. Still, an invisible force surrounding him exuded dominance. "Impatience is an individual motive. We serve as the face of fear and destruction for one reason and one reason alone. Destruction *must* come before creation."

"Together, we will rule." Passion rose in Wolf's chest, as it always did when he repeated their manifesto.

"Exactly. I will notify you when the time comes, but until then, stay far away from that woman. I already have scouts keeping watch on her every move."

Wolf's stomach flipped. He nodded, face still as stone. "Thank you for this opportunity, Spider."

"Don't make me regret it. Our window is approaching. One person, one error in judgment, can ruin it all. You will be accountable for controlling her."

"Yes, Spider."

Spider dismissed him, leaving Wolf alone in the empty stairwell.

Running a shaky hand over his eyes, he felt a sinking sensation drag his guts to the floor. He had a nagging feeling that of all the hostages he could've captured, Flynn Zarytsky was likely the most uncontrollable of them all.

16

FLYNN

By the time Flynn was released from the hospital, it was late spring. Her doctors and the authorities mutually agreed to keep her longer than anticipated to continue monitoring her. Avoiding the spotlight might have been easier, had her face not been plastered all over national television once the press identified her as the one REDS had taken hostage. She was slapped with a survivor label: the one who escaped the most horrendous act of violence ever witnessed by the city of Chicago. Never mind the thousands of other victims. The media painted her as a hero in a blatant attempt to heighten the potential of her story.

She was assigned a temporary security team to escort her from place to place "until the city had a chance to settle." The FBI relocated her and Cori, forcing them to vacate their walk-up apartment for a more secure high-rise building with a twenty-four-hour doorman and better surveillance. This only seemed to comfort her mother. Flynn knew that, despite all the safety precautions, the efforts were fruitless. Once she stepped outside the hospital, REDS would watch her every move.

"It's time we moved on." Cori tilted her head upward, taking in their old home. Nestled between two limestone mansions, the narrow, four-story brick building was often overlooked by passersby, their eyes skipping right over its shaded entrance guarded by a large maple tree. "It's been a great five years."

"Add it to the list," Flynn replied. "I'm so tired of this. No one asked me what I wanted. Everyone thinks they're acting in my best interest, but no one wants to hear what that might be."

Cori looked at her, mouth turning down in disapproval. "Hey, none of that. Onward and upward. Quite literally. I always wanted to live in a fancy high-rise on Lake Shore. You have to admit, the views don't suck." As they walked away, Cori took her hand. "This is for your safety, Flynn. It's better to be safe than sorry."

My safety? Flynn thought. *What about everyone else's?*

* * * *

The week following Flynn's release, reporters bombarded her, each wearing a pouty expression demonstrating trite remorse for her trauma. They trailed her everywhere she went, barely dissuaded by her security escort.

"Flynn, what was it like?!"

"Flynn, tell us about who did this to you!"

"Flynn, tell us how you made it out alive!"

"FLYNN! FLYNN!"

The questions were always the same. A rigid smile glued permanently to her face, Flynn repeated the response over and over like a skipping record.

"I'm sorry, there's really not much I remember."

News outlets offered huge sums of money for the rights to tell her story. TV networks offered red carpet events for one chance at an exclusive interview. If only she could sell her story to someone else so it would no longer be hers to bear.

The FBI provided occasional updates on the investigation. Two REDS members had died after detonating their suicide vests at Soldier Field, limiting their ability to narrow in on suspects. There was only one lead. The FBI released pieced-together surveillance footage of another two suspected REDS Enforcers operating as Soldier Field concert staff. Grainy images showed men wearing work crew vests smuggling in boxes of explosives. When the agents showed her the video, Flynn had no way of identifying either. All she could remember about the one who had found her under the concession stand was his bright green eyes, which weren't visible from the camera viewpoint.

The mayor issued a citywide alert that did little to help the dust settle: the men were still at large, probably within the Chicago area. Already tense, the city verged on panic. Right when it seemed like the blood was clotting, the scab was picked away, revealing a gaping wound.

✳ ✳ ✳ ✳

"Well, so much for discretion." Cori glanced over her shoulder at the two extremely large agents and gaggle of reporters trailing them on an early Sunday morning. "I mean, can a girl brunch in yoga pants and a messy bun?"

The clicking of distant cameras, like a small symphony of crickets, answered her question.

"When will this end?" Flynn groaned. "I can't believe tomorrow is my first day back at work. I already know how awkward it's going to be. What do I even say to people?" She dreaded the forced inquiries, the tentative sympathetic arm touches, and claustrophobic embraces.

Cori's lips slanted into a diagonal line, eyes shining. Worry seemed permanently glued to her face lately. "It will get better." Her voice was full of false promise. "Not many victory stories came out of that night. And I guess you can't really blame them. It *is* pretty remarkable you survived after everything . . ."

Staring straight ahead, Flynn shoved her hands deep into her jacket pockets. Lime green buds had sprouted in clumps overnight, poking out from winter's skeletal branches. Spring always ignited excitement in Chicago, drawing people out of hibernation. It was so easy to forget nature's thawing, musty smell, suppressed for so many months under winter's frozen tundra. Except this year, a hollow emptiness replaced the usual joy a new season brings.

"Those people," Cori continued, "they're heartless. It's easy to understand why everyone wonders why they didn't kill you."

Parents pushing children in strollers gaped at Flynn as they passed. Groups of friends staggered slightly as they walked by them, rubbernecking and leaning together in speculative whispers. Every stranger on the street was suddenly threatening and suspicious. Any gaze that lingered for more than a second triggered petrifying terror. Flynn's shoulders scrunched toward her ears. Her foot came into contact with a rock that had strayed into the middle of the sidewalk. It bounced merrily ahead of them.

"You know you can tell me if there's anything going on, right? I'm not some crazy reporter; I'm your best friend."

"I know, Cor." Flynn would give anything to tell Cori what had happened to her in the REDS holding cell, but it wasn't worth risking their lives. "All I want is for my life to go back to normal."

"Normal is over," Cori said. "After what happened at the Green Line concert, normal is over for Chicago."

Flynn shook her head. "Normal is what Chicago needs right now."

Cori dropped her forced cheeriness. "Chicago needs to wake up and stop spinning their wheels over two missing terrorists. They need to dig up the root of this organization or these attacks will keep happening."

Flynn frowned. "What do you mean?"

"So far, all of the targets leading up to the concert seem very calculated. That entire night was. Everyone seems to think that once we find these two monsters, the attacks will stop happening, but they won't. They're not addressing the overarching problem."

Cori was right, but Flynn remained quiet. She couldn't give any indication she was aware of REDS's size and force. It was true, REDS was strategic in their executions. The attacks leading up to Soldier Field were small and spread out. They were calculated tests to probe the law enforcement system for weaknesses, and, just as importantly, to amp up media coverage of the group, demonstrating clear intent to those who closely followed their path of destruction, which was pretty much no one except Cori, apparently.

"We should have seen this coming," Flynn admitted.

"Yeah." Linking arms, Cori exhaled loudly. "Well, how does that saying go again? Hindsight's always fifty-fifty?"

A chuckle bubbled up inside Flynn's throat. It felt good to laugh again, and it felt good having Cori's warmth beside her. For a brief moment, she savored it. "I think you mean twenty-twenty."

✳ ✳ ✳ ✳

Upon Flynn's return to work, friends and colleagues offered words of welcome and relief at her safety. But, as expected, no one knew how to address "the hostage situation." Eyes strayed from hers, unable to make contact. Postures shifted away to avoid brushing against her, as though she were a fragile antique. No office protocol existed on how to engage with a survivor of a devastating terrorist attack. She could see the wheels turning in people's heads during every conversation, speaking about her in hushed voices that hung in the air long after she'd walked away.

Should we ask her what happened?

Is asking how she's doing a dumb question?

Does she really not remember anything?

You think she's going to lose it? Maybe she's already lost it.

Flynn asked herself these same questions, especially when her train of thought wandered. Each day she wondered whether it would be the day REDS made contact with her again. She felt trapped in a barbaric waiting game, like she'd been strapped down to a merry-go-round that wouldn't stop spinning. Concentrating for long periods of time was difficult and, in moments of quiet, the voices of her captors resurfaced, whispering in her ear as she stared at her computer screen.

We'll find you when we need you.

You can't hide from us.

See you soon.

No one avoided her more than Ted. Every time they passed each other in a hallway, he cast his eyes downward. He'd exposed himself for who he was the second he left the team behind in that box. A coward. Rumor had it he and Nate's date, Victoria, were now hot and heavy. What a match, and also a relief. Flynn was grateful she no longer had to deter his advances on top of everything else.

But more than anything, Flynn was grateful for Nate. They took comfort in each other, eating lunch together every day and never speaking of the night at Soldier Field or their group therapy session at the hospital. There were moments his eyes clouded, as he quietly sank into an unknown depth of memories. Each time, her heart coughed to a stop. Nothing she could say would pull him back from the suffering. She knew how it felt to relive those moments in the stadium—letting go of his hand, watching him grab the two children and sprint toward survival. Nothing she could do would erase the limpness in his arms after the little boy died.

* * * *

Later that week, Flynn sat at Nate's desk reviewing feedback on two candidates. Her knee bounced up and down, jostling the computer resting on her lap. Magnetic's HR department had spent a month trying to fill a director role and, so far, no one had met the qualifications. Nate stopped speaking mid-sentence and hung his head, hand covering his mouth.

"What are we doing?"

Dragging her attention away from the laptop screen, she met his intense stare. Sunshine beating through the window forced her to squint. In the direct light, flecks of green ringed the brown epicenter of Nate's eyes. His unshaven jaw clenched, and a curl of his sandy blond hair fell across his forehead. Usually immaculately groomed, this unkempt version of Nate startled her every time she saw him.

"What do you mean? We need to give this hiring manager an answer by tomorrow . . ."

"It's hypocritical." His long fingers scratched the stubble on his chin, a scowl forming between his brows. His once pressed shirt was rumpled and creased. "You and I are hand-selecting and screening talent to propel forward a company neither of us believes in."

Biting her lip, she looked down at her hands resting limply on her keyboard. "Where is this coming from?"

They both felt similarly about their jobs. She and Nate had witnessed firsthand there were no checks and balances within a corporate organization like Magnetic. Slowly the company had inserted itself into almost every household in the country. Whether in their home or on their phones or computers, it gathered data about every aspect of people's lives. And when you know what makes someone tick, it's easy to influence and control them. The centralized network, praised for its conveniences and for providing efficiencies society now depended on, masked Magnetic's quiet agenda. It was difficult to accuse a company of monopolizing an industry when a country's entire economy relied on it to function. Astonishing internet speed and smart homes were once a luxury, but Magnetic had made them affordable for everyone.

"*We* are the ones who perpetuate what this company is doing." Nate waved a hand at his computer. "Magnetic continues to grow more powerful and it's us who allow it to happen."

Sighing, Flynn leaned back in her chair, massaging her temples. "It's our job. Someone else would do it if we didn't. Why does it matter?"

"Because these are our lives, and they're more important than a job. We of all people should know this company is spiraling. I mean, come on, how much longer can we empower this vicious cycle? We might as well be a narcotics company at this point. We know people's weaknesses and their fears and then we use that to bring them back for more."

"Alright, that seems a little dramatic. So, what do you want to do? Quit? You're working at one of the most reputable companies in the world. Golden handcuffs are a real thing."

Flynn had worked tirelessly after college in her last two jobs to become a recruiter for Magnetic. It had been a dream she could hardly fathom achieving, until she lost faith in the company she represented to hundreds of eager candidates all thirsting for the same position. There were certainly more rungs to climb on her career ladder, but up was no longer the direction she wanted to continue going. Problem was, she couldn't figure out how to get back down without landing on her ass.

"Who cares?" Nate tossed his phone onto his desk. It skated across the smooth plexiglass surface, pirouetting until it smacked into a mug. "That doesn't mean shit if we're not happy. We're bending over backward to grow a talent pool for a company that only views its employees as money-making cogs."

She shrugged. "Magnetic does some pretty amazing things for this world."

"Yeah, because of us! We're the bloodline to this place. We deceive all the bright-eyed, untainted candidates who walk in that door believing they'll work for a company that actually cares about making a difference instead of controlling their lives." He jabbed toward the door with his pointer finger.

Her skin tingled. She held her breath, scared Nate was going to do something drastic like quit. She couldn't bear the thought of enduring a day at work without him.

"Nate, after that night—" Faltering, her voice caught. "After everything, all I want to do is find my life again. Find a sense of normalcy. Right now, I can't care about what I have to do to get that back."

Shaking his head, he rested his elbows on his knees, intertwining his fingers behind his neck. "If anything, that night showed me life is short. We need to break away from this now while we can." His voice dropped. "Let's start our own talent agency. Only work for companies that *we* want to. Rediscover who we are and, better yet, who we want to be. We don't need to follow a predictable career path; we need to find what fulfills us."

"I don't want to break away from anything." She couldn't tell him it was impossible to focus on rediscovering herself. Not with REDS hovering nearby, waiting for the opportune moment to re-enlist her. She was still their prisoner. Clutching the armrest of her chair, she felt the room swaying.

"Flynn, I know this is something you always wanted to do." His face was raw and pleading. "You used to talk about it all the time before that night. If anything, this should prove to you there's no better time than now. Where's that old fire?"

Standing abruptly, she grabbed her bag, struggling to tame the tide of emotion rising within her. She couldn't listen to Nate talk about her distant ambitions. He was right; she'd always wanted to start her own agency. But that fire was gone. Extinguished. For her own sanity she needed this job, this rock of stability, if she was going to make it out of this alive.

It might be cowardly, but she walked away. It was the only thing she could do. She needed to get out of the office before her insides collapsed on themselves.

"Flynn," Nate called after her, "don't leave."

Hurrying down the hallway to the elevator bank, she glanced anxiously over her shoulder. Her security escort wasn't scheduled to pick her up for another two hours. Pulling on a baseball cap in an attempt to disguise herself, she hurried out of the building. The streets were bustling with the early afternoon rush. She darted south toward Millennium Park and the lake's fresh breeze. It was a long walk, but she didn't care; she needed to clear her head.

State Street's bridge extended across the shimmering Chicago River. As she crossed, she was amazed at how easily people's eyes slid past her when she wasn't flanked by giant bodyguards. The summer sun glinted off the reflective glass sides of skyscrapers looming above the river. Open-top boats floated lazily by, spotted with small clumps of passengers pointing and gawking up at the city overlooking them. Inhaling deeply, Flynn focused on the steamy heat pressing against her cold skin. Friendly bursts of wind greeted her, pushing back her hair.

After a little more than a mile, she reached Millennium Park. It was one of her favorite spots in the city when it wasn't teeming with tourists. As she meandered down a winding path, for a brief moment, the terror that had dictated her every move since the concert eased. Vines and leaves covered an aisle of wooden verandas, summoning her farther into their depths. Transported, lost in the green sea of shade, her anxiety dissolved. The beautiful gardens were foreign to the surrounding urban landscape, in the same way she now felt like a stranger trapped in her own body.

Flynn finally stopped at Buckingham Fountain. It overlooked Lake Shore Drive, sitting proudly along the edge of Lake Michigan. Shoots of water cascaded from the elaborate, three-tiered structure. Light shining on the smooth surface refracted a bright glare, and small rainbows bounced playfully off stray droplets. Closing her eyes, she listened to the soothing woosh of the fountain.

She knew Nate hadn't intended to challenge her complacency. Her response had been unwarranted, but she'd panicked. If anything, she was jealous of his newfound drive. Channeling his pain from the attack was exactly what she'd do if she were him. *If I wasn't weak—weak from the fear spreading in my organs like a metastasized tumor. Maybe REDS is full of empty threats.* A small spark of hope burst inside her. Should she have been so quick to resist his proposal?

"Beautiful day, isn't it?"

The silky voice ripped through her memory like scissors slicing through wrapping paper. She hadn't been sure she would even recognize the voice if she heard it again, but its sound submerged her in a rush. Every cell in her being threatened to peel away from her skeleton, but somehow, she remained standing. Her head spun from instant vertigo, her heartbeat spiked, and her stomach jerked into her throat, a rip cord yanked from a parachute.

It was as if REDS could read the doubt leaking from her thoughts. *How did REDS know I was on the verge of letting my guard down?*

Prying open her eyelids, she stared into the giant basin of water and the teal dragon rising out of its midst, spraying water from open jaws. She turned, body moving in slow motion, every instinct screaming at her to run. The same startling green she encountered beneath the concession stand gazed back at her. The color was so vivid the distant lake looked gray and lifeless in comparison. It was hard to believe these were the same eyes that bore into her soul the night her entire world fell apart.

17

WOLF

Wolf wasn't expecting the look on Flynn's face when she saw him for the first time since the stadium. Surprise. Not fear, but shock. Her expression transformed slowly to terror. Her eyes widened, her mouth leveled into a hard line.

"You," she whispered, barely audible over the fountain's steady stream.

There we go. That's more like it. That palpable fear was comforting. His lips twitched upward. "Me."

"I could scream at the top of my lungs. You'll be killed on the spot."

Yeah, yeah, yeah. An empty threat, he thought to himself. He knew better.

"You could. But you won't. Because you know we would still find a way to kill you if you did."

"How did you find me?" Her voice trembled.

A burst of lakefront wind collided with her body and blew toward him. Its floral scent was so familiar it immediately disarmed him. He resisted. "As promised, after our lovely introduction, we've been keeping close tabs on you."

Stepping away from him, she crossed her arms over her chest, hands shaking. "What do you want?"

"I could tell you now"—he paused as if actually considering it—"but I won't."

Something in her splintered. "Do you always play with your food before you eat it? Are you just here to fuck with my head some more?" Her gray eyes glinted in the bright sunlight.

She's interesting, this one. Even more defiant than I expected. Stronger than she gives herself credit for too.

"Come with me." He spun around, not waiting for her to follow. "Rules are simple. Number one, as already discussed, if you create a scene, there'll be consequences."

She hesitated. "And if I do?"

"You have a friend that you live with?" Flynn's skin paled to a sickly yellow. "Want her to continue living? Give me your hand."

"What?" Her voice cracked. She clutched her hand as if he'd burned her. "Why?"

"Rule number two, never—and I mean never—ask questions."

Slowly, she obliged, shoulders rounding forward. Her palms were sweaty, but her touch still had an electrifying effect. Tongue shriveling, the inside of his mouth lost all moisture.

"Relax, nothing's happening to you. At least not yet."

Her face flushed. "Relax? How can I relax around a psychotic terrorist who mass murdered hundreds of innocent people?"

Wolf shrugged. "I may be many things, but I assure you I am not psychotic."

"Just wait until the FBI finds you," she said, her voice weak.

"I'll make sure to sleep with one eye open."

Flynn's feet scuffed the sidewalk as if tied to cement blocks. They stuck close to Lake Shore Drive, a winding highway that ran parallel to the lake and encircled the city. From a distance, masts of docked sailboats swayed in the wind. They crossed over the busy street, hand in hand, on a walking path already teeming with runners sporting short-shorts and tight spandex that bunched awkwardly in weird places. Sweaty bikers whizzed by, eager to soak up Chicago's fleeting summer. To passersby, they appeared to be a normal couple enjoying a late afternoon stroll.

Normal, he thought. *What a concept. Is that what this feels like?* No one noticed his companion's grim face or tense posture.

As they neared the lake, he stopped, nodding toward her bag. "Call your security detail. Tell them you left work early with some friends."

Flynn bit her lip. "I'm never supposed to go anywhere without clearing it with them first."

"Maybe you should've thought of that earlier. They can pick you up at the Yacht Club."

Her eyebrows drew together. Reluctant, she reached into her bag for her phone and tapped the screen. After pressing the home button with her thumb, she scrolled through her long list of contacts.

Who talks to that many people?

"Hi, Scott? It's me, Flynn. I headed out of work a little early today. It's a friend's birthday and we surprised her with a boat ride on the lake." She paused, listening intently to her security's response. "Sorry I forgot to give you a ring; it honestly slipped my mind. It won't happen again." Another pause. "We all left together as a group and we're already on our way. You can pick me up later this evening. We'll be at the Chicago Yacht Club off Lake Shore."

What appeared to be triumph briefly crossed her face, until she looked at Wolf and seemed to realize her successful evasion meant spending time with him.

"Damn," Wolf said. "Pretty impressive. Who would've thought you'd be such a good liar? Looks like you have some bad blood in you after all."

"Comparatively speaking, next to you."

As much as he hated to admit it, she continued to surprise him. It was like she had this involuntary desire to challenge him. It amused him. It also made it so tempting to provoke her, just to see the fire light up her eyes again.

They approached the Chicago Yacht Club. He flashed his membership card at the security guard monitoring the stream of expensive cars inching into the parking lot.

"Welcome back, Mr. Mason," he greeted Wolf enthusiastically, bowing his head toward Flynn, trailing behind.

Wolf loved slipping in right under their noses, stuck so far up their asses they couldn't see past the deep layer of shit now replacing their brains. Nodding curtly, he bypassed the clubhouse altogether, heading straight to the docks.

"*Mister* Mason?" Flynn pulled her baseball cap off her head and shoved it into her bag, brushing her unruly hair out of her face. The hint of sarcasm in her voice was a feeble attempt to mock him. "Is that your name?"

His eyes shifted in her direction without breaking his stride. "Sure."

"Sure?"

"I'm not telling you my name." His tone signaled the conversation was over.

"Why is it such a big deal? It's just a name."

Just a name. He withheld a sneer. If only she could recognize her own privilege—to be so self-assured and confident in her identity. "Why don't you focus your energy on yourself? I already know everything I need to about you."

Her head cranked on her neck in disbelief. "Yeah, right. You're lying. A small militia organization like yours can't possibly have the resources or software to tap into every American citizen's background."

Does she really want to go there? He sighed, unable to resist. "You're twenty-seven. You've worked as a recruiter for Magnetic for two years. You live with your best friend of eight years, Cori Friedman. You met her in college. Indiana University. Your mother is Rachel Zarytsky. Your father is Sean Zarytsky. Your parents took your mother's surname after your father's parents disowned him for marrying a Jew. Your sister is Fiella Adland. Your brother-in-law is Jared Adland. Want me to give you their ages and addresses too?"

He glanced behind him. Flynn had slowed to a stop. Cold terror finally replaced the underlying hatred in her eyes. He faced her, walking backward. "Come on, gotta keep moving." An unfamiliar feeling crept over him, and he swallowed his sickening urge to comfort her. "We don't need our own software, not when it's so easy to hack into the government's. And 'a small militia organization'? Hardly. You know who we are. You heard what we're capable of. Just do what we say, and no one gets hurt."

She swayed dangerously. They were halfway down the dock farthest from the clubhouse.

"Hey, watch it. If you fall into the water, no way in hell I'm going in after you." He exhaled a deep breath through gritted teeth, waiting. She stood, paralyzed, staring past his shoulder into the distance. Impatient, he rolled his eyes. He marched back to retrieve her, his boots slapping hollowly over the dock's wooden boards. *I'll fucking carry her ass to the boat if I have to.*

He looped his arm around her, palm pressed between her shoulder blades, and gave a sharp push. She stumbled forward. Flynn was clever, resourceful. She must be watched closely. Contained. Wrapping his fingers around her thin bicep, he directed her to a small boat and untied it from the dock. She hesitated, considering the rocking bow. He gave her another push.

Catching herself, she whirled around, the fire reignited in her eyes. "Don't touch me."

Wolf leapt into the boat. She climbed awkwardly over the side railing and staggered, unsteady, as the floor tilted against his weight. He headed to the steering panel and Flynn took a seat toward the front, as far from him as possible, wearing a sullen frown.

He maneuvered the sleek MasterCraft speed boat away from the dock and into the harbor with ease. He slid on a pair of sunglasses, blocking the powerful rays beating down on them at an angle. The lake sparkled merrily, like thousands of glittering diamonds, coaxing them toward its horizon.

Flynn watched the bow slice through waves, unaware of how he was studying the way beams of sunlight reflected off her shiny, dark hair. Her slender fingers twisted it into a knot at the nape of her neck with a few flicks of her wrist, wrangling it from the gusty wind.

Beautiful, he marveled.

Once they left the no-wake zone, he shifted the boat into a higher gear. Flynn lurched backward, grabbing the railing. Glaring at him, she scrunched her nose in distaste.

As fucked up as it might be, her revulsion gave him a weird sense of encouragement. *She's exactly what we need, perfect for our next execution.*

"Where are we going?" she yelled over the roaring engine.

He decelerated the boat as they ventured farther from shore, relying mainly on the bouncing waves to propel them in the direction of the current. Although they were on a lake, it behaved like an ocean with its own rhythm and secrets. Wolf cut the engine and silence enveloped them, interrupted only by water lapping against the hull.

"From now on," Wolf began, "this will be our meeting place. Your escort will drop you off at the Chicago Yacht Club and I'll bring you to the boat. It'll be a different boat docked in a different location each time. I've enrolled you in a sailing course . . ." Flynn's eyebrows jumped in surprise. "Think of it as your alibi."

Though appearing uncertain, she nodded, fingers tangling back into her hair. "I still don't understand what you want from me. What is it you're trying to achieve?"

"What did I fucking say about questions? You'll be informed of our meetings twelve hours in advance. The date will never be negotiable. You will never be briefed, but we'll tell you exactly what's required of you."

"Why me?" she asked, ignoring him. "Of all the people you could have taken, what can someone like me possibly do to help you? I'm not some super whiz engineer. You already got the hostage money."

He scoffed. "That money was traceable—it went straight into the black market. Look, you wouldn't still be alive if I didn't think you could be of some use, alright? Your value is your direct access to Magnetic and its resources."

"For the millionth time, I'm just in recruiting," Flynn protested. "I don't have any influence. You have the wrong person. There's nothing I can do for you."

"Do you think I'm a fucking idiot? *You* are the insider we need to infiltrate the company. No one will suspect you."

"But they will suspect me." Her voice trembled. "Everyone knows I barely escaped as a hostage. The FBI is watching my every move." She searched for his eyes behind the black lenses. "I could lose my job, or, even worse, go to jail for helping you."

He stepped toward her, towering above her petite frame. The boat swayed, throwing her off-balance again. *I could break her in half with one arm.*

"Or you could lose everyone that makes your life worth living. You choose."

It was possible she might try to shove him overboard. Her smoky eyes were scanning his face, her distraught expression mirroring her new reality.

"But what about the FBI?" Desperate, she searched for a loophole, a final way out. "I can never be seen with you."

An involuntary smile inched across his lips. "Don't worry about that one. They won't be focused on you much longer."

18

WOLF

Spider found Wolf later that evening studying electromagnetic pulses in his room. His arrival filled the cramped space. Wolf stood at attention, body rigid. Spider rarely visited personal quarters.

The grate under his bed jumped immediately to mind. His heart accelerated. What would Spider do if he knew he'd hidden Bear there? He'd probably double over, hysterical with incredulity, right before killing him.

Spider walked to the shelf next to his cot, studying the row of textbooks closely. They were his sole personal belongings other than his uniform and weapons, stored neatly in a narrow locker and drawer. Uncomfortable silence sat between them while Wolf waited, attempting to normalize his erratic pulse. After several seconds, Spider finally turned to face him. "I have an update about Falcon's placement."

It took all of Wolf's strength to stop his shoulders from sagging with relief. Falcon had been in hiding since the evening of the Green Line concert at Soldier Field. He couldn't return to any of their outposts in case the Feds were tagging him, and also because he couldn't risk being compromised. Aside from Wolf and Spider, Falcon was the only one who knew the full plan of their upcoming attack. They had chosen not to share anything with the executive team to ensure complete secrecy. Teetering on the precipice of victory, they needed to have every single detail aligned before they could proceed.

"He's secure?" Wolf asked.

"Yes. One of our policemen offered to take him in until we're ready to move forward."

Spider had infiltrators throughout the city, stationed within almost every government organization. REDS tentacles stretched wide and deep long before they decided to expose themselves. It had taken years, but now the time had come. As their militia and support grew, the new order hovered within their grasp.

"We're close," Wolf said. "Everything we've worked toward for so long." For the first time, excitement expanded in his abdomen, lifting into his rib cage like rising helium. Although at times this journey had felt impossible, all the pieces were falling into place, and as the unbearable tension of the unknown eased, their future came into clear focus—the future of the country with REDS at the helm.

"Yes. The challenges we've overcome have led us to this point. As I knew it would." Spider approached Wolf, fingering his flat chin. "Redemption is within reach. Redemption for the evil society has inflicted upon our world."

"You've led us to this point, Spider."

"Don't think all your hard work has gone unnoticed, Wolf. You've proven yourself to me time and time again. You will be rewarded."

"I don't expect anything. This is my dream."

"This is *our* dream." The corner of Spider's mouth pinched into an almost-smile. "Do you want to know what separates us from the wannabes and the frauds?"

"Purpose?"

"Exactly. Years ago, when the KKK caught wind of us, they approached me about a partnership. But it was always important to me that REDS wasn't associated with any form of white supremacy. Those men, and what they stand for, are weak. They're pussies, threatened by others who are different from them." His face clouded with disgust. "Those men never amounted to anything because they never had an agenda. They never got anything done. All talk, no action. They fed their need for power with insecurities, and insecurities don't go away unless you look them in the face. But that takes courage. That takes self-reflection—something none of those assholes had."

Wolf gritted his teeth. "Cowards."

"That's why we only accept the best. It's not hard to stand out when the bar is always set so low, which is why we raised it."

Wolf thought back to the first day they met—sitting across from each other at the plastic cafeteria table in the reform center guest lounge. At that time, Spider was the recruitment lead. A small swell of pride filled Wolf. "I'm grateful to serve you."

Spider studied him with a thoughtful look, as if he might say something, but then appeared to reconsider. "I'll be in touch with Falcon. I'd like you to meet with him at one of our spots when you have an update about the hostage. I'll notify you of his whereabouts."

"Of course. When should we tell the others?"

"Soon. Very soon." Spider glanced at the book on Wolf's desk. He tented his long fingers on its pages. "I see you're continuing your research."

"I am."

"Missions can border on obsession. After a while, they become part of you. It's why we must die for them."

"The greatest of honors, Spider."

"Speaking of which, how did it go with the hostage today?"

"She has fire, but it can be controlled." Wolf paused, choosing his next words carefully. "She understands what will happen if she doesn't comply with our demands. She's the perfect mole."

He met Spider's gaze. The blue glow from his large double monitors painted strange shadows around his deep eye sockets and sunken cheekbones. "Good. When do you plan to kill her then?"

"Kill her?"

"Yes, once she gets you into Magnetic, will you wait until after you plant the malware?"

Wolf didn't reply, his tongue pinned to the bottom of his mouth as if with a stake.

"She knows too much already." Spider turned to exit, stopping at the door, his back to Wolf. "There will be no compromises. You'll continue to be merciless. Falcon's mission takes priority over yours for the time being."

"I understand."

"Never forget, we all have weaknesses. Overcoming them is what makes us stronger."

19

FLYNN

Scrabbling for her keys in the depths of her bag, Flynn felt a familiar dull ache throb behind her left eye. City sounds swirled with a pounding headache.

Is it my hands or is the whole world trembling? she wondered.

A million thoughts ricocheted through her brain, but the one that she kept returning to was the man's face. He didn't look like a terrorist. Not that she really knew what a terrorist should look like. Just that under any other circumstance, he would have come across as so . . . normal? Maybe even handsome. Okay, definitely handsome. How many others like him were posing as everyday people living out their seemingly regular lives—disguised by freshly pressed clothes and tapered haircuts? That duplicity clung to her like a filmy residue. She couldn't scrape its clammy chill from her skin. It unnerved her.

As she pressed her forehead against the cool, wooden door, a shaky groan surged from her throat. That terrorist had dropped her off at the Chicago Yacht Club and then sped off into the sunset to dock at another marina. Her security detail had been waiting for her in the parking lot, furious she'd left work unescorted.

"Need a little help there?"

She jumped, clutching her chest. "Cori! Jesus, you scared the crap out of me. Yeah, I can't find my keys," she muttered.

Cori watched her carefully. "You okay?" She inserted her key into the lock.

"Just tired." Exhaustion wound itself around Flynn's head, suffocating her thoughts. "Work is killing me."

"Maybe take tomorrow off? Go home and hang with the fam this weekend. Give yourself a break." Cori pushed the door open and took Flynn's arm to help her inside. She limped over the threshold, her flats digging into a blister that had burst on her heel.

The thought of leading REDS to her family home sickened her, although that man had made it clear they already knew where it was. "I'm okay," Flynn sighed. She slumped her shoulder, and her bag dropped to the floor with a thud. "Soo . . . I decided to sign up for sailing lessons at the Chicago Yacht Club. Who knows, maybe it'll help me." She kicked off her shoes, and their couch absorbed her weight, releasing what sounded like a surprised "Oof." Stupid flats. Maybe she shouldn't have chosen to break them in on the day she walked across the whole damn city. "At least it's something different."

"That's great!" Cori said, a little too enthusiastically. "Something to take your mind off things." She bustled around the kitchen, opening a bottle of wine while Flynn stared off into space. "So, uh . . . sailing, huh? Have you been sailing before?"

"No . . . but a bunch of us from work went out on a boat today and being on the water, I dunno, it soothed me."

Aside from his appearance, something else about that REDS guy stuck with her—beyond the revulsion at his very existence, a confusing emotion nagged her to chase it and pin it down. Every time it was within her grasp, it escaped her, floating further away.

"You, my friend, sound like you're in need of a drink." Cori set two full wine glasses on the coffee table then joined her on the couch, slim legs folded up under her, elbow propped on a pillow and cheek rested against her hand, her eyes studying Flynn. She couldn't meet Cori's penetrating gaze. In two seconds flat, her best friend would see right through her cracking exterior.

It was clear Flynn hadn't processed what happened to her the evening of REDS's attack. *Time is the only thing that can heal,* her parents continued to reassure her, *and the only way to make time move faster is to stay busy.* But her wounds couldn't mend when she was trapped in this nightmare. There couldn't be closure when it was still the beginning. Of what, she didn't know. The possibilities paralyzed her.

"Flynn," Cori said softly, "you've experienced something indescribably horrific. You don't need to pretend to be strong to make it through this."

Nestling a throw pillow in her lap, Flynn stroked its silky tassel. It was almost impossible to articulate the change she'd observed in herself over the past few weeks. Instead, she gulped a large swig of wine. Over the rim, ruby liquid reflected the light of the overhead lamp, reminding her of a goblet of blood. Her stomach rolled over. Wobbly, she placed the glass back on the coffee table.

"Sometimes I still can't believe this happened to me. It's as if my head and my body are never in the same place. One is always way ahead of the other and neither communicates about where to go or how to get there. I always end up feeling lost. I can't shake it."

Cori reached out and squeezed her arm, as if she could transmit strength through her touch. "I know what you're thinking. All you want is to go back to the way you were before all of this happened. But it's like I said after you got released from the hospital, life has changed. We all changed. Normal has to mean something different for you now. It's hard, but try to think of this as an opportunity."

Flynn's gaze wandered from the wine's depths to face her friend. Dark brown irises camouflaged Cori's pupils so they always appeared dilated in thrilled anticipation. The thought of what REDS might do to her turned Flynn's blood cold.

"What if I don't like the new me? I mean, it all happened so quickly. I never knew it was possible to transform into someone entirely different overnight."

Cori's fingers sifted through her bangs, eyebrows drawing together. She bit the inside of her cheek as she always did when concentrating intensely.

"Don't you think you're being a little harsh?" She sipped her wine. "What is it that changed about yourself that you don't like?"

Well, for starters, a shadow hovers over me constantly, she thought, *haunting me whether I'm awake or asleep.* "I don't know. I'm pessimistic, more bitter." Flynn paused, then finally admitted, "I think a big part of me is still in denial too."

Cori chuckled, but it didn't carry notes of humor. "My dad always says you know you're growing up when you begin to realize all the things that can go wrong in this world and there's nothing you can do about any of them."

"That's exactly it. I've always been in control of my life. Or at least I felt that way. Now, it's as if it's slipping through my fingers . . . like water," Flynn said. Her teeth dug into her lower lip, kneading its soft flesh. "There are times I feel so angry this happened to me, that I lived through that night and made it out alive against all odds. Countless people died, but somehow, *I* lived. How can I not become overwhelmed with that pressure? Which, by the way, only makes me feel even more helpless. All I can do is sit on the sidelines as the victim and wait for REDS to execute their next move."

"Loss of control and then anger at your loss of control," Cori interpreted, nodding, fingertips tapping her glass. "It's a vicious cycle."

"How do I get my life back?"

Cori leaned back into the couch so they were shoulder to shoulder and rested her head against Flynn's. She put her hand over Flynn's. Her hair smelled like the coconut conditioning mask she used to tame its thick blonde waves. Comforting and familiar, she was one of the last lifelines still tethering Flynn to her old self.

"You step back and let it fall into place on its own," Cori said. "Rather than resist this new version of you, try to understand her. She might not be nearly as bad as you think."

20

FLYNN

After their last heated exchange, Flynn avoided Nate at work for the next week. But when two dozen roses appeared at her desk the following Monday, he was drawn to investigate. They were a deep jam color. More red. She suppressed a dry heave.

"Looks like you have an admirer," he said. "So, you and Ted back on then?"

"Uh, yeah right," she scoffed, shaking her head, reaching for a cream-colored note embedded within the massive bouquet. The petals were velvety soft. Silky layers rested on top of each other, creating flawless blossoms. A hidden thorn unexpectedly pricked her, snagging her skin. Her hand jerked backward.

See you tonight. 6 p.m.

The note was written on thick card stock in rigid, block script. It wasn't an invitation or request. It was a demand. She exhaled slowly, sinking onto the edge of her chair, heart free-falling into her stomach.

"What's wrong? Date night round two seems to have you pumped." Nate's familiar sarcasm had returned.

"Turner, now is not the time." The words sounded weak and distant.

"Flynn." Nate's tone turned serious. "It's okay to keep moving forward, you know? It's time."

Her throat constricted. Swallowing hard, she nodded even though her time to move on was far away still. "Yeah."

He reached out awkwardly, grasping her shoulder. "It'll be good for you to have some fun. Relax a little." His smile had a shadow of sadness. "Whoever he is, he's a lucky guy."

"He sure is."

* * * *

Flynn's security detail dropped her off in front of the Yacht Club, under the impression it was her first sailing lesson. They instructed her to wait in the parking lot for their return in two hours. A tinge of annoyance crept over her. She felt like a child being dropped off at a birthday party. The sleek black car merged back onto Lake Shore Drive, disappearing into the blur of passing traffic.

"Right on time."

Dread shot through her veins. For a brief moment, her vision darkened. The voice had a smooth finish, almost seductive, but it carried an underlying, menacing threat. She faced him, gravel crunching beneath her feet. He stood beside a tall tree, unassuming in khaki shorts and a short-sleeve shirt, arms crossed casually across his broad chest. The curves of his muscles were pronounced even in his relaxed pose. She shuddered, sweat pricking her hairline.

"I figured it's best to be prompt for a terrorist. Do you kill me if I'm late?" Her voice caught. *Oh my god . . . did I really just say that? What is wrong with me? He could actually kill me. Dumb, Flynn, you are so freaking dumb.*

"Maybe." His lips turned upward in a mock smile. "Why don't you try it next time so we can find out?"

"I don't think that's necessary." Her voice was small, a squeaking dog toy that just got its stuffing shredded by uncompromising jaws.

"Let's get moving."

He led her down a swaying dock, different from the last one they'd visited. She staggered after him, falling behind, already breathless. Any sort of exercise had always been her worst enemy, and it didn't help her lungs still weren't functioning normally.

"Come on, keep up."

"Yes, master," she mumbled, so quietly the staccato wind swept the words away.

They finally reached a new cluster of boats, stopping in front of a small, sleek cabin cruiser. It bucked and dipped as the waves slapped against its side.

"Nice upgrade."

He hopped effortlessly into the boat, ignoring her, and headed straight for the steering console. His clothes rippled every time he moved, pressing against his body. She stared at his back for several seconds before scolding herself, appalled. Reluctant, she clambered in after him, tripping over her feet. Coordination had also never been her strong suit.

The sun hung low over the horizon, casting a warm evening glow upon them as they headed out toward the middle of the lake once again. Beams of light created masterpieces of art across the water's shimmering canvas. A breeze caressed her face, breathing into her a small tremor of courage.

After fifteen minutes they slowed to a stop, rocking in the cradle of passing waves. Terrorist Man wasted no time jumping right into it. "Time for your first assignment."

"Can we start by giving me something to call you?" It was a weak attempt to crack his icy façade. "If we're going to be spending all these lovely evenings together, it's awkward if I don't even know your name."

He stared at her with strange intensity. "Why does it matter? I have a job to do, you have a job to do, that's it. Purely business."

His irritated tone surprised her. "It's not purely business, at least not for me. This is my life you're hijacking, not some computer. I want to know your name." It was an interesting defense mechanism—building a wall around an untouchable space to keep her at a distance. Her fingers combed through her hair, rubbing the ends. "Alright, well, maybe it will assuage your fears if I'm clear with my intentions."

The word *fear* triggered an instant reaction. His face closed off, jaw set in defiance. "Intentions?"

"We're working together toward a common goal now, right? A name would help. Any name. Make one up if you like."

"If you're insinuating I'm afraid to tell you my name, you're barking up the wrong fucking tree."

"Then why won't you tell me what it is?"

He was quiet for several minutes. They swayed with the gentle motion of the boat. The anchor's metal chain clinked, breaking the long silence.

This man is a mass murderer and I need to know his name, she thought. *If I want to stay alive, he has to see me as a real person, which means I have to know him as a real person, even if he's the grimiest scum on earth.*

"I would kill you now if I could for what you did." The words poured from her mouth without thought. If only she could shove them back down her throat where they belonged. She might as well have "death wish" tattooed across her forehead.

The beginning of a smile played on his lips. Elbows resting on his knees, he leaned forward as if they were chatting about the summer weather. "I could put a gun in your hand right now and you still wouldn't be able to kill me."

She straightened, but her quaking voice exposed her. "You don't know anything about me or what I'm capable of."

Folding his arms, he barked out a laugh. "I think I have a real good idea of who you are. Trust me, I know a killer when I see one." He studied her for another second, his penetrating stare making her insides squirm. "Alright, fuck it," he continued. "You can call me Wolf."

"Wolf?" Flynn suddenly dropped back into a memory of the holding cell, listening to two voices argue. One wanted her dead. The other wanted her alive. They'd called each other strange names. Animal names she couldn't remember, until now. "Where did that come from?"

"REDS Enforcers don't have names. Names form identities, which we don't believe in. We operate under aliases."

"Why don't you believe in identities?"

"Identities procure attachments. Attachments make humans weak, makes them vulnerable."

For a small fraction of a moment she pitied him, until she thought about all he'd done. He seemed to have recognized her sympathy. She'd never had much of a poker face when it came to emotion.

"If you're feeling sorry for me, don't. Focus on worrying about yourself. You're the one who has to live with the fears and insecurities about your relationships and other useless shit. Wasteful *things* that bring no meaning to your life." His voice sounded brittle.

Taken aback, Flynn picked her cuticles. "But that's what it means to live . . . and love."

"Yeah, that's what you think. Anyway, I don't give a fuck about living. My mission is my life, and it will turn this corrupt, shitty world on its head."

His words crackled with anger mingled with a fiery hatred—a terrifying hatred. *What do I say to argue that?* she asked herself. *Who am I to tell this person how he should live his life? Unless it involves killing hundreds of innocent people.*

"Your alias . . . does it mean anything?"

Wolf's eyes narrowed. He plowed forward as if their most recent conversation never happened. "Enough of this shit. It's time to go over why we're here. Several months ago, the Magnetic Chicago office released an announcement about hiring more people to expand its smart home initiative into the cable and energy industry. The end goal is to transition Chicago's electrical management onto Magnetic's unified network, while deploying a smart grid system to maximize energy efficiency."

"You seem pretty smart for a brainwashed terrorist. Articulate too. Did you go to college?"

Scornful, his face scrunched inward, lines fissuring around his nose. "It's not hard to become an expert in a field you're interested in. I just never wasted my time with the other useless bullshit."

"Well, you've clearly done your research. To be honest, I don't know much about it other than it's cheaper and more sustainable. Supposedly, it will also help with having fewer electrical blackouts."

"If this proves to be successful, Magnetic will roll out similar electrical network mergers across other major cities. You're currently a recruiter for sales positions," he said.

"Yes . . ."

"Apply for Magnetic's electric and cable recruiting division. Secure a position in that org by next week."

"Wait," she protested, "you want me to switch jobs? Firstly, it's not that easy to change divisions internally, and secondly, I know nothing about engineering or what qualifications we're looking for in candidates. I'm not technical enough for that role."

"Guess it will be refreshing for you to try something new, won't it? This isn't an option. It's nonnegotiable. Figure it out and start doing research."

She stared at him, mouth hanging open. A mixture of emotions swirled in her stomach, causing a sickening taste to rise up into her throat. He had the power to manipulate her as though her life was meaningless. She swallowed, trying to subdue her queasiness. "I don't understand. How will this help with anything?"

A soft smile brightened his menacing expression. Chills snaked around her shoulders and slithered down her spine. "You'll see."

* * * *

On the car ride home, the city flashed by, a blur of twinkling windows and passing headlights. High-rises stretched upward, disappearing into a somber navy sky. Loneliness engulfed her and she sank into its depths, disappearing beneath the shifting surface of what felt like her old life. *Is this the type of isolation that has shaped Wolf into the person he is?* she wondered. *No one to confide in. No one to share his deepest fears with. Left to confront this terrifying world on his own.*

Tilting her head back, she pressed it into the soft headrest, closing her eyes. Instead of darkness behind her lids, she saw striking green. Once more, she was transported back to the cold cement floor, Wolf's voice whispering in her ear.

You will be ripped apart. We have no rules.

She dug her fingernails into the leather seats. She had been too delirious then to process Wolf's warning. Had he been trying to save her? Had he cared whether she made it out of that cell alive? The questions sprinted through her head again and again.

You need medical help. This is your only shot at getting out of here.

Shaking her head, she wanted to scream to drown out his voice, but it continued to echo through her conscious, a haunting prophecy.

Is he truly one of them? Is there a chance he has a sliver of humanity left? she wondered. *Or is he completely soulless?*

He had already discovered her pressure point, so there had to be a way to uncover his. Wolf kept his cards close to his chest, but all she had to do was discover his tell in order to win. Fire versus fire created a bigger flame. What she didn't know was whether manipulation versus manipulation would have the same outcome.

21

WOLF

Only two days in Wolf's life still haunted him. One was, of course, his first encounter with Flynn. But the second had never really numbed over time.

It hung in the back of his mind, reminding him that as much as he hated to admit it, he had some form of a conscience. He'd done everything possible to rid himself of the memory, but no matter how hard he tried to push it aside, it lingered on the periphery, stalking him.

It had happened during initiation. After six months of grueling training, the remaining recruits had been transformed into merciless machines. They'd lost all sense of time. No one knew if it was a Monday or a Thursday, five o'clock in the evening or five o'clock in the morning. Disoriented, they followed orders to function—training, lectures, eat, sleep, repeat. Until one day, Cobra announced they had only one final task awaiting them before they could call themselves REDS Enforcers. Wolf had never anticipated the last challenge would be the worst of them all.

The details of that day remained vivid, refusing to fade with the grace of time. Sticky air had clung to his skin, leaving a thin sheen of sweat. Suffocating heat and a blindfold wrapped around his head made a doubly oppressive combination. Charged bodies shoved against each other, damp flesh pressing into damp flesh, a herd of slippery hogs guided to a butcher. He shuffled forward, arms slightly outstretched, not knowing what awaited just steps away. Someone shoved him. Staggering, his shins collided with stairs. Stinging pain sizzled up into his kneecap.

Rough hands arranged the recruits, positioning them shoulder to shoulder, before removing their blindfolds. Wolf tensed, preparing for an onslaught. His eyes flicked back and forth. Once they'd adjusted to the dim, windowless room, he saw they were on a small platform, a tight ring of faces wearing crimson masks staring up at them. Grim reapers waiting for death, they wore long black cloaks, blending into the darkness, their forms motionless.

Wolf's heavy breathing sounded like screaming. A palpable, crazed energy spread down his arms. The scent of adrenaline mingled with salty sweat seeped from their skin. Invigorating. Dangerous.

Control the physical response, he told himself, practicing what they'd learned in their training. *Convert it into something powerful.*

Beta bumped against him. Hair shaved close to his head, his once waspy body now carried a bulk of muscle. Beta had grown to be Wolf's only friend, something he never anticipated during a process equivalent to hell.

"Maybe today's the day I get to be the alpha," Beta muttered out of the corner of his mouth.

Wolf's lips twitched. "Not a chance."

A member stepped forward, his wide and bulky outline commanding immediate attention. He spoke in a deep, unfamiliar voice. "The time has come; your final initiation challenge. In order to join us, you must prove your loyalty one last time."

A second member broke rank, raising his arms in an outward expression of welcome. He was smaller than the first, his broad shoulders jutted into a sharp T. Although his raspy voice barely reached a whisper, in the stillness, every word rang as audibly as a yell. "The test will prove your resilience and mental fortitude. It will demonstrate your commitment to our ultimate mission."

The recruits fidgeted, feverish racehorses prancing behind the starting gate. Wolf's muscles clenched so tightly his limbs trembled. Mouth salivating, he could finally taste membership's savory honor. Nothing would stop him. Nothing. He needed this to complete him, to validate the shit he'd endured—to give him purpose.

"Take a look around," the raspy voice continued. "This is the last time you will stand together as one. Soon, only the strongest will remain."

The cluster of REDS parted, creating a narrow aisle. An Enforcer approached them, his cloak billowing around him as he emerged from the sea of black. He removed his mask. It was Cobra.

"During these final moments, reflect back on the recruits you experienced this journey with." Indifferent to the weight of their hungry stares, Cobra paced in front of them. "Never forget, your legacy as a warrior is about choosing to live or choosing to die an honorable death. Which will you choose today? Will you live or will you die?"

In unison, the initiates responded, "Live!"

Wolf glanced at Beta, fingers tingling. His glassy eyes shone, void of color in the darkness. Wolf balled his hands into tight fists, his spine straightening in rigid determination.

"To proceed to the Acceptance Ceremony, you must overcome weakness. You must overcome attachment. You've spent the past few months severing all ties to the outside world; now it's time to prove your strength. It's time to prove you're a warrior. Your final challenge is to kill"—Cobra paused—"your living partner."

Shocked silence rang throughout the room. Then action ensued as quickly as if someone had flipped on the lights. Wolf turned to Beta, grabbing his knife in the same motion. The receptors in his fingertips weren't working. They didn't register the blade's weight or its smooth antler handle as it sliced a thin line in Beta's neck, summoning a waterfall of fresh blood.

Stepping back, Wolf stared straight ahead as Beta fell to his knees.

Bodies hitting the platform thumped around them. It took less than a second to slit his throat.

Wolf couldn't breathe. The command had been given. He'd followed orders. He never questioned, doubted, or considered its consequences. Desperation rose within him, roaring flames doused with gasoline. Hanging limply by his side, his knife dropped with a clatter.

Do not fucking feel, he told himself. *Don't give into the weakness. Shut it off.* Like the gears of a car, he shifted his focus to the present.

Fuck you. He whispered to the piece-of-shit, self-loathing demon thrashing inside him. Its claws scaled the rungs of his rib cage, forcing entry into his airway. Its fiery breath shoved against gritted teeth. *I'm stronger than you.* He smothered its scream. *I'm more powerful than you.*

Those who paused for a second thought, a slight hesitation, were the ones who died. Half the recruit class lay dead on the floor, their blood soaking the survivors' feet. Wolf refused to look at Beta's face. If he glanced down, he would never be able to unsee the last seconds draining from his eyes.

The world is harsh, Beta, he wanted to tell him. *You of all people should know that.*

Beta was faster than him. He had defter knife skills than him. But he hadn't taken a single step toward him. It was as if he knew he needed to be sacrificed.

The REDS Enforcers detached from their tight formation, joining the surviving recruits on the platform. After dipping their hands into the blood of the dead, they brushed the warm, sticky liquid onto the new members' faces like war paint.

"Remember and celebrate this moment," Cobra's triumphant voice rang from the back of the room. "You are true warriors!" Cheers of raucous approval roared out. "You've set yourselves free. You've demonstrated your pledge is not to each other, but to our mission. Redemption. Execution. Deliverance. Salvation."

A deep chant rose from their lungs, joining together, as they covered their faces with blood. Their first crimson mask. A coiled spring of excitement released, shivering through Wolf.

REDS. REDS. REDS!

Their uncompromising purpose that had once unified them now lay shattered at their feet. Wolf had failed to predict how contradictory forming a relationship with someone would be while attempting to eradicate the emotional components of himself. REDS secured them within their ranks using the most fucked-up ploy of all—irreversible damage to their souls, like black ink pooling over white satin. He'd murdered Beta simply because he'd been ordered to, killing a part of himself along with him. There was no going back. They were finally warriors, and they were there to start a war.

Wolf had seen a lot of shit since that day, but for some reason Beta's death stuck with him. Maybe because for the first time he understood how it felt to lose someone, to feel the direct blow that killing lands on those left behind. He'd proved his commitment to REDS so it hadn't been an act of betrayal.

Yet, Beta had made a different choice. He had chosen Wolf. Their decisions had been tested for a reason—to see what they could fight through and live with. Because what they couldn't know then that Wolf knew now was that this pain was nothing compared to what would come next.

22

FLYNN

Wolf's eyes were everywhere, watching from the darkness, waiting for Flynn to be alone. She woke in the middle of the night searching for him, drenched in cold sweat, convinced she would find him standing over her bed. Not knowing was most terrifying—not having any idea when he'd want to meet next, where he'd show up, or what he was planning. Some days it was so daunting that just getting out of bed took all her strength. An imaginary clock hovered over her, ticking away the seconds, bringing her closer to their next inevitable encounter.

She scheduled time to meet with her manager, Jon, the next day to discuss her proposed career change. His office overflowed with tech journals, papers, and magazines. Two plush chairs shoved in the corner hugged an oval coffee table. Mounds of files sandwiching resumes covered the clear plexiglass surface. His disheveled appearance matched his surroundings, but his eyes smiled as he ushered her into the room with a warm welcome. Dread squeezed her chest, tightening like a snare.

"Flynn, glad you sent me a note. I apologize, I realize it's been a week or two since our last one-on-one, but I've been terribly busy. How are you coping with being back?"

His genuine concern made this even harder. One of Magnetic's co-founders beamed down on them from a framed poster on the white wall. "Well, uh, I was actually hoping to talk to you about that. I've been thinking, Jon . . . that I need a new challenge. I've decided to go for a role on the E&C team. As you know, it's Magnetic's next big push. I figured it might be the perfect opportunity for me to start fresh and try something different."

He frowned, running a hand through the patch of sandy brown hair remaining on his crown. The partially concealed bald circle on the back of his head had not yet expanded to meet his receding hairline. "Ah. I had no idea you were unhappy." He cleared his throat, gesturing to the chair. "Please have a seat." Its cushion sucked her into its center. She pressed her thighs together, unsure how she would get back up again. "Flynn, let's talk about this. You're one of our best. You've been in sales recruiting for years. You develop such a great rapport with these types of candidates. I've gotta tell you, it will be entirely different working with engineering candidates and finding those types of qualifications."

He's right. I know nothing about engineering, especially in this division. A frustrated groan blistered the back of her throat. She stared at her knees, concentrating on the moisture gathering underneath them. "It'll be different, that's for sure. But this is something I have to do. For myself."

His expression softened. Maybe he would refuse to let her go. Maybe he would give her an ultimatum and ask her to leave the company. Pinpoints of hope prickled her scalp. "Well, as long as Magnetic can still rely on you as the face of the company, then we're lucky," he said.

Flynn leaned back, deflated. The chair's backrest cocooned her shoulders, making it even harder to move. She'd dreamed of putting in her resignation for a while now. But on the other side was always an exciting new opportunity, not blackmail. She'd be lucky to be alive, let alone still have a career after Wolf got through with her. "Thanks, Jon. I knew you'd understand. I've done sales for so long it's time for me to try something outside of my comfort zone. Interviewing for the E&C team is a long shot, but I wanted your blessing before I try."

"That team's growing massively. They'll need someone like you to lead the charge. I'll make sure to reach out to the hiring manager and sing your praises."

Jon might be skeptical, but he couldn't argue a hostage victim suffering from PTSD wasn't in need of a refreshing change of pace. Intimidation sloshed inside her like water in a fishbowl. She didn't know anything about the cable industry, or any of their technology, for that matter. She didn't even know where to start.

"Thanks, Jon, I'll need all the help I can get."

* * * *

"You're leaving the team?" Nate's eyebrows shot upward upon hearing the news.

"Yeah." Too exhausted to muster any enthusiasm, Flynn sat on the edge of her desk. "If I'm being honest, I can't believe I got the position."

"Well, they're pretty desperate to start building out that team, right?"

She eyed him, annoyed. "Or maybe I'm good at my job and have a decent reputation here." Avoiding his gaze, she started tossing items on her desk into a cardboard box. "I've been thinking a lot since our last conversation and I figured now's the best time to make the move. It'll be good for me. Sales is getting old."

If anyone could see right through her false positivity, it would be Nate. He watched her pack. "You sure? I thought you were hoping things would fall back into place."

Forcing a smile, she lifted a shoulder, stacking framed pictures of her family at her sister's wedding on top of her keyboard. "Time to give you a shot at the limelight, Turner."

"Alright, alright. The least I can do is buy you a drink to celebrate. Call that security escort of yours and tell them to join us off duty."

She was supposed to meet Wolf at the Chicago Yacht Club after work, but dark clouds in the distance threatened a downpour. It was doubtful they'd head out on the lake today, and she had no way of contacting him to confirm. Digging through her foggy memory, she searched for the last time she'd gone out and enjoyed herself. A rebellious, devilish spark ignited deep within her.

Why not? she thought. *I just kissed my job goodbye.* If they left now, she could always meet Wolf after one or two drinks. Maybe it would even make him bearable.

"Sure, I'd love to."

* * * *

Four drinks later, they'd moved on to their second stop in the West Loop. The exhilaration of escaping others' scrutiny in a crowded and overly loud bar felt too good to stop now. Now that she was blissfully buzzed, the past few weeks seemed like a hazy dream. As Flynn sipped her fifth gin and tonic, the bite of alcohol tickled Flynn's throat. Nothing tasted better.

"I should have resorted to booze sooner," she told Nate, unable to hold back a snort of laughter. The world tilted slightly.

"I'm tellin' you," he said, raising his glass toward her in a sloppy salute, "there's nothing better than a good stiff drink to take the edge off this twisted world."

Nodding in drunken agreement, she rested her head on her hand. "What happened? This world didn't always feel so twisted."

Nate frowned, concentrating hard on her question. The perfect skin on his forehead folded into creased lines. "People got meaner."

"That is profound, Turner." Pursing her lips, she considered his response. "But why? People drink as much as they did twenty years ago—shouldn't that make them happy?" The ice cubes in her almost empty glass sang thirstily.

"True! But things also used to be simpler. There's no mystery anymore, no joy in seeing anything in real time. Social media creates the illusion that life is all sunflowers and rainbows, when in reality everyone is in miserable competition with each other in a game no one can possibly win."

"Wow, blaming the good ol' technology vice. Real original, soapbox."

"When was the last time you saw a beautiful sunset and simply savored it instead of reaching for your phone?"

She squinted her eyes in thought. She couldn't even recall the last time she'd noticed the setting sun's popsicle colors melting across the sky. Over the past weeks, she'd been so consumed with fear and anxiety that everything was tinted dark gray.

"I don't think I can remember," she admitted.

"Being present is no longer something that comes naturally. It's something that has to be taught and learned because we're so wired to our devices." Nate flung his cell phone onto the bar counter in melodramatic disgust. "Living is no longer about enjoying life; it's about who has a better one according to the internet."

"Preach!" She clinked her glass against his, sloshing a small puddle of liquid onto the bar, before downing the rest of her drink. "People are shallow assholes."

"Everything is shifting toward automation. All of this access to information—people just abuse it," Nate continued, now lost in a full-blown rant. "They can't be trusted with it."

Swaying on her barstool, she laughed. "Okay, okay, what are we supposed to do, put padlocks on Magnetic's search engine? People have always had equal access to information. At least, for the most part."

"Maybe, but technology evens the playing field. It makes everyone more powerful, an equal threat hiding behind a computer screen like a coward."

She swatted his arm playfully, noticing at the same time her painful inability to flirt. "Since when did you become so serious and paranoid? You used to be *such* an ass, but at least you were funny."

"I'm still funny," Nate argued, defensive. "But for good reason my humor has taken on a darker tone." He paused, signaling to the bartender for another beer. "And maybe after my near-death experience, I decided to experiment with being a nicer person and see if that brings me better karma."

"Yeah, okay." She rolled her eyes and tossed an ice cube into her mouth. It slid over her tongue, melting into a cool trickle. "Let's see how long you can stick to that."

"What's that supposed to mean?"

"You can put lipstick on a pig." She poked his arm.

"Alright, well you're not exactly your old bubbly, optimistic, altruistic self either."

She leaned back, hanging on to the side of the bar to stabilize herself. "Yup, yup, I think you're right. See, at least I admit it. Except . . . I've never been bubbly, let's be honest."

Nate grabbed her wrist, pulling her upright, their faces dangerously close. "In other words, you're throwing in the towel. You're going to let REDS win?"

His voice was low, but she could hear him clearly above the loud chorus of boisterous laughter and reverberating music. She couldn't help but stare at the perfect lines of his eyebrows and the golden coloring of his long eyelashes. Both were a shade lighter than his wavy hair. His skin took on a dewy caramel hue in the bar's dim light. She'd never forget the first time they saw each other at the hospital therapy session, after they both thought they would never make it out of the stadium alive. They were different people now.

"I can't fight what they did to me," she whispered. "They changed me."

"Yes, you can," he urged, eyes widening. His face pinpointed in and out of focus. "You're stronger than them. You have more to offer than they have to take."

Sensing the danger in their closeness, she snorted uneasily, pulling her wrist from his grip. Trying not to topple off the stool, she stood. She stumbled forward, the floor pitching under her. Nate grabbed her, holding her steady, while the world spun violently.

"You know what I think, Turner? I think it might be time to call it a night. Let me text my driver."

"This is what we get for not eating anything at that last bar."

"There were no good vegetarian options."

"Since when have you been a vegetarian?"

"Since I now understand what it feels like to be a cow herded to slaughter."

"Hmm, fair, I guess." He led Flynn outside, one arm wrapped around her shoulders to gently guide her toward the street.

The earthy smell of rain enveloped them and fresh air pushed their hair back from their sticky faces. A black sedan sidled to the curb. "Gentlemen!" she called to her security escort. "It's time to go! No judgment of my current state allowed."

"I'll make sure you get back okay." Nate started to help her into the car.

"Turner, I have my own ride sponsored by our lovely friends at the FBI. No offense, but what can you contribute to this entourage?"

"It's not your physical safety I'm worried about."

She patted his arm. "I got this, Turns."

"Turns?"

"And that's my cue to leave. You're officially on your own! Don't miss me too much, now that you have no one to torment anymore. How will you ever get on without me?"

Flynn practically dive-bombed into the back seat. As she struggled to a seated position, Nate leaned forward, forearm against the open door, grinning at her. His smile was sad.

"I have to admit, I'm not sure I will."

23

WOLF

Flynn wasn't even a little fazed to find Wolf standing in her dark apartment when she stumbled through the door.

"Oh, you?" She staggered past him into her room. No questions about how he got in, where her roommate was, or any goddamn account-ability for her earlier absence. A nauseating stench of alcohol wafted from her like sickly perfume.

Blinding red filled his vision. *She cannot be fucking serious*, he wanted to scream. Taking a deep breath, he flexed his hands, digging his fingernails into his palms. The building pain re-centered him. Storming into the room after her, he grabbed her shoulder and spun her around to face him.

"Where the fuck were you?"

Her bleary eyes studied him, an unfocused expression glossed over her slack face. "I forgot," she slurred.

"You *forgot*?" He clenched her brittle, toothpick arms. "Do you think this is a fucking game, Flynn? Some sort of social club you get to *decide* if you want to attend? For fuck's sake. Lives are at stake. Apparently, that means nothing to you."

A part of him craved the fire that ignited when he provoked her. Instead, her body was limp, her drooped mouth expanding into a bored yawn. His grip tightened.

"Why don't you kill me instead? No one else has to die, only me. I mean, come on, wouldn't that make your life a million times easier?"

A vein in his neck throbbed. She was completely oblivious. "No. No, I'm not going to kill you," he fumbled over the words. "We're not done with you. At least not yet."

"Yeah, yeah, yeah." She pried his hands off her. After kicking her shoes across the room, she hopped onto her bed, patting the spot next to her. "Wait 'til you find out I'm useless. Come on over. Have a seat; relax a little for once, why don't ya?"

The girl was hammered. Ass wasted. Nothing he said was going to register with her. Suddenly claustrophobic, he paced up and down the length of her small room. Her plush carpet sucked at his feet, tripping him. Next he collided with the edge of her dresser. Tubes of makeup spilled onto the floor. A bottle of perfume clattered to its side. Her mirror oscillated on pewter legs, swaying his reflection. A stranger glared back at him, panic in his eyes. Hot fury twisted like a stake driven into his throat.

Shit. Get it together, he scolded himself.

He grabbed a turquoise vase from a small table and hurled it onto her bed. The fluffy, cream-colored duvet absorbed the impact with a sigh. She raised an eyebrow, unimpressed.

"You're not a fucking child." He swallowed hard. His breath puffed in short bursts, flaring his nostrils. "There will be repercussions for this bullshit."

"Stop cussing. Will you take a chill pill? Jeez, you're always so uptight and angry. It's *exhausting*. Do you ever have any fun?" She flung herself against a stack of propped-up pillows but continued to squint at him as if he stood far away. "There are a lot of you right now."

He buried his hand into his hair. Grabbing a fistful, he tugged at its roots against his scalp. "The word *fun* isn't in my vocabulary."

"You know what? I think I know what you need." Flynn pushed herself back upright with what looked like a great amount of effort. "Do you need a hug? Would that help?" The corners of her mouth turned down in a mock pout.

What the actual fuck, he thought, disgusted. *This bitch is crazy.* Recoiling, he stumbled over the carpet again. *Stupid fucking carpet.* Through her drunken stupor, her eyes lit up. Seemingly encouraged by his defensive body language, she rolled off the bed and lurched in his direction.

"Flynn, stay back," he warned. "Don't touch me."

A surge of adrenaline rocketed into the base of his skull. Before she could reach him, he extended his arm, palm pressing into her forehead. Her arms flailed in front of her, swiping through the air like windshield wipers as she struggled to overcome his strength.

"Oh, come on. What's the harm in giving you a hug? You obviously need it."

"Don't fucking test me."

"Fine." She stopped struggling and pivoted, shoving tousled hair off her face. Without warning, she dove toward him again, wrapping herself around his torso.

Her warm body pressed against him, squeezing out the space separating them. Air was sucked from his lungs as she turned her head to rest it against the breadth of his chest. His muscles melted, leaving only wired nerves wrapped around bone. She held on tightly, as if trying to keep him from running away—a boxer tying up an opponent by getting close. Too close to fight his way out.

"You're hard." Wolf's black, lightweight jacket muffled her voice. "Not much give to you."

How the fuck do I get out of this? he asked himself. His limbs wouldn't respond to his brain. Truth be told, she was pretty damn strong. *An escape route . . . there has to be one.* Keeping his arms raised, he threw his head back, mouth open in a silent yell. *It's fight or flight. Kill her, damnit. Do it now. This is what you've been trained to do. What you're meant to do.* Two dark clouds collided inside him, forming a swirling tornado. It would be easy to wrap his fingers around her throat. Twist and crack. Squeeze until deafening silence. *No. I can't. I won't. Not her.* His hands twitched, responding to the instinctual urge to kill when threatened. Something fought back. Something stronger.

That familiar floral smell drifted up from her hair, bringing with it waves of inexplicable emotion. Claustrophobia overwhelmed him. Could she hear his heart? Desperate, he ripped her arms away from his sides, dragging her back to bed.

"Shit, Flynn. I'm not your friend. You have no idea what I'm capable of."

She stared up at him, head tilted back limply. Her dark eyelashes were magnetic, ashy tones dancing in her irises.

"You saved me that night of the concert," she whispered. "You wanted me to live."

Something in Wolf untethered, floating away into the depths of the sky like a freed balloon. *How would it feel to hug her back?* he wondered. *How can I live my entire life resenting and hating every single fucking human, only to encounter one and have it change everything?* Pressure built behind his eyes, pressing against his temples.

"I don't . . . I don't know what you mean. You're wrong. I took advantage of the opportunity." His voice was strained and foreign, as if it was being wrung out of his body. "I saw your work badge."

"No." She shook her head. "You know I should have died right there along with everyone else. You kept me alive then, and you kept me alive in that cell. You could've taken anyone at Magnetic whenever you wanted, but you took me. Why *me*?"

He started to back away. She lunged, grabbed his hand with both of hers, reeling him back in. Her palm was soft and warm. Unfamiliar. His arm jumped, like she'd shot him with a Taser.

"Wolf, don't be afraid, I'm trying to talk to you."

Fury electrified him the second the word "afraid" escaped her lips. He yanked his hand from her grasp, raising it above him to strike her. She'd crossed a line. For the first time, she cowered. A small sliver of sobriety returned as she ducked, covering her head. He squeezed his eyes closed.

"I'm not afraid," he hissed. "I'm getting the fuck outta here. This is going nowhere."

"Why did you come?" she spluttered, her voice full of loathing.

Rushing from the room, Wolf slammed the door behind him. Breathing heavily, sweat peppering his forehead.

Fuck, he cursed to himself. *Fuck. Fuck. Fuck.* It was too late. His cover was blown.

She'd already seen right through him.

24

FLYNN

"Flynn? Flyyyynnnn? FLYNN!"

Heavy weights anchored Flynn's eyelids closed. Head pounding, tiny knives slicing her throat, she struggled to the surface. Groaning, Flynn cracked open one eye. Cori's form swirled above her.

"What the hell did you do last night?" Cori demanded. "I came home from happy hour and you were snoring so loudly I could hear you from the kitchen. I yelled your name and you still didn't move."

"I'm going to puke," Flynn mumbled.

"Oh my god." Realization washed over Cori's face. "You're hungover? I'm so proud of you! When was the last time you went out and got drunk?"

She pressed the heels of her hands against her eye sockets. "Cori, I need quiet. I need you to leave."

"Um, I'm sorry, no way." She jumped onto the bed and crossed her legs. Flynn's stomach bungeed with the bouncing motion. "Who were you with? Was it a guy? Did you meet a sexy sailor during one of your lessons?"

"No. Dear lord, where do you come up with this shit? I was with my coworker. Nate. Remember him? We went out to celebrate my last day on our team." Cori's high-pitched squeal pierced Flynn's ears. Wincing, she shushed her. "Can you please not be annoying about this?"

"Sorry, I can't help it! Did you guys hook up?"

"What? No! We're just friends."

Cori's shoulders sagged, eyes flicking upward in patronizing impatience. "So what? You can be friends and still hook up. Let your hair down! You need a wild night out on the town."

Flynn refrained from reminding Cori about what happened the last time she pushed her to go out on a date with someone she worked with. "For the millionth time, no. Like I've told you *before*, I'm not interested in dating a coworker."

"Flyyynn." Cori flopped down beside her. "I don't understand why you think that matters. Who cares if you guys work together? You're not even on the same team anymore. Work hookups are super convenient. Trust me, I know. They happen all the time. You might notice if you would just pay attention."

"Not at Magnetic. Everyone is married with kids."

"Okay, well how else are you supposed to meet a guy then?"

"You know, that's really not top priority at the moment."

Cori shimmied closer, her tan summer skin a tone darker than Flynn's. "But you're so gosh darn cute. Who could resist you?"

Flynn groaned. "Will you settle down? How many espressos have you had this morning?"

"Only two shots, with a swig of tequila." She fluttered her lashes. "You know me so well."

An instant burning sensation filled Flynn's throat at the mention of alcohol. Scrambling out of bed, she sprinted to the bathroom.

* * * *

During her ride to work later that morning, Flynn tried to piece together the previous evening's events. Flashes of Nate's face only inches from hers, and then the memory of Wolf's solid body. It was enough to make her vomit again. She chewed at her thumb, gnawing her nail into a jagged edge.

Ugh. What have I done? Shame oozed from her pores, more pungent than the booze. *I should just bury myself in bed for the rest of the year.*

"Hey, Scott," she called up to her escort. "What kind of state was I in last night? Isn't it your responsibility to make sure I don't get that intoxicated?"

Their eyes met in the rearview mirror, and a smile widened across his face. "Well, Miss Zarytsky, let's put it this way—I'm surprised to see you heading into the office this morning."

Leaning her head against the warm window, Flynn felt the sun's spotlight beaming down on her. "That makes two of us."

✳ ✳ ✳ ✳

Flynn hibernated in Magnetic's upstairs café for most of the day, poring over research about open positions she'd be tasked with filling on the cable team. Magnetic's smart grid initiative was as foreign to her as her former team's fantasy football league, but the development plans were fascinating. Maybe this position would be a refreshing new beginning for her, away from the politics of the sales organization that were as deep-seated as weeds.

As she read about the benefits of building an improved energy infrastructure, unease nagged at the back of her mind, distracting her. Each sentence might as well have been written in Hebrew, which she'd refused to learn growing up. She'd been terrified of giving the kids at school another reason to tease her. Another reason to see her as different.

What could Wolf's motivation be for me to join this team? How could this division be of any interest to REDS? She closed her eyes and, racking her brain, recalled blurry images of him standing in her room, filling the space with his imposing form. He'd looked so out of place amid the soft white curtains, his black jacket and pants starkly contrasting her duvet and patterned rug. She massaged her forehead, still able to feel Wolf's palm pressing against it, pushing her away, keeping her at a distance.

I can't believe I tried to hug him. What the fuck was I thinking? Stupid. I'm so stupid. I swear, I get this mindless audacity from my batshit crazy mother. Face hot with embarrassment, her head fell back against the wall behind her. Her bruised brain rattled around in her skull. She would do anything to erase the foggy memory. *No alcohol ever again. Well . . . okay, let's be realistic, at least for a while.*

"Hey there." Nate stood in front of her, hands shoved deep into the pockets of his navy slacks. His white collared shirt, the top two buttons undone, exposed a glimpse of bronzed chest. Despite his impeccable style, his appearance always looked effortless. Flynn suddenly felt self-conscious in her plain black pants and loose blouse. "How're you feeling?" His greeting carried a more awkward air than usual.

"Mission accomplished on Operation Get Flynn Hammered. If you can't already tell by my lackluster appearance, I'm struggling."

Nate's crooked grin was slow and seductive. She could never tell whether the expression was calculated or natural.

"Last night was great," he said. "I haven't had fun like that in a while."

She forced a grimace. "Yeah, it was fun, despite the hangover. I'm glad you convinced me to go out." Tapping her pen, she waited for him to continue on and get a coffee, or do whatever else he came upstairs to do, but he didn't move. She shifted in her chair, her already queasy stomach churning. He took a seat opposite her.

Damnit.

"Tell me about the new division. You look overwhelmed."

Her eyes skirted his face, unable to meet his gaze. "Um, what do you want to know?"

"What are the goals for the team? I don't really know anything about cable; I just keep hearing they're hiring like crazy."

"Well," she said, exhaling sharply, "management wants to invest in smart meter hardware and then expand into cable. I guess the cyclical nature of how the two pair together leads to more sustainable and renewable electricity." She paused, angling her laptop screen in his direction. Nate leaned forward. His aftershave smelled clean and masculine, like pine trees on a crisp winter day. "T-To start, they're using Chicago as a test market, and helping the city invest in a more modernized smart grid. Almost like a case study to see the benefits and outcomes of improving the reliability and affordability of energy."

"Sounds like admirable work. Wonder what's in it for them."

"Guess we'll find out, won't we?"

They sat, sinking into a long pause. Crossing one leg over the other, Flynn shoved her hands between them. Nate slid both forearms onto the table.

"So, uh, I was thinking . . . Now that we're not on the same team anymore, maybe you'd like to go out to dinner sometime?" The words flooded from Nate's mouth, jumbling together.

It took a few seconds for Flynn to process his ask. Her stomach dropped. "Oh, um, you mean like a date?" she asked, flustered.

"No, Flynn, like an awkward, forced conference call." His wit came to him so quickly it was no wonder women found him irresistible. "Yes, like a date."

She searched for words. If she was being honest with herself, she kind of liked the idea of dating Nate. She loved spending time with him and how he challenged her, in a good way. But . . . *Flynn, stop that*, she thought. *No. Impossible. Dating Nate would put him in serious danger.* She shuddered at the thought of him becoming another person on REDS's hit list—a perfect target because of his proximity to her.

"I don't know if I'm ready yet, Turner," she finally replied in a small voice. "I'm sorry."

He held up his hands. "Fair enough. I don't mind a bit of a wait. If anything, it makes the main event even more enjoyable." Undeterred, he grinned cheerfully. "Hey, mind if I catch a ride home with you and your driver today? I think I only live a few blocks from your new place so I can walk home from there."

Flynn blinked. Talk about whiplash. "Uh, yeah, sure."

"Great." He knocked the table with his knuckles and stood. "Swing by my desk before you head out."

He sauntered away, posture relaxed and gait slow, pulling his phone from his back pocket, as if he had all the time in the world. Pinching her brow, she gnawed on her lip. A part of her wished he would stay.

* * * *

During their ride home together later that afternoon, Nate and Flynn offhandedly discussed her initial thoughts about her new manager. It was as if his earlier date proposal never happened. He joked about having a shot at a promotion since she was no longer a contender in the running. When she ignored him, he moved on to complain about Ted's insufferable team meetings that could be heard from the other end of the office. Soon enough, they pulled into her building's curved driveway.

"Scott, I don't plan on leaving the rest of the evening, so you can head home." They clambered out of the car, legs squeaking across dry leather. "I'll text you tomorrow with my plans for the weekend."

As he drove away, Nate glanced at her. "How much longer are you going to have to deal with that? Must get old having a babysitter all the time."

"Not much longer. I put in a request a month ago to terminate their services. My mom wasn't too happy about that one."

"At least you get free rides everywhere. Your own personal Uber service."

"I guess. They're finally scaling back. I'm sure they only kept it up this long because the FBI's keeping tabs on me." Shielding her eyes from the sun with a hand, she tilted her head in his direction. "It's hard for life to go back to normal when that night follows me everywhere I go. Quite literally, I mean."

He nudged her, winking. "Kind of an awkward opener on dates, I'm sure."

"There are no dates," she sighed, exasperated.

"What about those roses?" Flynn didn't respond. "I'm kidding, I'm kidding," Nate said. "Will you relax?"

Shifting from one foot to the other, she was suddenly eager to get inside. Everyone needed to stop telling her to relax.

Nate scratched the back of his neck. "You sure you don't want to grab a bite to eat?"

"Turner, you nearly drowned me to death in booze yesterday."

"Alright, fine," he said in mock dismay. "As you can probably tell, I'm not used to rejection."

"Oh, please. I didn't reject you."

"Yeah, yeah, it's okay. Like I said, I enjoy a bit of a challenge."

Standing over her, he grazed the side of her face with a hand. Unexpectedly serious, he took a loose piece of her hair between his thumb and finger, studying it. All she could hear was her breath colliding against clenched teeth. Her eyelids fluttered closed.

He'll see right through me, she thought. *Straight through the lies and into my rotted, blackened core.* He would never forgive her if he knew her involvement with REDS. He wouldn't understand. He wouldn't be this weak. Nate wanted to help her heal, to make the pain melt away. But he couldn't. She stepped back, wrapping her arms around her boiling midsection.

"You need to know," he said, "I am serious about what I said last night." Tense energy radiated from his body, as if probing for kinks in her flimsy armor.

She finally met his gaze. "About what? Last night is a bit of a blur."

"About continuing to live your life." He moved closer. "A little boy died in my arms that night at Soldier Field. I think about him every single day. When I want to give up, I think about those men in masks—about how they murdered all those people. I won't let them kill my will to live too. I won't let them kill everything that's good in our world."

Fiery and fervent, Nate's eyes shifted, searching for missing pieces of her that were stolen weeks ago.

"REDS is still out there," Flynn whispered. "You know that night is only the beginning. It's a warning, showing us what they're capable of. Now they're watching to see how the world responds."

In one short breath, he cradled her face in his hands, thumbs resting on her cheekbones. His touch was gentle, palms warm against her clammy skin. She wanted to fall into his embrace like she did when they first saw each other in the hospital. "There's something you're not telling me. I know it."

Her ears filled with rapid machine-gun fire. *Is it a flashback or my heartbeat? Save him. This is all to save him.* "Nate, please leave."

"I was there with you. If anyone knows how those memories haunt you, it's me. You can tell me anything."

For the first time in weeks, tears filled her eyes like water sinking a ship. The moisture behind her lashes blurred her surroundings into a palette of glossy colors. *Don't let them fall*, she warned herself. *Once they start, they may never stop.*

"You weren't there the whole time. You weren't with me in that cell." A zip tie squeezed her throat shut. Blinking, she pulled away. "I can't do this right now. I'll talk to you on Monday."

As she turned toward the rotating doors, each step felt heavier than the last. Her sole defense was to run. And hide. Pathetic. She was sick of people prying, saying she could tell them anything, like it was that simple.

Nate grabbed her hand as she moved away. "I know I wasn't, Flynn, but you walk away every time I try to talk to you about what's happened to us. About what we lived through." Two lines pushed his brows into a deep V. "It's because you know I'm right."

Why couldn't he move on and forget about her? Instead, he was adding another complex layer to her already messy life. How could he not understand there was nothing he could do to help her?

"Nate, look, there's a before Flynn and an after Flynn. Period. There's no going back. Now please . . . drop it." The hard finality in her voice was more forceful than she'd intended. Shaking his head, he released a sharp exhale, lips crumpling into a lopsided frown. He scratched the stubble speckling his jaw.

"You can keep pushing me away, but I'm not going anywhere. And despite what you might think, you're not alone." His thumb pressed into her palm. The firm pressure shot warmth up the length of her arm. "Be brave, Flynn. It won't be easy. It's never easy. But if anyone can do it, it's you."

He's wrong, she thought. *I'm a coward. A selfish coward, who would do anything to keep him alive.*

25

WOLF

"When can you get in?" Falcon asked.

He sat across from Wolf in a cramped booth hidden in the back of a bar. The dimly lit room covered half of Falcon's face in shadows. Windows caked with grime kept any natural light from peeking through the panes. Two other men occupied a table close to the door, draining large glasses of foamy beer before slamming them down for another.

"Give me three weeks." Wolf sipped his whiskey. He rarely drank, didn't like anything subduing his senses, but on the occasion he did, he savored it. The warm liquid rolled over his tongue, coating it with a rich, oaky flavor.

"*Three* weeks? Fuck, you need to get in faster than that. The Feds are hot on my ass. I can't hold out that much longer."

Wolf glared at him over the rim of his glass. Falcon had grown a shaggy beard, concealing his haggard face. "The mole moved into the new position today. I can get in within the next few weeks. The hiring process at a place that size takes time."

"Then we move forward without your placement." Falcon's gaze was piercing, his voice steely. He rubbed a hand wearily across his forehead and over his hooked nose. Falcon had taken Wolf under his wing and mentored him over the past few years. Enigmatic aloofness superseded his usual boisterous energy.

"I need to get in to implement the malware and take over the network," Wolf said, watching the beer drinkers at the front door. "We can't fucking wing this. The substation is only supposed to serve as a test."

"Yeah? Well, what about *my* mission?" Falcon leaned forward, jabbing at his chest. His reddened eyes, the ones that inspired his name, blazed.

"We have a common goal." Wolf's voice was low and urgent. "You know the manifesto—we have to destroy this system together. It's not about you or me. These are Spider's orders. There's too much at stake to be careless now."

"Yeah, coming from someone who's not hiding out in a fucking basement. Spider had no idea it would take you over a month to get in the door at that place. We need to keep the wheels moving. You're stalling us."

"Spider understands," Wolf said, swirling the amber-brown liquid in the cloudy glass. "He knows we need to be patient to see this through the right way."

"Yeah? We'll see about that." Falcon pushed himself up from the table. Flipping his hood over his head, he disappeared into the night.

* * * *

Early Friday morning Spider found Wolf eating breakfast in the arena. Tables, placed in a circle within the cavernous room, surrounded the same platform they'd stood on for initiation.

The arena was located in the basement of an old, abandoned church on the south side of Chicago. It was one of their many outposts. The first REDS members had discovered it over fifteen years ago and converted it into a soup kitchen. It served as the perfect cover for scoping out new talent. They'd evaluated the bastards drifting through the door, searching for anyone capable of serving as an Enforcer. The pickings were usually slim. They didn't want minds muddled with addiction. They wanted bitter outcasts with nothing to live for and full of fury toward all the assholes who viewed them as the ringworm of society—contagious, pitiful, an eyesore.

Members rotated soup shift on a monthly basis. It was a required duty to ensure they remained camouflaged. But staying inconspicuous was easy in an area that city officials marked off due to dangerous gang violence. The gangs never bothered them since they didn't deal drugs, and REDS kept to themselves. One could call it mutual respect—each looking to survive in a different way.

An enormous sign hanging over the melted stained-glass window greeted anyone entering the church. The words scrawled in red on the canvas declared their organization's insignia to the outside world: *Redemption. Execution. Deliverance. Salvation.* Everyone was too blind to see it for what it really was, how ominous those biblical promises turned when used in a different context. Like changing a single spice in a dish to give it a totally new dimension of flavor. Wolf had always loved its irony.

A unified wave of soldiers stood at attention when Spider entered, an army saluting their general. He approached Wolf, eyes locking on his face. His target.

"Wolf, come with me."

Shit. What does he know? he wondered. *Well, that's a dumb fucking question. He knows everything.*

He left his plate of food behind without question and followed Spider into the Leadership Chamber. It was a plain room adjacent to the arena where executive members gathered for consultation. Hard wooden chairs surrounded a single round table in the center of the room. Austerity was one of REDS's tenets.

"Take a seat."

Without hesitation, Wolf sat, back erect. Veins running down the length of his forearms pulsed, blood surging from his spiked heart rate. It was unusual to sit in their leader's presence.

"I've spoken with Falcon. He said you're still three weeks away from gaining employment at Magnetic. Time is not on our side. We need to accelerate." Spider tented his long fingers. "Falcon could be compromised before he completes his mission, and it's a necessary trial before we move forward with your operation. We *cannot* have one of our members taken prisoner."

His voice offered no room for discussion. Wolf silently cursed Falcon. "Yes, Spider."

"I understand your main priority is your mission, but these are crucial steps. Never forget the big picture, but do not underestimate the strategic details."

Wolf's eyes remained glued on the opposite wall. "Yes, Spider."

"Speak your mind," he permitted after a pause, studying Wolf's profile.

"I can't manipulate Magnetic's hiring process. I can secure the position, but it might take time."

"You can manipulate the hostage, so you can manipulate the process. We need you in by the beginning of next week. No excuses. Once you're granted clearance, we will work with Falcon and move forward with taking out the substation."

"Yes, Spider." Wolf nodded, a small, swift motion, and waited to be dismissed. Flynn won yesterday. She'd outmaneuvered him without even fucking trying. She had home field advantage. Her smell, her blasé attitude, the soft colors of her room, had disarmed him. *I should be in control, not her*, he thought. *I should be calling the fucking shots.*

"One more thing." The air crackled with staticky tension. Spider continued to scrutinize him. "The council has discussed nominating you to replace Falcon on the executive committee. Are you willing to accept?"

Wolf blinked, while the remainder of his facial muscles stayed frozen in place. "It would be an honor, Spider."

"I promised a reward for your dedication and creativity. Both are invaluable assets to our organization. It has taken us to places we never thought achievable. Your relentless commitment to our cause is admirable. But"— he paused—"you must not succumb to temptation. It is dangerous and short-sighted."

Wolf didn't respond. A warning snaked deep within Spider's words. The muscles in his jaw were so tight they might snap.

"You've always stood out from other Enforcers. Your potential is limitless. I see a great deal of myself in you." Spider towered over him, broad chest blocking the light. "I hope to mentor you one day, when the time comes, so you're prepared to take over for me."

Become the leader of REDS? Impossible. He didn't have the presence to inspire or terrify. He didn't have the charisma to set forth a movement or captivate an audience. Both were necessary to maintain complete control. Head swimming, Wolf could feel his composure wobble. Hairline cracks spread over the thick walls he'd built to safeguard his vulnerabilities. Vulnerabilities he hadn't known he had. Doubt peeked through the fissures, exposing tiny glimmers of light.

"You honor me, Spider, but I'm . . . I'm not worthy to lead REDS." His neck bent, pushed by an invisible hand. The words tasted sour, scraping his tongue raw.

Spider took a seat across from him. Their eyes locked. Wolf's breathing became shallow. Spider's face could transform dangerously fast from callous and menacing to beguiling and warm. His allure was deceptive, carefully crafted into a practiced persona.

"You will never see yourself as worthy. That's the type of man you are. But true greatness is only achieved when the final result is never enough."

"I am not a leader," Wolf said. "I will never be able to uphold your legacy."

"Others respect you, so you are a leader," Spider corrected. "Building the confidence to lead is a choice."

His resolve hardened. Spider's approval was validation, something he'd never received from anyone before. It replenished him like water pouring over parched earth. Spider would never mislead him. Ferocity roared within him, reawakened. Unleashed from captivity, it burst forth with new resolve.

"There's only one requirement." Spider reached forward, grasping his shoulder. Even through his vest's thick fabric, Spider's fingers burned a handprint into his skin. "You must pass the ultimate test."

* * * *

Later that evening, Wolf waited in the shadow of Flynn's building for her to return from work. The rusty bike rack serving as his perch snagged his jeans whenever he moved. Silent headphones rested in his ears, so it looked as if he was listening to music while waiting for a friend. Usually, he would never risk meeting this openly in public, but after Flynn blew him off to drink herself into oblivion, consequences were critical. That, and they were now operating under an expedited timeline.

His arm hairs prickled; he was unaccustomed to the casual attire required to blend into his surroundings. People strolled by, yammering into their phones. They were as foreign to him as a different species.

Assholes, he sneered to himself.

Finally, Flynn's security escort pulled into the building's driveway. She stepped out of the car, followed by a tall man. He lingered next to her even after the vehicle pulled away. A nerve jumped painfully above Wolf's brow, drawn over squinted eyes. At first their conversation seemed light, but the intensity in the man's expression deepened.

Who is this prick? An unfamiliar sensation crawled over his skin, squeezing around his chest. The guy was close enough to Flynn he could touch her. Wolf watched as his hand traveled to her face.

An urge to pulverize him into bloody shreds blinded Wolf. It came as unexpectedly as a train barreling through a thick wall of fog. Flynn attempted to walk away, but Prick grabbed her hand, stopping her. Again, condensing all his strength, Wolf fought the impulse to beat him into the sidewalk until his organs stained the cracked cement. It would be so easy to end his life. Wolf turned his back to them and braced himself on the bike rack. His fingers wrapped around the rusty metal, tightening like they would around the asshole's throat. He inhaled, trying on the long exhale to quiet the rage hijacking his entire body. Sucking in more oxygen, he tensed, risking a quick glance under his arm.

Flynn's gaze cast downward as the man backed away. The shifting, dappled sunlight shone upon her blank expression, barren of emotion. It was as if she was lost in thought about something different. It took a second for Wolf to finally admit to himself that he'd underestimated Flynn's power over him. Something wild and frantic pulled him toward her. After killing Beta, he thought he'd escaped all bullshit trivial emotion, but he was wrong.

Spider's voice broke through the screaming chaos between his ears.

You must not succumb to temptation.

A familiar pain spread through his nerves touching every limb. It was hollow, empty, a gaping crevasse with no end . . . a deep, insatiable longing. Hunger that couldn't be satisfied. Thirst that couldn't be quenched. A craving that consumed every goddamn waking moment, gnawing at his insides until there was nothing left. It was how he'd felt before REDS found him. Before he belonged.

26

FLYNN

"Flynn. Walk with me."

Flynn's heart froze mid-beat, as if Wolf had reached in and ripped it from her rib cage. Wolf stood casually by the bike rack, his usual reflective sunglasses masking his green eyes. The background murmur of passing traffic faded, disappearing into a black hole.

Did he just see Nate leave? Her lungs collapsed, severing her ability to breathe. *Focus*, she told herself. *Inhale. Exhale.* She glanced over both shoulders. She had no choice but to follow him. Her knees threatened to give out with each step. *I'm such an idiot. How could I have forgotten that I never showed up to our meeting yesterday?*

They turned onto a shaded street lined with beautiful brownstones and modern duplexes. Tree branches waved above them in quiet glee, filling the street with low, shushing whispers. A couple pushing a stroller wheeled by them, eyes locked on the little pink bundle cooing inside. She might as well have been walking a tightrope in a parallel universe.

Flynn remained quiet, too terrified and humiliated to be the first to speak. *He's going to kill me. Here. Now. For the entire world to see. Good— put me out of my misery.* Last night was still such a blur. Fuzzy images of Wolf standing in her bedroom taunted her like a fly buzzing against a screen door. Her cheeks scalded. *Smooth, Flynn. Way to throw yourself at a mass murderer.*

"Who's that man you were with?" His voice was even, measured almost.

That was the question he chose to lead with? Stunned, Flynn glanced at him, heartbeat pulsing in her fingertips. "No one. He's no one."

"We can make this hard or we can make this easy. You can fucking tell me, or I go and find out for myself."

Her tongue suddenly lost all ability to function. "We, um, we work together. He was with me the night of the Green Line concert."

"Ah, must've missed him."

Clearly Wolf's biting remark was an attempt to provoke her, but she was too exhausted to take his bait no matter how disgusting he might be.

"Wolf, about me not showing up yesterday, I promise it won't happen again. I officially started my position today within our E&C division. I completed your request. I already have ten different positions to fill."

"You bail on our meeting, go get annihilated, and I'm supposed to let you off free? Shit, maybe I should talk to your friend and get another opinion."

His voice simmered with a violent undertone that made her shiver. On the edge of hyperventilating, Flynn struggled to smother her building panic. Making sure no one approached on the sidewalk, she pulled Wolf in the direction of an elementary school playground deserted in the early evening hours.

"What do you want me to do, drop to my knees and beg for forgiveness? Surrender myself to you so you can take me back to REDS's lair and torture me again?"

Wolf stalked toward a swing set, its black plastic seats baking in the setting sun. She watched him, still finding it hard to reconcile that a wanted fugitive could look so deceiving, blending in seamlessly with the rest of the world. Shoulders tense beneath his thin shirt, he seemed uncomfortable in his clothes, like he knew he didn't belong. His face from last night filled her head, appearing before her like a vivid dream. Trepidation had spread from his mouth to his eyes after he'd extracted himself from her embrace. His impenetrable guard had cracked, revealing a glimpse of susceptibility.

He doesn't know what to do with me, she realized.

A small seed of courage sprouted deep within her. Maybe she needed to lure him into just the right position to penetrate his reptilian skin.

He faced her, unreadable, eyes shielded from view. "We've been over this already. We're letting you live because you have a job to do."

Why couldn't he touch me last night? He always made a noticeable effort to stand far away, as if she was contagious. Deciding she had nothing to lose, Flynn charged toward him across the playground's dense mulch, prepared to confront him. His fingers curled into tight fists as he backed into a swing. The seat bounced against his legs, jangling. She'd trapped him.

"What are you so afraid of?" she asked, incredulous.

His contemptuous laugh stung like a slap. "I'm not afraid."

"Then let me touch you." She crossed her arms over her chest.

His long stride closed the remaining distance between them quickly. Within seconds they were standing less than a foot apart. Wolf loomed over her, the breadth of his shoulders threatening. His fingers twisted into her hair, yanking her head backward. They wrapped around the back of her neck, squeezing harder and harder. Trapped within his lenses, her wide-eyed reflection stared back at her. The pressure intensified and she locked her jaw against the gasp of pain.

He's everything he says he is, including a murderer. If he killed her, he would not get the satisfaction of watching her cower. *Just get it over with. Let it be fast.*

"I have nothing to prove to you. You work for us, got it? Stand me up again and we'll find a new way to break into Magnetic that doesn't require *your* assistance. The only reason you're still alive is because it would be too suspicious if you were to suddenly disappear."

Vision blurred with adrenaline, she placed both her hands on Wolf's chest, nails digging through the fabric. He was so still he might have stopped breathing, his body as motionless as a marble pillar.

Something changes when I touch him.

"Oh, look," he said, voice laced with venom. "I somehow survived that one."

He released her roughly. Flynn gasped, massaging her throbbing neck.

"Oh, yeah. You're such a fucking hardass. You're such a big macho man. What? Do you get off on going after people weaker than you? Smaller than you? You can deny it all you want, but you saved me that night at the Green Line concert. You wanted me to live." She wished her voice didn't sound so pleading.

He ripped off his sunglasses. His clear eyes refracted the last rays of sunlight peering down on them.

"REDS don't have *individual* desires. I have one mission. One. And it's all I fucking care about."

"Everyone wants something for themselves; it's in our nature."

"I don't associate myself with our worthless species," Wolf spat.

"But you can't deny you're human."

"A superior one, maybe." He grinned knowingly, as if she'd wandered into his trap. "You'll see soon enough the effect *individual* desires have on humanity."

"You're always hinting at something. Why can't you just tell me what you're planning?"

"That's never going to happen."

"Why not? I'm a part of this now too," Flynn said.

"Stop asking questions. I'll say it once more.... You have *one* role in this and that's it."

"And then what? You'll leave me alone forever?" The last word trembled as it dropped from her lips. He tore his eyes from hers, staring into the distance. She had no delusions about what her future held as a result of her involvement with REDS. Her body seized with an involuntary shudder.

"That doesn't matter," he said. "What matters is what comes next, which is why I'm here. On Monday, you'll find a new submission in your application system from Chris Newman. You will coordinate an in-person interview with him by Wednesday and extend an offer to him by Friday."

"Friday? I've . . . I've never been able to get an offer out that fast."

"You can if he's an exceptional candidate with two other pressing job offers that require you to be extremely competitive."

"Even then, it has to be approved by our hiring committee."

"Guess you'll have to figure that out then," Wolf snapped.

There's no way. I've only been on this new team for a freaking day. What he's asking me to do is impossible. "What about references, security clearance, a background check?" She ticked them off on her fingers.

His lips curled into a small, forced smile. "Oh, I'm sorry, did I tell you this was going to be easy?"

"I don't need your condescension. I'm trying to be realistic."

"And I don't need your bullshit or your whining. Glad we can come to a mutual understanding. Figure it out. I'm not going to tell you how to do your job."

Children's shrieks of delight in a nearby yard cut through the silence.

"Alright. I'll see what I can do. Can I go home now?" Flynn asked.

"Are we clear about expectations for next week?"

"Yes." She pushed the word through clenched teeth, digging her nails into the length of her collarbone. She'd been beaten into submission. She never understood until this moment how degrading it felt to be enslaved. Victimized, dehumanized, coerced by evil forces.

Jaw rigid, Wolf slid his sunglasses back on. "You're alive, Flynn. Be grateful."

A scream boiled up in the back of her throat. He was testing, probing for her trigger points, and he'd found one.

"Grateful? You're telling me to be grateful? I watched hundreds of people die, people that *you* killed!" She gasped for air as her vocal chords strained against the constricting anger. "You tortured me for days for *no* reason, and as if that wasn't enough, now you're controlling every aspect of my life!" Blinded by mounting hysteria, she shoved Wolf with all her weight. It was like crashing into a brick wall. He barely tilted backward. "Be grateful? For what? That a murderer didn't kill me when he could have? That he's just waiting to kill me when he's done using me?"

She wound her elbow back to punch him, but before her knuckles could accelerate forward, he grabbed her wrist in an iron grip. She jerked her arm, twisting her body to break free, but it was hopeless.

"Let. Me. Go!" she choked.

"Yesterday you try to hug me and today this is the reaction I get?" Face cracking, Wolf couldn't hide his amusement. "Unbelievable. Looks like you could use some work keeping those emotions in check . . . and on your form."

Rage sliced deeper into her chest, like a butcher knife wedged in between her ribs. He yanked her toward him, grabbing her other wrist, subduing her thrashing limbs. "You still think you could kill me?"

She squirmed to free herself. "I hate you," she said, channeling her remaining strength, hopeful the words would pierce his black soul.

He leaned in with a sardonic smile. "You think you know what it means to hate? You think you know how it feels to detest something so fucking deeply it becomes part of you?" His silky voice was mesmerizing. A charmed snake frozen in place, Flynn couldn't rip her gaze from his face. "Imagine killing me a thousand times over in every way possible. That's how I felt walking into that concert. That's how I felt toward all of those faceless, insignificant assholes, because that's all they were to me—faceless." He pushed her away from him. She staggered backward, clutching her wrist to her chest.

"None of those people deserved what you did to them. No matter what lies you tell yourself to justify your actions." Hollow defeat slowly replaced her fiery hot anger.

He laughed. The desolate sound jarred her insides. The thrill he got from controlling her was sickening.

"Fuck, Flynn, I don't need to justify my actions. Everyone's done something to someone. *Everyone.*"

"But to kill someone? To end their life?" The small, battered circle of survivors in the hospital therapy sessions materialized before her. "You have no idea, do you? You also ruined the lives of all the people who loved them."

His hooded stare was unsympathetic. "Would you rather die, or would you rather live your life alone in total isolation? Which is worse?"

"Life is about choices. You can still choose to make your life meaningful."

"Isn't it obvious? I already have."

She squinted at him, trying to read his expression. "You don't have a sliver of a conscience that compels you to think differently?"

"All I need is my purpose."

Flynn thought back to her conversation with Cori in their apartment after she encountered Wolf for the first time. She'd admitted REDS's attack on Soldier Field had morphed her into a different person. At first, she'd attributed this to being victimized as a hostage. But in reality, it was Wolf who had ripped her entire life out from beneath her as effortlessly and carelessly as someone taking out the trash.

"You underestimate me," she said, "but that's okay. I'll use that to my advantage when I kill you."

A flicker of surprise registered on his face before vanishing as quickly as it came. "Once more I'll get the last laugh. Like I said, you don't have the guts."

Every person has a breaking point, and Flynn felt seconds away from reaching hers. Like water trembling just below a boil, it was simply a matter of time before she erupted. Her life was now a constant seesaw, tipping back and forth between terror and outrage at the injustice of Wolf's demands. She refused to let herself roll over and succumb to someone so evil.

Fight back, she told herself. *You can do this. You're probably going to die anyway.*

He stalked away without looking back, a black silhouette fading into the fiery sunset. Birds sang evening lullabies in nearby trees. Their melody was sweet, haunting. Standing alone in the abandoned playground watching the distance between them grow, she felt as though the fabric of her soul was being sliced by an invisible razor, leaving a gaping hole that would be impossible to sew back together. It seemed obvious, glaring—the first thing anyone would notice even if she could slap a patch over it. Where a big piece of her once had been now was empty, lost forever. She had no idea how to fill it, and when she tried to examine it more closely, she could hardly distinguish the feelings swirling around inside that void—guilt, pain, fear. They all became one, living in the hole that she knew would grow bigger every day.

27

WOLF

As promised, Flynn delivered. Early the following week, Wolf had an on-site interview at Magnetic. When he arrived at the office, it took everything in him not to yawn in disdain. Its modern interior was just another show to the outside world. A way to convince its employees they were members of some elitist club full of arrogant douchebags. The large atrium was dotted with sharp-edged furniture and strange-shaped cubicle sofas and chairs, mainly in white with occasional "pops of color"—all of it so fucking pretentious. Typical of a company with an inflated ego. If only these assholes knew the fancy space was just another way for their employer to exert control over them. Distract them with sparkly objects. Sheep were predictable.

During a quick tour of the expansive lobby, a chatty receptionist explained how the white theme exemplified Magnetic's viewpoint that the world was a blank canvas ready to be re-created into a masterpiece. "Creativity is the epicenter of our values here at Magnetic," she chirped. The woman was at least a foot and a half shorter than Wolf, her hair pulled back so tight it lifted her face into an expression of constant surprise. She reminded him of a cricket you trapped in a jar just to watch it suffocate. "The spaces were designed to encourage spontaneous collaboration."

What a way to convince people to identify with a self-serving lie, he thought. *It's comical how quickly they fall for this shit.*

"How poetic," he said with a close-lipped smile, tipping forward in feigned interest.

The second she turned away, his eyes rolled upward. She led him to a sitting area next to the floor-to-ceiling windows covering the length of the back wall. The office was located on the outer west side of the city, so the entire Chicago skyline spanned before them as serene as a landscape portrait.

"Your recruiter will be here momentarily. She'll escort you to the room reserved for your interview. Can I get you a coffee or water?"

"I'm fine, thank you."

Her chin dipped in a cursory nod. Still eyeing him curiously, she strutted behind a desk made of clear plastic. When she sat in her chair, her razor-sharp heels barely skimmed the floor's surface.

Wolf watched the city move by soundlessly below him. A few minutes later, the quiet hum of sliding doors and the clack of heels against the gray marble floor alerted him to Flynn's arrival. She crossed the room, her face hard and impassive. Wedged shoes showed off her slender legs. A denim top tied in a loose knot at her waist draped over tense shoulders. Her fingers fidgeted, sliding down the length of her black cotton skirt and up through her hair. She had a habit of doing that—touching her hair when she was on edge.

Flynn smiled at the receptionist, who tilted her head toward Wolf and mouthed, "So hot." Flynn's grin promptly vanished. Her lips puckered in disapproval. When she reached his chair, he beamed up at her, rubbing his hands over his knees in pretend anticipation.

"You must be *Mr. Newman*." Surprise crossed her face as she took in his khaki slacks, white button-down shirt, and navy blazer. "Welcome to Magnetic. You certainly look nice."

"Well, thank you, *Ms. Zarytsky*. You know what they say, dress for the job you want."

Her grimace evaporated into a forced, pleasant smile. "Flynn. Please."

"Ah, yes, right."

"Follow me." She walked toward a glass door leading to a floating staircase. It spiraled over their heads through the center of the building. Flynn pressed her badge against a small square card reader, waiting for a beep and a green light before guiding him down to a lower floor.

"Flynn," Wolf said slowly, tasting the syllable as it rolled off his tongue. "Isn't that a boy's name?"

"Apparently not."

A chuckle bubbled up his throat. "No, of course not. Did you know the name Flynn is derived from an Irish surname meaning 'descendant of Flann'?"

Balancing on a wedged leg as she descended to the next step, hand hovering above the delicate wrought iron railing, she replied, "Thank you for that thrilling historical tidbit, Mr. Newman. That would make sense considering my father is Irish. Let's hope you're as familiar with electric infrastructure as name genealogy."

"Well, Flynn, you didn't let me finish. 'Descendant of Flann.'" He paused, the smell of fresh-pressed espresso and bagels rising to meet them. "Do you happen to know what 'Flann' means in Irish Gaelic?"

"No. Please enlighten me."

"Red. It means red. How appropriate."

Silence rang between them like a reverberating gong. Faltering, Flynn's foot slipped over the last step's shiny wood surface. She stumbled and, in a flash, Wolf grabbed her elbow, catching her right before she fell. Coming into contact with her skin stung his palm. Blowing out a rattling breath, she avoided his gaze.

"This . . . " Straightening, Flynn coughed a few times, attempting to regain her composure. "This is one of our six kitchenettes. Our café is on the ninth floor, where you would receive free breakfast and lunch every day *if* you are extended an offer."

"*When* I receive an offer," he corrected her, nodding in fake interest at the surrounding shelves of organic snacks. Flynn's hair cascaded down her back in thick, luminous waves, juxtaposed against the stark white walls.

"Hey, Flynn," a voice called across the kitchenette. A young man holding a steaming mug wandered toward them. He was attractive, and his confident stride suggested he knew it. As he approached, it dawned on Wolf that this was the same guy who had grabbed Flynn outside her apartment building last week.

"Hi, Nate." Flynn pivoted away, eager to keep walking. Her voice carried a nervous edge that wasn't present earlier. "Sorry, can't really chat, we're headed to an interview."

His wavy, light brown hair was tousled a little too perfectly and he exuded a strong, masculine smell of cologne.

Does this prick blow-dry his hair? he wondered.

"Oh, no worries, I won't keep you two. I'm about to head to that Leadership in Tech conference you bailed on last minute. Come meet us for drinks after? Should be a lot of cool people there. Might be a good networking opportunity."

"Um, I don't think so." She crossed her arms over her chest, shifting her weight into one hip. "We're trying to hire ten new heads this week. Things are pretty crazy, and I'll have to work late."

"Alright, cool, let me know if you change your mind." He took a long, drawn-out sip from his mug. "You might pick up some good candidates at the conference for those positions you're trying to fill."

Grinning playfully, he drank in her unsuspecting beauty, ignoring Wolf's presence. He was like a manicured mannequin; it was as if he'd never known pain. Clenching his hands into tight fists inside his pockets, Wolf suppressed the urge to punch this asshole square in the jaw. When Flynn glanced at Wolf, eyes wide, Nate finally acknowledged him.

"Sorry, man. Forgot to introduce myself." He extended a hand. "Nate Turner. Flynn and I worked on the same team before she moved over to our E&C division. We lost a good one."

Flynn's face paled as she waited for Wolf's reaction.

Accepting his handshake, Wolf squeezed his grip tighter than necessary. "Chris Newman. I'm interviewing for one of the field manager roles."

"Well, good luck with this one." Nate nodded toward Flynn, taking a step closer to her. "She'll grill you."

He flashed her a lazy smile. Adoration filled his eyes, as well as a hint of longing. The urge to smash his face into the counter almost overpowered Wolf. His control was slipping.

Flynn stared at her feet, shaking her head. "Please, right this way, Chris."

She guided Wolf down a hallway into the interview room, closing the door behind her. Motioning for him to take a seat, she wrung her hands, sinking into a chair as far from his as possible. Her voice was anxious when she spoke.

"What are you really doing here, Wo—Chris?"

Leaning back into the white leather chair, he tried to shake the lingering rage provoked by Nate. His relaxed confidence. His easy smile. A superficial pretty boy with his head lodged too far up his own ass.

"I'm interviewing." Wolf's knee bounced up and down.

"You're risking exposure."

"Chris Newman will pass your background check with flying colors."

"That's because Chris Newman isn't a real person," she hissed. Running shaky hands down the length of her skirt, her posture tensed. "Listen, I can't get you in here if you don't impress the interviewers. This won't be a walk in the park. These interviews are extremely difficult and comprehensive, especially for such a technical position like this."

"Don't worry about me." He shrugged. "It'll be a breeze."

Flynn's pointed disgust gave him a spark of smugness. Riling her up never got old. "I don't care about you. It's me I'm worried about if you don't get this position."

"That guy, Nate." He tried to keep his tone indifferent. "He likes you."

Fear materialized on her face. The same fear as when he'd mentioned her family at the Yacht Club a few weeks ago.

Bingo, he realized. *So she does care for him.*

She shook her head. "No, trust me, he's just a flirt. He's the type of guy who always wants what he can't have."

"That means he must want you?"

"Wh-what do you mean? No, of course not." She squirmed under his scrutiny. "Regardless, it's none of your business."

Blood boiling, his fingers dug into the chair's armrest as though to rip away its faux leather skin. "Maybe it's time Nate and I have a . . . talk."

Her breathing changed, eyes staring into his, hate and helplessness swimming together. "Dating is the furthest thing from my mind, Wolf."

Puckering her lips as if she just bit into something sour, she picked at the knot in her shirt. "You of all people should know that."

"Don't fucking call me that in public again." He leaned forward, glowering. "It's a fair question after the last little stunt you pulled. Getting blackout drunk and blowing me off. I'm making sure you're maintaining your focus. The last thing we need is for you to get distracted. I need you to take this seriously."

"Seriously? My life, my family's life, is on the line and you don't think I'm taking this seriously?" Her whisper was hard and pressed. "You're already controlling every other aspect of my life. Are you really going to dictate who I associate with or talk to?"

She stood abruptly and then stormed from the room, slamming the door behind her. It vibrated in its frame. Releasing a frustrated grunt, he threw up his hands.

Fuck me, he fumed. *Her temper has a shorter fuse than mine.*

Flynn had an irritating habit of walking away whenever conflict arose. He watched her stomp off through the clear glass walls of the conference room.

He should be preparing for the interview, but his thoughts followed her down the hall, reminding him how he'd never questioned his life with REDS until Flynn came to his defense in the coffee shop years ago. Even if the deceitful thought only occurred for a split second, it was hard to ignore when it resurfaced every time he saw her. And each time, a tingle of fear lingered in its wake. Right when he'd convinced himself he had disassociated any feeling toward her, she drew him back, a siren singing to a ship destined for destruction. Flynn embodied a path that could lead his life in an entirely different direction if he chased her whenever she walked away.

Wolf drummed his nails on the table, filling the room with rhythmic tapping. *No*, he thought to himself, *she isn't going to win this one too. She doesn't get to have the last word.* He exploded to his feet, slamming a fist on the table, preparing to rush after her. *I don't know what it's going to take to scare some fucking sense into her, but hopefully it involves blowing Nate into a million pieces.*

Right as he reached the door, he stopped, hand suspended over the handle. Shoving a breath through gritted teeth, he spun back around and kicked the chair closest to him. It twirled on its axel, its backboard banging into its neighbors. He was letting his rage get the best of him. *Flynn* was getting the best of him.

She doesn't matter. He harnessed his anger before it peaked into fury, wrangling it back into its enclosure. *Getting into Magnetic is what matters.*

He had shit to do. Too much rested on this opportunity to let it slip past him. Besides, if Spider found out, saying goodbye to his spot on the executive committee would be the least of his concerns.

28

FLYNN

Suffocating disappointment pressed in on Flynn from all angles. She'd collected the interviewers' feedback. Wolf had received rave reviews.

"He studied electrical engineering at Purdue, just got his masters from MIT, oh, oh, and I loved his responses to my brain teasers." Dan, the hiring manager, listed the interview highlights with buoyant enthusiasm. "We haven't seen anyone like him. He was professional and, let me tell you, *great* sense of humor. Got a kick outta all my puns. He meets all of our qualifications. What a find, Flynn! Super impressive for your first week."

"You don't think he was a little too . . . I don't know, young?" Jutting her chin, she frowned in mock concern. Anything to dissuade him from Wolf's candidacy. "What about that other engineer you met with? He has fifteen years of industry experience and *two* master's degrees. He was extremely impressive!"

"Eh, age is just a number, especially at a company like Magnetic." Dan's glasses slid down his slick, bulbous nose. He shoved them back into position with stubby fingers. "If anything, it means we'll be able to keep his offer much lower compared to the other candidate, who wanted double what Chris asked. Plus, did you see all his extracurricular activities? He's very involved in the community. Such a refreshing change of pace. We need more young blood like him."

"Oh, yeah . . . I got that impression as well." As she struggled to keep the sarcasm from her voice, her shoulders drooped. "Well, I just heard from Chris, actually. He has two other competitive offers that require a response by the end of the week. If we want him, we need to act quickly, but I don't know how we'll get this past the hiring committee."

Dan waved his hand. "Leave it to me."

Great, she mused. *The one time things actually move quickly around here happens to be now. Thanks, Dan.*

* * * *

By the time Friday rolled around, Wolf's approved offer sat in her inbox. A dark undertow of fear dragged her focus in a million directions.

I could lie to the internal team . . . say Chris accepted another offer. Would Wolf know? What if Dan gets involved and tries to counter? She mentally scrolled through her limited options. There would be consequences if she didn't get Wolf into Magnetic. She tried to foresee what those might be. *Murdering me would be easy. Too quick. No, REDS would kill my family. Nate. Cori. They'd pick them off one by one. But what could happen to the city if we do hire him is equally horrific.*

The grim image of the man crawling toward her at the Green Line concert rose before her like a movie on a giant projector screen. His wild eyes. His life extinguished in an instant. More people would die just to keep those she loved alive. No one was safe.

An ache crept up her side, wringing her muscles. The pain lingered, a cramp that wouldn't ease.

"What's the status?" Dan materialized by her desk with no warning, face glowing, red forehead perpetually shiny. She jumped, splashing coffee onto her keyboard. Reaching for a napkin, she ducked her head, hiding her annoyance. "Did he accept the offer or did he counter?"

"I'm—I'm about to extend it now."

He stroked his thick mustache. "Yes! Call him, call him!" His nasally voice cracked with excitement. "What if he already accepted one of the other offers?"

"Trust me, I don't think he's going to turn us down."

"You never know with these things, Fiona. A bright, young man like that is a rare find. Try to aim for the earlier start date, too, if possible."

She glared after him as he practically skipped back to his office, pale yellow shirt stretched snugly over his eggplant-shaped body. *Did he seriously just call me Fiona?*

"Oh, he's a rare one," she mumbled under her breath.

Eyeing her phone, she rubbed a finger over an eyebrow. After several long seconds, she snatched it off the stand. Dan had confirmed her suspicion—if she lied and told him Wolf declined, it would result in an onslaught of counter offers.

The call went straight to an automated voicemail. She left a message, requesting he call her back immediately. Guilt pricked her skin like hundreds of invisible needles jabbing into a pincushion. Her phone rang as soon as she turned back to her computer monitor. Startled, she picked up the receiver.

"Hello, Flynn? It's Chris Newman. I received your voicemail. I'm hoping for some good news."

His honeyed voice was cool and calm. It unnerved her.

Sociopath.

"Well, you're in luck." She cleared her throat. "Excuse me. I mean, on behalf of Magnetic, we're excited to extend you an offer. I'll send formal details, including a proposed start date, over to your email via a secure link." She recited the words, a monotone, robotic script she used for every new job offer. "We can then schedule a follow-up call to discuss any questions you might have."

"How about an in-person meeting to discuss questions?"

Jaw clenched, she paused, exhaling through her nose. "I don't think that will be necessary."

She'd brought Wolf in for an interview, a nearly impossible feat considering his tenure and age. Still, he'd proved her wrong. He was a mastermind chameleon, transforming into whoever he needed to be to get a job done. She'd dangerously underestimated him, and now she wanted nothing more to do with him.

"What are you doing tonight?" he asked, ignoring her rebuttal.

Tugging at her braid, she searched for any excuse to avoid him. Her gaze landed on a picture sitting on her desk. It was of her old team at last year's holiday party. Nate's face grinned back with easy confidence. There was clearly something about him that dug under Wolf's rhino-thick skin. It blinded him. Threw him off the scent. Distracted him from whatever it was he was planning.

"Ah, I'm sorry, I'm unavailable."

"Unavailable?" he repeated, voice brittle.

"Yeah, um . . . you know, been a long week. What with trying to get all these positions filled under a time crunch. I think I'm going to lie low tonight. Get some rest. Congratulations on your offer, Chris! I look forward to connecting soon and having you join us."

The nausea that had been creeping up on her intensified as she hung up the phone, hands shaking.

What was she doing? She wasn't messing around with a crazy ex-boyfriend; she was provoking a terrorist who'd murder her and anyone else without blinking an eye. Her forehead dropping to her palm, a groan lengthened from her throat. *Calm down*, she told herself. *Wolf is about to start at Magnetic. He can't compromise his employment by murdering someone now.* Yet she was sick of it—all of it. She'd done her job. She'd met each one of Wolf's demands and, still, he was intent on continuing to torment and scare her into submission.

Nerves too shot to sit still, she wandered to the staircase, descending a floor in search of Nate. She missed his friendship; its warm solace thawed frozen parts of her old self. Maybe she should ask if he was available for a drink. . . . It would be a much-needed distraction.

Nate was sitting at his desk, wrapping up an interview. Leaning back in his chair, he cradled his phone between his ear and shoulder, twirling a pen around his forefinger. His calm, easygoing demeanor was contagious, warming her like a sip of hot coffee. "Ahh, yes, that is *very* impressive." His bored expression implied he wasn't impressed with the candidate. "Well, thanks again for chatting. I appreciate your time. I'll be in touch regarding possible next steps."

Sagging against his cube's low partition, she stared longingly at her old desk adjacent to his. He placed the phone back on its stand, then looked up at her with a raised eyebrow. She struggled to rearrange her face into a smile.

"What's wrong?" he asked.

"What do you mean? Nothing's wrong."

"Flynn." He swiveled his chair to face her, running a hand through his thick hair. Hair any girl would die for. "I know when something's on your mind."

Her inner self warned her not to pursue Nate. *What kind of message would it send?* it whispered in her ear.

Maybe we could run away together, she argued back. *Escape. Grab Cori and hightail it back to Indy before REDS found out. Wolf made it into Magnetic; what more could he need?*

Wolf is always one step ahead, her conscience taunted. *He'd find you. He always does.*

But all she wanted was more carefree hours like the ones they'd shared at the bar last week. Those blissful moments when the world outside their bubble had melted away. Her desperation for a night of normalcy before Wolf's presence haunted Magnetic won.

"What are you doing tonight?" she asked, ignoring his question.

This time he raised both eyebrows, locking his hands behind his head. "I'm going to watch the Cubs game in Wrigleyville. Wanna come?"

Anxiety tugged at her insides. Since the Green Line concert, she had a difficult time being in large crowds. The only benefit her escort service provided was avoiding Chicago's packed public transportation, and the last thing she wanted to do was go somewhere with hordes of people standing too close and elbowing each other. . . . *But lots of people around could be perfect, easier to blend in.*

"Yeah, sure. Why not?"

Excitement flooded his face, lighting up his eyes and tinting his cheeks a rosy color. She instantly regretted her decision.

"Is this finally our first date?"

She rolled her eyes. "Don't push it, Turner."

* * * *

Later that evening, Flynn's escort dropped them off at a bar on the north side of Chicago, close to Wrigley Field. Slamming the door behind her, she called in through the open front window. "Thanks, Scott. I'll give you a ring when we're ready for pickup."

Hot, steamy July air engulfed them as they strolled down streets teeming with boisterous fans heading to the game. Crowds laughed and jostled each other in eager anticipation, forming long lines to enter the baseball stadium. Scalpers carrying flimsy cardboard signs stood outside apparel stores, flashing paper tickets and calling out prices, hoping for a last-minute sale.

The pressure of so many bodies, the venue, the night, sparked memories she couldn't suppress. Flynn heaved a sigh without meaning to. "After the Green Line concert, the thought of going to a game with all those people makes me want to scream."

Nate glanced at her, the corners of his mouth drooping into a small frown. She never discussed that night at Soldier Field. He observed the throngs of people sporting Cubs jerseys and hats, waiting to go through metal detectors manned by armed policemen.

"It's amazing how quickly people move on," he admitted, "how they choose to forget. I can't tell if it's a good thing or if, one day, it will be the end of us."

She let his morbid comment sink in. They walked along a fence soaring over the stadium's bleacher seats, her fingertips strumming its chain-link diamonds. They passed crammed bars, their windows and doors open wide in celebration of the glorious summer evening. Tables stacked with people stared up at televisions, cold beers slippery with condensation gripped in their hands.

"I know it might be wrong to say this, but I'm glad you were with me that night. I'm sorry . . . I never said thank you. Thank you for saving me." Tucking a chunk of hair behind her ear, she locked her attention on to her white Converse shoes shuffling over the pavement.

When she finally glanced in his direction, his light brown curls glowed in the lowering sun's glare. Pain creased his face, as if she'd punched him in the gut.

"I didn't save you. It's my fault, what happened to you. I submitted you to worse than death. I left you to them . . ." His haunted eyes told her it was something he had lived over and over again.

"Nate." Slowing to a stop, she grabbed his arm, forcing him to face her. He scratched the stubble dotting his jawline. His shoulders slumped, still carrying the weight of insolvable sadness. "Do you really blame yourself for what happened to me?"

"Of course I do. I'll never forgive myself for what they did to you. They should have taken me instead."

She shook her head. "They would have killed you."

"So why didn't they kill you?" His lips hardened.

She looked away, the distant hum of the city calling to them. Opening her mouth, she hesitated, then closed it again. "I don't know." Her stomach writhed under the intensity of his stare. It suddenly dawned on her— Nate knew she remembered those days she lay gagged and blindfolded in REDS's cell. Cori probably did too. Her two best friends could read her like an open book.

She dropped her gaze, concentrating on the tufts of grass peeking through the cracked cement. "Do you ever think about what you would do if you saw one of them again?" Her question blended into the raucous yells from a nearby sports bar.

"REDS?"

An invisible rope noosed her throat. "Yes. The things you would do to them . . . for everything they did?"

"I used to," he said, then paused. "But now I try not to think of them. I like to pretend they don't even exist."

Searching his face, she expected to see anger, even sadness. Instead, his mouth slid into his mischievous sideways grin.

"Isn't that the same thing as forgetting?" she asked.

"No, I'll never forget. But if I let myself get caught up in hating them and feeling vengeful, I become like them. I end up perpetuating their terror. That's exactly what they want—to control us."

"You really think that's what they want?"

"I do," he said. "Control is power."

"Well, how do you stop them then?"

"By doing the opposite of them," Nate said. "By spreading all the things they are trying so hard to get rid of."

"Okay . . ." She felt like a nagging child asking the same question over and over. "Like what?"

"Compassion seems like a good start. Usually people who do hateful things haven't experienced much of that in their lives. I also think the media is way off about them. Think about it. Everything about the Green Line concert was carefully orchestrated and to pull that off—that's no easy feat. REDS is strategic. Something else is coming. But if everyone keeps downplaying what their capable of, we can't prepare for it."

Something else is coming. A cold chill breathed against the back of her neck like a whispered warning. They ambled farther into the depths of a small park a few blocks past the stadium. Trees swayed gently overhead. The green canopy shifted above the bench-lined path, exposing glimpses of twilight sky through its dancing leaves. Cars honked in the distance, accompanied by barking dogs. Other than that, they were alone, nestled amid the peaceful whirr of cicadas.

"Hmm, compassion. No offense, but I hardly think one random act of kindness a day is going to make much of a difference."

"Maybe not," he said, "but you never know. What's the alternative?"

A burst of wind rustled the branches overhead, conducting a symphony of low whooshing murmurs. "I guess I'm finally coming to terms with the fact that I haven't moved on."

"It takes time, and work, to change yourself. You have to put yourself into an entirely different frame of mind."

"How? How can you make it sound so easy?"

"It's not easy. A while ago, I started reading to sick children over at Lurie Children's Hospital. At first, I couldn't bear to be around them . . . to see all these innocent kids suffer. But I made myself go back. Soon I realized that they're the ones who are actually helping me. They reconnect me, give me new perspective on what it means to be strong. And talk about resilient. They make adults look like such wimps."

Her face burned with shame. Guilt. Betrayal. Secrets. They all boiled to the surface.

"I had no idea you did that."

He smiled sadly. "I don't do it for the praise, Flynn. It helps put me in that different frame of mind, and it also gives me a sense of purpose. Even if only for an hour."

She stopped walking, her legs unable to move any farther. Soft moonlight illuminated one side of Nate's striking profile, casting the other half in dark shadows. Longing built in her chest, breaking through the last frayed strands of restraint. She leaned in to kiss him, wrapping herself around his body, and falling against him like she did the first time she saw him after the attack.

He staggered back in surprise, catching himself, tangling his fingers in her hair, pulling her closer. The urge to jump into his arms and lock her legs around him was overwhelming—to push her body so hard against his that all her pain and fear would melt into ether. His hands were warm and strong, offering protection against the most vulnerable parts of herself. His touch ignited a flame of hope deep inside her. Maybe together they could erase the past and re-create an entirely new future.

For the first time in what seemed like months, a faint glow of happiness rose within her like a sunrise peaking over the horizon. It stretched through her, reaching to fill the empty craters punctuating her body.

I should tell him everything, she thought. If he wasn't holding on to her, there was no way she would still be standing. *He can make everything right again. He can make me whole again.*

In a sudden flash of movement, a steel grip grabbed her waist, ripping her from Nate and hurling her to the ground. Gravel scraped against her cheek as Flynn skidded across the pavement. A loud crack rang through the darkness—fist colliding with bone. She pushed herself onto her heels, jagged cement digging into her palms. Nate reeled backward, his body collapsing in slow motion.

Her lips parted. She contracted her abdomen, preparing to scream. A large hand enveloped the lower half of her face, clamping down on her nose and mouth so tightly no air could escape. She clawed at the thick forearm, digging her nails into tough skin.

"Scream and I'll kill you."

Wolf's voice sent spikes piercing straight into her heart. He shoved her away from him. She staggered and fell to her knees. The same crimson mask stalking her dreams loomed over her. A black hood shielded his eyes.

"Who do you think I am, Flynn? Do you think I'm fucking around?" His voice trembled with rage.

Wolf yanked her into a standing position. She struggled against his iron grip, thrusting an elbow forward, aiming for his throat. He deflected it with ease, grabbed her arm, and twisted it behind her back.

"I told you to stay away from him."

He tossed her next to Nate's motionless body. Gasping, she rolled onto her back. Wolf's black pants blended into the tree trunks towering above him. One of his boots materialized, resting on Nate's throat. He pulled a gun from his belt, aiming it directly above his forehead.

"No! Wolf, please!" Diving forward, she used her body as a shield. "This isn't about him. This is about me. I thought . . . I thought we were done." Panic barricaded her throat so words could hardly escape. "I did everything you asked!"

"Your work for us is not over. It isn't over until I say it's over." He crouched down so they were eye to eye. A glimmer of green glinted from beneath his hood. She stared into the black hole of his gun. "I don't believe in second chances. Consider this your final warning."

He reached into Nate's pocket, digging for his wallet.

"Give me your bag," Wolf said.

She handed over her purse. Her arms, covering Nate, shook violently. Relief washed over her when she felt the faint rise and fall of his chest. Wolf started to stomp off, the night obscuring his immense figure.

"Why did it have to be him? Why can't you just kill me and be done with it?" She hadn't thought it possible, but like water gushing from a burst pipe, her hate for him came pouring out. It hemorrhaged into her bloodstream.

He stopped mid-stride. Spinning around, he lunged forward. With one hand, he flung her off Nate.

"Because that's not what will break you." He cocked his knee and delivered a swift, heavy kick to Nate's side. "This is what will break you."

She launched herself against Wolf, tears streaming down her face. She might as well have collided with concrete. He pulled his foot back again, as if she weren't even there, aiming a blow at Nate's head. Flynn dropped to the ground in front of him, a sob heaving from her chest.

"Please don't hurt him. Please. Hurt me. Hurt me instead. I'll do anything!"

He placed his foot back down. His hood fell to his shoulders, revealing eyes narrowed into thin slits. His mouth contorted into a sneer.

"Call your escort. Tell them you got mugged. Mention anything about REDS and he dies." Wolf stormed away, rocks crunching beneath his boots. "Oh," he called quietly over his shoulder, "see you Monday."

Within seconds, the darkness swallowed him.

PART TWO

★ ★ ★ ★

THE CONSEQUENCE

29

WOLF

The Naming Ceremony was the acceptance ritual into REDS following the final initiation test. After seemingly endless weeks of torture, they were gifted an identification alias and officially inducted. By the time Wolf's group had reached their Naming Ceremony, only five remained.

Beta had kept him moving forward, yet in the end Wolf sat waiting to take his pledge alone. He hadn't been remorseful; he had been thirsty. The back of his throat itched, scratching the roof of his mouth. He could taste membership, like a hound seconds away from closing its jaws around a rabbit's neck. The promise of a new beginning, a new family, finally hovered within his reach.

No one had ever incentivized him to do anything meaningful with his life. School had always been easy. Too easy. Every year, teachers asked why he didn't apply himself, insisted he was smart enough to excel. He told them their curriculum wasn't applicable to his future. What did they know about what he wanted to do or who he wanted to become? No one had cared enough to dig deeper. They were conventional, teaching the same lesson class after class, forcing conformity down their throats. He'd wanted a different education, and REDS gave it to him.

On the brink of becoming an Enforcer, Wolf was ablaze with passion—mind ignited with unleashed potential. Killing Beta had been a mutual act of allegiance and self-destruction. He couldn't turn back. Murdering his living partner had sealed his fate. But in its wake, glory awaited. Relief flooded his veins as he bid farewell to Alpha forever.

The new initiates sat in straight-backed wooden chairs with elaborate armrests that twisted into roaring lions' heads. Wolf's fingertips, still sticky with Beta's blood, had curled around their open jaws, digging into the pointy fangs. The damp smell of rot clung to his nostrils.

REDS Enforcers circled them, stacked in tightly packed rows, their faces a sea of crimson silk. The Ritual Chamber was only used for select ceremonies, mainly to honor the dead. In the cramped cellar of an abandoned historic home, the stone-walled room's thick wooden beams supported its dropped ceiling. Chandeliers held dripping candles, the chamber's only source of light. Their flames danced and flickered in the drafts, sputtered in the steamy air.

Cobra opened the ceremony by reciting REDS's manifesto, symbolizing the initiation's conclusion. The new members had never heard the creed. Wolf felt suspended in time. Destiny had led him to this sacred moment, where his future now lay clearly before him.

No more questions, he thought. *No more doubt.*

"You are more than the world has allowed you to believe. You are worthy." Cobra surveyed them, eyes shining, chin raised in approval. "Among REDS, you serve as an integral part of our purpose. We were once lost, victims of an unjust system. Now, we stand as one, soldiers championing those oppressed by tyranny." Sweat snaked down Wolf's back. "We create a binding heart, pulsing fear into society. Destruction must come before creation, and from the ashes of despair, a new order will rise. Together, we will rule." He raised a clenched fist into the air and began pounding his chest. Slow at first, the hollow, rhythmic thumping gained speed like a drummer summoning troops to battle. *Thump. Thump. Thump.* "Redemption for the oppressed. Execution for the unjust. Deliverance for the guilty. Salvation for the lost."

"REDS. REDS. REDS." The surrounding voices roared in unison.

A small tremor shook Wolf's shoulders, vibrating deep into his core.

Cobra melted back into the congregation and Rhino, their Master of Ceremony, took his place. Black floor-length robes curtained his stocky frame. He had a similar shape to a squat, walking boulder, but his burly form masked his dangerous speed. Face devoid of a mask, his leathery skin glowed orange in the candlelight.

"There is no greater honor than to live within these ranks. We are an unbeatable army, trained to expose society's true nature. Each of us has an individual mission, and when the time comes, we will sacrifice ourselves to fulfill it. Remember, to serve as the face of fear and destruction means you will never be forgotten. There is no greater legacy." A long, spear-like piercing above the bridge of his nose glinted black in the candlelight. "Each new member is gifted an alias based on the growth and skills you displayed throughout the initiation process. This is who you are and what you've become." His gravelly voice came in short, grunting bursts. Wolf held his breath, desperate to capture every word. "Your alias is an earned title, unlike a meaningless name given at birth. We honor animals for their powerful natural instincts—behaviors that evolved over time purely for survival and self-preservation. We strive to emulate them and eradicate our human weaknesses."

Like a priest behind his pulpit, Rhino spread his thick arms wide, mouth set in a smug smile. The lions' fangs pierced the flesh under Wolf's fingernails, but he couldn't feel it. His skin crawled, alive with feverish frenzy.

"Your new alias is symbolic of your transformation. Allow it to serve as a constant reminder of the new order we strive to build as one. Who you were before this night no longer exists. We have much to learn from our animal ancestors. Honor their resolve to survive."

Rhino called them forward individually by their recruit names. Wolf's turn came. Blood thumping in his ears, he rose to his feet. As he approached Rhino, his surroundings dissolved, melting into the stone walls. Something unfamiliar burned inside him.

Is it pride? he wondered, awestruck. *Joy?*

Rhino extended his right arm to clasp Wolf's left shoulder—the REDS sign of respect. "Do you swear to seek redemption for the evil society has inflicted upon our world? To expose and execute those responsible for corrupting humanity? To contribute to society's downfall? To deliver yourself in the name and honor of this organization?"

"I do." He'd never felt so sure of anything in his entire life. The burning heat inside him ignited, a gas burner lit by a single match.

Rhino's clear blue eyes bore into his soul. "Do you swear to bring salvation to those who are oppressed? To assist us in building a new empire?"

"I do." Wolf's voice rang through the cellar clear and strong.

"As the elected Master of Ceremony, I grant you the official alias . . . Wolf."

Deep, hollow voices echoed around them. "Redemption. Wolf. Execution. Wolf. Deliverance. Wolf. Salvation. Wolf. REDS!"

The chant branded the name deep into his psyche. His heartbeat accelerated with each declaration.

REDS. REDS. REDS.

Rhino extended his hands toward him, palms facing upward as an offer. Wolf rested his bloodstained fingers on his. Rhino guided them over a cluster of smoking coals in an iron bowl resting on a tall pedestal. Their black edges glowed electric orange.

"Let your old identity burn away with your fingerprints," Rhino announced, triumphant.

Plunging his hands into the fiery depths, Wolf wrapped his fingers around the scorching coals. His jaw clenched against the gasp of searing pain clawing to rip itself free. He bit down hard on his tongue as the heat melted away the last remnants of his old self. His stomach rolled, the acrid stench of burning flesh overpowering him. A hazy fog briefly clouded his vision. He relished it.

"May you remain indistinguishable and untouchable to outside forces," Rhino whispered into his ear, pulling a silky mask over his face, "and may you always be protected by the crimson mask."

* * * *

In the weeks following the Naming Ceremony, new members were responsible for formulating missions. The end goal was the same for each—societal breakdown. Destruction before creation. REDS's executive committee would review, judge, and vote on the most exemplary. The most lethal.

When he'd killed Beta, Wolf vowed to fulfill his promise to seek revenge. He threw all his energy into a plan to honor him—to destroy those who had dismissed them. The world would cower at the sight of their crimson masks.

Spider had just taken over as the new leader of REDS when Wolf presented his mission to the executive committee. Jittery, Wolf paced the room, nerves fried from exhaustion, his mouth so dry it hurt to swallow. Complex definitions and facts raced around his mind like cars speeding around a track. He grappled with stringing them together to form cohesive thoughts. His mission was ambitious. It would take many years to execute. But once it succeeded, it would be the catalyst to the fulfillment of their coveted end goal. And he would be the master of its genesis.

His proposal had been thorough, elaborate. Detailed research, supported with charts and maps, outlined a full analysis of potential outcomes. His plan had only one requirement—for him to attend a nearby community college to study computer science. His mission required training and specialized skills. After he finished his presentation, the executive committee discussed among themselves. Moisture gathered on his upper lip, its sharp, salty taste pricking the tip of his tongue. A few members eyed Spider. Others shook their heads, mouths frozen into skeptical lines.

Spider sat in silence, his face unreadable. After what felt like hours, his icy façade slowly melted away. His thin lips pulled back into a small grin. The foreign expression turned Wolf's legs numb.

"I knew from the second I sat across from you at the Abbott Juvenile Reform Center you possessed potential." Spider crossed his arms, leaning back in his chair. A choked laugh rose from his chest, an empty, joyless sound. "But I couldn't have known its extent. Already you live up to your alias. Once you lock your jaws upon your prey, the smell of blood awakens an insatiable hunger and there is no hope for escape."

Ten years later, Wolf succeeded in the first installment of his plan. The evening of the Green Line concert, he didn't feel pity or doubt. Not even hate. It was a thirst for vengeance. The same thirst Beta had passed on to him. The legacy of Beta's suffering, of all their suffering, had fueled him. As he gunned down bodies in the stadium hallway, people fell to the ground in a growing ripple, like after a stone is dropped into the middle of a glassy pond. Everyone wore the same terrified expression. In a split second, they were exposed for who they really were—mindless, bleating sheep.

30

FLYNN

When Flynn was young, she'd been fearless.

Her father always used to tell her, "Life is a sum of the decisions we make."

She and Fiella would waggle their fingers at each other, mimicking his thick accent under their breath. It was a warning to make good choices or expect repercussions, but over time it had taken on an entirely different meaning. As Flynn rode with Nate in the back of an ambulance, the consequences of her decisions lay before her on a narrow stretcher. Her choices had the power to put other people in danger.

Nate's eyes flickered open. The clear oxygen mask covering his nose and mouth fogged with each exhale. A medic wearing cornflower-blue elastic gloves worked quickly, sticking a syringe into a small bottle of clear liquid. He inserted the needle into a vein bulging from the crook of Nate's elbow. Her heart stuttered, skipping several beats.

"Nate." Gasping, she leaned forward in the jump seat as far as the seatbelt harness would allow. She grabbed his hand with both her own as a wrecking ball of guilt slammed into her gut, winding her.

How do I explain what just happened to him?

Surprisingly, he didn't ask. He simply stared at her, dazed, pupils dilating and contracting. In the bright, swirling ambulance lights, his skin adopted a ghostly ashen hue. His eyelids lowered.

It's all my fault. His pain is all my fault.

"Tell me a story," he said. The mask muffled his weak voice. Inside the claustrophobic space, his body seemed to double in size.

"A story?" She brushed a thick curl back from his forehead. His nod was almost imperceptible. "About what?"

"Anything."

Wheels below them sped over concrete, bumping and jostling against any irregularity in the pavement. Desperate, she scanned her memory for something that might distract him from his pain, even for a second. Her mind blanked, overstimulated by clamoring nerves.

I got nothing. "Well . . ." She cleared her throat. *Might as well just talk.* "Despite what you might think, I was pretty nerdy growing up." A small smile broke his misery, emerging beneath the steamed plastic. "Fitting in at school never came easily." Her thumb drew small circles over the back of his hand. "I never knew where I belonged. My family had just moved to Indiana so my mom could get her PhD, and I was the only Jewish girl in my class. Kids there had never even met a Jewish person before. While they got to go to Sunday school and church, we had to drive forty-five minutes to go to Hebrew school and learn the Torah. We were the only family that didn't celebrate Christmas, and when my parents pulled me from school during High Holidays, I wanted to curl up and disappear. No matter what I wore or how I did my hair to try to blend in, I was always different. Almost like I wore some kind of invisible scarlet letter. No one wants to be associated with the weirdo."

Nate opened his eyes. Watching her, he seemed to relax at the sound of her voice. "But you're beautiful."

Her lips twitched. "So, I read. All the time. I read to lose myself in different worlds. Different times. History and biographies were my favorite. I soaked up everything I could about all the other misfits out there. It made me feel less alone. Leaders that defied the status quo and made an impact on the world. George Washington. Da Vinci. Harriet Tubman. Aristotle. Einstein. Michelangelo. Susan B. Anthony." The medic, the chaotic ambulance innards, the crackling radio set—all of it—disappeared. Words flowed effortlessly, like she was recounting a story she'd bottled up for a long time. "I wanted to understand where their greatness came from, to teach myself how to be just like them, to live by their example and change the world . . ."

"Keep going," Nate urged, squeezing her hand. The ambulance made a sharp turn, throwing her against the nylon straps. Nate lifted his chin upward, knuckles springing into rigid claws. She unbuckled her harness and wrapped her arms around his hard torso, resting her head on his chest, trying to absorb his pain.

If only humans could perform osmosis.

"Then I grew up," she said sadly. "I became what I'd always wanted to be—just like everyone else. Falling into a conventional life was so easy. So comfortable. I became complacent . . . too afraid of the unknown, I guess. I decided I wasn't strong enough to be like the heroes in my stories."

After she'd almost lost Nate, it had become clearer the most unbearable hardships in life were no longer what might happen to her, but to those she loved. Self-preservation revolved around protecting her family and friends. If she wanted to change the world, merely sacrificing herself would never be enough. She had to be willing to sacrifice everything. That was something she couldn't do.

"There's still time," Nate whispered over the siren. His strong heartbeat thumped under her ear. "There's always time."

The ambulance slowed, rolling to a stop. Muffled shouts replaced the wailing. Back doors flew open, releasing a flurry of urgent movement. The medic pushed Nate's stretcher into waiting hands, guiding him away from her. Silence lingered in his place, expanding inside the empty cabin.

★ ★ ★ ★

Flynn had avoided the hospital since her release over a month ago. The subdued voices, fluorescent lights, sticky magazines, and strong antiseptic smell brought back waves of raw emotion. Squeezing her eyes shut, she attempted to transport herself somewhere else. Anywhere else.

Resting in bed, Nate's chest rose and fell in perfect synchrony with beeps of the machines attached to him. The left half of his face was swollen, black and purple bruises tainting his usual perfectly tanned complexion.

I did this to you. How could I have been so unbelievably selfish?

A short nurse in green scrubs bustled in, humming a tune to herself. Checking Nate's vitals, she made notes on a chart with thoughtful and routine purpose. Glancing in Flynn's direction, she offered an encouraging smile.

"He's going to be okay. A couple of badly bruised ribs and a fractured eye socket . . . We've seen much worse, trust me." Flynn tried to muster a smile in return, but all she could manage was a grimace. The nurse gave a sympathetic shake of her head. "Some people are so cruel," she rattled on. "How did they get to a place in their life where they think it's okay to hurt others just to get at a wallet? You've got to wonder what made them that way. I tell you, if someone wants my money, all they need to do is ask. No need to hurt me, I'll hand it right over."

Flynn's fingertips grazed the side of her face, covered with scratches from falling on sharp rocks. She still didn't know what Nate had seen or heard. Everything happened so quickly. One moment they were kissing, the next Wolf knocked him unconscious. Vomit swelled up her throat at the thought of Wolf's gun angled at Nate's forehead.

The nurse patted Flynn on the shoulder, her gentle touch startling back tears that had been threatening to fall. "Do you remember what the person looked like?"

"No. It happened too quickly. He threw me to the ground, punched Nate, grabbed our stuff, and ran."

"Well, my dear, I always tell my children that belongings are only things, and things are replaceable."

Teeth clamping the inside of her cheek, Flynn nodded as the nurse left the room, humming to herself once more. Reaching forward, she intertwined her fingers with Nate's. His palm enveloped hers, the warmth of his skin pulsing strength into her veins.

"Please be okay," she whispered.

Her phone pinged with a text from Cori.

Flynn! What is going on?? Everything OK? Your bad luck is suspicious. I'm worried about you. CALL ME!

She'd texted Cori her whereabouts in the ambulance so she wouldn't panic when Flynn didn't come home. Ignoring Cori's accusatory tone, Flynn rested her forehead on the edge of Nate's hospital bed, exhausted. A cloudy haze muddled her thoughts, dulling her emotions. Her phone pinged again, but this time it began vibrating.

Jolting upright, she flipped it over trying to read the screen. *Can Cori just chill out for one second?* she thought.

It took a few fuzzy seconds to process the call wasn't from Cori. It was an unknown number. Brows sinking, she tapped the green "Accept" circle.

"Hello?" Her voice cracked.

Silence.

Clearing her throat, she tried again, this time more forceful. "Hello?"

"Next time, he dies. I'll be watching."

The phone stayed pressed to her ear long after Wolf's call ended. Its cool screen gradually grew slick as tears began to fall, slow at first, then faster and stronger. Unable to staunch the steady stream, Flynn folded her arms on top of the bed and buried her face, shoulders convulsing, as more tears gushed through the broken dam. She sobbed until she couldn't anymore. Until her eyelids grew so heavy they wouldn't lift. Her cheeks went numb, raw from the salt water scalding her fresh scratches. Wavering in and out of consciousness, she drifted into temporary darkness.

* * * *

Twitching, Flynn woke with a gasp, blinking away the crimson mask staring down at her from her restless dream. Nate stroked her hair.

"Whoa there, it's okay, it's just me."

She stared at him, his face bleary and unfocused. *Ugh. How long has he been watching me sleep?*

"You're okay?" she croaked.

"Seems like it." Wearing his usual wry smile, he winced, gingerly rubbing his ribs. "I don't know how you dealt with having more than one of these broken."

"Nate." Sliding her hand from his, she smoothed back her hair, wiping traces of drool from her sticky mouth. Her cheeks still stung. "Nate, I'm so sorry, I don't know what happened."

He studied her with bloodshot eyes, the skin around them swollen and purple. "Flynn, come on. I saw the mask. That crimson color. I know it was them."

Her breathing stopped. A puddle of words swirled in the back of her throat, trapped, like water trying to escape a clogged drain.

"You're okay, that's all that matters," he continued, "but I know that we weren't randomly mugged. You're being watched."

Glued to her chair, Flynn realized for the first time she couldn't walk away from this conversation.

"You need to tell me what's going on," he pushed.

"No." She shook her head. "N-nothing is going on."

"Stop lying to me. You've been lying to me since the concert. What did they do to you when they took you?" His bludgeoned lips twisted into a scowl. "What are you hiding?"

She continued shaking her head even though pain ping-ponged back and forth between her temples. "Nate, I wanted to tell you I'm sorry. For this. For everything." She paused, and then blurted out what had been on her mind the entire evening. "We can't continue to see each other. Only at work. Whatever it might be that was starting between us has to end. Even our friendship."

"No. Not going to happen." His voice rose in anger. "You think that's the answer? After everything we've been through? I know what's happening here; it's them—REDS is controlling you."

Hugging herself, she rose, trudging to the sink in the corner of the hospital room.

Next time, he dies. I'll be watching.

Wolf's whisper was less a threat than a promise. She clutched the porcelain to keep from doubling over. In the mirror above the dripping faucet, she hardly recognized herself. Gaping back at her was an aged hound, leading its hunter straight to the kill. Mottled skin, eyes hollow, deep lines dug straight into her forehead. But something else rested there. Something she scrubbed and still couldn't erase. Terror. Haunted terror that had been tattooed onto her, reminding her of its existence every time she caught a glimpse of herself.

Exhausted, she turned. Nate observed her, muscles in his neck loosening. His tight expression softened into concern. Silent communication passed between them. A thousand words that had been waiting to be said.

At the sound of their heightened voices, a doctor hurried into the room, followed by the same nurse who had tended to Nate earlier. "Mr. Turner, you're awake. I'm Dr. Jefferson. How are you feeling?"

Jaw rigid beneath his swollen, discolored face, Nate kept his gaze on Flynn. She looked down at her cuticles, avoiding his stare. "Been better."

Dr. Jefferson turned Nate's chin toward her with two gentle fingertips. Shining a light into his red eyes, she offered succinct comments to the nurse. She recorded them in a computer, keyboard taps and clicks joining the chorus of whirring machines hooked to Nate. "You were lucky, Mr. Turner. Your assailant barely missed your eye." Dr. Jefferson probed the glands under Nate's neck. "Could've blinded you. We'll send you home with some medication to help with the pain and swelling. The socket fracture and bruised ribs will heal with time. Any intense head pain?"

"A little. Just really sore."

"Yes, that's to be expected for a while. We'll keep you overnight as a precaution. Monitor you in case of undetected internal bleeding. We can discuss physical therapy options tomorrow before we release you." The doctor handed her otoscope to the nurse and turned to Flynn. "I understand you two were robbed. While I have you both in the room, would you like me to call the police so you can file a formal report? We can provide them with Mr. Turner's medical write-up if you choose to disclose it."

She met Dr. Jefferson's kind eyes, continuing to avoid Nate's gaze. She could feel it burning into her forehead. "I'll leave it up to Nate. He's the one who got hurt."

His brows sinking, a muscle ticked in Nate's temple. She waited, limbs taut, nails digging into her arm. If he reported Wolf's assault, it would trigger another FBI investigation. She would be exposed, and possibly arrested for being an accomplice in a terrorist plot. He sighed, defeated. "No. There's no point going through all that for a wallet. It's probably too late now."

"Can't hurt in case it happens to someone else in the area," Dr. Jefferson urged. "It will also help your case with insurance coverage."

Nate slumped against his pillow, fingers curling into fists over the bedsheets. "The Chicago PD have bigger fish to fry . . . but, I'll think about it."

Sensing Nate and Flynn's tense energy, Dr. Jefferson looked back and forth between them. She scratched the cornrows lining her head. "Alright, I'll leave you two alone to discuss. Let me know if you need anything."

The nurse cast furtive glances over her shoulder as they exited the room.

"Nate," Flynn pleaded, finally breaking the deafening silence. She went to Nate and sat on the edge of his bed. "I can't stop you from speculating . . . but I'm ending our friendship so this never happens again."

"I'm not a kid, Flynn. I can take care of myself. Whatever it is you're up against, you think you can handle it on your own? Regardless of what's going on between us, I care about you. Let me help you."

Nate's voice was earnest and persuasive. Wrapping his fingers around hers, he pulled her closer. *He's using his charm to crack you, and it's working.* All she wanted was to lose herself in kissing him again.

As if reading her mind, Nate reached up, placing his hand on the side of her face, thumb hooking under her jaw. He guided her mouth closer to meet his. His lips flattened her defiance like a house of cards. Both Nate and Wolf knew exactly what it took to break her.

You're going to kill him, she screamed at herself. *You're going to kill him, and you'll never forgive yourself.*

Behind closed lids, she saw Wolf's steely eyes glaring from under his shadowy hood. She could feel his wild and frenzied rage as he pressed his boot into the nape of Nate's neck. His warning rang in her ears as clearly as if he stood beside her.

I don't believe in second chances.

Trembling, she pulled away, withdrawing her hand from Nate's grasp. Wolf would kill him without a second thought, given the opportunity.

"I'm not going to risk losing you. This is goodbye . . . I'm sorry. I'm sorry I did this to you. I'm sorry for everything."

His expression grew stormy as she backed toward the door.

"Don't do this." His voice dropped, as if speaking to a frantic, wounded animal. "Let me help you."

She tried to tear her eyes from his, but she fell into their endless depths. They shifted in color—somber brown to playful green to wondrous yellow—shining beacons in the room's muted light.

"You can't help me." Self-loathing rained over her, a shower of dirt burying her alive. "No one can."

31

FLYNN

Flynn sat outside Nate's room for an hour before finally leaving the hospital. Something inside her felt fractured, broken. Eventually she wandered home, every step delivering a stab to her bruised hip and her conscience. When she arrived back at their apartment, she pushed open the door, her keys jangling in the lock. "Cori?" she called. "You home?"

Depleted of all energy, she shuffled down the narrow hallway leading to their living room, secretly hoping she had the apartment to herself. She didn't want to have to explain everything to Cori, and nothing sounded better than a moment of uninterrupted quiet. Right before she swerved into their kitchen, she stopped mid-stride. Blood rushed to her ears, muffling the usual chorus of car horns blaring outside their windows. Cori sat on their couch, surrounded by three FBI officers. The same ones who'd visited her in the hospital. They hovered awkwardly around the coffee table, positioned in a strange oblong triangle.

Lowering her foot, Flynn didn't register when it came into contact with the floor. Her entire body had gone numb. "What's going on?" she asked.

"Your driver informed us of your hospital admittance," Kind Agent said. She still didn't know his name, but he had more gray streaks in his dark hair than the last time she'd seen him.

"I'm fine. I wasn't admitted. My friend was."

Agent Rich's scrutiny flicked to Cori and back to Flynn. Slumping into the pillows, Cori crossed her arms, avoiding eye contact with Flynn. "But you were *both* mugged, correct?"

Flynn leaned against the kitchen counter. Her legs were seconds from giving way. "Cori? What have you told them?"

"I haven't told them anything!" Cori pointed at her chest defensively.

"So, what is it you'd like to know now?" Flynn asked, clutching the cool granite. "What do you want to rip out of me this time? You sure as hell don't care how I'm doing." The broken part of her sprung to life. She didn't know where the outburst came from or how to harness its sudden force. "You clearly couldn't give two shits about that!" Spittle flew from her lips as she flung the accusation in their shocked faces.

"Flynn, that's not true—" Cori stood, but Agent Rich motioned for her to sit. Rolling her eyes, she flopped back onto the couch.

"Then why are they here? Because *you* told them to come?"

"No!"

"You're wrong. It *is* true," Flynn seethed, her anger whipping out of control. "They're here to interrogate me. Again. All they want is to keep squeezing me for information."

"We want information to save innocent lives," Agent Craig said. "To prevent another incident like Soldier Field from happening again."

He looked thinner than the last time she'd seen him. His banana roll had deflated, his belt cinched tightly around his waist to compensate for his baggy pants.

"How many times do I have to tell you?" she said. "I know *nothing*."

The agents exchanged dubious glances. "We have reason to believe you were attacked by a REDS member tonight. You're still being targeted," Agent Rich said.

Wow, took you long enough to figure that one out, she fumed inwardly.

"People get mugged in Chicago all the time," she countered. "Welcome to the most dangerous city in the US."

"That may be so, but something isn't adding up here," Kind Agent said in a pacifying yet equally condescending tone, enraging Flynn even more. "Not when there are still two REDS individuals at large," he added.

"You should be the ones figuring that out; you're the *professionals*," she air quoted.

"We've gotten a few leads but nothing substantial. We can't pin them. We can't pin any of them. They know we're on to them and they're covering their tracks," Agent Craig said, leaning against the TV stand. He lurched upright when it wobbled precariously. "You can help us."

Flynn threw her head back, exhausted by this dance—a dance she couldn't learn the steps to, no matter how hard she tried. Right when she thought she might be on the verge of nailing the choreography, she stumbled and fell. Right on her face.

Maybe they're right. Maybe this is my out. I could finally throw in the towel. The second the thoughts entered her mind, the image of Nate lying bruised and battered in his hospital bed came into clear focus.

Next time, he dies. I'll be watching. Wolf's voice spoke clearly into her ear again, as if he were following her. She jumped, half expecting Wolf's shadow to emerge from the corner of the kitchen.

No. She had come too far to give up now. She had sacrificed too much. The FBI had proven their incompetence. They wouldn't be able to protect her or anyone she loved. It was time to take things into her own hands. This wasn't about her anymore.

"Just tell them what happened," Cori urged. "They can help you."

Flynn lasered Cori with a glare so deathly she paled, shrinking into the cushions. The FBI couldn't help her. Not when REDS had a system in place more nimble and ruthless than the sloth-like "intelligence" of a fucking bureaucratic, political, government-run organization. *They* were the ones who had underestimated REDS for too long, chasing foreign threats instead of domestic ones. They'd been too busy comparing dick sizes with Russia and China instead of noticing REDS's deft accumulation of power right under their noses.

"There's nothing to tell." Flynn's patience dwindled to a frayed thread. "Maybe you should focus your energy on tangible evidence instead of following around a twenty-seven-year-old hostage hoping she'll bounce back from her drugged, PTSD state and remember something."

"Should I remind you that withholding information from authorities is considered the same thing as conspiring with this enemy of the state?" Agent Rich scowled, his brow sinking so low over his eyes as they compressed into slivers. "In other words, treason."

"Threaten me all you want. I have nothing to share," Flynn's voice rose. She would take on the FBI over REDS any day. "And, on that note, my escort service you've so generously sponsored ends today. You should know by now that trying to use me as bait isn't going to work. The fact that you haven't figured out REDS is smarter than your little game is what's most concerning."

She stormed into her room, slamming the door behind her. Gasping, she collapsed backward, sliding down the length of smooth wood until she sat crumpled on the floor.

I can't trust anyone. The thought splintered her heart into a thousand pieces. Each time she was sure she'd reached her breaking point, she'd turn a corner and find another obstacle towering before her, higher than the last. Apparently, unraveling doesn't happen all at once. It's the slow, twisting process that eventually breaks you.

* * * *

Eventually, the FBI finally left their apartment. Lying on her bed, right cheek throbbing, she stared at the ceiling in self-inflicted pain. It was as if she lived with a monster curled inside her stomach, gorging itself on her intestines. Images of Nate, unconscious on the ground, helpless on the ambulance stretcher, wouldn't stop replaying in her mind.

Never again, she promised herself. Wolf had played her. A checkmate. Now, how could she play him? How could she turn his game on its head?

Cori barged into her room, unannounced. "Flynn?"

"Yeah, Cori?" Her voice was hollow. *Would it kill her to at least knock?*

She strode over to Flynn's bed and glared down at her, hands on her hips. Flynn tore her gaze away from the pimpled popcorn ceiling to meet her accusatory frown. Cori's brown eyes were ablaze. Flynn heaved a sigh, bracing herself for another confrontation.

Might as well get it over with, she thought.

"Look, I'm sorry, I know I shouldn't have let them in, but I didn't know what else to do."

"Why did they come here looking for me in the first place?"

"You heard what they said. Your driver called them after you went to the hospital. I didn't contact them, I swear. You know I would never do that to you."

Groaning, Flynn thumped a pillow over her face. Fighting with Cori was pointless; she never won. She was worse than a dog who wouldn't let go of its chew toy. "I'm so sick of them hounding me."

"Do you really believe that?" Cori ripped the pillow from her hands and flung it across the room.

"Believe what?"

"That the FBI has been using you to bait REDS?"

Defeated, Flynn shrugged. "Yeah, I do. They didn't tag me with someone to follow me everywhere I go to look out for my best interest. They wanted to see if I was being watched. They wanted to lure them out of hiding."

Exhaling sharply through her nose, Cori sat on the bed, chewing the inside of her cheek. "What even happened?"

She knew this was coming. There was no escaping it. "Nate and I went to Wrigleyville after work to watch the Cubs game. We took a walk and then, out of nowhere, someone attacked us and took Nate's wallet and my bag. He was knocked unconscious, so I rode with him in the ambulance to the hospital. I wanted to stay with him until he woke up." Cori opened her mouth, but Flynn interrupted her. "I'm fine, I promise, and so is he. A little shaken up, but we're okay."

Flynn could tell Cori was debating whether to continue pushing. "I know I keep saying this," Cori said, "but when will you realize whatever it is you're going through, you don't have to carry it alone?"

It was eerie how similar Cori and Nate sounded. At times when Flynn's fear threatened to drown her, Nate's soft words offered soothing comfort.

Be brave, Flynn. I'm not going anywhere. You're not alone.

But terrorists were watching her every step. One foot in the wrong direction could trigger a landmine of devastating outcomes. She'd learned that the hard way.

"I know, but there are things I need to figure out for myself." Flynn's voice was strong despite the nagging fear leaking poison into her bloodstream. "I can do this."

I've got to protect Cori, she told herself. *I might have failed Nate, but I can't fail her.*

The anger on Cori's face faded. A small smile played on her lips. "I know you can. You've always been a fighter."

Flynn snorted and shook her head, rustling the pillowcase. "Who are you kidding? Me, a fighter? Maybe once. I used to think I knew what it takes to be one, but it's hard when I'm always on the losing team."

Cori grasped her arm, face rigid with determination. "If you never give up, then you're a fighter."

"You think?" Flynn's chest deflated. "I feel like I'm fighting in an entirely new game. . . . Some nights, right before I fall asleep, the explosions at the concert start, and I can't stop them. It's like I'm trapped in that glass box, my brain forcing me to live it over and over. Sometimes I wonder if I'll ever know peace again."

Cori leaned against the pillows, legs folded beside her. They lay shoulder to shoulder, inhaling and exhaling in rhythmic synchrony. "You know, sometimes I think back to when I was a kid. I had the craziest imagination. I would play for hours by myself, making up the most elaborate stories in my head. I'd slip into the bushes behind our house, searching for fairy villages. I made giant couch forts, waiting for a prince to come save me. I even ate a dog treat once because I wanted to be a dog." Flynn coughed a puff of laughter. She glanced at Cori out of the corner of her eye. Although she smiled fondly, Cori's voice carried a layer of sadness. "But, as I got older, my imagination disappeared. It vanished. Does it even still exist? I dunno. Maybe reality destroyed it. I mean, why don't we play anymore? Why don't we use our imaginations?"

Flynn thought back to the last time she'd indulged in any form of art or creativity. Had it been, what, maybe fifteen years ago? Ten? Over time, age had herded and locked away her wild, rampant imagination into a tiny cell. Now, giant walls built of fear and trepidation surrounded it.

"I dunno," Flynn admitted. "I guess it's because after a certain point, we're not taught to use our imagination. We're told we need to learn certain subjects and work hard in order to succeed. That's what it must mean to grow up." They were both quiet. "Evil has taken on a whole new meaning, hasn't it?" she said. "It's no longer monsters and dragons. The future used to be exciting. Now, it's morphed into something threatening . . . ominous."

"True. But we're all in this together. No one is exempt from life's hardships."

"Yes, but it's hard to be playful and reckless when we know life's consequences. We're all living in a giant waiting game, waiting for the next bad thing to happen."

Flynn rolled on her side to face her friend. Cori's eyes were still lifted upward. Early morning sunlight shining through the window contoured her high cheekbones, powdering a natural shimmer over her skin. Flynn bit her lip, tempted once more to tell her everything.

"You can't live your life like that," Cori said. "You'll drive yourself crazy. Plus you're forgetting about all the *joy*—the love." She met Flynn's gaze, squares of white light skating around her dark brown irises. "Maybe our choices dictate our destiny . . . but maybe, that's only half the story."

32
WOLF

Misery. Pure misery. That was the best way to describe Wolf's first few days working at Magnetic. They were full of orientation material. Videos on humanitarian projects and "revolutionary" technology advances that strategically positioned the company as one of the thought leaders of the world.

It's all bullshit, he thought.

Then there was the security protocol, direct deposits, and retirement options. This was what these bougies concerned themselves with? Which portfolio to invest their 401(k) in?

It was all smoke and mirrors anyway, especially Magnetic's claim that it was a "flat" organization. Easier job fluidity, they promised, more mobility without the focus on fancy titles. Yeah, right. Even REDS had a hierarchical structure. It could be viewed as operating similarly to a corporate organization. The executive committee reported to Spider and oversaw line workers. But their system worked. It yielded results. And, most importantly, their creed and manifesto extended beyond self-indulgent promotions and myopic paychecks. They had a vision of a new world. A new system. With them at the helm, all working together to achieve it.

Magnetic had their own vision of control, but their approach was more obscure and deceitful. At least REDS was forthright about their intentions to rebuild society in a way that evened the playing field and didn't revolve around keeping only the elite in power. Magnetic masked their agenda as a way of helping the world, when in reality, they wanted more money at any cost—a buffer to protect the elite.

Far worse than reviewing irrelevant corporate benefits was having to participate in team breakout activities. Avoiding his new, obnoxiously enthusiastic colleagues at all costs, Wolf sulked on the outskirts. His teammates were perfectly happy to overlook his sullen demeanor as "typical subdued engineer type." By the third day of new-hire training, he wanted to claw his eyes out.

I don't belong here, he realized, *among these fake egotistical assholes.*

Flynn's desk sat on a different floor than his, so he hadn't seen her since starting. Brainwash boot camp could also be a contributing factor. But on the last day of orientation, as he waited in the lunch line, he caught her watching him from across the café. His tapping foot hovered midair, no longer impatient with the person in front of him conspicuously judging each dish's nutrition label. Flynn's face darkened when their eyes met. He grinned and raised his hand in a mock wave.

Flynn turned on her heel, scurrying away. He abandoned his place in line, hurrying to catch her amid the throng of employees crowding into the cafeteria. It was strange for her to greet him with fear rather than bristly defiance.

"Flynn. You're not going to welcome Magnetic's brightest new star?"

His voice echoed throughout the atrium, cornering her. Located in the center of the building, glass walls enclosed the floating staircase connecting Magnetic's ten floors like a human spinal cord. Pausing mid-stride, Flynn eyed the herd of people moving around her, a rock lodged in the midst of a gushing stream. He stopped beside her.

"I can't believe you." Her hand fluttered to her lips. Each word she uttered appeared painful.

"What? What can't you believe?" Tilting his head, he frowned, feigning innocence.

"You almost murdered Nate right in front of me." Her voice pressed into a whisper. "You almost compromised all of *this*."

"I can still finish the job." He wondered if she knew how tempting the idea was.

Flynn glared at him, the familiar fire turning her eyes an ashy hue. It drew him to her each time, a wave crashing to the shore over and over, sucking away his resistance.

"Leave him out of this, Wolf."

"Chris," he corrected her with a hiss. "*You* were the one who brought him into this."

Her expression was weary, her pale skin an unusual sickly color. She nodded toward the door, signaling him to follow her down a flight of stairs. She walked with a stiff posture; her shoulders hardly swayed with each robotic step. When they reached the landing, she pulled him past the kitchenette and into a nook around the corner where two plush, red chairs sat huddled around a digital whiteboard. The screen cast a blue light over her profile, painting one side of her face in an ethereal glow.

"I didn't involve him. I'm . . . I'm simply trying to live my life. It looks suspicious for me to go about my days in complete isolation, especially with the FBI still watching my every move."

He leaned over her. "Wake up. It's time to come to terms with your new life. It's no longer yours. It's ours."

Eyes narrowing, she clenched her jaw. "I'm doing everything you ask. You know you didn't have to hurt him. Nate isn't a threat to you."

He couldn't tell her harming Nate was never part of REDS's plan. Spider would be livid if he knew Wolf had attacked him and possibly compromised himself. But when he saw them kissing, he had been consumed by slicing hot rage so uncontrollable he hardly knew what he was doing.

"You provoked me," he snapped. "Don't tell me you didn't know exactly what you were doing."

"Nate is harmless." Her hands leapt upward, gesticulating wildly. "What's your problem with him?"

"I warned you to stay away from him. He's getting too close. He could jeopardize everything. That, and you purposefully defied me. You wanted to see how I would react."

"Everyone okay over here? Sounded like things were getting a little heated." A calm voice behind them interrupted their boiling exchange. Nate stood at the entry of their hidden nook, thumbs hooking the pockets of dark, perfectly tailored jeans. His eyebrows jumped toward his immaculate hairline when he recognized Wolf. "Wow, you got the job already? That must be record timing."

The greenish tinge of fading bruises covered his face, and both eyes were still bloodshot from the trauma of colliding with concrete.

"Yeah, I was lucky. Magnetic wanted to move pretty fast." Wolf's posture tensed. "You're a little more roughed up than the last time I saw you."

"Bad biking accident." He stepped closer to them, his ironclad stare locked onto Wolf. "Today's my first day back in the office. Chris, right?"

Flynn's mouth slid into an unnatural smile as she fought to maintain her composure. She intercepted Nate, blocking his path. "You're back! We were so worried about you."

Her voice was several pitches too high. Nate glanced at her before his eyes flicked back to Wolf.

"I've never seen anyone make it through the hiring process so quickly here. Wasn't your in-person interview only a week ago?" He didn't mask his accusatory tone, his suspicion palpable. "You must be something special."

Wolf could smell a challenge from a mile away. He squared his body, unable to resist Nate's provocation. "I like to think so. It helped I had two other offers on the table."

"Definitely one of my best candidates to date," Flynn interjected enthusiastically.

Nate directed his attention to her. "Ah, that's right he's *your* candidate. How did you come across such a great find?"

"Oh, uh, you know . . . some college career fair. Chris just got his master's. He was in our system and must've been overlooked a few times. Probably his age." After a few beats of uncomfortable silence, she added, "Figured it couldn't hurt to bring him in."

Nate looked Wolf up and down, sizing up his opponent. His shoulders retracted. "You do seem young for a field manager position. You must be, what, twenty-eight? Twenty-nine?"

Wolf's fingers twitched, desperate to encircle themselves around Nate's throat. *Who does this entitled prick think he is?* "Twenty-seven," he said. "I tend to find I'm the exception, not the rule."

Wolf saw Flynn's eyes dance back and forth between Wolf and Nate, as though calculating how to diffuse the tension growing between them.

"And you passed the background test?" Nate pressed.

"What's that supposed to mean?" Wolf snapped.

"It means there's something not right about you."

Wolf laughed, his upper lip curling into a snarl. "Are all assholes this insecure here? Listen, it sounds like this is a *you* problem, not a me problem."

Nate advanced toward them. "This has everything to do with you."

Flynn jumped between them, clapping both hands together. "Well, looks like we're not exactly getting off on the right foot." Both men ignored her, two snorting bulls circling each other, probing for an opening to charge. "Chris, I'll show you how to get back to orientation. This building can be confusing at first."

Nate's chin lifted an inch, the muscles in his neck straining. "I've got a bad feeling about you. I can't put my finger on it, but I'll figure it out. Until then, watch yourself, Chris."

"If I were you, I'd focus my energy on staying on my bicycle instead."

Wolf stiffened, preparing for Nate to swing a hook straight to his nose. If Flynn wasn't standing right in front of him, it wouldn't have been out of the question. Instead, Nate smirked and walked past them to the staircase, taking steps two at a time, leaving behind a not-so-subtle warning as a farewell. Unaccustomed to showing restraint when he wanted to bash someone's face in, Wolf gritted his teeth. Flynn's hands visibly trembled, her eyes as round as two nickels.

"What. Does. He. Know?"

"Nothing. He knows nothing."

"Don't lie to me. He knows I'm the one who attacked him. What else does he know?"

Torn, she rubbed her lips together. He could see the wheels in her head turning as she tried to formulate a story to refute his claim. It took seconds before she gave up, sighing.

"I think . . . I think he's been suspicious since I was released from the hospital. He seemed to know I remember everything after the concert. Then, I switched teams with no explanation. Seeing you here probably confirmed some of his suspicions."

Squeezing the bridge of his nose, Wolf forced a loud hissing exhale. *Stupid*, he cursed himself. *I can't believe I was so fucking stupid.*

"Flynn. This is exactly what I was talking about. He needs to go. He knows too much."

"No! Please, no." She grabbed his arm. He jerked it away, her touch startling him. Her fingers hovered in the space between them, reaching for him, before dropping to her side. She straightened. "I will go to the FBI. I will tell them everything."

"Then I will kill you too."

"Good. At least I would finally be free again." Moisture built in her eyes. A single tear spilled over, tangling in her lashes then shimmying down her cheek. "I wouldn't have to be your puppet anymore. I wouldn't have to be a part of your fucked-up plan."

A piece of Wolf broke, cracking along a fault line, releasing seismic tremors that shook him to the core. She meant it. She knew he could have killed her by now. He *should* have killed her.

But I won't. I can't. Nate and her family, on the other hand . . . I can, he thought. *That threat is the only thing keeping her in check.*

"If he keeps this up, if he gets involved . . . I'll kill him. And I'll kill your roommate and your family too. I can't risk someone running their mouth. I can't risk him exposing me."

She sniffed loudly, swiping the heel of her hand across her cheek. "He has no evidence; he's only making assumptions. I already told him we can't see each other anymore or be friends."

A bitter laugh coated his tongue. "Are you trying to convince me? Am I supposed to be reassured by that? You're the one fueling his suspicions."

"What do you want me to do?"

Her plea hacked into him, a blunt butcher knife slamming into an animal carcass. She cared for him, even though she would never admit it.

"If I see you two alone together, that'll be the last time he breathes."

33

WOLF

Executing catastrophic damage to society was simple for Wolf. The one necessary ingredient for success? Determination. Calculated determination.

Creating explosives required a basic understanding of chemistry and some time spent trolling online encyclopedias for recipes for mass destruction. It only took him a little research. The internet willingly shared its information without bias or censorship. Sites piloted by groups with subversive agendas provided a platform on which to rally an audience. Algorithms were easy to manipulate.

Online, it was easy to destroy someone. Not by ending a life, but by hijacking a system. Stealing an identity. With a few keystrokes, infinite information was at his fingertips. Within five minutes, he uncovered video tutorials of how to conduct a train, located documents on network upgrades to its system, and found diagrams of a model train station. Innocuous materials that could be devastating if the wrong person stumbled upon them. In a few clicks, the options for inflicting unprecedented horror were overwhelming—especially when he had nothing to lose.

* * * *

"I'm in," Wolf reported to Spider and two other executive members in the Leadership Chamber. "Give me a few days to get into Magnetic's system and implement the malware. We'll be in the clear to proceed the week following Falcon's attack on the substation."

"Good." Spider pushed his chair back from the table and strode toward the amplified map of the Chicago Transit Authority train system projected on the wall. He studied it carefully even though they'd pored over the interwoven web of tracks so often that Wolf had memorized it. "And the hostage, is she still complying?" His head swiveled on his neck to face Wolf. "We'll need to dispose of her soon."

Wolf hesitated, his pulse spiking at the mention of Flynn. His tongue was suddenly swollen, useless. "Of course. Timing will be of the utmost importance to ensure we don't draw unnecessary attention to ourselves."

Spider narrowed his eyes, probing for gaps in Wolf's plan that could cave to unseen errors, to the detriment of their whole plan. "And there's no possibility the electrical grid is stronger than you anticipated?"

Wolf's lips flicked upward. "It's almost a hundred years old. I'm confident I could take down the entire system without testing."

"Take down Chicago's electrical grid?" Weasel, Executive Director of Operations, joined Spider at the map. He was a thin man with beady eyes and long gray hair pulled back into a loose ponytail. One of the eldest and most respected members of REDS, he'd overseen the execution of almost every mission throughout the past fifteen years.

Wolf once heard about how Weasel's fellow recruits had written him off during initiation due to his small size. Underestimated, he advanced with astonishing speed and finished at the top of his initiate class. One of the smallest carnivores, a weasel can take down prey five times its size. He'd earned an alias worthy of his stealthy power.

In the dim lighting, Spider's mouth blended into his skin, making it impossible to read his expression. "Yes. Without access to power, we'll be able to take control of the city and cut it off from the rest of the country. Wolf, you'll need to inform Falcon that he must be prepared to act at any time."

Weasel pointed a ragged black fingernail to a circle on the map. "Why this substation instead of the others?"

"I want to be cautious," Wolf said. "We've never used Semtex explosives on a target this large. We need to ensure it can wipe out the entire electrical substation." Wolf swept his palm over the strategic coordinates. "We need to observe how the main network responds to the removal of one station. From there, we can calculate how many we'll need to destroy in order to overload the larger system, with the assistance of the malware I'm going to plant in Magnetic's system. The fewer substations we need to target the better." As he paced up and down the length of the room, everyone seemed to disappear, dissolving into their surroundings. All he could see was his mission unfolding before his eyes. "Weasel, it will be crucial to monitor how long it takes to reroute the power. This substation also controls the communication network and power grid surrounding the bridge, freezing train number two in place. Timing must be perfect to position it for the river attack."

Weasel furrowed his brow. "Attack on the river? Who's running point on a river assault?"

Glancing at Spider, Wolf waited for his confirmation to speak.

"Yes." Spider's attention remained glued to the map, his voice distant. "While Falcon hijacks the first train directly from the station, Croc will captain a boat on the river. He'll detonate a second Semtex bomb here, taking out the bridge and the other stalled train." He rested his long, pointed fingertips on the map over the small representation of a bridge extending over the Chicago River.

Weasel considered this, rubbing his chin. "It's risky. How do we plan to generate enough shock or friction to detonate the Semtex explosives?"

"An electromagnetic pulse," Wolf said. "Hyena and I have been working together on a new EMP for quite some time now."

Weasel turned to face Hyena, REDS's Executive Director of Weapon Advancement. He hadn't moved from his observation point at the back of the room. Massive arms crossed in front of his chest, and two grooves bracketed his downturned mouth, as if he was pondering his next move in a chess game. Hyena had earned his alias during initiation due to his strong affinity for human corpses.

"Hyena," Spider ordered, "debrief."

Hyena leaned forward, placing three small mounds of white, putty-like substance on the table in front of them. "As you all know, up to this point, we've relied on C-4 explosives for smaller-scale attacks. For this mission, we needed to develop a bomb that can produce a much larger chemical reaction with less material than a comparable C-4." His voice crescendoed, from low to high, replicating the eerie, cackling laughter of the animal that inspired his name. "So I started experimenting with Semtex. It has similar malleability to a C-4 but a higher percentage of RDX. The amount here"— he flipped a piece no bigger than a penny over in his fingers—"should be able to destroy a commercial plane. It's also more difficult to detect."

An ex-Army veteran, Hyena was discharged from the military due to mental instability after two years of deployment in Iraq. He'd tried to blow up his own camp, his mind so muddled he'd confused it with the enemy's. He might have been successful had he not lit himself on fire. Abandoned and homeless, he'd come across REDS's radar right as he prepared to leap off a highway overpass.

"Will the EMP's shock waves be enough to detonate the Semtex?" Spider picked up a piece of putty, examining it. "Now I'm sure you can understand why I pushed you so aggressively on its development."

Hyena nodded once, eyes round with excitement. A deep, red scar ran down the entire length of his face. Glimpses of warped tissue wrapped around his neck, extending up to his cheekbones. His skin had darkened in those places, like strips of leather plastered haphazardly over his visage. Scars from his old burns and battle wounds. Only a thin line of cartilage separated the large, gaping holes that used to be his nostrils.

"It's ready. I told Falcon how to activate it. We just need to make sure he's in the designated area when the time comes to detonate the bomb." He gnawed one of his knobby knuckles. "He must be within range."

Spider tilted his head in Wolf's direction. "Where will you be positioned?"

"With your permission, Spider, I want to assist Falcon on the platform."

"No. Too risky. We can't compromise you. We're already sacrificing Croc and Falcon."

Wolf rejoined Spider at the map, running his finger along one of the tracks, stopping at a train station inside the Chicago Loop. Nestled right in the center of the bustling financial district, high-rise buildings surrounded it on all sides.

"Falcon will be here, on this elevated platform, to hijack the train. This station will get him close enough to the substation in the shortest amount of time. As Hyena mentioned, if he's not within range, activating the EMP might not detonate the Semtex explosive. I hacked into the security cameras in that area to study the surveillance coverage. If I stay between the elevator bank and the stairwell leading to the street, I'll be concealed."

"It doesn't matter. Others in the area could see you," Weasel said. The lines around his eyes multiplied with disapproval. "Once Falcon takes control of the train, pigs will be there within minutes."

"Not if I'm able to take out this entire platform." Wolf waved toward the train station on the map. "After Falcon's train leaves the station, I can destroy it, distracting the Feds from the other targets. It will create an easier escape route for everyone else."

This mission is part of me, he thought. *It's been my entire life. I deserve to be in the center of the chaos as it unfolds, breathing it in.*

After these past few weeks with Flynn, he needed to remember the reverberating purpose killing gave him. Taking from those who took from him. Reminding the sheep that that's all they've ever been—mindless animals.

Weasel glanced at Spider, waiting for him to dismiss Wolf's idea. "Spider, permission to speak?"

"Granted." His lips barely moved in reply. Spider kept his attention fixated on the map, wide-legged stance unmoving. A mountain unbreakable by the elements.

"We're getting greedy. Our goal is to take out the electrical substation. Attacking two separate targets and having Wolf make a hit significantly increases our potential for error and jeopardizes his identity."

Spider began to walk around the table, circling the perimeter in just a few long strides. His giant presence made the room and everyone in it shrink. "Wolf, state the significance of taking out this platform."

Wolf pointed at the surrounding buildings. "Falcon's collision point by the electrical substation and the bridge are removed from the center of the city. Destroying the platform will result in a greater impact and maximize casualties."

He had played into Spider's blind spot—his thirst for mass destruction.

"How do you plan to take out that entire station while keeping yourself intact?" Hyena's question seemed curious rather than critical.

"By testing the malware I plan to implement within Magnetic's main network."

"We built it to hijack and paralyze Magnetic's system," Hyena said. Shoulders rounded in a permanent hunch, he dipped his head, emphasizing a mane of hair gelled into a mohawk. "The malware's only intended to act as an isolated computer virus."

Shaking his head, Wolf swallowed, summoning a last-ditch effort. "This will be a different kind of test. One I've experimented with on a smaller scale. I can hack into wireless devices connected to unsecured Wi-Fi networks in the area. By activating them all at once, we can use them to emit an electromagnetic pulse to detonate another Semtex bomb hidden on the platform. The trigger will come from multiple signals all around the station, making it nearly impossible for the Feds to pinpoint a source during investigations."

"A spontaneous EMP," Hyena observed, his voice pitching an entire octave higher.

Weasel and Hyena looked at each other, silently weighing potential benefits and consequences. Tension ricocheted throughout the room as they waited for Spider to make the final call.

"Wolf, you may accompany Falcon to the platform on one condition." Spider's full attention fastened a heavy yoke around Wolf's neck. "If he's detained before the train hijack, you will not expose yourself. We will not gamble your role in our larger mission recklessly. Not at this pivotal time." Wolf nodded once, knowing better than to disobey him. "We cannot compromise your identity."

A subtle warning tinged his words. Wolf's stomach nose-dived. Did Spider know he'd attacked Nate? It was likely. He had spies everywhere, giving him full access to the city's inner workings, including those of his own people.

"Weasel, finalize timing and location targets," Spider continued. "Hyena, arrange bomb placement. You're all dismissed."

The three Enforcers stood at attention, bending into slight bows before exiting the room.

"Oh, and Wolf," Spider called after him, "there will be no hostages this time."

34

FLYNN

Wolf's presence in the office hung over Flynn's head, circling her like a starved vulture. She avoided Nate at all costs, but he didn't make it easy for her. Every day he sought her out. Whenever he came by, she pretended to be distracted by calls with recruits. His face would fall, eyes and mouth turning down in disappointment. If she wasn't at her desk, he left urgent notes begging to speak with her.

We NEED to talk. Come find me. Please.—N

Each time she ignored him, a part of her chipped away. She threw herself into work, hiding in conference rooms long after interviews were complete, remaining glued to the phone while she sat at her desk. The nagging guilt was unbearable, a giant sponge lodged deep in her stomach soaking up any desire to eat or drink. The only way to maintain a sliver of sanity was to direct her focus to what Wolf might be planning. Now that he'd officially infiltrated the company, it positioned him one step closer to completing his operation. The thought was sickening enough to make her double over in pain.

One afternoon, while escorting an interviewee to the elevator bank, she passed Wolf standing in the micro-kitchen. He was listening intently to a cluster of engineers, body rigid, defensive, as if one of them might thrust a knife into his gut at any moment. Their eyes met and an electric current passed through her. It was startling, almost how she imagined a defibrillator pressed to her chest might feel—jolting, painful—paralyzing and awakening all at once.

There were fleeting moments when he looked at her and his expression seemed to soften, before vanishing again behind a tightly controlled façade. Confused, she would relive that hazy, drunken night when Wolf stood in her room. The angst on his face when she'd hugged him was the only glimmer of vulnerability he'd ever exposed, revealing a possible weakness, despite his attempt to conceal it.

Ever since their first meeting at Buckingham Fountain, she'd pushed Wolf away. Rather than learn more about him and REDS, fear and repulsion had immobilized her. He tore her down, diminished her, convinced her she was nothing—an insignificant puzzle piece dropped into position. Wolf exposed her for the coward she was by dangling people's lives over her. Terror had the power to do that. But, after everything, she was still alive. That fear had become a friend she'd grown accustomed to living with. Now, it awakened her. She was rising, even if she was merely a sapling below a towering oak.

It's my turn to break him down piece by piece. No one else could stop him, and while she could live with the fear, she didn't know whether she could live with the regret. There had to be a way to figure out his mission, or at least weaken his defenses. Attacking them was her only shot.

* * * *

As the end of the day approached, Flynn wandered down to Wolf's desk. She found him bowed over his computer frantically typing strings of code. The numbers and letters jumbled together to form an alien language.

"Hey," she greeted him, forcing her arms to hang neutrally by her side.

Jumping, he blinked up at her, adjusting back to reality. "Hey," he said, wary, glancing back at his screen.

"So, um . . . what're you working on?" She knew this wasn't going to be easy.

Why must I always be so awkward?

His brows pinched together. He tapped his desk with a fingernail, distracted. "What do you want, Flynn?"

She fidgeted, picking invisible lint from her navy shirt. "I told my security escort I have a sailing lesson at the Yacht Club today. I was hoping you could take me out on the lake."

His voice turned suspicious. "Why?"

She shrugged. Every movement felt mechanical and forced, as if she were a marionette with severed strings. Lying had never been her strong suit. "I dunno. It's a gorgeous Friday. No work tomorrow. Have to take advantage of Chicago summers while we can."

Wolf's eyes scanned over her. "We have nothing to discuss today," he concluded, turning back to his computer.

Nope, she told herself. *No way I'm giving up that easily.*

"Maybe not, but I thought it might be nice to hang out."

His jaw hardened. "I told you, I don't do 'having fun' or 'hanging out.'" He air quoted each phrase in disdain. "Both are a waste of time."

"We can celebrate you getting the job." Her forced enthusiasm was half-hearted at best. "Or we can view it as an obligatory favor since I got you a job here."

He glanced around the office to make sure they were alone. "Do you actually think I owe you something for getting me into Magnetic?" His voice lowered. "You're lucky to be alive."

Her heart sank, a fluttering butterfly with a torn wing. "Alright, fine," she sighed in pretend defeat. "There's something I need to tell you. The FBI came by my place again a few days ago."

His tapping fingernail picked up speed. Swiveling in his chair, he began to bounce his left knee too. "Tell me here," he hissed.

She shook her head, dropping her voice to match his. "I can't. It's too risky. We can't be overheard."

Wolf's thorny glare wilted. "Fine, if you'll leave me alone, fine. Now let me get back to work."

Note to self: he's easier to wear down while he's focused on another task.

"Perfect. I'll have my escort drop me off at the Yacht Club at six. See you there."

He ignored her, already engrossed in the indecipherable rows of numbers on his screen. She walked back to her desk, ignoring her sparking nerves. This might be her only chance to crack Wolf. Who knew what he'd do when he discovered she had lured him out under a false pretense.

Should I try to kill him while we're on the lake? she wondered. *No one would hear us. No one would even know he had gone missing . . . except REDS.*

Her fingers dug into her scalp. Considering how easily he had deflected her attempts to attack him in the past, she would need a weapon.

"Flynn."

She stumbled, Nate's voice behind her causing her legs to freeze. Most of the bruising on his face had faded except around the fractured eye socket. He shoehorned his fists into the crooks of his armpits. Even in his most vulnerable state he exuded confidence.

"Nate." His name was the only word she could muster.

"You're avoiding me."

She cast a conspiratorial glance over her shoulder toward Wolf's desk. A familiar guilt crept over her, roasting her skin like she were on a spit. His voice wasn't accusatory or angry, but she winced as if he'd slapped her. "I'm sorry . . . I've just been super busy."

He crossed the space between them. Her muscles tensed. If Wolf saw them together it would be catastrophic. As if sensing her unease, he pulled her around the corner into an empty conference room and closed the door. Frosted privacy glass surrounded them, but it didn't stop the panic from swelling inside her.

"I'm worried about you," he said. "Look, I know you can't tell me anything, but something isn't right, and it has to do with that new Chris guy."

Flynn wanted to shake Nate, beg him to forget about her. She'd already entangled him in the same inescapable web trapping her. Now, he carried a target on his back, and, worse, he didn't even realize it. It was in both their best interests to move on.

"You need to forget about me and what's going on here. This is bigger than you think. You have to trust me when I ask you to stay away from me."

"No. I'm sorry, I can't." He searched her face. "Isn't it time to come clean? To stop the lying, at least to me."

She groaned. "Nate, this is dangerous, what you're doing. You're going to get yourself killed and I can't, I just can't be responsible for your death."

"My life isn't your responsibility. I can take care of myself. This is about me making sure nothing happens to you or to hundreds of innocent people again." His eyes changed color to chocolate brown, emulating his intensity. "You can make it easy and let me help you, or you can waste time and risk others' lives trying to do this alone."

How could Nate possibly understand? Even if he did, he would never forgive her. She had contributed to setting REDS's plan into motion. She couldn't confide in anyone without risking their safety. The temptation to tell him everything—to finally release the relentless fear she'd contained for months, to quiet the torture that raged long after leaving REDS's holding cell—was overwhelming.

"No. I almost watched you die, and I won't do it again."

His face darkened. "What about you? I'm supposed to sit back on my ass while you self-destruct? You're deteriorating. I can't watch it any longer."

Knees shaking, she sank into the nearest chair. Loneliness crushed down on her. "I'm not worried about myself. I'm scared about losing you." Her head fell forward into her palm, her neck unable to withstand its sudden weight. The clammy cradle offered momentary relief, a cool compress against her hot skin. "Please, help me. I'm begging you. Stay away from me and don't involve yourself."

He slammed a fist on the table. The thud sent shock waves through her arms. She immediately regretted meeting his gaze. The coldness embalmed itself into her memory. "You know me. You know I've never been one to sit around and do nothing."

Inhaling deeply, she wedged her fingers under her thighs. She held on to the breath.

Nothing is going to stop him, she realized.

"Alright, let me just . . . think through this." There had to be a way to throw him off Wolf's scent so he didn't do something drastic. Anything to appease him, to keep him occupied and out of any real danger. "Give me a week to work out a few things. There's something I need to do."

I need a way to protect us, she said to herself.

"We don't have a week, Flynn. Time isn't on our side."

Her mind spun in circles. "Alright, can you at least give me until Monday?"

"Why? Why Monday? Why can't you just tell me now?"

"Because I need to figure out how we can get through this together."

Shaking his head, he massaged his jaw, agitated nails scraping against scruff. "Each minute that passes, you're in danger. We're all in danger."

"If we go to the FBI now, they'll arrest me in a heartbeat," Flynn blurted, unable to stop herself.

Nate's hand skidded to a stop over his chin. "What do you mean? Why would they arrest you?"

"After we were attacked in the park, they became suspicious. They think I'm withholding information."

"Well, are you?"

"Am I what?"

"Withholding information."

"I dunno . . . I mean to some extent, yes."

"Jesus, Flynn!" Clutching the back of a chair, he leaned forward. "What the hell are you thinking?"

"What? You think this is something I want to be doing? That this is something I chose? I'm doing what I need to do to stay alive—to keep the people I care about alive."

"What about all the other people out there?" He stretched his arms wide, gesturing to the walls around them. "What about them?!"

Flynn sprang to her feet. "I don't care about them! I care about my family. Cori. You." Her voice trembled so violently she had to pause before continuing. "Just give me the weekend, that's all I ask. On Monday, I'll tell you everything."

His shoulders lowered, relaxing a centimeter into her deceitful assurance. "Fine," he relented, although his expression hung heavy with doubt.

"Nate," she pleaded, begging him with her eyes to understand. "How can the two of us go up against an entire militant terrorist organization on our own? You of all people know what REDS is capable of."

Nate turned to leave but paused in the doorway. "That's exactly why I have to try."

35

FLYNN

From the entrance of the Chicago Yacht Club, Wolf watched Flynn approach with a guarded expression. She tapped her phone screen, pretending to answer a call until her Uber pulled away.

"Hey," she greeted him, careful to ensure she didn't sound like she was trying too hard.

"Where's your escort buddy?"

"I fired him."

"You fired him?" He eyed her before turning to head past security toward the docks. "I thought you told them you had a sailing lesson today."

Shit, she thought. *Busted*. The FBI had relented to ending her escort service after she accused them of baiting REDS. "I did . . . it's uh, it's a long story. I'll explain when we're out on the water."

"You're up to something. I'm not as oblivious as you think."

A spark of annoyance flared inside her. He always saw right through her. Was she that predictable?

"Maybe that's what I want you to believe by luring you out here. Maybe you won't make it off the boat alive."

He barked a desolate laugh. "I'll take my chances."

He led her to a smaller cabin cruiser this time. Sleek and sporty in design, it glinted vainly in the sunlight.

"Where do you get all these boats?" she asked.

"Nice try."

"I'm not probing, I'm curious."

"Accept that you'll never know the answer."

The boat rocked as she made a small leap over the starboard side. Of course, she landed without an ounce of grace or coordination. "So, you stole it then."

He thought for a second, lips curving into the smallest smile. "No. Our boats are all gifts."

Rather than sitting up front, as far from Wolf as possible, Flynn sat beside him in a cushioned chair by the captain's seat. He maintained cool indifference, but his posture was vigilant, as if she might spring on him at any moment.

"That's one word for it," she said dryly.

"You're welcome to believe anything you want. You've already formed your own judgments about who we are regardless of what I say."

Keeping his eyes straight ahead, he navigated out of the busy harbor teeming with boats floating eagerly toward the open lake. His hair had grown longer and its color lighter since they'd met. The wind's fingers combed through its rippling ends. Faint golden stubble covered his neck and chin.

"Judgment." She let the word play over her tongue. "I don't know if I'd call it that. I would call it educated assessments based on historical activity."

His small shadow of a smile returned. "How concise."

They left the wake zone and Wolf accelerated. Balancing on her seat, she gripped the counter beneath the glass windshield. They bounced over waves, and a light spray settled on their faces. As the wind whipped around them, she relished this newfound feeling of freedom. For a brief moment, she couldn't remember why she'd asked Wolf out here. The fresh water released boundless energy, rejuvenating her soul.

Eventually he slowed the boat, the engine's roar quieting to a murmur before he cut it completely. The close space between them hung uncomfortably, waiting to be acknowledged. A full minute passed, and she became more desperate.

"You know what you've shown me over the past few weeks?" The question poured from her mouth without thought.

He glanced in her direction. His round knuckles protruded from his skin like a mountain range as he clutched the steering wheel. "That you should be terrified for the future of this city?"

Her mouth crooked into a grimace. "No. You've shown me we're not as different from each other as you might think."

Inhaling the damp breeze, she closed her eyes. The air was intoxicating. It brought a piece of her to life, a small part she thought might be dead. She would do anything to stay on this boat, floating amid the seemingly endless lake forever. When she opened her eyes, Wolf was quietly watching her.

"We don't share a single thing in common," he said.

His sharp-edged voice colored his words with bitterness, stabbing through her reverie. "But we *are* similar. We all have basic needs. Everyone wants a roof over their head, food on the table . . . protection. We all want to belong somehow."

"How philosophical."

"You're so damn predictable." She rolled her head backward. "You just focus on the differences. You're blind to similarities even when they're staring you right in the face."

His upper lip arched into a barbarous snarl. "I share nothing with anyone from this fucked-up, hypocritical society. I'm better than them, all of them."

"I know what it feels like to be an outsider too, you know. And I chose not to let that define me."

"Oh, poor Flynn. Did you get left out of a high school slumber party?"

"You can't see it, but that's almost worse." She fingered the small Star of David hanging from her neck, its six-pointed edges pricking her skin. In Hebrew it was called the Shield of David. Now, she needed it more than ever. "My scars are invisible, just like yours. I'm a Jewish woman in a society controlled by white Christian men. You don't think I know how it feels to be taunted, stereotyped, and . . . and demeaned?" Her voice wobbled, choking with unexpected emotion. "Being a minority is something I've lived with every day. I've felt insignificant . . . alone . . . like I'm somehow less than them because of the god I worship. But I *chose* to move past that and keep living my life. Some of us have to be the ones to bridge the divide."

Her breath released in tight spurts. She rarely talked about her religion. Not with friends. Definitely not with strangers. She hated drawing attention to the fact that she was different, unlike them in both belief and history. Sometimes she still found herself wishing she was like everyone else. Never knowing what it was like to walk into a room full of people and feel out of place. Never being that one person who doesn't belong.

He scanned her face as if seeing her for the first time. Something lingered in his eyes, an expression she'd never seen before. He remained enigmatic, but the coldness thawed slightly.

"All this bullshit over a 'god,'" Wolf air quoted. "That one is better or more real than the other. As if there's one in the first place. It's all just another hoax to mind fuck people and steal their money. Regardless, boo-hoo. Anyone can make it through hardship with a support system. You have a family. You had money . . . an uppity education. You always knew where your next meal would come from. At least you had a chance."

Flynn's eyes narrowed. She turned in her seat and edged forward. "Okay, so, because of that I can't know hardship? Resources can make things easier, yes, but it doesn't always mean you make it."

The boat tipped back and forth in gentle, rhythmic motions, bobbing over rolling whitecaps. It rocked her balance, tossing her into him. His back tensed, hands clasped around the wheel. They were so close the scent of soap floating off Wolf's skin tickled her nose. He pushed away and she shot back into her seat. Flynn still couldn't figure out why he always seemed so uneasy. . . . Did he only act this way around her?

"Life is hard," he mocked her. "Like you have any idea. You and your fucking privileged life."

"Did you not hear a single thing I just said? I carry an identity and stereotypes that define me everywhere I go. I constantly have to prove myself." Wolf might know her trigger points, but she had her own tricks up her sleeve. His walls might not come down on their own, but she could knock them down, or, better yet, incite his own anger to knock them down for her. "At least you can hide your face behind a mask like the fucking coward you are. You can hide behind your white masculinity. At least I don't put my blame on everyone else. I hold myself accountable. I don't let the assholes of this world define me like you have."

Like she predicted, something in Wolf snapped, unleashed from Pandora's box. "You have no idea what it's like to truly be alone. You pretend empathy or sympathy or whatever, but you have no idea. It's worse than any prejudice or injustice."

"How would *you* know?"

He loomed over her, fury decomposing his aloofness. "How would *I* know? Because I was passed around from home to home like some unwanted puppy until eventually, they threw me into a reform center. No one ever cared. No one's ever loved me. You can never understand that emptiness."

Stunned, she recoiled. *Maybe he's right.* The unwelcome thought nudged against her hatred toward him. She didn't know what it was like to live her whole life haunted by the knowledge that she was unwanted. Everyone wrote him off, so he wrote them off too.

Although they were so close she could touch him, he was unreachable, their universes far apart. Part of her wanted to hold him like a hurt child, to absorb some of his cold loneliness and replace it with human warmth. But her limbs were frozen, arms hugging herself tightly. She couldn't let herself forget what he really was—a murderer.

Wolf glared at the sadness spreading across her face. "I told you before, I don't want your sympathy. Is that what you think I need?" He jabbed a finger at his sternum, eyes flashing. "My whole life people looked down on me with pity but did *nothing.* That's why this world will never change—too many people do nothing. They just go about their lives buying shit they don't need and trolling people on Facebook to make themselves feel better."

It dawned on her suddenly that humanizing Wolf would require a more thoughtful, offensive strategy. Poking a bear only stirred him into a frenzy and fending off his attacks depleted too much of her energy. Taming a beast required deception. She would have to beat him into submission while allowing him to believe he was still in control.

Forcing herself to meet his accusatory stare, she straightened her shoulders, ready to reinstate emotional restraint. "I'm trying to do something now. I'm trying to understand you."

"It's too late. I don't need your *understanding*. REDS filled that hole years ago. They channeled my strengths into something meaningful when everyone else only gave a shit about themselves."

"Meaningful?" Her brows shot upward. "You call mass murdering innocent people *meaningful*?"

"Okay, whatever, fine, let's call it *effective action*."

The triumph on his face made her want to punch him. She used to think the barriers around Wolf's heart were insurmountable, but it was possible he just never had one to start with.

Don't let him win, she urged herself. *Take back control.*

"You're trying to make me hate you." She traced the floral pattern splattered over her silky pants. "You're pushing me away, like you've done with everyone else. How do you know people didn't try to help you, but you refused to see it?"

"I'm not *trying* to do anything. This is who I am." He shifted his weight, breaking their eye contact to stare out at the blue backdrop. Twinkling water rose to meet an infinite sky. "I don't give a shit what other people think, or what you think, and that right there is the definition of freedom."

Shit. Her front teeth raked over her bottom lip. Here she was focusing all her energy on changing Wolf, changing his point of view. But wasn't this what everyone had done his entire life—mold him into someone he never wanted to be? No. That's exactly what REDS did. They took advantage of him. They were the ones who distorted his view of the world.

She knew nothing about his past or what had led him to want to kill without a second thought. Who knew how many people he'd encountered who kicked him around, shoved him into the shadows, saw him as just a number, another lost child, until REDS seized the opportunity and radicalized him. How clever to shape it into something he viewed as empowerment instead of brainwashing.

"Have you ever considered maybe you're as bad as the people you hate?"

she asked. "You think your pain is the only injustice in this world. That no one else has ever felt abandoned. Don't you see? It's like I said; even those are shared experiences."

"REDS don't believe in feeling."

"Why? That's impossible."

"Because it's a weakness," he said.

Wolf had finally made it clear why he possessed such an impenetrable guard. His resistance toward emotion was a core principle of his livelihood. His all-consuming hatred was embedded so deeply within him it seemed irreversible. An unexpected urge to save him from REDS cut through the sickening revulsion Flynn had accumulated the past few weeks, unleashing fresh rage. "What have they done to you? Do you realize how brainwashed *you* sound?"

"Is this why you brought me out here, to lecture me? To convince me this world is a great place? To act like you actually *know* me?" His scowl wrinkled the smooth skin on his forehead into deep rows. "You told me you had something to tell me about the FBI. Alright, let's hear it."

She dropped her gaze to fidgeting fingers that wouldn't lay still. Sharp-beaked gulls dove and swooped around them, screaming at each other in high-pitched cries. "I just . . . I don't believe you're the emotionless person you say you are." She thought back to his racing heart the night she'd hugged him. "No matter what you say, we're all hardwired to seek human connection. It's a part of our evolution, our survival. I know there's more to you than hatred."

His brows dropped low over his eyes. "You're wrong. Save your psycho-analysis for someone who gives a shit."

"Sometimes it takes someone else to show you there are other paths you can take in life. You don't have to stay on the same one."

"Flynn." He rested his forearm on the steering wheel, ran a hand through his hair. "I know what you're trying to do. Nothing you say will change my mind about this mission."

"Let me show you there's still good in this world—a side to human-ity you haven't seen," she pleaded, grabbing his wrist. It was so thick her fingertips didn't touch. "A side you're blind to. It's not as simple as black and white. Like me, like you, sometimes our scars live under the surface of our skin." She searched his face, desperate for a trace of reconsideration.

He jerked his arm backward, freeing himself from her grasp, eyes resuming their glassy vacancy. Turning back to the control panel, he flipped a switch labeled "Blower." The boat hummed to life.

"If I haven't found good in humanity after twenty-seven years, I have a hard time believing you can show it to me now." Wolf pressed the ignition. The engine's roar sliced through the tumbling waves. A sharp gasoline odor overpowered the fresh breeze. "Wake up, Flynn. You can't solve this by sitting around in a circle holding hands and singing 'Kumbaya.' It's about time you come to terms with the fact that at the core, everyone is the same. They're all selfish assholes."

Sitting back in her chair, she braced for the lurching acceleration. *What the fuck was I thinking; this is impossible . . .*

"I don't understand what REDS's end goal is in all this," she yelled over the deep, guttural rumble. "What is it they want to achieve?"

"Societal breakdown." Wolf's voice was eerily casual.

"Wh-what?" she coughed, words stumbling in her throat. "Societal breakdown? How?"

A familiar shadow of a smile transformed his face, sending a shiver quaking through her. Evening had crept over them, spreading its languorous cloak. The lake's horizon blended into an indigo sky, melting into violet twilight. "You'll see."

"But, why?"

He yanked hard on the steering wheel, commanding the bow to point back to shore. "Destruction must come before creation, and from despair's ashes, a new order will rise."

Terror gripped her heart, freezing the blood coursing through her veins. "What does that mean?"

"Redemption for the oppressed. Execution for the unjust. Deliverance for the guilty. Salvation for the lost."

He recited the words mechanically, as if reading from a prayer book.

A cog jammed into a spinning gear, halting her body's ability to function. Redemption. Execution. Deliverance. Salvation. She had no idea the name REDS possessed a hidden meaning. Except it wasn't simply an acronym; it was a promise. A mission. "REDS . . ." she whispered.

The carnage at Soldier Field replayed in her memory, an endless recording that would never stop. The sensation of bodies falling around her—people's lives ending before screams could escape their open lips—would always haunt her. Gripping her empty stomach, she fought the urge to dry heave. Flynn was Wolf's last chess piece moved into position.

The question is whether I'm a pawn or the queen.

36

WOLF

Flynn kept quiet during the boat ride back to shore. In the fading sunlight she looked defeated, but Wolf knew she was scheming. Her twiglike arms wrapped around bony shins belied her power.

"I told you we aren't the same, Flynn," he yelled over the engine's bursts.

She tilted her head to watch him, chin resting on knees tucked tight against her chest. Sadness muted her eyes' usual luminous glow. Her body rocked as the boat skipped over waves.

"But we are," her voice floated between them, barely audible. "We're both driven; we just have different motivations. We're both passionate about what we care most about in this world, but we're . . . I dunno, we're fueled by different fires."

A flare of resentment shot through him. *She's using our similarities to her advantage, but she's not wrong,* he realized. *We're on an even playing field, and she knows it.* She was the first person he'd recognized as a counterpoint, an equal. An epiphany washed over him, shining a bright spotlight on the solution to an equation that he could never solve until now. *It's why I can't let her go.*

"We're also both afraid. Afraid of being vulnerable." Lowering her legs, she straightened, feet planted on the deck. Her head hovered right below his shoulder. "There. I said it. It's taken a long time to admit it, but getting to know you, I've come to recognize it in myself."

Something stirred deep in his core, jumping to life like an exposed animal darting for the safety of its den. "You don't know me."

"It takes courage to be vulnerable. Maybe we're both too afraid of what will happen if we allow ourselves to let our guard down. We think we have to lock everything inside to preserve ourselves, kinda like some fucked-up defense mechanism, but we don't. We won't collapse. It'll make us braver. Stronger."

"You have it backward. Vulnerability is weakness," he growled, clenching the throttle, pushing it forward. The motor revved, vibrating, propelling them faster. They skimmed over the water's surface, jerking forward when the bow bumped over frothy churn. "All of that emotional bullshit gets you nowhere; it just gets you hurt. It allows you to be manipulated."

"So what's the alternative then?" Flynn's question wasn't combative. Her voice carried a weight of exhaustion.

Wolf could see straight through her attempts to befriend him. He knew she had an ulterior motive to break him down, but a small part of him wondered if her efforts were genuine.

"Resilience," he said.

Wind whipped her hair around her face. Sighing, she blinked her long lashes against the strands. "Hmm. Can't say I know much about that one."

Could she be right when she accused me of not recognizing others' attempts to reach out to me? he wondered. As a child, he'd lived in an abyss of loneliness. He'd grown accustomed to its emptiness, and eventually its darkness had blinded him. *Am I still blind?*

Her lips twitched into a sad smile. "To be resilient you have to push through the hard stuff.... You have to bounce back from it. But I always let my fear get the better of me. I have too much to lose. It's why I can't make sacrifices or take risks, even if it's for something I believe in."

He decelerated the boat as they entered the wake zone. Her confession took him aback. *But she is resilient.* He scratched the prickly hairs sprouting over his neck. *Way more resilient than I could ever allow her to believe.*

"At least you know your limits. Probably for the best, anyway," he said. "If two opposing parties are uncompromising, no one ever wins."

Flynn turned her attention to the approaching city as they entered the harbor. Tiny lights blinked to life from the buildings, awakened by the dimming sky. Cutting the engine, he let the current carry them to the pier.

"Have people always tried to change you?" Her voice stretched tight with emotion, no longer having to shout above the wind. "Has anyone, including REDS, ever let you be who you wanted to be?"

Frowning, he shrugged. "REDS showed me who I was. They showed me how powerful I really am."

"But did they? They took a part of you and formed it the way they wanted. I guess what I mean is . . . they got what they wanted out of you, but did *you* get what you wanted?"

"You don't get it. I never liked who I was before them," Wolf said.

"Why not?"

It unsettled him how Flynn's authenticity disarmed him. Her raw questions lowered his defenses. "I dunno. No one liked or respected me, so how could I like myself?"

The sudden pain bludgeoning his abdomen knocked the wind out of him. Her probing questions forced him to say those words aloud, words he'd never even allowed himself to think. He'd compartmentalized the shame that once stalked him, locked it away for the sake of self-preservation. Their eyes met. He tried to pull his away. Something drew him to her, imprisoning him under her control. Panic tightened around his chest, recognizing danger.

"Do you like who you've become?" she asked.

"Haven't thought about it. You can't survive in REDS if you doubt yourself."

He hopped onto the dock and tied the boat in place. Flynn followed, stumbling out of the bucking cruiser. He steadied her as she clambered over its bow. She staggered forward into his arms, their skin colliding. The discreet lilac scent of her hair smacked him in the face. Every cell in his body screamed to pull away, but he stood paralyzed.

I never should have touched her. Fight it. Fight back.

Flynn stared up at him. Moisture clouded her eyes, triggering a deep primal instinct inside him—the need to protect her from everything, including himself.

How have I been so fucking stupid?

He'd been too preoccupied—too obsessed—with winning, convinced Flynn couldn't beat him at his own game. Except this entire time, she'd been playing her own. A different game, with different rules.

"You never had anything to tell me about the FBI, did you?" Despite his attempt to make his voice harsh and accusatory, it betrayed him, releasing as a whisper.

"There doesn't always need to be a winner, Wolf. Before I knew you, I didn't understand that people could be multifaceted. I formed my own judgments of you, like people have done your entire life. I never realized how easy it is for people to become what others believe of them." Her warm breath stroked his face. Orbed tears slid down her cheeks.

Have I finally broken her? Wolf thought. *If I did, it wasn't in the way I intended.*

"Instead of changing the world around you, others tried to change you, as if you were responsible." Flynn swiped at the stream, smearing wet mascara. "I never tried to understand what your life was like or to see it through your eyes. But I get it now—the empty loneliness. In the end, there's no winning or losing in this life. There's only living."

The rising moon cast a soft glow over them. His skin tingled, as if a bomb he'd spent months creating was seconds away from exploding in his face. He couldn't fight it anymore. Maybe he could surrender, just this once. It would be a loss that might yield to a later victory. He reached out to touch her, unable to resist her radiance, shining under the luminous warmth. All the blame—all the hate that had consumed him—melted to the dock beneath his feet. In its place, awe filled him, illuminating dark corners throughout his entire being.

She stepped closer, tears glistening. Without thinking, he let his lips find hers, heart fumbling in his chest. Cradling her face in his hands, she wrapped her arms around his torso, melding her body into his, erasing a pain Wolf had thought was ingrained in him forever. Bliss rumbled through him, spiking his endorphins, fogging his mind like a crazy high—a high he would never stop chasing.

She knew what she was doing this entire time, but I don't care.

Since the moment he first saw Flynn in the coffee shop years ago, he'd repressed all memory of her. He did everything in his power to escape her. But now here he was, back in the exact same place. She'd found him and weakened every defense he'd spent a lifetime creating.

37

WOLF

Later that evening, new recruits filtered into the training center for their first day of conditioning. There were fifteen of them. If five made it, Wolf would be impressed. Their eyes flitted back and forth, taking in their surroundings. Their knees were locked, mouths pressed into trembling grimaces as they tried to hide their fear, but their dilated pupils exposed them. They all wore familiar wounds, carried in their sloped posture, like broken soldiers returning from war. He knew those wounds. They never went away, but he'd learned to channel and feed off their residual pain.

Flynn was wrong when she said she and Wolf were the same. She didn't understand, could never understand, how their pasts divided them. His life had been sucked clean of all brightness. Its colors were muted, distorted . . . sometimes gone entirely. He stopped seeing people as humans long ago. Probably because they stopped seeing him as one.

It wasn't always that way. As a child, Wolf had been convinced he was a superhero. He'd waited for his powers to reveal themselves so he could save the world. In his imaginary landscape, he'd pretended to kill countless evil villains. He stood over their battered bodies, triumphant, while they suffered until their last breath.

Years later, he learned other kinds of brutality could destroy a person. True villains preyed on the depths of a human soul. They reached in and ripped it apart. Manipulation was their ultimate weapon, far more dangerous than physical harm. Villains preyed on the emotions that separated humans from animals. They went after the unimaginable—to places impossible to conjure in childhood fantasies.

* * * *

Wolf's first memory of his mother was blurred around the edges, so distant that he questioned at times if it happened at all. ComEd had cut the heat and electricity in their house . . . again. But that was typical. He couldn't remember where they lived, but he remembered the cold. His breath had formed small clouds, suspended in front of him momentarily before melting into darkness. He and Mom huddled on a thin mattress in the corner of an empty room lit by a single candle. Strange shapes danced around them in the light of its flickering flame, guardians against the surrounding gloom.

Rocking him on her lap, she sang a quiet melody, her voice a soothing conductor for the shadows' eerie choreography.

Hush little baby, don't say a word, Mommy's gonna buy you a mockingbird . . .

"It's time to leave, baby," she whispered into his ear.

She extinguished the candle's flame, summoning the lurking darkness. He clutched his one belonging, a stuffed bear wearing a lopsided smile. The fuzzy patches of fur that remained had become mangled and dirty; its missing eye and ear were evidence of foul play, but he hadn't cared.

"No, sweetie. Bear has to stay here."

"Mommy, I can't leave him. He's my only friend."

Bundling him against her chest, she crouched below the partially boarded window. An aroma of fresh flowers mingled in her sandy blonde hair.

"Shhhh, okay, we can bring Bear, but now it's time to play a game. If you keep very, very quiet until Mommy says so, we'll share your favorite chocolate bar."

He puckered his lips, and his stomach rumbled. It'd been another day without food. Mom crept into their tiny kitchen, ragged socks muting her footsteps. She held him to her so tightly her fingers left white, circular indentations on his skin.

"Mommy, you forgot my shoes."

Deep voices approached their front steps. She froze, body morphing into a statue. Pounding echoed through the empty house, shattering the silence. It matched her heartbeat hammering against his cheek. He peered over her shoulder as she skated toward the back door.

"Baby, don't say a word," she breathed.

They slipped out into the cold night. The warmth of her body was a sanctuary, the sway of her running lulling him to sleep. He woke to his mother lifting him away from her. Tears streamed down her pale cheeks. She pressed her lips to his head, body convulsing in sobs. White light from a nearby window streamed onto the stoop where she laid him, casting them in a holy glow. It was impossible to forget her hollow eyes, identical to his. Every day they stared back at him in the mirror. As she ran away, monsters waiting in the darkness swallowed her whole.

It was the last time he saw her.

✶ ✶ ✶ ✶

Things got worse in school. Wolf had been an outcast, the invisible blemishes on his personality driving everyone away. Kids avoided him. Teachers didn't know what to do with him. The administration threw in the towel. He was expelled for good in third grade.

He had punched Tony Barilli in the nose. Probably broke it. That was the final straw. Bruised knuckles swelling, he clasped his hands in his lap, eager to get another lecture over with. His legs swung back and forth under his seat, scuffing the floor.

Mr. Perkins sighed, slid his square glasses onto his forehead, and rubbed his eyes. "There's no excuse, *ever*, to respond physically and harm a classmate. That's why we teach you to use your words."

"Words hurt more. You don't forget words, Principal Perkins," Wolf argued.

The stern line of Mr. Perkins's mouth turned down into a frown. "This is your *fifth* incident this month. Your foster parents have threatened to surrender you unless you clean up your act." He waited for Wolf to show some sign of regret. "I'm disappointed in you."

Wolf peered up at him through his fringe of dirty blonde hair. "I don't care. I hate Mr. and Mrs. Mercer and I hate it here. I want to get suspended. I don't want to come back."

"You don't mean that, son. I know you can be a good boy. You're very bright and if you would just apply yourself, you'd have a great future ahead of you."

"I am not your son! I am nobody's son!" Wolf yelled, his ten-year-old frame shaking with rage. A familiar ugly beast swelled within him.

Mr. Perkins's shoulders sagged and he shook his head, rising to his feet. "I'll call the Mercers to pick you up."

Wolf shrugged, picked at a growing hole in his sweatpants. The bell rang, signaling the end of the school day. The hallways flooded with children, filling the air with gleeful yells, stampeding footsteps, and shouts of triumph. He stared out the office window overlooking the crammed line of cars winding in front of the school. Parents greeted their children, arms outstretched for warm embraces. Wolf hovered, scowling, on the outskirts of a reality entirely separate from his own, never participating, never invited.

When everyone else gave up on him, it was easy to give up on himself.

* * * *

So, what's left when no one wants you? *Nothing.* That's how Wolf got used to feeling nothing. It was better than feeling alone. Mrs. Mercer eventually took him to the Abbott Juvenile Reform Center, handing him back over to the state—returning a kid like how one would return an ugly coat.

The center director shuffled through mounds of paperwork scattered over his desk, oversized round glasses resting on the tip of his stumpy nose. He was a large man, visibly uncomfortable in his bulky form. Any movement required a significant amount of effort and a concentrated exertion of energy. After five minutes, he managed to extract Wolf's file from a stack of battered folders balanced precariously on a filing cabinet. He flipped through it, breathing heavily in short huffs. Wolf remembered hating his sausage fingers and the way the man seemed to be looking for any opportunity to point at him . . . always staring with his bushy eyebrows folded in.

"Hmm," the director wheezed, "it doesn't look like there's any background information included in the paperwork faxed over by the state. No documented parents. No social security number. Not even a bloody birthday." He stared down at Wolf with doubtful scrutiny, as if he were a whining puppy in the pound. "His mother could have birthed him in the back of a truck for all we know."

"The fire department found him outside their door when he was about four years old. That's the extent of what the Illinois State Department told us," Mrs. Mercer chimed in for context. "All he had were the clothes on his back. We're the eighth family to foster him since then."

Wolf ignored the adults talking about him as if he weren't right there and concentrated on the wave of resentment coursing through him at the mention of his mother.

"Mrs. . . . umm—"

"Mercer."

"Right. Mrs. Mercer, I'm sorry, but we're at full capacity. We don't have room to take on another child in his age group. Especially one with so many documented behavioral issues."

"Please. There's nothing else we can do for him. He needs a professional facility to help him. He received full psychiatric testing and his results came back normal, whatever that means. His IQ is off the charts; it's just his emotional intelligence that seems . . . well, nonexistent. He needs some solid structure and we have too many other kids in our care to give him the undivided attention he needs."

The director's gaze roamed over Wolf, taking in his small, unassuming form. Wolf busied himself tracing the orange spiral patterns trailing over the shag carpet with his toe.

"I suppose we can squeeze him into Ward C with some of the younger boys."

* * * *

Wolf had never flown in an airplane, but he often wondered what was hovering on the other side of clouds. Did the sun shine up there even on rainy days? Kissing Flynn was the most awakening moment he'd ever experienced. It was how he imagined bursting through a thick wall of storms into a world of blue skies would feel.

Maybe Flynn's right, Wolf admitted to himself. *Maybe it is my fault I'm alone.* After all, he'd been socially inept from the beginning. He'd spent his time at the reform center wandering the halls of Ward C, a ghost drifting through empty space, a hollow shell incapable of feeling. It didn't take long for reality to thwart his dream of becoming a superhero. The world he lived in was no longer worth saving. In his childhood comic books, battles raged between good and evil with no gray area between the two. He decided that if he couldn't be the superhero, then he'd take control of his destiny another way. He didn't want to merely exist. He wanted to follow the new path that called to him with seductive promise.

He wanted to become the villain.

38

FLYNN

Glancing over both shoulders as she stepped out from under the train station's covered platform, Flynn pulled her hood lower over her head. A late-summer storm poured sheets of rain over the gloomy city. It was the perfect Sunday to curl up on the couch and binge-watch an entire Netflix series. Brisk air carried the promise of an early fall. Summer's long days of hazy warmth were numbered. Time now seemed muddled together, and she couldn't believe it had been almost three months since the Green Line concert.

Since she was no longer burdened by the FBI's watchful scrutiny after basically firing them, a small part of her basked in this freedom she once took for granted. But right as she felt herself rising, lifting upward with lightness, her chains yanked her back to earth, shackling her to the ground. That freedom was an illusion; it didn't exist. She was still REDS's prisoner.

Flynn crossed a bridge spanning over a busy highway. Cars whizzed by below, leaving hissing trails of spray in their wake. The vehicles' whoosh and rumbling were the only sounds echoing through the streets, other than her squelching footsteps on uneven concrete. The orange glow of a nearby streetlamp cast strange shadows on the neighboring buildings.

Three blocks past the bridge, she reached a battered mid-rise apartment complex. Peeling block letters clung to the main storefront's window. "Mike's Barbershop." A faded welcome mat waited forlornly outside the door, as if it hadn't seen foot traffic in years. She squinted at it in the dim light, obscured by the building's overhang, trying to read the nearly illegible joke stamped on top. "The neighbors have better stuff."

The barber pole beside the door no longer displayed blue-and-red stripes twisting in an endless candy-cane ribbon; a faded white cylinder flecked with spots of color was all that remained. She pushed open the door. Had the homeless man given her the right tip, or had he delivered her straight to a drug lord?

Five other homeless people had ignored her, dismissing her request with angry grunts and waves. She'd finally come across an old man under a walking bridge in the park across from her building. His meager belongings, probably salvaged from the garbage, were stacked around him like a fortress. A sharp, moldy stench radiated from his body, forcing her to breathe through her mouth. His bleary eyes had looked her up and down in paranoid speculation. He didn't ask any questions. He simply replied to her request, "World's a darker place now, 'init?"

A little bell signaled her entrance into a small room with a single barber chair positioned before a cloudy mirror. An old box TV hosting a thin film of dust sat on an overturned bucket in the corner. The scraping of a chair against laminate shrieked in the adjacent room.

"Now don't come traipsing your wet boots all over my floor!"

A heavyset man blundered through the swinging door. He staggered to a halt when he saw her. Shallow breath huffing in her intimidated silence, he scratched his scraggly, reddish beard, taking her in. His hair was parted to the side, wild curls expanding outward in the humidity so it looked like two giant balls of frizz sat on either side of his head. A pair of weathered suspenders held his jeans in place around his expansive waist. He met the exact description the homeless man had provided.

"You got an appointment?"

She glanced around the vacant salon. "No, sir."

"Well, what'd you want then?"

"I'm h-here for a clean back shaving." Stumbling over the bizarre request, her voice cracked.

Mike the Barber squinted at her, doubt creasing his forehead. "Honey, a girl like you can get one of those straight."

"It can't be documented."

He didn't take his eyes off her face. "Sorry, lady, I got nothin' for ya."

"You do." Flynn kept her voice even. "I know from a reliable source you're always well stocked."

"Who told you 'bout this?"

"I found the right person."

He released a long puff through gritted teeth. The forced air made a high-pitched whistle. His thumbs looped around his suspenders. "I don' take fancy credit cards."

"I have cash."

"How much you got?"

"Enough."

He deliberated for a full minute as she stood her ground, legs trembling. Finally, he scratched his head and turned toward the door, waving for her to follow.

"Eh, if you were a cop, you woulda busted me by now."

She kept her mouth shut. It was probably best not to inform Mike if she was a cop waiting to arrest him, she would need a plausible reason.

He led her into a tiny kitchen dominated by a table and two chairs crammed together in its center. Their shoulders brushed against each other uncomfortably, but there was no room to spread out farther. He yanked open a door leading to a shallow pantry with a dirty mop and a corn broom tucked inside. Tossing the cleaning tools behind them, he grabbed a beaded chain dangling from an empty lightbulb socket. Grunting, he gave it a sharp pull. The ceiling dropped, extending into a set of steep stairs.

Mike sucked in a breath in an attempt to flatten his stomach and squeezed himself through the doorway. He heaved himself onto the first few steps. The wood bent, groaning under his weight. He glanced down at her.

"You coming?"

"Guess I have no choice," she mumbled, terrified Mike would come crashing down and squish her. Clutching the ancient stairs in front for balance, she started her ascent.

The stuffy attic bore a low-hanging ceiling. Mike stooped over to avoid hitting his head. A skylight in the sloping roof provided the only source of dim light, diffused by overhanging clouds. Sheets of rain streaked down the dirty pane of glass in streaming trails that diverged into new ones as the raindrops continued drumming down, their sound amplified in the confined space.

Mike reached inside a large wooden cabinet for a pair of thick gloves. Panting, he pushed the piece of furniture to the other side of the room. He returned to the wall, prying away thin plywood and cotton candy insulation to reveal a safe wedged between two beams.

In a few flicks of Mike's wrist, the safe swung open. She tried to peek around him, but he blocked her view. He withdrew three guns and placed them on a rickety table covered with rusty tools.

"Never had someone like you in here before. What's a city girl like you need one of these for?"

She stared in disbelief at the array of weapons displayed in front of her.

"Personal business," she said. She gnawed her lower lip, her eyes scanned the table. "I don't know what any of these are."

He released an impatient sigh and pointed to two black guns. They were pernicious and intimidating, with what looked like matchboxes protruding from their sleek bellies. She assumed that was what held the ammunition— the bullets that sliced into people and ended their lives as quickly and effortlessly as turning off a light.

"Submachine guns. This right here is an Uzi and this one's an MP5."

Shuddering, she recalled the chilling, tightly packed bursts reverberating through Soldier Field. "No, none of those."

"Alright." He moved on to the larger one with a nylon strap and a wooden handle. "How about an assault rifle? This here's an AK-47. If you wanna do some real damage, this is your gal."

A tsunami of panic threatened to pour out of her chest. Her breathing became shallow. Unable to look away from the illegal arsenal, she felt her hands grow slick with cold sweat.

"No. No assault rifles either," she croaked, her hoarse voice weak. "I only need one or two shots."

Grumbling, Mike turned back to his safe and removed a small black handgun. He held it out to her. She stared at it, loathing and disgust swirling together at the thought of what these sorts of weapons had done to her—what they'd done to so many innocent people.

"You gonna take it or what?"

Finally, she reached out and accepted it, stomach lurching when the smooth metal rested against her skin.

"It's basic, but it'll do the trick. An M9." She swallowed down the acid rising in her throat. He nodded toward the gun hanging limply from her grasp. "You ever use one of these before?"

She shook her head. Beads of sweat from the thick, humid air dotted his brow. His dark eyes widened. "Just point and pull the trigger. That's all there is to it."

39

FLYNN

Monday mornings were rough enough for Flynn without having to figure out how to confront Wolf. They hadn't spoken since Friday evening . . . the evening of their boat ride. *Do we talk about it, or do we pretend like it never happened?* Quintessential female relationship analysis. Oh, the irony. It was enough to make her burst out in uncontrollable laughter. Not fun, hysterical laughter. Frantic, crazed laughter.

Then there was Nate. She'd promised she would tell him something by today. Mollifying him was no longer an option. He'd demand answers. No doubt the kiss was successful, a home run even. A fissure of Wolf's humanity had finally expanded into a crack. Problem was, who knew what would emerge from its depths. Lava? A bubbling spring? Sunlight? The strange conflicting feelings that followed were worse than she expected. Guilt and determination had jabbed at each other the entire weekend. On the one hand, she had broken him down, exactly as she'd intended. On the other, she'd finally gotten a glimpse behind the curtain into his previous life, and it had been so utterly sad. She'd danced back and forth between wanting to kill Wolf and wanting to hold him again—to expunge his pain. Given this paradox, there were moments she questioned her sanity.

When she arrived at the office, she sought him out immediately. Her stomach rolled with queasiness and her limbs shook as if she'd downed three shots of espresso.

Better get this over with. Saliva stuck to the roof of her mouth, building in the back of her throat. The gun's weight in her bag was a silent reminder of her pending decision. *How am I going to look into Wolf's eyes and kill him?* she wondered. He wouldn't expect it. He'd made it clear that he didn't think she had it in her. And did she? There were times it unnerved her how easily he seemed to be able to read her.

But something in her moved when Wolf had kissed her—something she would do anything to smother into nothing. Maybe there was more to him, more than she could've imagined. Maybe the kiss broke some evil spell feeding on his soul. Or maybe this was yet another crazy fantasy she'd whipped up in her head.

When she got to his desk, it was empty.

He's usually here by now. Glancing around, she waited several minutes, praying he'd appear wearing his usual hostile scowl. *What's scarier than knowing where Wolf is? Not knowing.*

Unsettled, she headed to the café for breakfast, doing her best not to jump to conclusions. He could be working up there, trying hard to avoid her. *Don't think about him. Focus on the day ahead. Knock off items on the to-do list.* She bit down hard on the inside of her cheek.

By lunchtime, Wolf still hadn't shown up. His computer and chair remained untouched, vacant since last Friday. Panic blistered her lungs. What if he was dead? Pushing a deep breath through her nostrils, she tried to calm her wired nervous system. That could be a good thing. It would relieve her of that pressure. She approached the small office diagonal from Wolf's desk. Clear floor-to-ceiling glass separated it from the main sitting area. Dan, the hiring manager she'd worked with to hire Wolf, was hunched over a keyboard, fingers pecking furiously.

Peeking through the open door, she knocked, startling him.

"Yes?"

"Any idea whether Chris is coming in today? I wanted to speak with him about possibly interviewing a few candidates."

Scratching his balding head, he craned it toward Wolf's desk, eyebrows creasing. "Hmm, I don't know. I can't remember if he asked off today or not.

Seems unlike him to not show only two weeks in. Must be sick." His magnified eyes scanned over her from behind thick glasses. "He might've emailed me. I haven't gotten through my inbox yet. Needed to address some other pressing matters. Also, I need those three open heads we discussed last week filled. We're dying over here."

He returned to his screen, lips moving silently, signaling an end to their conversation. *Thanks for nothing, Dan*, she thought to herself.

Annoyed, she walked into a nearby conference room to watch and wait for Wolf. Any hope of getting work done now was shot. This was so typical of him—operating on his own schedule. Keeping her in the dark, per usual. If she'd pulled this shit, he would be livid. She'd have to deal with a weeklong string of threats.

Over an hour later, Wolf was still absent.

Something's wrong. Magnetic is a new job; he can't risk drawing unnecessary attention to himself by not showing up. Not while he's still pursuing his own agenda. Unless . . . he's already succeeded.

Frantic, she pulled his calendar up on her laptop. Today was outlined in red.

And on there he'd written: "Game Day."

Her hand froze over her mouth. Wolf had mentioned it the other evening with disturbing detachment. The clock over her head read two o'clock. Its needle-thin second hand ticked by with uncompromising certitude, inching closer to an unknown fate. Wolf could be one step away from inflicting unthinkable harm. He could be minutes from achieving his mission.

She bolted for the door. There was only one person in the world she could confide in. Even though they technically weren't on speaking terms, Nate would never turn away from helping her. Flynn sprinted to the floating staircase, tripping forward as she descended two flights as fast as her feet could carry her.

"Nate!"

Nate looked up from his computer, fear flooding his face when he saw her expression. She gulped for air.

"What's wrong?"

"We need to get out of here," she whispered, working hard to keep her voice steady.

"What? Now? And go where?"

"I think something's about to happen."

Nate rocketed to his feet. "What do you mean? Are we in danger?"

She shook her head. "Not here, but others might be somewhere else."

"Can we call your escort to pick us up?"

"Their services ended last week."

He rubbed his jaw, scrutinizing her desperation.

"Alright." He clicked off his monitor. "Let's go."

They swung by her desk so she could drop off her computer and grab her bag before exiting the building. Magnetic's office sat on the outskirts of downtown, in the West Loop neighborhood. Once an industrial area, it had transitioned into a modern hub full of tech start-ups and trendy restaurants. They headed toward the city's center, walking at an unnaturally brisk pace. Rush hour traffic had already filled the streets. Roads teemed with cars, drivers honking irritably as they headed home at the end of their workday. Swarms of people brushed past, muttering into their phones or mouthing into the air on Bluetooth headphones.

"Where are we going?" Nate dodged a swinging purse.

"Don't know," she admitted, already out of breath. "My gut says head to the area with the most people."

"The Loop," he said. "Is this about REDS?"

She nodded, unable to speak. Fresh fear washed over her at the mention of their name. "Chris never showed up to work today. I have no way of tracking him down."

"Wait, the new guy? So he *is* one of them?"

Wincing, she tried to repress memories of Soldier Field—of the horror REDS was capable of committing. They crossed onto a bridge leading to the financial district. On either side of them, neighboring bridges spanned the length of the Chicago River, connecting the Loop with outer parts of the city.

Nate stopped, grabbed her shoulders. "Flynn, you hired him? You let one of them into Magnetic?"

The bridge vibrated as cars barreled past. Beneath their feet, the rippling river winked through the metal grates. She forced herself to meet Nate's gaze. It wasn't accusatory or angry. It was a look of terror.

"Yes." Her voice caught, as if invisible hands had wrapped around her throat. He stiffened, absorbing the blow of her response. "I had to. REDS threatened to kill everyone. My family. Cori. You."

They stood there, staring at each other, when a *pop, pop, pop* interrupted the usual city noise. Nate opened his mouth, lips forming a silent "O." They both instantly recognized the sound piercing through the bustling rush hour commotion. His grip on her arms tightened, face draining of color.

The distinct clips turned into a steady stream of machine gunfire.

"N-n-no!" Her heart surged. "No, it can't be . . . " She grabbed Nate's shirt as the world tilted.

They took off in the direction of the shots, their feet floating over the pavement seemingly in slow motion. They didn't have a plan, but they knew REDS was the source and countless people were in extreme danger. Maybe there was an inkling of a chance they could help. The bridge began to tremble. A train on the tracks above them groaned to a halt with a series of reverberating clanks, suspended over the river. Streams of people walking against them swiveled their heads toward the staccato bursts, faces squinting in confusion. Flynn and Nate shoved past, dodging two women pushing strollers, and kept running at full speed toward the city center.

At Wacker Drive, a curving, four-lane highway framing the perimeter of the Loop, a throng of pedestrians clustered at the crosswalk waiting for the walk signal. The light turned red. Flynn and Nate bulldozed through the thick crowd.

"Turn around!" Nate yelled. "Don't go into the city!"

Cars crept to a halt behind a growing stalemate, landlocked by the surrounding river.

Suddenly, a blast on their right surged down the length of the street. Nate shoved Flynn against the side of a marble building, shielding her body with his own. Screams carried over the crackling aftermath. Drivers threw open their vehicle doors, leaving them abandoned in the middle of the street as they fled. People swarmed over the bridge, desperate to escape the city.

Another deafening explosion pitched the two of them forward. They staggered against each other, almost falling to their knees. Crouching against the side of the marble building, Flynn threw her hands over her ears. The bridge behind them blazed, completely engulfed in flames. Angry black smoke billowed upward into the sky, expanding outward like fiery demons escaping from hell. The metal beams groaned as they weakened in the fiery furnace, unable to withstand the crushing heat.

Nate's face slackened with shock. "Oh my god."

Dismembered body parts, caught within the explosion's force, scattered over the street with sickening thuds. People flailed wildly, unable to shed the flames destroying their bodies, wailing in prolonged agony. They charged into the river, filling the air with the nauseating smell of singed skin, hair, and bones. Bellowing pedestrians retreated from the severed bridge and sprinted down Wacker Drive, lunging over each other in their panic.

Nate stared helplessly as the train hanging from the bridge's underbelly fell away and tumbled into the river. It floated on the surface for an instant before slowly sinking into the watery depths. He inched toward the scene, watching as people scrambled and clawed their way out of the few open doors or cracked windows. He pivoted to face Flynn. Sweat streamed down his pale forehead into hollow, empty eyes.

"Go!" she yelled. "Go help them! Someone needs to!"

"I'm not leaving you." His voice was fierce. "Not again!"

A siren's scream accentuated the surrounding chaos. Fire trucks blared their horns into inert traffic, red lights swirling. Flynn dropped her backpack and tore it open. Her throat closed as the gun's heavy metal touched her skin.

"Nate, go! There's something I need to do!"

"Flynn." Nate reached for her gun.

"GO!" She yanked it away. "Those people in the river . . . We don't have time to argue. But I . . . I might be able to stop him."

"You can't stop him." His fingers gripped her wrist. "It's too late."

"No!" she screamed, ripping her arm free. "I have to try. These people"— she pointed to a woman dragging her child from the train compartment as it disappeared beneath the water's surface—"help them! They need you more than I do. Don't follow me; I'll come back. Meet at the river."

Flynn dove into the crowd before he could respond. As she sprinted to the train station two blocks ahead, more people spilled out of buildings, some pulling off high-heeled shoes to run barefoot along the concrete.

Right as she was about to cross under the elevated platform, a third explosion threw her sideways. The overhead tracks ignited in a giant scorching ball of light. The air was sucked from her lungs, displaced by smoke. Coughing, heaving, she crawled forward, gun scraping the pavement. The world dipped as she staggered to her feet. Bloodied, dazed faces floated by. Metal and wood cascaded down on them. She stumbled, dizzy, ears ringing, unsure of where to go. A burning sensation grazed her scalp from above. Sparks rained over her shoulders, briefly illuminating the thick wall of smoke. Her eyes and nostrils stung with every scorching inhale.

She blindly shuffled toward a gray clearing, her mouth sealed against the thick snowfall of soot and debris. *Just a bit farther,* she told herself. *Only a few more steps. Push through the darkness. He has to be close. He has to be.*

Suddenly, her heart stammered to a stop. A tall form materialized before her, appearing out of thick air. Wolf's distinct, rigid posture emerged from the alcove of a storefront entryway. Tears streamed down her face, partially from the smoke and partially from the pain ripping into her chest like razor-sharp talons. Fury roared inside her, so powerful her limbs trembled. It was blinding, uncontrollable—toxic unless released. Gasping for breath, she aimed the gun at his back.

Sensing her presence, Wolf turned. It took less than a second for him to register that she held a loaded weapon. But his response didn't look like fear. His expression was curious, as though he wondered what her next move might be.

He was waiting for her to pull the trigger.

40

WOLF

The sharp sound of flying shrapnel echoed off the surrounding buildings. Mass panic had ensued on the street below the elevated train platform. Police sirens wailed in the distance. Wolf walked against throngs of people sprinting away from the city center, tearing in every direction. He breathed in the smell of fear, allowing a wave of calm to wash over him.

Yes. This is what I'm meant to do, he thought, triumphant. *This is where I'm meant to be. Finally, normalcy.*

A halfblock from the station, he stepped off the street into the doorway of a small eatery, abandoned in the frenzy. Cracking his neck, he waited for the sound of the Semtex explosion, signaling the electrical substation's destruction. Tension released from his body. Flynn's presence over the past few weeks had frayed his nerves, splitting them into wiry strands.

I have control again. Complete control. Nothing could compare to the comfort of knowing that nothing in his way stood a fucking chance.

"Wolf in position," he growled into the microphone.

He leaned out of his alcove, watching the station. Above its entrance, a sign in white block letters against a brown background announced its location, "Washington & Wells." Sweat dripped down his back. Humidity wrapped a blanket of suffocating heat around him. A small breeze from the nearby lake carried with it momentary relief before it retreated, leaving the thick air stickier than before.

Falcon's timing was crucial, choreographed to align with Croc reaching his target on the river.

"Approaching target now," Falcon said. "Sayonara, folks. Been an honor doing business with ya. Hit in three, two, one—"

An eruption reverberated through the streets. Falcon had detonated the EMP right before bulldozing straight into another train stopped on the tracks in front of him. Tremors from the impact rippled through the city's epicenter. A cloud of thick black smoke unfurled into the sky. People screamed, dove for cover, looked up for the source of the sound. Electricity flickered in nearby shops before extinguishing in exhausted defeat.

"Croc, what's your status?" Wolf asked.

"Under target. Second detonation in three, two, one—"

Another boom rolled over the city. Flooded streets crawled with bodies, a school of minnows scattering away from hungry sharks. No one knew which way was safe. No one knew where the next explosion might be. Eyes wild, they ran in all directions, streaming around abandoned vehicles. A laugh bubbled up Wolf's throat. He clenched his jaw against it but couldn't help releasing a large grin.

Sheep. In the end, they're always sheep. No matter what skins they hide under, their true nature will be revealed.

Static from Falcon's and Croc's microphones crackled in his earpiece. Pulling a small tablet from his vest, he activated the test malware, signaling phones in the area to emit an electromagnetic pulse. Another Semtex bomb waited in the station's handicap elevator bank. One of Weasel's men had placed it there, posing as a technician during a routine maintenance check. He braced his body against the oncoming blast. Several long seconds passed. The bomb ignited within the elevator shaft. A massive eruption traveled upward like lava shooting from a volcano, enrobing the platform in flame. With a deafening roar, the explosion's force sent people flying. The platform caved in two. Fiery plumes erupted into the sky, twisting the steel frame into a strange sculpture. Thick, billowing smoke enveloped the area.

People staggered past him, coughing and covered in soot, some dragging others along with them. Bright blood streamed down their faces, trickling over their ears and lips. Missing limbs spouted gushing arteries and burns revealed marbled muscle. Waves of rubble cascaded onto the street.

Now this is a goddamn glorious scene.

Beautiful as it might be, Wolf only had a few minutes to make his way to the river to meet Weasel for pickup. Their getaway window was small. Ducking out from his alcove, he prepared to jog toward the city outskirts. As he relished the madness all around him, excitement flared inside his chest, filling his lungs. Until a small form behind him caught his eye.

No. It can't be her.

His stomach plummeted, a bird shot down after taking flight. Flynn stood before the smoldering platform, her figure barely distinguishable in the screen of smoke. He could make out the faint outline of her face, her features set in rigid determination. She raised her arms in front of her, pointing a gun straight at him.

41

FLYNN

Three. Two. One, Flynn counted down in her head. Amid the sea of people flowing through the intersection, a tide of bodies pushing onward, she kept her eyes locked on Wolf.

The platform behind her burst into flames, crackling and roaring. Debris and rubble tumbled around them. *Do it. Just do it. You can't let him live. How many more will die if you let him live?* She gritted her teeth, screamed at herself to pull the fucking trigger. To kill him.

Gloved fingers emerged from the smoke screen, grabbing her wrist. The gun clattered to the pavement. A rough hand twisted her arm behind her. She cried out, back arching against the pain radiating down her shoulder. A razor blade pressed against her throat. One swipe, one flick of the wrist, and it would all be over. Through the hazy mirage of heat and ash, she saw fear materialize on Wolf's face. Fear? She'd never seen him wear that emotion so starkly. Holding her breath, she lifted her chin away from the sharp edge. Head swimming, she waited. She waited for the gushing blood.

Please be quick, Flynn prayed. *Please be painless.*

Wolf sprinted toward them. The ferocity in his eyes sent chills skating over her scalp. He pulled a gun from a thin vest underneath his shirt.

Shoot me. Spare me from a slow, miserable death. She closed her eyes. Fate kept leading her back to this moment. *I'm meant to die. Here. At the mercy of REDS.*

A shot sounded, echoing through the now deserted streets. She braced herself for the bullet's impact, tensing against the pain about to rip through her. The razor blade clattered beside her feet; at the same time, the grip holding her slackened. Coughing and choking, she staggered forward, falling to her knees. Behind her, the lifeless Enforcer slumped on his back, his spilled blood leaving a black trail over his silk mask.

Wolf grabbed her, dragging her away from the body. Her legs buckled, mind woozy and numb.

"Flynn, what the fuck are you doing here?" His voice was low and urgent. "We need to run. We've gotta get out of here."

"Don't touch me!" she spluttered, pitching sideways. Her palms hit the pavement. Gravel dug into her skin. She wanted him to leave her. She wanted to give up. "I can't. I don't want to go any further."

He pulled one of her arms over his shoulder, wrapping a hand around her waist. Each time she came into contact with his body, it always surprised her how hard it was, like pressing against a wooden plank. A vest, strapped around his torso, was its sole cushioning.

"You're just gonna give up, huh? After all that? Come on, move!"

Flynn didn't have the energy to fight him. "Leave me. Just leave me alone!"

"I'm not leaving you here. It's too dangerous."

He's dangerous. More dangerous than the burning buildings.

Piercing fury exploded through her exhausted muscles, giving them new life. "You did this." The words released in sharp bursts. Her anger was so overpowering she could barely form a sentence. "You—*you* did all of this."

"Yeah, and? I told you this was coming."

He dragged her down a narrow alleyway, one of the last unobstructed paths leading away from the city. Smoke had seeped through the streets, spreading with merciless speed. It blanketed the area in an eerie, haunted silence. The only sounds were of their feet pounding over the pavement and ringing sirens in the distance.

Gasping for air, Flynn struggled to breathe through the thick ash pressing against her mouth like a wet cloth. Wolf pulled her around large dumpsters and parked cars. He half carried her as if she weighed as much as a preschool backpack. Her feet tripped over each other, trying to keep up. He leaned down and scooped her up. No longer inhibited by her clumsiness, he ran faster.

Fresh rage smoldered inside her chest, growing with each second she lay helpless in his arms. She wanted to resist. She wanted to kick and scream like a tantrumming child until he put her down. No matter what she did, Wolf was steps ahead of her. And exactly like he'd predicted, she couldn't kill him. Instead, he'd saved her. Again. *Or had he?* If he'd just let her die, she wouldn't still be stuck in this nightmare.

"We need to get to the Yacht Club." Sweat ran down Wolf's face and neck, staining his dark gray shirt with rings of black. The moisture rubbed against her bare skin. Turning a corner, they headed east toward the lake. "Just a little farther."

"Put me down," she demanded. "I never want to see you again."

Abruptly, they staggered to a halt. Wolf's grip on her tightened. Five enormous figures emerged from the haze several yards in front of them. A row of identical crimson masks blocked their path, carrying raised guns. For a second, her vision went dark, heart crumbling to the pavement. She couldn't escape them. Wolf placed Flynn back on her feet, shifting his body to shield her. Her fingers wrapped around the fabric of his shirt, binding them together. She dropped her forehead against his back, overcome with dread.

Make it end.

"Another hostage, Wolf? Looks like the same one we've been dealing with."

Flynn peered over his shoulder. An Enforcer walked toward them, gun trained on Wolf's heart. His shrouded eyes shone beneath his black hood.

Wolf's shoulders were so tense they might snap. He surveyed the line of men, probing for an exit strategy. She clenched her jaw to quiet her teeth's violent chattering.

"Tiger. This is none of your fucking business."

"Hyena told me about this one. I thought your work with her was done. It's time to get rid of her. Or do you need me to do it for you?"

"Touch her and I kill you."

Tiger's lip curled into a snarl. Puckered red scars were visible through the eye holes of his mask. Flynn made herself as small as possible, trying to disappear behind Wolf. "Where's Puma? He radioed us to come get you."

Wolf swallowed. "He didn't make it."

Tiger raised the gun to Wolf's temple. "Try again."

"We lost him," Wolf said.

Tiger aimed the gun in her direction. In a flash, Wolf disarmed him, slamming him to the ground. The remaining Enforcers closed on them, guns angled in from all directions. One of them grabbed her from behind, pulling her toward him. Wolf's shirt ripped from her fingers. He spun around, lunging for her. An Enforcer intercepted him, smashing the butt of his gun into Wolf's temple. He collapsed to his knees.

A piece of her shattered as the gun collided with Wolf's head. "Get off me!" she yelled. She tore at the arms holding her in place. "Let me go!"

Wheezing, Tiger rose to his feet. He looked down at Wolf with disgust. "Interesting turn of events." He rubbed the back of his neck, eyes dancing back and forth between them. "I can't decide which of you I want to kill more."

Flynn strained against the iron grip. Wolf remained on all fours, unmoving, a thin trail of blood sliding down his cheek. Desperate, she sunk her teeth into her captor's forearm.

"Ah! Dumb bitch," he cursed, releasing her.

Tiger grabbed her around the waist before she could sprint away. "No, no. Time to come with us. Spider's been waiting for you. He thought you two might be a package deal."

42

WOLF

Blindfolded, hands cuffed in front of her, Flynn's pale skin was coated in a sheen of sweat. Enforcers towered over her, ogres guarding a fawn. The night was steamy with no moon as the van's tires crunched up the gravel drive. Taking her by the arms, two REDS dragged her through the back service door of the abandoned church. Her feet skimmed stray pebbles, shoes leaving a dull line in her wake.

Wolf's head pounded. Searing pain rested, pulsing, behind his right eye. His mind spun, the events moving too quickly for him to come up with a plan of escape. *Fucking shit. Neither of us would be here if I'd just let her go.* Disgust sat in the base of his throat, impossible to swallow.

They were shoved into a small kitchen and down a narrow staircase to an underground pantry. The escort party made it a tight squeeze. This place had always been Wolf's sanctuary. His home. Now, it was as if the walls were caving in, intent on crushing the life from him.

The largest Enforcer shoved Flynn into a giant, rusted walk-in refrigerator. She stumbled forward, gasping. Wolf grabbed her arm, steadying her.

"Wolf?" she breathed. "Don't leave me. Don't let them take me again."

Her tiny voice sparked his fury. Wolf's curled fist slammed into the guard's face. *Dick.* He fell back against a metal shelf, cans raining over him, clattering loudly as they collided with his head and the floor.

Doesn't he know who he's fucking with?

"Don't touch her," Wolf warned, voice venomous.

Two sets of rough hands closed over his shoulders, forcing him back.

"Watch it, Wolf. She's no longer your prisoner."

He didn't recognize the voice. Three REDS restrained him as others shuffled into the fridge now operating as an elevator leading to their main encampment. They pinned Flynn against the opposite wall. Defeated, lips pressed into a grimace, she didn't resist.

"Let me go or I'll tear you apart," Wolf said, but an elbow locked against his throat strangled his words.

A guard pulled a handgun from his vest and pointed it at his forehead. "I have permission to do this." He grabbed Flynn, yanking her to his chest. Her neck hooked in the crook of his forearm, he shifted the barrel to her temple. "Or, even better, this."

"Do it," she hissed through gritted teeth. "It's better than what's waiting for us."

Wolf stopped struggling, knuckles numb. The metallic taste of blood rested on the tip of his tongue. The heavy door groaned closed behind them. Another guard twisted a large padlock dial embedded above the handle. Once the correct combination clicked into place, the floor beneath them began to vibrate. They descended down the shaft, the loud clank of clomping gears filling the silence. A screech of metal grinding against concrete signaled their arrival. Adrenaline spiked Wolf's heart rate. His neck muscles were as taut as drawn bowstrings.

The door swung open, revealing a familiar corridor lit by bare, murky bulbs strung in a single line along the low ceiling. A burst of stale air greeted them. Jerking his arm free from his escort's grip as they exited the chiller, Wolf straightened his shoulders. He knew what lay ahead. A fast death was a mercy act atypical of REDS. Bloody ghosts from past victims swam before his eyes.

They still need you, a small voice whispered in his head. *Prove it. It's your only chance.*

Approaching the arena was like surreal déjà vu. Only a week ago, he'd ventured down these halls alone in search of Hyena to discuss their most recent attack. Now, it was quite possible he was being led to his execution. How ironic, that the people who had saved him would be so willing to destroy him—to turn on him. He tried not to think of Beta, but inhaling suddenly burned his chest.

In the arena, the entire organization awaited their arrival, flanked in rows around Spider. Their crimson faces floated on a black ocean. Clearly, a newly elected executive member betraying his comrades was a rare attraction. Bloodthirst must be quenched. Wolf's eyes locked with Spider's. His uniform was identical to the group's other than a small golden spider pinned on his vest. Dangerous energy radiated like clouds of poisonous gas from his rigid body. Their guards led them to the center of the room and forced Wolf and Flynn to their knees before melting back into the surrounding ranks. The concrete's damp chill seeped through Wolf's ripped pants.

Flynn swayed beside him, bound hands resting in her lap. Her top was soaked with sweat and dirt, revealing her light, delicate skin underneath. A long, ragged scratch extended over her collarbone and up the length of her neck, bleeding through the fabric. Torn and singed by burning debris, a hole in her jeans exposed her right thigh.

Spider surveyed them through narrowed eyes as he approached. His slow, foreboding footsteps echoed throughout the cavernous space. Flynn flinched as each step grew inescapably closer.

"Welcome back, Ms. Zarytsky! We expected your return, although admittedly we did not presume you would be alive." He walked toward Flynn, but his dark eyes remained lasered on Wolf. Wolf's hands cramped from the pressure of clenching his fists. Spider gripped her chin, tilting her head up. He peered at her blindfolded face. "And you, Wolf. You betrayed us all. Six men I sent after you. I risked six men for *you*. I thought the pigs might have gotten you. Then I heard your microphone." Wolf couldn't move, an ant trapped beneath a magnifying glass, with Spider's glare slowly burning him alive. "Now one of our own is dead. Dead because of you." The corners of Spider's mouth dragged into a small smile. "Let's make you pay, shall we?"

SMACK. He struck Flynn across the face so hard her body skidded over the concrete. It was like watching sand slip through an hourglass in slow motion. Wolf doubled over, unable to breathe. Her yell saturated the silence, shredding his insides. The sensation that hijacked him months ago, after Spider beat Flynn the first time, returned in full force. Wolf scrambled toward them—half lunging, half crawling. Spider raised the heel of his boot, resting it on Flynn's throat. Wolf froze on all fours. "Come any closer and she dies," he threatened, voice calm. Her chest heaved with choked sobs.

It was the exact tactic Wolf used on Flynn only a couple weeks ago with Nate—forcing her to surrender, playing on her weakness.

"You were meant to be my successor, Wolf. You were destined to lead this organization to great heights." Spider's weight shifted forward, pressing harder against Flynn's windpipe. A pitiful yelp squeaked from her throat. "Come. Put this behind you. Let us celebrate our well-deserved victory."

Wolf rocked back on his heels. Sweat streamed down his face, dripping into the cuts crisscrossing his knuckles. The salt stung his rosy-red flesh.

"Let her go."

Spider's upper lip curled into a sneer. "You're weak," he spat, voice full of loathing. He removed his foot. Coughing and gasping for air, Flynn rolled to her side. "Kill her. Kill her now. I prepared you for this moment." He cranked back his leg, then sent his boot colliding into her mid-back with a deafening thud. A blow right to her kidneys. Flynn's scream sent Wolf's heart slamming into the roof of his mouth. "This is the test. The ultimate test. Remember what I've always told you: *the connections tying us to another person are debilitating, blinding—powerful enough to destroy us.* Now is your chance. Prove yourself. Show the entire organization what you're capable of!"

Flynn's moans paralyzed him. The bones in his hands crunched against the concrete. Wolf's vision tunneled in and out of focus, the surrounding crimson smearing against black. Spider stalked toward him, ready to strike, zeroing in on his moment of disarmed weakness.

"Why is this so hard for you? Do you actually love the girl?" Heavy boots materialized before him. Scuffed metal decorated their tips. Spider's words fell on the back of his neck like scalding water. "You're blind. She's using you." He stooped down, face hovering inches from Wolf's. His teeth bared into a snarl. "This is why we taught you to *control* your emotions. You're allowing her to manipulate you. She's pulling you into a trap. She's one of them. A sheep. A piece of the evil we detest. Either you kill her, or we kill both of you. Which do you prefer?"

Wolf's hand shot out and closed around Spider's throat. REDS shifted around them. If Enforcers fought, it was a strict rule only those who engaged could end it. No outside party should interfere, no matter the outcome. But no one had ever challenged a leader before.

Shock drained Spider's lips of color. "I . . . raised you," he spluttered, voice rattling.

"I don't need you," Wolf hissed through clenched teeth, squeezing harder. "I need her."

"We all . . . have someone we want . . . not *need*." He gasped, his airflow growing more constricted. "You are a REDS . . . Enforcer. You need no one."

Forearm swelling, Wolf stood, dragging him upward. "She needs to stay alive if you want me to see this through." There it was, the mission dangling over their heads, the carrot Spider would lunge for each and every time it caught his eye.

"She . . . kil-killed one of your brothers. There must . . . be consequences."

"Her security will be all over us the second she disappears."

"You and I bo-both know her security detail *ended*," Spider stammered.

"If I disappear, the Feds will put two and two together." Flynn's whisper floated over them, so soft it could barely be heard. She rolled over with diffi- culty, angling her body toward the sound of their voices. "They'll figure out REDS infiltrated Magnetic. Wolf's cover will be blown. You need us both. Now, more than ever."

The pressure mounted. Spider's eyes bulged, black orbs protruding from his face. "I need . . . no one."

"You need us if you want your plan to succeed. I'm the only one who knows how to activate the Magnetic malware," Wolf said.

Spider slammed his elbow down on Wolf's outstretched arm, attempting to break his grip. Wolf delivered a blow straight to his side. Spider's knees crumbled. Fingers tightening, Wolf held him in a standing position.

"You know our ru-rules—a life for a life." Spider gagged, choking. Wolf could see his mind working. He was losing control and Wolf was too strong. Spider couldn't overpower him. He had to make a choice. "If she doesn't die . . . someone must . . . die in her place."

Limbs shaking with rage, Wolf dug his nails deeper into Spider's pulsing arteries. "That's something we can discuss."

All remaining color seeped from Spider's face. "You think this is strength? Turning on me? Be-betraying me? No. You're a coward. You—you will never be REDS's leader unless you kill her."

"Fine. It doesn't have to be me."

"It is you." It was almost impossible to make out his words. His exhales released in labored bursts, shuddering inhales like sucking air through a straw. "I chose you."

Sharp pain sliced through Wolf's chest. His grip faltered. "I told you I wasn't worthy."

Spider was the only father figure he had ever known. He'd saved him from the reform center. He'd recognized what Wolf was capable of when everyone else only saw a number. If it weren't for him, who knew where he would be.

Wolf shoved him aside. Heaving, Spider staggered backward, struggling for air. Wolf's hands tingled, wrists pulsing. His violent anger subsided into despair. Spider straightened, adjusting his vest with one hand, massaging his neck with the other. A thick choker of dark purple bruises already encircled his throat.

"We'll proceed without you." Spider's voice emerged as a gravelly whisper.

"Flynn's right," Wolf said. "If she disappears, they'll raise the alarm. We can't risk being discovered when we're this close."

"Then we act now and move forward sooner than we'd planned to."

"I told you, I'm the only one who can activate the malware."

"Hyena can do it. Consider yourself on probation while the executive committee determines whether your time with us is done."

"No!" Wolf stormed toward him until they stood practically nose to nose. Spider held his ground. "I've worked toward this moment for eight years."

"You forfeited your chance!" Spider tried to yell, but his crushed vocal cords blocked the sound.

"I designed the malware so no one else could activate it. I made sure that if anyone detected it in the system, they wouldn't know how to disable it."

Spider gritted his yellowed teeth. "We don't need the malware. We can just take down more substations with EMPs."

"It's too risky. The Feds will be watching the other stations like fucking hawks after what we just pulled. We'd be walking right into their open arms." Convincing Spider to spare him and Flynn might be impossible if Wolf couldn't prove the mission would be compromised without him. "We're too close for something like this to stop us. It would have all been for nothing."

Wolf and Spider stared at each other, gridlocked. Neither moved a centimeter, until Spider finally blinked. "She can live," he croaked, "for now. Tomorrow we revisit the final installment of our plan. If it is not executed flawlessly, we'll tear her to pieces. Bit by bit. And you will watch." His strained voice dissolved into a cough. Wolf's chin lowered in silent assent. "Get her out of here. If you're not back within twelve hours, we will hunt you down. Both of you."

Flynn lay on the ground, drifting in and out of consciousness. A guard approached Wolf with the key to her handcuffs. Bloody rings wrapped around her thin wrists. Wolf gathered her limp body, cradling it against his chest.

The eyes of the entire organization followed them as they left the arena. His arms, almost too weak to carry Flynn, trembled. An unbearable weight pressed down on him, heavy as a suit of forged steel. He had been so focused on keeping her alive, but he'd only succeeded in hurting her again and again. He'd failed her. He'd failed Spider. He'd failed REDS.

Worthless. I'm worthless.

His insides hollow and empty, each step he took formed a trail of misery. In minutes, the reputation he worked for his entire life was gone. Vanished. Replaced by smug accusations of treason. He was no longer an

Enforcer. He was a traitor. A disposable traitor. The word seared through his skin.

My identity is a lie.

When he first took Flynn hostage, Wolf had thought he had to choose between completing his mission or saving her. Now, everything had changed.

He could save Flynn, or he could save himself.

43

FLYNN

Cori emitted a shocked cry when she opened their apartment door to a ragged Wolf. Flynn clung to his neck, bracing her body in an upright position, lips pressed together in a razor-thin line. Frantic, Cori wasted no time barraging them with questions, demanding to know what happened and threatening to drag them to the hospital. Flynn did her best to mask the intense pain radiating through her body as Wolf carefully set her on the bed.

"Cor, downtown is completely shut down. Besides, hospitals are overloaded with people who really need help. I'm just a little bumped and bruised." Flynn winced. "I was running down a flight of stairs at the train station after the first explosion and pretty much got blown onto the street, and then a stampede almost trampled me. Thankfully Chris was there to help me."

Cori's mouth drew into a tight pucker, her face pale. She glanced at Wolf as if she just realized he was there. He stood in the corner of Flynn's room, shifting from one foot to the other. She took in his tall, muscular form. Splotches of dried blood covered his hands and face. Soot shaded his skin a tone darker.

"And who are you?" she demanded, her tone abrasive, as if he was to blame for Flynn's injuries.

Wolf hesitated, about to speak, but Flynn cut him off. "We work together. Will you please relax? I promise, I'm okay."

"Stop telling me to fucking relax. How are you so accident prone? I mean, the mugging and now this? I don't get it." She sighed, collapsing against the doorway. "Your parents have called me like ten times. What were you even doing downtown? Magnetic is in the West Loop."

A twinge of annoyance twisted a screw in between her temples. Cori's unrelenting scrutiny was exhausting, and it was the last thing she needed piled on top of everything else right now. "Seriously, Cor? I have to take the Brown Line to get home now that I don't have my security escort anymore." Appealing to her big-sister concern, Flynn switched tactics. "I promise if I don't feel better tomorrow, I'll go see a doctor. You know there's no point going now. Who knows if it's even safe. I honestly just need rest."

Cori ran a shaking hand down her face, a meager attempt to wipe away her panicked despair. "I can't . . . I mean, I can't believe this happened. Again. The streets were full of people. Everyone running. The explosions . . . they wouldn't stop. They kept coming." Her voice choked. "It was a nightmare. A nightmare. I can't bear to turn on the news. I don't—I don't understand what's happening. How has this happened *again*?"

Wolf and Flynn listened in silence as Cori repeated herself. Her words washed over them.

"A group from work is meeting down the street to head back to the Loop. We're going to bring water and some food for the first responders. See if there's anything we can do." Rubbing her lined forehead, she crossed the room to take Flynn's hand. "Are you okay here on your own? I can be back in a few hours to check in on you."

"You're going now? It's like one in the morning."

"Yeah, no one has been able to sleep. It's the least we can do. Everyone working out there is probably exhausted."

Flynn squeezed her hand back in reassurance. "Don't worry about me. Be careful, okay?"

Cori nodded, her eyes brimming with tears. "I'll have my cell. Not sure it's working, but don't you *dare* leave this apartment until I get back."

"I won't," Flynn replied obediently.

"Oh, and at least text your parents to let them know you're okay. Knowing them, they're probably already on their way to Chicago."

When the door finally closed behind Cori, Flynn collapsed back into her pillow with a groan. Shock waves of pain washed over her body every time she moved.

"Advil. I need Advil," she mumbled through gritted teeth. "Either that or a fifth of booze, whatever you find first."

Wolf perched on the edge of the bed, cautious. He reached for her, reconsidered, then tentatively placed a hand on her side. His touch was gentle. It felt strange to have him willingly approach her, his closeness intimate yet foreign.

"Can you roll over? I should check your kidney." Peeling her damp shirt away from her skin, he examined her mid-back. His fingers left a cool trail, as if every skin cell he touched had its own life. "I did this," he said, so softly she almost missed it. "I did this to you."

Flynn's nerve endings went numb. She hadn't expected that, just like she'd never expected to find Wolf back in her room. They were alive. They'd overcome the seemingly impossible and escaped REDS. Together. Now the impossible was happening again, this time right before her. *Could people really change?* she wondered. She'd changed to survive. She'd done things she hadn't known she was capable of doing. *Is that what he's been doing all along? Surviving?*

Sensing an opportunity, she rested her palm on his face, thumb smudging small circles of dirt on his cheek. Their eyes met. Once more the green depths hypnotized her, and a sad smile crossed her lips. Her pain faded for a brief moment.

"You can't go back there."

"Flynn, you don't understand. It's not that simple."

"What's there to understand?"

"I can't walk away from the only family I've ever known."

His breath steamed her skin. "How can you say that? That man is crazy. Psychotic. He threatened to kill you." She lowered her hand. "He almost killed *me*. He's clearly only using you to execute his plans."

"And you aren't using me now?"

Wolf's tone wasn't wounded, but she flinched, taken aback by the straightforward question. Guilt crystallized in her heart. "What do you mean? You think I'm using you?"

"You lure me out onto a boat, attempt to disarm me by making yourself emotionally vulnerable, and then come after me with a loaded gun to try to kill me. I'm not an idiot."

Her fingers bunched into her palms. *No point in denying it*, she thought. It might make her seem more ingenuine, blowing her cover. "Of course I'm motivated to prevent you from killing more people." She tried not to sound defensive. "You backed me into a corner. What else could I have done? I had to try to stop you."

"Even if it meant killing me?"

Her neck flushed, the heat creeping up to her cheeks. "I knew it was only a matter of time before you killed me, so I . . . guess I tried to beat you to it." Swallowing the golf ball wedged in her throat, she dropped her gaze. "But I couldn't. You've known all along I wouldn't be able to. You said so on the boat the first time we met."

"That wasn't the first time we met," Wolf said, eyes unfocused, reliving a distant memory.

She frowned. "After the Green Line concert, I mean."

"We'd met before then as well."

Flynn racked her brain. When could she have possibly come into contact with a terrorist without knowing it?

After several long moments of silence, Wolf relented. "It was years ago. You wouldn't remember. You served me once at a coffee shop where you used to work."

"What?" Shocked, she stared at him. How could she have forgotten those eyes?

How many other people have I encountered without truly seeing them— without thinking twice about their stories? she wondered.

"I'm used to it." Wolf lifted a shoulder. "No one ever noticed me." He said it matter-of-factly, without a hint of self-deprecation. The hatred Flynn had spent the past weeks crafting crumbled into a thousand pieces. "Some douchebag spat at me and you put him in his place." He half grinned. "Pretty sure he was your boyfriend at the time, too. You stuck up for me. No one had done that for me before." He paused, lost in thought. "After everything I've done, you still couldn't kill me. But REDS would . . . my own brothers would without a second thought. And I would too if I were in their shoes."

Now, it finally made sense—why after an attack as brutal as the Green Line concert she was still alive. Wolf had recognized her that night. Something she had done almost a decade ago, something she still didn't really remember, had saved her. An undeniable force pulled her to him, as invisible and strong as gravity. She couldn't argue why Wolf was compelled to evil—it was all he'd ever known. That, coupled with loneliness and abandonment, brewed the perfect storm—a hurricane of hate that wiped out everything in its path. The urge to protect him, to prove to him that there was a different world than what he knew, harpooned her heart.

Now's not the time for pity, a voice whispered in her head. *Now's the time to lunge for the throat. Grab him by the jugular and finish him.*

But his weakness was different. It was hidden, and it required a different weapon to reach it. She searched inside herself, summoning her last bit of strength to yank the grappling hook firmly into its hold. "Has anyone ever shown you kindness? Like real, genuine kindness?"

His brows lowered over guarded eyes, the drawbridge raising as it did whenever she probed too deeply. "Not genuine, no. At least not that I remember. There was always an agenda."

"Well, then I'll be the first." She cleared her throat, attempting to prop herself higher on her pillows. Her back spasmed, screaming in protest. "Let's start by talking about the ways in which you're good. Throughout your life, all you've been told over and over is you're bad. You became that narrative. But, really, you're the smartest person I've ever met. You're not afraid of anything. And, while you definitely lack most endearing qualities, your wit and sarcasm are rather . . . undeniable."

Wolf softened, his rigidness melting, the way someone does when relaxing into a long exhale. "I guess I'll take that as a compliment."

Her guilt reared its ugly head again, refusing to be ignored. She traced the river delta of veins trailing his wrist. He didn't resist her touch. Closing her eyes, she pulled his palm back to her cheek, inhaling his calming scent. Plain soap and sweat. His calloused skin was rough, soothing. This was a dangerous path. All signs warned her against pursuing it because beyond the horizon was nothing but devastation.

"What now?" she asked, groggy, her mind drifting toward sleep.

"Worse is coming. That was a test run."

She opened her eyes, blinking at him. "What?"

His body stiffened again. "That attack was strategic. We needed to identify gaps, vulnerable spots in the electrical grid by targeting specific substations."

Um, what the fuck did he just say? "So . . . what does that mean? What's next?"

"Societal breakdown."

Panic catapulted into the depths of her stomach. "How do we stop it?"

"We don't. Especially if we want to live."

"We can't just let it happen, Wolf. There has to be something we can do, somewhere we can go to escape them."

"We'll never be able to hide from them. They're watching our every move. I can't protect you from all of them."

An urgent pounding filled the apartment. Wolf's hand jumped to the gun hidden in his vest. His other arm shot over her body protectively.

"Help me toward the door," Flynn whispered, fingernails digging into his bicep.

"Let me answer it."

"No! No one can know you're here. It could be the FBI."

Avoiding her bruised back, he looped his arm around her hips, practically carrying her down the hallway. Closing one eye, she pressed the other to the peephole, heart drumming in her ears. Sickening guilt dragged her stomach to the floor like a weighted anchor.

Nate's face filled the magnified monocle.

44

FLYNN

"Flynn?" Nate called through the door, his voice wavering. She turned to Wolf. "It's Nate. I need to let him in."

"What? You still talk to him?"

"Of course I do. I have to see him. We came after you together. Before you blew up the whole freaking city." Motionless, Wolf's expression darkened. She pushed him back toward her room. "Wolf, please. No matter what, don't think about touching him. He'll go to the police if he thinks I'm unaccounted for. He deserves to know I'm okay."

Wolf retreated reluctantly down the narrow corridor into the living room, brows plunging into a deep V. Forcing an exhale from puffed cheeks, Flynn opened the door. As soon as Nate saw her, relief flooded his face. Dirt covered every inch of his skin and his hair was matted with sweat and grime. His eyes shone like stars exploding in a dark sky. A gun hung loosely from one of his hands. Nate pulled her to him, wrapping his arms around her fiercely.

The pressure sent an earthquake of pain down her back. Yelling out, she fell against the wall. Nate caught her, alarmed, lips parting in concern. "Flynn, are you okay? What's wrong?"

Wolf came lurching toward the sound of Flynn's distress. Seeing him, Nate jumped in surprise. He threw his body in front of her, shielding her from Wolf's advance.

"What the fuck did you do to her?" Nate's voice trembled. He pointed his gun at Wolf's chest. "Come any closer and I'll blow your fucking brains out."

Wolf stopped several strides short of them, face hard and impassive. "She's hurt. She needs to lay down."

"Flynn, what the hell is he doing here? What did he do to you?"

When she didn't respond, Nate lunged at Wolf. Flynn threw herself forward, blocking him. Wolf ripped his handgun from his vest, raising it to Nate's forehead, tensing against an attack.

"Nate, no! Stop. He saved me."

"What?" Nate's neck was a deep shade of red. "What're you talking about? He did this." He gestured out the far window. "All of this! He killed those people. Again! He destroyed our city!"

How do I navigate this? she thought. *How can I possibly explain this strange, disgusting tie connecting me and Wolf?*

Slumping, her face tipped into her hands. "I know. I'm not . . . I'm not excusing what he's done. But I'd be dead if it wasn't for him."

"Don't let him brainwash you into feeling sorry for him." Nate grabbed her wrist, dragging her fingers away from her eyes. Bright spots erupted across her vision like dancing fireworks. She couldn't meet his stare. "You wouldn't even be in this mess if it weren't for them kidnapping you and taking you hostage. He's manipulating you."

"It's not that simple," she pleaded.

Nate's mouth fell open, aghast. "Fine. If you can't do it, I'll kill him for you." He pointed his gun at Wolf again and Flynn wondered if he had any idea how to use it.

"Where did you get that thing? We're not killing anyone. That's not the answer."

Flattening her palm against the wall, her locked arm barricaded the doorway. Nate hurled a look of disgust in Wolf's direction, then ran a despairing hand through his hair. The grime froze its ends upright, giving him another inch of height.

"When you set foot outside this apartment, I will find you," he warned, voice low and menacing. "I will find you, and I will fucking rip you to shreds."

Wolf smirked. The drawbridge lifted again, separating him from Flynn. Within seconds he'd transformed back into a ruthless REDS Enforcer, instantly unreachable. "Oh, really? You're going to come after me? I'll be sure to watch my back considering where you ended up last time."

"I *knew* it was you, you son of a—"

"Stop!" Flynn resisted the urge to clap her hands over her ears and scream. "Both of you, stop."

Shaking his head, Nate backed away, eyes widening. "Who are you, Flynn? How can you associate with this piece of shit after everything he's done? What about all those people he killed?" He jabbed his gun in Wolf's direction, slamming his other fist into the drywall. It left a small crater, cracks of plaster fissuring around its edges. "What about them?"

She recoiled as his accusation came crashing over her. "This isn't something I expect you to understand. It didn't happen overnight. But if we want to prevent more attacks from happening, we need to work together."

"No. Nothing you say can possibly justify what he has done."

"I'm not trying to make excuses, but you need to listen to me. We can't fight REDS with more hate. You said so yourself. This has to stop. Don't you see? We're stuck in this vicious cycle, blaming others who are different from us. We can't change people unless we take a step back and see the world from their perspective."

"You *are* brainwashed." Nate's eyes scanned over her, halting on the purple bruises flowering over her skin. His lip curled. "What have they done to you? You're telling me we're supposed to overlook everything a terrorist has done because he's *misunderstood*?"

"I'm trying to do what you said!" Her voice climbed, shrill and desperate. "You were the one who told me if we want to change this world, we have to spread everything REDS is trying to destroy."

"I didn't mean by actually associating with one of them."

"But how is that different?"

She reached for Nate, but he yanked away. "Because he isn't a person. He's a monster." He studied her with sadness etched into his features. "I won't lose you to them. Not again."

"Nate . . ."

He slammed the door. The hanging light fixture oscillated above the entryway. Bending over, she steadied herself, breathing shakily. The world slanted. Head reeling, she sank to her knees. *What have I done? I knew he would never forgive me. I don't know if I'll ever be able to forgive myself.*

Wolf lifted her effortlessly to a standing position and guided her back to bed. Her feet shuffled forward in a zombie-like trance—unfeeling, unseeing. As he laid her down, sizzling nerves wrenched her back to life. A groan of pain shoved against her clenched jaw. Nate was one of her best friends. She was pushing him away because of a man she hardly knew. A man responsible for killing innocent people. How could she explain to him that this was the only way to get into Wolf's head? Her insides twisted together into a tangle of knots.

"Do you want to change who you are?" she asked.

Wolf sat back on the edge of the bed. For several silent seconds, he wore the same unreadable expression, no sign of torment or regret on his face. Flynn frowned. *Who is this man?* Quiet and removed one second, alluring the next. His ability to morph into a mindless soldier was terrifying. It was almost as if there was an unpredictable switch deep within him. He seemed to process emotion toward her—he'd shown that by saving her— but remained detached from everyone else. Anxiety ballooned inside her chest, expanding against her rib cage, cracking it apart piece by piece.

"No. But sometimes, when I'm with you . . . I wonder."

Flynn absorbed his confession, unsure of how to respond. It was working—her plan of attack was working. Flynn smothered the conflict fighting to engulf her. If she could break through to him, it might be worth it— Nate, the most recent attack, all of it. *Keep going,* she told herself. *You have to keep going.*

"It's not just you," she sighed. "We all need to change. You were right about what you said the other day in the boat. Society has remained complacent for too long. We've empowered REDS by giving them a motive. We created them."

"It's not in our nature to be selfless," Wolf said. "Societal correction has always been led by outsiders. People seen as threats or rejects."

He was right. Wrapped within the intricate code of each person's DNA were stereotypes and biases that corrupted people's judgments, allowing them to justify the pain they inflicted upon others. Inherent differences prevented people from showing empathy to those who needed it most.

An avalanche of tears slid down Flynn's cheeks. Tasting their salty bitterness, she pressed the heels of her palms into her eyes, trying to staunch their flow. Wolf lifted her hands, leaning down to kiss her. She knew now that seeing her cry triggered something in him, gifting her another piece of ammo for her arsenal.

Wrapping her arms around his neck, she pulled him closer, hungry. When Wolf kissed her, she forgot who he was. She forgot who *she* was. She even forgot why she'd kissed him in the first place—to disarm him, to beat him, to win.

I don't care anymore, she thought, dissolving into the moment. It wasn't over. None of this was over. But for one second, she wanted to sink into the mind-numbing warmth and stay there forever.

He hovered over her, as if afraid to touch her. She skimmed her body against his. Strapped to his chest was a thin mesh military vest that holstered two handguns and a jagged knife. Flynn stopped, staring at the weapons, lowering back into her pillow. Reality slammed into her with painful speed. Wolf wasn't afraid of pain. He took power in knowing what made other people weaker made him stronger. It reminded her of what she had to do.

He watched her beneath long, golden brown eyelashes, his breathing heavy. He unstrapped the vest, tossing it to the floor. She clawed at his shirt and then yanked it over his head. Powerful muscles curved gracefully over his shoulders and chest. Long scars ran down the entire length of his body like strokes of paint. She reached up, fingers floating inches away from his bare torso. Unable to resist, she traced the puckered skin.

"What happened?"

Wolf dodged the question, eyes shifting. He shrugged. "Learning how to resist torture is more important than learning how to inflict it."

Before she could respond, he kissed her again, pulling off her tattered shirt. Their hot skin collided. The smell of his breath sucked her in—the last little inhale before their lips met. Calmness illuminated the corners of her haunted mind.

I'm in control now. I've tamed the beast.

Flynn never understood addiction before this moment. She'd always wondered how the thing that made someone crazy, that slowly destroyed them, was the only thing that also brought temporary peace. Now, she held similar power as that intoxicating drug. They both led to potentially devastating outcomes. They both didn't have the luxury to morally evaluate whether their purpose was right or wrong. They kept giving when the user came back asking for more. They gave knowing it would waste them away. They gave knowing it would kill them.

I can do this, she told herself. *I have to do this.*

45

WOLF

At first, the smell of lilacs on Flynn's pillow seduced Wolf. He was so entranced by the aroma he wasn't sure he'd find his way out of their sweet purplish haze. But slowly it transformed, enclosing him in a poisonous, suffocating trap. He awoke with a start, choking, strangled lungs coughing for air. He blinked away a faded dream of his mother, his forehead tingling where her phantom lips pressed to his head. Her green eyes, full of unkept promises, sank into the darkness.

He attempted to calm his breathing. As he ran a hand over his slick face, sweat gathered behind his neck. He turned toward Flynn. Her dark curls brushed against his cheek. He slid his fingers through their glossy strands, the texture coarse and soft at the same time. He finally knew why the smell of Flynn's hair had such an unsettling effect—it reminded him of his mother.

Flynn lay asleep on her side, her face turned toward him in innocent appeal. It was easy to get lost in studying her perfect features. He wanted to trace the delicate, symmetrical shapes just to make sure she wasn't an illusion. Her eyebrows formed a perfect arch, matching the curve of her lips, the same cupid's bow that drew him to her in the coffee shop.

A nearby streetlamp's soft light peeked through partially open shades. Long shadows glowered against the wall. The numbers on his watch glowed—five in the morning. Wolf contracted his muscles to avoid shifting the bed as he climbed over Flynn. After groping for his discarded shirt and vest, he dressed in silence. Flynn still hadn't moved, succumbed to exhaustion. He zipped his vest slowly, watching her sleep.

Should I wake her to say goodbye? he asked himself. If he kissed her again, it would make leaving harder. The second she reached for him, he would never be able to walk away.

What awaited back at REDS headquarters wasn't going to be pretty. He'd betrayed his family. Worst of all, Spider.

What if he just didn't go back? Could he convince Flynn to run away together before REDS gained a firm foothold on the city? Spider was intent on grooming Wolf to take over REDS, and he had made it clear only Flynn stood in the way. Spider probably would have killed her himself, but he knew it would be more effective to have her die by Wolf's hand instead.

He's a monster.

Nate's damning judgment bore into him. Sacrificing himself wouldn't protect Flynn. REDS would still destroy her. The only way to keep her alive was to move forward with the plan. REDS needed him to complete the final stage. Their mission was his only leverage to safeguard her. At least, for now. A jagged spear pierced into each of his organs, snagging and peeling back the filmy skin. He stepped toward her, arm extended.

Fingers hovering centimeters from hers, he hesitated. Just one more time. Trembling, they curled into a fist, then dropped limply to his side.

He had to stop. Shut off the leaking faucet. Fill the cracked pipe with cement. End these fucked-up emotions spilling toxins into his body like a sinking oil barge. Turning, he slipped out of the room, leaving behind the last person he cared about in the world.

* * * *

Back at REDS headquarters, Wolf considered heading straight to his room. Strange, his first impulse was to seek out Bear. The ache to destroy him and hold him diverged into two dark storm clouds. Bear. An inconsequential toy. But nonetheless, it was Wolf's only tie to his past. Just like

REDS was his only tie to his present. After a few moments of brief hesitation, he made his way to the Leadership Chamber. Spider stood over the round table in the center of the room, deep in discussion with Hyena and Weasel as they examined a large diagram. Wolf's unacknowledged knock on the open door hung in the small space, hollow and unwelcome.

"Spider. Permission to enter?" He stood at attention, waiting.

They turned to stare, faces impassive. Crackling energy radiated from their bodies. The shadow of bruises encircling Spider's neck had transformed into a dark purple manacle.

Spider's brows peaked, steely eyes glinting. "Come join us, Wolf." His voice creaked, squeezed from a swollen throat. "Sit." He nodded toward the table. "But first, present your weapons."

Wolf unzipped his vest, placing it in front of him. He took a seat, hands gripped, knuckles white. Aiming their guns at his head, Hyena and Weasel rose simultaneously.

"Surely you knew there would be serious repercussions for blatant mutiny." Spider's usual cool demeanor dissipated. His face erupted in blotchy red patches. "You betrayed your brotherhood. You put the entire organization in danger. You showed me disrespect worthy of an immediate death sentence."

After several seconds, Wolf met Spider's electrocuting stare. Spider loomed over him, motionless except for the rapid rise and fall of his shoulders. "I failed you, Spider. There is nothing I can say to change that. I returned because I deserve punishment, but I won't kill Flynn. If that means you will take my life instead, then so be it. You of all people know I don't fear death."

"You think that would save her? Sacrificing yourself?" Spider slammed both fists on the table. His mouth twisted into a scowl. "That girl would be dead within an hour of us killing you. Or at least partially dead. We would leave a trail of her body parts scattered throughout the city." He glared down at Wolf, his wide forehead shining. "But we would keep her organs intact long enough for her to live for a few more days—suffering until the very end."

It took everything in Wolf's power not to throw himself at Spider again. *I'll rip your fucking throat out with my own two hands*, he thought. Wolf pressed his knees together to hide their tremor.

"What do you want me to do?" Wolf asked. Enunciating each word required a huge amount of effort. "Without me, you won't be able to collapse the power grid."

"I want you back." Spider grasped Wolf's shoulder, digging to the bone. "I want your complete unwavering loyalty back." He dropped his arm to his side. "You've made it clear that's not possible unless we dispose of the girl. So maybe . . . we can come to an agreement."

The muscles spanning Wolf's shoulders and neck tightened. Spider's terms were almost always lose-lose. "What kind of agreement?"

"If we agree not to kill her, you must get rid of her another way. Distance yourself from her so that she never comes into contact with you again."

"How?"

"By killing all the people she cares about."

Wolf's breathing slowed to a stop, as if Spider had sunk a dagger straight into his gut. "I don't understand," he said, even though he did.

"If you want her alive, so be it, but you will turn her against you. You will kill her roommate, you will kill that boy you attacked in Wrigleyville, and you will kill her family."

All sensation melted from Wolf's skin. He struggled to piece together an alternative, but every turn came to the same dead end. It was too late. REDS had their scent. They would stop at nothing until they hunted him and Flynn down and destroyed them. When he'd sacrificed everything to save Flynn, he had no idea it would only mean a different type of death sentence.

"If I kill the others . . . *If* I kill them . . . you agree not to harm her?"

Spider stared down his angular nose. "Yes. However, if you fail to follow through with any of the assassinations or the final installment of our mission, the girl will be tortured." The creak in his voice dropped to a rasping whisper. "You will watch her die, a slow, merciless death, and there will be nothing you can do to stop it."

His threat was straightforward—a nonnegotiable agreement solely on his terms and conditions. Wolf nodded once, jaw clenched so tight a sharp pain shot up his neck into his temple.

As long as Flynn lived, he could bear his existence. No one else mattered. "Done."

46

WOLF

"Moving on." Spider broke his unremitting gaze and began to circle the table. His left foot dragged, giving him a small limp. He stroked his neck, fingers faltering over the swollen bruises. "Let's review the victories from the latest attack and go from there." He signaled for Hyena and Weasel to holster their weapons and take their seats next to Wolf. "The Semtex bombs Hyena developed proved to be extremely successful in destroying the substation and bridge from the distances we projected. Both Croc and Falcon's EMPs worked as detonators for the bombs, and Wolf's makeshift EMP detonated the explosive on the train platform. This is a wild victory." He paused, eyeing each of them, the corners of his mouth tugging upward. "So, I'm willing to overlook the contempt and betrayal you've shown me, Wolf. We will move on from what happened, especially in the wake of our brothers' deaths. Weasel, proceed."

Weasel extracted a small pane of glass from his jacket pocket and positioned it over the diagram on the table. He pressed a button and a magnified, three-dimension replica of the Chicago electrical grid projected in front of them.

"The code name of our mission's final phase is Operation Blackhole." With a swiping motion, Weasel expanded the image. Rotating, it spun on an invisible axis. "The key is to decide which of the surrounding substations to attack, and, most importantly, to elect a time when we enact the malware Wolf has embedded within Magnetic's system."

Hyena turned to Wolf. "We need to know exactly how the malware will perform."

"It signals all the devices connected to Magnetic's network at once, creating an energy pull. It will be so powerful the entire system will shut down." Wolf's voice fell flat, empty of its usual confidence. "Originally, I planned to hack directly into the grid from Magnetic's network. But Magnetic has the network's connectivity air-gapped from the power generation, forcing me to come up with an alternative plan. Luckily, after a few days, I found a new vulnerability and developed a malware—a zero-day virus. No one will be able to detect it until it's too late."

"You're sure?" Spider rested his fingertips on the table and leaned toward him, as if sniffing him for any deviation.

Nodding, Wolf withheld a shudder. "It will paralyze the entire network. That, coupled with taking out the substations, will destroy the grid completely."

"Which substations should we target?" Weasel asked. "Once you identify them, I can coordinate our plan of attack."

Wolf paused, passing a hand over his face, his vision tunneling. His brain pulsed from the earlier blow to his head. "I need to review the grid's response to the substation Falcon destroyed. The fewer we have to destroy the better. The Feds will be watching the remaining ones closely."

Spider watched him, but Wolf kept his attention lasered on the diagram. He'd memorized it over a year ago, along with the map of the CTA train stations. This mission had been his entire life. He tried to summon the old fire that had burned so fiercely within him.

Do you want to change who you are? Flynn's voice whispered in his ear, startling him.

Spider hobbled to the table and sat. His movements were slow and deliberate, as if he'd aged ten years overnight. "Weasel, Hyena, good work. It's crucial we take advantage of the city's current state of weakness to deliver our most crippling blow. But we'll need to proceed carefully.

We may have exposed our motive with our latest attack. Like Wolf said, the Feds will be hot on our trail. We need to act fast. Let's reconvene tomorrow morning after Wolf has had a chance to review the grid's behavior following the substation blowout. You're both dismissed. Wolf, not you; you stay."

Weasel nodded and deactivated the virtual reality pane. He and Hyena bowed in Spider's direction before leaving Wolf and Spider alone. Thick, endless silence wrapped around them, pressing into Wolf's ears like a world muted under a heavy blanket of snow.

Spider leaned back in his chair. "Have you forgotten the lessons we ingrained in you? After years of training? Have you forgotten the oath you pledged to REDS?"

"I have not, Spider."

"Despite what you might think, we've all had moments of weakness. That's what it means to be human. It's why we teach you about the danger of giving in to emotion." He intertwined his hands on the table, studying them. "It's why we teach you resilience. Our training had a purpose. So, in moments like this, when you feel lost, you can resort back to the values we instilled in you."

It hurt to process Spider's words. Could it be possible their fearless leader once carried shadows of self-doubt?

"You had a weakness?"

Spider nodded. A glimmer of pain passed over his face, disappearing as quickly as it appeared. "Yes, but like all things, we decide how we react to our weaknesses. I chose to reflect on it, and then changed my perception of it so that instead I viewed it as a challenge I needed to overcome."

"I never understood the effect emotions could have on me until now," Wolf admitted. "I couldn't anticipate their burden . . . even after all our training."

"I've always known you were a rarity," said Spider. "It's not often someone hasn't experienced emotional conflict until this point in their career. You were always different from the rest, uncompromisingly sure of yourself. Until now."

Wolf slid wet palms over his pants. "What was your weakness? If you want me to be your successor, I need to understand how you overcame it."

Spider rubbed his bony knuckles beneath his chin, considering Wolf. "I also cared for someone, as you do now."

"You cared for someone?" Surprise rolled off Wolf's tongue before he could stop it.

"I did." Spider's mouth twitched. "She died in my arms on a freezing January day. It was so cold outside it hurt to breathe. A terrible illness took her life slowly, callously." Darkness passed over his empty eyes. "I had no way of getting her to the hospital. No method to even call an ambulance. The homeless shelters were too full, so they turned us away. Families were prioritized. Women who had produced too many children just to suckle off the state. The police scorned us, accusing me of being mad, calling us addicts who were too fucked up to function. I couldn't carry her to the hospital. I was too weak. No one would help us. I even stooped so low as to beg." He paused, deep in thought, reliving his hidden memory. "After I lost her, I thought it would only be a matter of days before I joined her. I was alone when REDS found me. I don't believe in divine intervention, but I do believe in fate. Her death led me to REDS. It showed me the corrupt system that has infected our society for too long. So I vowed to seek revenge."

Chills cascaded down Wolf's arms in an unexpected landslide. He never knew how Spider had come to join REDS. He was such a natural, as if he'd been incubated and hatched into the organization like some rare bird. "How is killing Flynn different than you losing the woman you loved?"

Spider stood abruptly, chair skidding over the concrete floor. His mouth contorted into a grimace. "Because I learned loving someone is a sick waste of the human soul. It brought me nothing but pain. You can't trust her, Wolf; she'll manipulate you to get whatever she wants. Think about it. Think about all the times she's needed something from you. Has she ever given you anything in return? Has she ever given you what *we* have?"

Wolf stared at the table. He missed the religious self-control he'd possessed only a few months ago. He longed for the indifference he once felt toward everyone and everything. It had been so much simpler.

I knew exactly what I wanted.

Flynn's power over him was unnerving. Unnatural. She muddied the water that used to clearly reflect his future, a future that had always revolved around REDS.

"Now, we stand as one, soldiers championing those oppressed by tyranny." Wolf recited their manifesto. Its familiarity warmed the bottom of his stomach like a hot drink. He met Spider's gaze. "She's a victim, Spider. Oppressed just like we were. She's different. It's my duty to protect her."

Spider stalked toward him, nostrils flaring. "Your duty is to REDS. She's *not* different. She's not oppressed. She's disguising herself as a victim, posing as an outcast when really it's only a matter of time until she abandons you. Then you'll be alone, exactly as I was. Exactly how I found you."

His words sucked Wolf back in time, forcing him to relive a nightmare. Except he was awake, limbs paralyzed, unable to fight the contrived visions spawned by his mind. When Spider had found him, he had no one. If he left REDS, he'd have no one again.

"What kind of life would you be able to lead with her?" Spider asked.

Wolf's resistance crumbled. He'd never been able to trust anyone. Why start now? It would lead to the same disappointment he'd already experienced over and over in the past. He shook his head, voice lodged in his throat.

"We took a vow, Wolf. We pledged ourselves to REDS. We swore the organization's needs would come before our own. Always. Emotion, attachment . . . they both create selfishness. Selfishness destroys *everything* we've worked toward. It destroys our united vision." Spider stood in front of him, leaning against the table, eyes burning into his. "Alone we are nothing, but together we are formidable. Together, we will rule." Spider paused, lips turning upward into a small smile. He crossed his long, sinewy arms over his chest. "You know, I don't regret that this happened to you, or to us. If anything, I'm pleased."

Wolf's head screamed, attacked by a blizzard of emotions. Serving Spider had always been his greatest honor. *Who would I be without him?* he asked himself. *Who would I be without what Spider has taught me? He showed me the thrill of setting the world on fire. He brought me to life.*

But Flynn also awakened something he'd never experienced. Something he never knew existed and still couldn't identify.

"You're pleased?" Wolf finally asked.

"I know you. This is a setback. Overcoming it will make you a stronger warrior. I have no doubt this pain will serve you well, just as it served me." Spider wrapped a hand around the back of Wolf's neck, clasped it softly. "You have what it takes, but you must prove yourself. Prove your loyalty to me and to REDS. If you succeed, you will lead this organization one day. You will lead us all to victory."

47

FLYNN

Who are you, Flynn?

Staring at the ceiling, Flynn pondered Nate's question, wondering how to dig into the depths of herself and unearth an answer. It almost felt like she was watching a documentary about someone else's life. Wolf had an entirely different worldview from her own. Was there a way to bridge the two? It would require her to give up everything she thought she once knew, everything she'd been working toward, and start fresh. If only the rest of life worked that way—erase the past to create a new beginning.

Would we continue making the same dangerous mistakes? she wondered. *Would history keep repeating itself? Isn't that what's already happening?*

Questions swirled about her head like the floating pyramid in a Magic 8 Ball, bouncing off the walls in hopes of procuring an answer. Maybe humans were too weak to hold on to the pain of their past. Maybe that was why they were selective in what they chose to remember. Maybe Wolf was right, and humanity was evil and selfish. Her stomach twisted at the thought.

"You up?"

Turning onto her side, she grimaced. Cori leaned against the doorway, hair slicked back in a greasy ponytail. Green-tinged circles ringed her eyes.

"Yeah," Flynn mumbled. She couldn't muster much else.

Cori crossed the room and sat on her bed. "How're you feeling?"

Exhausted, Flynn groaned, rubbing her face. Flipping back, she did her best to ignore the dull aches pulsing through her limbs. "Kind of like I got hit by a bus, if I'm being honest."

Cori reached over and grabbed her forearm, examining the fresh red rings encircling her wrists.

"You gonna tell me what actually happened to you and who that guy who slept over actually is? He was like a life-size G.I. Joe."

Flynn's heart jackhammered in her chest. She stuffed her other hand under the sheets. She didn't have the energy for this conversation again. "Drop it, Cor."

Cori's lower jaw slid forward. "When are you going to learn you're a horrible liar? I don't understand, you used to tell me everything. We never kept secrets from each other."

"This is different," Flynn said.

"How? How is this different? Help me understand."

Flynn sighed and winced as pain darted through her lower back. It was quite possible she had a ruptured kidney. "I'll be able to explain soon, I promise."

A sad smile dimmed Cori's face. "If this conversation isn't déjà vu, I don't know what is. I'm trying to trust you, but I dunno, this might be the last straw. I can't keep giving you the benefit of the doubt for much longer. I'm really worried about you."

"Just give me a little more time. I promise I'm . . . I'm trying to figure this out."

Cori dropped her chin, long lashes fluttering in exasperation. "Alright, alright, I give up. But can you at least tell me who that guy was? Talk about hot, holy shit. You've been on a roll lately, my friend. A roll downhill."

Flynn rolled back on her side, hiding her expression.

"Again, he's someone I work with. He was one of my first hires after I moved into the new role. He happened to be at the station when it blew. He brought me home."

"Wow, I don't know who you are anymore," Cori said. "Coming from someone who refused to mix work with pleasure."

"Yeah, you're telling me. I'm a changed woman."

Cori clambered over her to sit cross-legged, back leaned against the wall. "Did you guys sleep together?"

Her face burned at the memory of kissing Wolf. "No. I was a little too sore after yesterday's nightmare for much exertion, if I'm being honest."

Cori shot her a disbelieving look. "He slept in your bed . . ."

"Yeah, but it was nothing more than that. I think we both needed to hold on to something, so we held on to each other."

Cori's expression clouded at the recollection of yesterday, her lips pressing into a line of fresh pain. She looked down at her hands resting on her lap, the tips of her fingers still stained brown. "You know, it's the same terrorist organization that led the attack on Soldier Field. They already claimed responsibility. It was the group who took you hostage and tortured you. I can't believe people can be so evil."

Flynn nodded, stomach pitching as if she'd dropped unexpectedly on a roller coaster. Wolf spearheaded yesterday's horror. No wonder Nate was disgusted at her. She had defended a man who murdered a new roster of innocent victims. Except to him, they weren't innocent. The thought almost made her violently sick.

"I don't understand why." Cori's eyes brimmed with tears, their brown depths magnified by shining pools. She wiped them away with the back of her hand. "You should have seen it out there yesterday when we went to help. It was like a war zone . . ."

Her voice trailed off. Flynn didn't need to see the attack's aftermath to remind her what REDS was capable of. This was the second time she'd witnessed it firsthand.

"Do you ever think about what drives a person to the point where they believe society is so horrible they feel compelled to destroy it?" Flynn asked. "I dunno . . . that maybe . . . we created the kind of people that could do this to others?"

Cori frowned, jerking her head back as if Flynn had slapped her. "No."

"But these people are so alone. They have nothing to lose. It's what makes them dangerous."

"Are you . . . are you actually defending these guys? The same ones that tortured you?"

"No! No, of course not. It just makes you wonder, what makes these people resort to this kind of violence? It doesn't make sense. Everyone keeps asking the wrong questions. They keep asking, 'How did this happen?' instead of '*Why* did this happen?'"

"It doesn't matter," Cori said. "Nothing excuses killing hundreds of people."

Flynn rolled over onto her back. Cori and Nate's perception of REDS was the exact same. Black or white. Good or evil.

"Yeah, but . . . how can we expect others to change if we're also unwilling to see things from a different perspective?"

Cori stared at her like she was crazy. She climbed over her, got up, and walked away from the bed. "You know what I think? I think you must have hit your head when you fell down that staircase yesterday."

"Cori! Don't *you* ask yourself why? They're people, right? Fucked-up people, but people."

Cori shrugged. "I really don't give a shit anymore."

★ ★ ★ ★

Magnetic closed the office for the remainder of the week while the city struggled to get back on its feet. Illinois declared a state of emergency as the authorities again failed to detain anyone responsible for the attacks. The stock market plummeted, a knee-jerk reaction to panic spreading throughout the nation after the worst terrorist attack since 9/11. Chicago residents refused to leave their homes, too afraid to venture outside. Nowhere was safe anymore. Speculation spread like an uncontained plague, its symptoms made worse by incessant media coverage. Who would be the next target? Would REDS activity bleed into other states? Would there be copycats? Why had REDS attacks remained isolated to the Midwest? Why was it taking authorities so long to find them? What was their motive?

Public transportation screeched to a halt while construction crews repaired damage to the bridges and train lines. Teams worked around the clock to restore electricity to areas impacted by the decimated electrical substation. Police set up perimeters around the city, filling the streets with checkpoints, so it was almost impossible to commute anywhere except on foot. A thick film of soot from remnant smoke and debris settled over pockets of downtown, a ghostly reminder of the horrors of the recent carnage.

For days, cruisers floated up and down the Chicago River. Vigilant spotlights glided over dark, glassy water, paying quiet respect to the hallowed depths. Shock mingled with terror and intense mourning, descending upon the city like a thick fog. People grappled with the loss of those killed in the explosions and on the two decimated trains. Everyone seemed to know someone who died that day. Their grief seemed inconsolable, the pain running as deeply as the fresh gashes carved into the high-rise buildings by the bombs.

★ ★ ★ ★

Every time Flynn left the apartment, nausea threatened to drive her back inside. Similar to the city itself, she felt shattered with no method to pick up the pieces.

Look what you helped set into motion, she told herself. *Look what you did.*

No matter where she went or what she did, Wolf's warning continued to loop in her mind. *Worse is coming. That was a test run.*

What did he mean? How could she stop Wolf, or better yet convince Wolf to stop REDS? Her helplessness crippled her. She had no idea where he was or how to find him. The FBI came by her apartment twice. They brought pictures of suspects and recordings of voices, searching for confirmation of potential leads. Their desperation bordered on rage. She contemplated revealing Wolf's true identity, but the thought of admitting everything she did to help him infiltrate Magnetic ignited another intense wave of nausea. That, and she'd received a note, slid under their apartment door and addressed to her. It contained a threat that ironed her mouth closed for good.

Cori is next.

48

FLYNN

Flynn returned to the office the following week, desperate for the normalcy that had disappeared overnight. Heavily armed policemen greeted her outside Magnetic's doors. Sticky phlegm coated her throat at the sight of their holstered guns and thick padded vests. She still hadn't heard from Wolf since he left her apartment without saying goodbye.

"Can we see your work badge, miss?"

Startled, she jumped, gaping up at the tall guard blocking her entrance into the building. Digging into her bag, her fingers trembled as she fumbled for her ID. When she finally extracted it, he examined her bouncing face before nodding and stepping aside to let her through. Stumbling into the elevator, she squeezed her eyes shut. The doors slid closed behind her. In the boxed space, anxiety pressed against her chest, threatening to crack the thin ice and release the silent scream resting on her tongue.

The same vicious voice reappeared. *Your lies. Look what they've caused. How many have died because you wanted to protect the people you love?*

She'd been struggling to pick apart the memory of her and Wolf's return to REDS's headquarters. There were brief gaps between the pain when she could recall Wolf convincing someone to spare her life, but once more the blindfold and mind-numbing terror had disoriented her. One tangible statement rang through her mind, as disjointed as her fuzzy reflection in the elevator's shiny metallic wall.

I'm the only one who knows how to activate the malware.

After she badged through the doors leading to her floor, her feet carried her in the direction of her desk, even though she didn't see any of her surroundings. She clutched her purse, sweat built behind her fingers. Wolf had proved time and time again he was always several steps ahead of her. Her heart sank. Whatever his plan, it was likely too late to stop him.

★ ★ ★ ★

After dropping her stuff at her desk, Flynn wandered aimlessly in search of Nate, desperate to corner him. She had no idea what she was going to say, but she had to at least try to repair the damage. She had to warn him.

His desk was empty.

Panic simmered inside her. Hot tears sprang to her eyes. She yanked a Post-it note from a pad and quickly scribbled him a note.

Please come find me. We need to talk. Meet at park outside my apt building.—F

Turning away, she headed up to the café for breakfast.

He's okay, she told herself. *Don't jump to conclusions. Nate is fine.*

The usual lively and bustling atmosphere was subdued and quiet. Hollow eyes glided over each other, lost in the collective struggle to move on. Slack faces huddled around tables, whispering in hushed voices, trying to process the trauma from the past week.

"You know Mary? She just got back from maternity leave a week ago," a short woman in front of her at the omelet station whispered to a friend. "Her husband was on the train that got hijacked. Their baby is only a few months old."

"No!"

"Mm-hmm. Can you think of anything more tragic?"

Flynn's appetite vanished, replaced by sharp, ragged pain. What had Wolf done? Over the past week, she'd felt as if she was severing herself from an abusive relationship. Confused one moment, she would make excuses to justify Wolf's erratic behavior. The next moment, her anger would be so overpowering she wanted to hurl anything she got her hands on across the room.

A small, secret part of her also wondered about him. He'd committed an unthinkable act of betrayal by saving her life. How could he possibly escape REDS's brutal retaliation? The image of the thin white scars trailing Wolf's body burned into her subconscious.

She sat at her desk for an hour staring numbly at her phone, debating whether to pack up her stuff and head home. It was impossible to focus. How could she reach out to candidates about new opportunities in the wake of such a tragedy? She took several breaks to walk back to Nate's desk. It remained empty. Giving up all self-restraint, she texted him.

You coming in today? We need to talk. Meet at my apartment later?

Her teeth clamped down on her lower lip as she waited for his response. A sudden low buzz distracted her. Her computer flickered, the screen filling with grainy pixels. Frowning, she tapped a few keyboard buttons. Nothing. The screen turned white.

Great, she thought. *This is exactly what I need right now.*

She scanned the surrounding workstations. One after another, rows of computers flared the same bright, stark white. She clicked her mouse in frantic Morse code. In response, the hard drive's fan began to whir. Either it was rebooting or getting ready to lift off.

Annoyed, she sighed. "Seriously? Come on."

Holding down the power button, she reached for her phone and gasped. The small, rectangular screen squirmed with the same static.

What's happening?

The room abruptly darkened, overhead lights and white monitors extinguishing in unison. An eerie silence pulsed throughout the floor. Bewildered, people migrated toward the windows, straining to see what might have caused the sudden power outage.

A manager emerged from her office, face bright red with agitation. "Okay, okay, everyone, remain calm. One of the crews fixing electricity in the area must have caused a blackout."

"It looks like the power is down on the entire block," someone toward the back of the room observed.

"Yeah, well, that would make sense, wouldn't it?" the manager responded, tapping her unresponsive phone. "Is anyone getting cell service?"

Everyone shook their heads, murmuring to each other. The sudden loss of communication began to settle uncomfortably. One of the police officers patrolling outside the office that morning pushed through the door leading to the emergency exit stairwell. He surveyed the scene.

"Alright, as you can see by now, the power in the building is down," he called out, raising his voice so it carried the length of the floor. "Please gather your belongings and proceed down the stairs. Stay calm. The elevators aren't in working order. We recommend everyone return home at this time. We're not sure when the issue will be resolved. Crews are already stretched thin, but we'll provide an update as soon as we have one."

"Don't we have a generator?" the manager asked, the color of her face shifting to a deeper beet red.

The officer shook his head. "It's not working. IT is saying something about the system being unresponsive."

I'm the only one who knows how to activate the malware.

Flynn swayed on her feet, clutching the back of her chair to stay upright. She didn't really know what malware was, but working at a tech company, she knew it was some sort of computer virus. She had to get home *now*. If the power outage was a result of REDS's final mission installment, Wolf was still alive. He might be waiting for her back at the apartment.

She had to convince him to stop this. She would do anything to convince him.

49

WOLF

Wolf had burned Bear. Finally.

In a matter of seconds, he was free. Liberated. The clumps of matted stuffing had disintegrated into ash as flames devoured his last ties to his past. A similar fire grew within him. Its scorching hunger destroyed everything in its path. Everything.

It was time to forget Flynn, forget how his pain dissolved when he touched her. The day he slit Beta's throat, he had sealed his fate. Hesitating outside her apartment, he grappled with the inevitability of losing her. He had no other option. This was the only way to keep her alive, to keep her breathing. For his own sanity, he told himself that.

"Let's go." Spider's hand pushed him forward.

Leaning his forehead against the door, he clung to the handle, Spider's presence evoking a churn of emotions.

Killing had always been easy. Effortless. He'd been blind to its consequences until now. But Flynn would refuse to give up on him unless he showed her he was unreachable. Her stubbornness was relentless. He'd already robbed her of leading a normal life, and Spider was right; he would never be able to give her the love she deserved. They would continue to take from each other until they had nothing left.

I need to show her that she can't save me. No matter the cost.

"It's time, Wolf. Time to prove yourself," Spider said.

Reaching into his jacket, Wolf's fingers closed around the familiar, silky fabric of his mask. Dragging it over his face, he allowed himself to fold into the identity it magically created. He couldn't have both worlds—Flynn and REDS. Water and oil always separated. One floated to the surface. Jet black. Easily ignitable. The other dragged to the bottom, the base it sat on. Pure.

When Flynn had looked up at him from her bed and asked if he wanted to change, the answer was simple. He couldn't. Everyone had demons, but his defined him. Destroying them terrified him more than living with them. What would be left in their absence? He already had a void inside him so deep it was impossible to decipher where it started or ended. Escape wasn't an option. Silencing the emptiness in his heart, he whispered goodbye to Flynn forever.

Maybe we're all destined to have at least one weakness, to serve as a constant reminder that we're human, Wolf thought. *Maybe the most difficult lesson in life is learning how to move on once the blood dries.*

50

CORI

The damn, fucking power. Cori belly-flopped onto the couch face-first, puffing. She despised all forms of exercise, so walking up seventeen flights of steps wasn't really her cup of tea. *What's happening now?*

Breathing in the musty cushion smell, the Taft fabric sopping up the moisture slicked to her forehead, she had a bad feeling about this. It was the same feeling that had been lurking around their apartment for months. Ever since Flynn returned from the hospital.

She had been waiting for Flynn's haunted look to disappear, for her old warmth to find its way back. Except it hadn't. Something closed off replaced it. Something hidden, like a secret too dangerous to unleash into the world. Guilt slithered up the back of her calves to the nape of her neck.

It's all my fault. The thought entered her mind for the hundredth time, a now familiar daily meditation.

Flynn would never have gone to that concert if it wasn't for her. She'd pressured her into going, and now who knew if her best friend would ever recover. At times her self-revulsion was so sickening all sound disappeared. Without warning, people walking by on the streets would zoom past at warp speed, leaving her in the dust. It reminded her of an old cartoon, where the coyote chased the roadrunner straight off a cliff only to drop into a ravine with a whistling splat.

No matter what she did, no matter who she was with, she couldn't shake it.

After the most recent attack, Cori almost caved. She'd debated calling Flynn's parents. She considered staging an intervention to send her back home to Indiana for a few months. Yeah, when the FBI agents showed up unannounced, she'd even almost told them how Flynn screamed in her sleep.

"Wolf, no! Please, no!"

Countless times, Cori hovered on the verge of asking Flynn who or what Wolf was. Was she referring to some animal? Had REDS manifested itself as a beast in her dreams? Each time, that look in Flynn's eyes stopped her. It crushed her. Afraid Flynn might snap, she resisted prying. She resisted because she would do anything to make that look go away. She'd kept her lips shut.

The apartment door opened and clicked closed.

Thank god she's home.

Groaning, Cori moved to get up from the couch. She buried her self-pitying thoughts and slapped on a happy façade—one she reserved for whenever Flynn was around. "Flynn? I don't know whose brilliant idea it was to live on the seventeenth floor, but I'm sure as hell regretting that decision."

A strong hand grasped her shoulder, yanked her off the couch. Before she could yelp, another hand crunched her lips against her teeth, pressing so hard air could barely escape her nostrils.

"Do it. Do it now, Wolf," a husky voice commanded.

Wolf . . . That name.

A towering figure stood before her, face concealed by a dark red mask. A hood cast rectangular shadows over his eyes. Terror gripped her abdomen like a clenched fist, squeezing all feeling from her legs. Thrashing, she clawed at the hand, ripping into rough skin.

"NOW, Wolf!"

The man before her raised a gun to her forehead. She tried to scream, condensing all her strength into exerting a gurgle that couldn't escape. She bit down on the fleshy palm.

"Not with a gun," the voice growled behind her. "I want you to feel her die."

Die? I can't die. I'm not supposed to die. Not me.

Wolf reached for his belt, withdrawing a long, jagged knife. It trembled in his grip. She thrashed harder, trying to swing her arms free. Her captor's hold was too strong. A wild, instinctual urge to stay alive, to keep breathing, commanded her limbs to fight. Her senses ignited, fueled by the crazed panic possessing her.

NO. Her throat burned under pressure of her barricaded scream. *NO.*

The knife rested in the space before them, as if Wolf were second-guessing himself. "If she doesn't die," the voice behind her whispered, "Flynn will."

Flynn? Something in Cori quieted. *Is this a sacrifice to save Flynn?*

Wolf drew back his elbow, preparing to strike. She stopped struggling, waiting, eyes squeezed shut against her fate. An angry growl snarled behind her and the pair of hands released her, shoving her face down into the couch. There were sounds of a scuffle and, for a brief moment, she wondered whether she could escape, until sudden pain exploded through the center of her back, a bomb shattering her nerves. A gasp forced itself from her lungs. She slid to the floor, legs unresponsive. Her head lolled back, her neck unable to support its heavy weight. Green eyes stared down at her. Haunted . . . they looked so haunted. Tears leaked down her cheeks. Maybe they were from the pain, or maybe it was because she couldn't hold on any longer.

The man named Wolf crouched down and withdrew the knife, ripping her open and extracting the last few seconds of her life along with it. Blood poured from her gaping wound. Hot. Sticky. Unnatural. Her agony subsided to hazy, fuzzy gray.

Flynn, she thought. *I'm sorry, Flynn. See you when you get here. Wherever that might be.*

51

FLYNN

Flynn weaved through throngs of her coworkers shuffling down the emergency stairwell, sweat gathering at the base of her neck. She'd avoided small, crowded spaces ever since the Green Line concert. Jostling bodies pressed up against each other, hot breath fluttered against her cheeks. The pressure of it all accumulated until she felt like the walls might collapse, trapping her within the narrow stairwell.

After what felt like hours, she burst outside. People streamed out of neighboring buildings, forming clusters on the sidewalks, speaking in anxious, muffled tones. Others walked to their parked cars or followed her toward the bus stop, since the train lines were down. Honking horns and sirens blared in the distance. Glancing around, everyone watched for each other's reactions, the past week's events still raw and fresh.

Flynn waited for fifteen minutes with no sign of a bus. She finally headed home on foot after another ten minutes of failing to hail down a cab. The brisk, early fall air was an overdue and welcome relief from the last few days of suffocating heat. She walked north, eager to put the two miles behind her.

It didn't take long for her to realize the power outage extended far beyond Magnetic's office and the West Loop. Neon lights hanging in storefronts were nothing more than dark, squiggly shapes. At every intersection, cars inched past nonoperating traffic lights. Stacked rows of shadowy windows stretched down each block like vacant eyes, casting their solemn judgment over the quiet street. The late afternoon sun refracted off the darkened building faces, the city's only light coming from that brilliant orange orb suspended mid-descent.

✷ ✷ ✷ ✷

When she finally made it back to their apartment, the doorman, Roger, was pacing back and forth, taking brief pauses to peer outside the glass doors. Perspiration pebbled his forehead from the lobby's lack of air circulation.

Flynn groaned. "Ugh, the electricity is down here too?"

"The entire area has been out for the past hour and a half. No way to get ahold of anyone. Sorry, Flynn, you gotta take the stairs to your apartment."

Suppressing another groan, she mentally prepared herself for the seventeen flights of stairs ahead. Her body still sore and bruised, any amount of exertion was daunting. Dragging her feet up each step, she thought about what Roger said. How could she get in touch with her family to let them know she was okay? Her parents had spent the past week begging her to return to the Indianapolis suburbs and live at home for a while. Her involvement in two separate assaults within the span of a few months had been enough to send her mother into hysterics. This would be the final straw.

By the time she reached their apartment she was gulping for air. Moisture prickled her collarbone and glued her shirt to her lower back. She twisted the handle, heaving a sigh of relief when the unlocked door swung open.

"Cori?" she wheezed, rushing into the kitchen, desperate for water. Her parched throat scratched. The door clamped shut behind her with a dull thud. "Cori? Cor, we're going to have to stay put for a while because there is no way I'm walking up those damn stairs again."

Silence filled the small apartment.

Strange, she thought. *Cori's usually home by now.*

She grabbed a cup from the cabinet, but when she flipped the sink handle only a few drops spilled from the faucet. Frowning, she peered down to examine the thin stream. Then she saw her. On the other side of the counter, Cori's body stretched over the living room floor in a pool of blood.

Flynn's cup slipped from her hand. It fell with a crash, exploding shards of glass over the tile floor. Her mouth unhinged, opening to scream, but no sound escaped.

52

FLYNN

The world spun at frightening speed, slanting at an angle that pitched Flynn sideways. Grasping the counter, she fell to her knees, unable to stand any longer. A riptide sucked her out to sea—an enormous hand pushing her head under, filling her lungs, drowning her.

"Cori?" she sobbed, crawling toward her, knocking a stool out of her way. Glass shards clinked against the hardwood floor, slicing into her palms and knees. She didn't feel it. Her body was numb. Lurching over her, Flynn pulled Cori to her chest, searching for the source of the blood. "Cori! Answer me!"

Flynn's trembling fingers found Cori's neck, desperately seeking a pulse. Her clammy skin sprung like putty. It was rubbery, a damp sponge retaining too much liquid. Uncontrollable tears streamed down Flynn's face.

"No. Cori, no. Hold on! Just hold on!"

She choked for air, unable to breathe, her mind losing control. She grabbed her phone to call an ambulance.

Wait. The cell towers are down. Vomit rose in her throat.

"Help me!" she screamed like a lost child. Cradling Cori in her lap, she gripped the empty shell of her friend's body, burying her head against her chest, searching one more time for a heartbeat. Anything to indicate she had a whisper of life remaining. Blood seeping from the puncture wound in Cori's back stuck to Flynn's hands, coating them in wet gloves. It soaked into the ends of her hair, matting them into a wet clump. Nothing. No sign of warmth. Cori's dark brown eyes, usually full of vibrancy and humor, were dull within her sickly white face. "Someone please help me!"

"Flynn. You need to leave here now."

Wiping her cheeks, she blinked up in disbelief, smearing tears and blood into diluted face paint. An unmistakable form stood in her bedroom's doorway. Against the tangerine sunset filtering through her open window, Wolf's silhouette flung a long shadow over her. His black hood shrouded his eyes from view. Covering the remainder of his face, his mask transformed him into someone she hardly recognized.

"Wolf." Her voice sounded far away. "Please. I need your help." She willed herself not to faint, her stomach writhed from the metallic smell of Cori's blood.

He stared down at her in silence.

It only took a second. Then it clicked. "Did . . . did you do this?" She plummeted toward earth, nose-diving in a burning plane, the change in air pressure crushing her skull. "Tell me this wasn't you. Tell me you got here too late to save her."

"She's gone, Flynn."

Seizing Cori, she used her legs to propel her limp body backward. Sharp glass slivers speared her calves. Bright red droplets sprung to her skin's surface, mingling with Cori's trail on the floor.

"Stay away from her!" Her back collided with the living room wall. Cornered, she released Cori and sprang to her feet. Launching herself over the kitchen counter, she grabbed a knife from the butcher block beside the sink. Standing over Cori's body, she brandished it in front of her, hand shaking so badly she could barely maintain a grip on its handle. Her other hand clutched the counter to keep from collapsing.

"Did. You. Do. This?" Her swollen tongue stumbled over the words. "Tell me this wasn't you."

"I had to make a choice." Wolf's whisper was soft, but she winced as if he'd yelled. "This is what I had to do to keep you alive."

An anguished scream tore from her chest, ripping her apart piece by piece, slicing away fragments of her heart.

"No! No, you should have killed me instead. Why didn't you kill me instead?"

"Because I can't. You know I can't."

"Do it now!" she screamed, throat burning. "I want you to do it now."

Unable to control herself any longer, she lunged at him, knife aimed straight for his throat. She wanted him to feel the agony coursing through every inch of her soul. Wolf seized her wrist, suspending the blade an inch from his face. From beneath his hood his green eyes shone with strange intensity.

It's no use, she realized. *I can't overpower him. I can't outmaneuver him. I can't escape him. He's won.*

"How could you?" she sobbed.

The knife dropped to the floor with a clatter. Wolf remained unmoving, as if an invisible shield protected him from her rage. Her knees buckled and she sank. Wolf's grip on her wrist tightened, almost as if he couldn't let her go.

"You fucking coward," Flynn said. "Wearing that mask to disguise yourself from the world. You're really only hiding from yourself. You're disgusting!"

Suddenly a voice spoke that sent her heart cannonballing into her chest. "Let her go."

Standing in the doorway, Nate inched forward, his gun aimed at Wolf.

Nate? No. Not him too. Anyone but him.

He was breathing heavily, sweat pouring down his forehead from exertion, but his aim was steady. Wolf released her wrist.

"Touch her and I blow your brains out," he warned, pressing the barrel against Wolf's temple.

In a flash of limbs, Wolf grabbed Nate's arm, delivering a crushing blow to his elbow. The gun spun past her. Nate threw his body weight against Wolf, bulldozing him into the wall. A loud crash shook the room. He swung a hard punch straight to Wolf's jaw, slamming his head backward into a hanging mirror. Cracks lightning bolted across the glass before it showered to the floor. Wolf hurled himself at Nate. They tumbled back into the kitchen—two trucks colliding in a crunch of warped metal. Straining against each other, their feet skated over shards of broken glass. Wolf dove for the butcher block, but Nate intercepted him, smashing into his side, knocking him to the floor.

Flynn scrambled into the dark living room, searching for Nate's gun. He was no match for Wolf's strength and superior fighting skills. Blood pounded in her ears. Adrenaline took control of her limbs.

Focus, Flynn, focus, she told herself. *You're running out of time.*

A dull, matte object caught her eye, nestled in the shag rug by the couch. She leapt toward it, her hand finally closing around its grip. Whirling around, she stumbled to her feet right as Wolf shoved Nate against the counter, a serrated bread knife pressed against his throat.

"Let him go." Pointing the gun at Wolf's forehead, she maintained a safe distance. "Let him go, or you're dead."

Both men stopped, panting, their shoulders rising and falling with each rattled breath. Wolf's bloodshot eyes remained locked on Nate.

"Drop the knife," she repeated. "Or else I'll kill you."

Wolf glanced at her, lip curling. "You can't kill me. We both know this by now."

"I have no problem killing a monster."

Dropping the knife, Wolf pivoted to face her, yanking Nate into a chokehold. With one quick twist he could snap his neck. Taking another step closer, she aimed the gun between Wolf's eyes. Her hands failed her, shaking uncontrollably again. Cori's corpse lay at her feet.

If I had pulled the trigger a week ago, could I have protected her? she wondered. *REDS would have killed me, but Cori would be alive. If I shoot Wolf now, how many others will I save?* Scanning his face, she searched one last time for the man who had sacrificed himself for her, but he was nowhere to be found.

Wolf's bicep asphyxiated Nate, turning him ghostly pale. Keeping the gun trained on Wolf's forehead, she sidestepped slowly around the counter. Glass crunched under her shoes like fresh snow.

Come on. Do it. Pull the trigger, she told herself. *Kill him. Just kill him.* Violent rage flooded her entire being, so powerful she almost threw her head back and screamed. She hated him. But, even worse, she hated herself.

Wolf held her gaze for what seemed an eternity. Then she saw it. Her own tortured reflection staring back at her, trapped. Locked away. A prisoner. She could finally feel the pain he hid so well. Pain built upon hate. It conflated with her own, emerging from her soul's darkest depths, blinding her with earth-shattering clarity. They were the same—two forces fused by an uncompromising drive to destroy what each considered evil.

I'm a monster too.

"There was a reason," she choked, throat collapsing. "There was a reason I could never kill you and you could never kill me. We used each other . . . chasing each other around and around, until we collided."

Wolf's arm relaxed a hair, releasing the pressure around Nate's neck. Something in his eyes shifted. Sweeping up the last remnants of her heart, she deposited them in front of Wolf. They were her last shot. The bullet she could never release. His face swam before her, glossed over by a thin film of tears.

"I gave you everything you asked for." She gasped, and her lungs shriveled. "I—I saw you as your true self—as a human being. But it didn't change you . . . it only changed *me*. You're still unreachable. You got what you wanted. Now, I've become a monster just like you."

Wolf froze, her words casting a brief spell over him. Without warning, Nate ducked free of his hold, spun, and landed an uppercut straight to Wolf's jaw. It bought him enough time to leap forward and snatch the gun from Flynn's hand.

"She might not be able to kill you, but I can, you fucking asshole."

"Nate, NO!" Flynn jumped, shoving his arm right as an ear-crackling bang exploded. Wolf reeled from the impact of the bullet lodging into his shoulder. Panting in pain, he slid to the floor. His palm compressed the blood oozing from his wound. Flynn blundered between them. "No! Nate, don't!"

"Get out of the way, Flynn!" Nate yelled. "You'll thank me for this one day."

She knew she'd stepped over a line. She had gone beyond manipulation into uncharted territory. No matter how demented Wolf might be, she had seen him through different eyes.

"Let him suffer alone," she said. "Don't let him change *you*, too. Don't become the monster he is—the monster he's turned me into. If you kill him, you might not come back from that."

Nate steadied himself, sucking in gulps of air. She approached him cautiously, extracting the gun from his grip. Circling an arm around his waist, she pulled him away. He followed reluctantly, guided by the firm pressure of her hand.

Arduously, Wolf rose to his feet, his fingers doing little to staunch the steady stream of blood. "Get out of the city. Now," Wolf said, his voice thick as Flynn and Nate staggered down the hall toward the door. "Worse is coming. This is only the beginning."

His warning lingered in their wake, but Flynn didn't look back. There was nothing left to see. She squeezed Nate's hand tighter, binding herself to him, knowing that without him she would tip into a black hole of despair and never find her way out. She'd left behind a piece of her soul. It lay next to Cori on their living room floor. She'd never even had the chance to say goodbye—to hold her one last time, to touch her face, to promise she would avenge her death.

Wolf had made his decision.

Now, it was time to make hers.

END OF BOOK ONE

ACKNOWLEDGMENTS

JUSTIN, this book is as much yours as it is mine. It's taken us six long years to get here, and I never could have kept going if you hadn't pushed me every step of the way. Thank you for your unflinching support and for loving me in a way that I've never doubted.

Tanya and Bill, we did it. You and your friendships made this journey beautiful, and, dare I say it, fun? You both made me a better writer, reader, and editor. I owe almost everything I've learned to you two.

Thank you, Mums, for telling me to go for it, and Dad, who still loved me anyway. My big sister, Emily, you know what it feels like to be compelled to write, to touch others with words, and to never give up the compulsion to seek out that connection.

Thank you to Ryan Steck; you have been a cheerleader and a champion for this story. You dealt with a lot of whining and commiserating, all while helping me navigate the industry and teaching me how to keep the pages turning. Who knows where this book would be without you, or, let's be honest, what shape it would be in.

To my beautiful children. You both slowed down this process (rather significantly), but during that time, I found myself through you two. You gave me so much joy and love throughout this process, as well as meaning. You two were always a source of light in a cavern of resounding nos. I hope this book shows you the power of dreams, and the power of resilience and courage. I hope that, like me, one day you will take that leap and never look back.

Thank you to my family, friends, and confidantes who never stopped asking about my characters or reading these pages—to those who lifted me up and believed in me when I gave up on myself, you know who you are, and I am so damn lucky to have you. If I can impart any wisdom to those reading these pages, it's to find your village and cherish it—find the people who will lug you to the ends of the earth and make you laugh through the pain. In the end, that's all that matters. And to all the strangers who read this story in its earliest form and loved it, you are the true reason that, after all these years, I never gave up on this book.

Thank you to my amazing team at Greenleaf Book Group. I couldn't have asked for a better crew to take this book to the next level and carry it with me over the finish line. Thank you for giving me and this story a chance, and for instantly recognizing what it could offer the world. My editorial team—Lee, Liz, Tenyia, and Stephanie; you sharpened my words and focus, while also preserving my vision. You gave me the last bit of confidence I needed that I was ready to send this book out into the world, and I am so grateful for the time and energy you put into myself and this book.

To Christian Picciolini, thank you for dedicating your life to ending the vicious cycle of hate that has become so prevalent in this world. Thank you for taking the time to share your experiences with me and validate my characters in this story. To anyone interested in learning more about the dangers of extremism and intervention resources, I encourage you to visit his website and read his fantastic books: *White American Youth* and *Breaking Hate, Confronting the New Culture of Extremism*.

Lastly, to those out there who feel lost and alone, to those working toward a different life for yourself, keep going. Keep moving forward.

THERE IS A PLACE FOR YOU HERE.

ABOUT THE AUTHOR

CLAIRE ISENTHAL lives in the suburbs of Indianapolis with her husband, their two children, and a mutt. She graduated magna cum laude from Purdue University and is an account executive at a Fortune 500 tech company. She has worked in digital marketing for over ten years. *The Rising Order* is her first novel, and she is in the midst of writing its sequel, *The New Order*. Visit her website, www.claireisenthal.com, or follow @claireisenthal on Instagram or Twitter.